Also Published by HarperPrism

Isaac Asimov's
HISTORY OF I-BOTICS

Isaac Asimov's I-Bo

TIME WA

Isaac Asimov's I-Bots

TIME WAS

STEVE PERRY & GARY A. BRAUNBECK

HarperPrism

ACKNOWLEDGMENTS

The authors would like to acknowledge some of the people who helped us along the way as we wrote this book. First, thanks to Denise Little, for her enthusiasm and some much needed shots in the ego. Next, thanks go to Larry Segriff, for continuously putting Gary in his place. Thanks to Ed Gorman, for being a fine teacher by example. And last but hardly least, thanks to Isaac Asimov, for the legacy he left us, and in the sincere hope that this minor footnote is worthy of his memory.

HarperPrism
A Division of HarperCollins*Publishers*
10 East 53rd Street, New York, NY 10022-5299

ISBN 0-06-105295-7

HarperCollins®, 📖®, and HarperPrism® are trademarks of HarperCollins Publishers, Inc.

HarperPrism books may be purchased for educational, business, or sales promotional use. For information, please write: Special Markets Department, HarperCollins Publishers, Inc., 10 East 53rd Street, New York, NY 10022-5299.

Designed by Jeannette Jacobs

First printing: June 1998
Printed in the United States of America
Library of Congress Cataloging in Publication Data is available from the publisher.

Visit HarperPrism on the World Wide Web at http://www.harperprism.com

98 99 00 01 02 ❖ 10 9 8 7 6 5 4 3 2 1

For Dianne

> *—Steve Perry*

For Eric Robert Dickey and Kylie Ann Connor. Someday you'll be old enough to read this, and then you'll understand why everyone looks nervous when Uncle Gary comes around.

> *—Gary A. Braunbeck*

ALL THIS DARKNESS

"It is one of the greatest tragedies of this age that as soon as Man invented a machine he began to starve."

—*Oscar Wilde,* THE SOUL OF MAN UNDER SOCIALISM

1

Time was he knew happiness, hope, and acceptance.

But now . . .

Now, in the grave-silent, ink-black darkness where even the deepest shadows would shine brightly, the child thought: If only I could scream.

Blackness above, below, all around him.

Or so he imagined.

This darkness had been his home for so long he could no longer tell if his eyes were open or closed. Sometimes he wondered if he still had *eyes; he had no sensations of blinking, of crying, of fluttering lids—he couldn't even reach up to rub them, to find out if they were still there or if Father had blinded him.*

If only he could scream . . . but there was just numbness, a consuming nothingness where he knew his mouth should be. He'd long ago forgotten what it felt like to whistle, to click his teeth together, to moisten his lips with the tip of his tongue before letting fly with a good, loud raspberry.

Why did you do this to me, Father? *he thought.* If I did something bad, I'm sorry. Just, please . . . *please* let me out of here. It's so dark.

I'm scared.

I hurt.

Please, someone, come get me.

He remembered the faces of other children he'd seen (though he could never be sure where *it was he'd seen them), faces filled with joy, mischief, glowing with laughter, and he wondered if any of them had noticed him, if they remembered what he looked like, if they were now,* right now, *asking their mother or father where that little boy was, if he was coming back.*

The memory made him smile (he thought/hoped), because that meant he wasn't blind, after all. The darkness had just lasted a lot longer this time, but maybe that was okay because then he'd appreciate the Light all the more, and maybe, just maybe, if he appreciated it enough, then Father would never put him back here in this awful, dead, silent, dark, and lonely, lonely place.

Sometimes, when he remembered the threat (and Father had made it, hadn't he?) and the Bad Feeling came over him, the child would think about his own face. He thought he knew what he would look like, and the face he gave himself was a good one, yes it was; a good, friendly face, the face of someone another child would want to have as their bestest buddy in the whole wide world.

He pictured his face now and felt a little better.

But only a little.

Only a little was often all he had.

He remembered ice cream, and hot dogs with mustard (he didn't think he liked mustard), and big, juicy cheeseburgers. It all looked so good and tasty.

He could not remember the last time he'd eaten anything.

He couldn't even remember what they tasted like.

Or even if he'd ever tasted anything.

Why wasn't he hungry? He should have been starving—but then he remembered seeing pictures of other children in faraway countries, their bellies bloated from starvation, and some voice telling him that these deprived children reached a point where their hunger was so great they were no longer aware of how hungry they were.

Was that why he didn't feel hungry? Below him, somewhere in the darkness, was his stomach swollen?

He slowly became aware of occasional flickers of dim light piercing the darkness, flowing inward, and for a moment he thought Father had come back for him, smiling forgiveness and understanding, and Father was going to turn on the lights and say, "All right, then, you've learned your lesson. Now come on out. There are a bunch of your friends waiting outside, see? Run along, have fun. But behave yourself. You know what happens when you misbehave, don't you?"

The child waited, so excited and happy he could barely contain himself.

If he could have felt his hands, he would have clapped them together with glee.

If he could have found his legs, he would have bent his knees and bounced on his toes with anticipation.

If he could have laughed, that would have made everything all right. Forever.

Never again this darkness.

He tried to laugh, to force the sound out from the back of his throat and make everything All Right.

He thought about strands of cotton candy swirling onto paper cones.

He thought about playing catch with his friends in open summer fields when night was kept away by the buzzing lights surrounding the baseball diamond.

He thought about the music of a calliope and wondered why he couldn't remember ever hearing it.

Above him the blackness snowed a blizzard of images from his memory as the lens of night burned, blinding him once again with white-hot darkness in his eyes. Then:

Silence.

The crackle of fear.

Loneliness.

Abandonment.

No echo of laughter, for there had been none.

The child remained still, almost lifeless, and knew that he'd made a mistake about that light, those images and memories. It was part of his Forever-punishment. Father would show him all the things he was missing, all the joy and happiness and fun that would never include him, and it was mean and hurt so much and made him want to cry or shout or raise his fists and strike out or maybe smash through one of the windows in this room if it had windows, if it was a room, if he could move, if . . . if . . .

. . . if only he could scream.

But he knew he couldn't.

He also knew what Father was planning to do to him.

Soon.

Very soon.

Please don't, *he silently called out to the night.*

. . . and as much as he was capable, the child began to whimper, wishing for the release of tears. . . .

2

There was something in the air, something more than the humidity of another seventy-one-degree night; not quite tension, perhaps, but a sense of something unnameable impending. In the city below, it beckoned solitary figures to their windows to watch the murky light of the streets, their gazes following it upward to stare transfixed at the massive, brightly lit compound atop the somber hill, motionless as some ancient sleeping animal on the edge of civilization. There was a great insect humming in the air, singing in ceaseless, bumbling tones, rising a bit, falling a bit, but keeping the same pitch.

The breeze soughed and leaves fell silently from trees, tumbling with dry whispers, the rattling sound of a paper cup caught in the wind.

Crickets chirruped.

Frogs croaked.

Dogs howled mournfully in the distance.

The moth was unaware of any of it, save for the light.

It fluttered in ever-smaller circles toward the light, only the light, allowing nothing else to draw its attention away from a destiny its race was genetically predisposed to fulfill.

It felt the force of the light and, beneath it, something thrumming.

So close now, circling, so near to the light—

—the tip of its left wing touched the electrified chain-link fence and in a millisecond its fate was realized in a flashing *crackle-buzz* burst of two hundred and ten thousand volts that reduced the moth to ashes before its remains hit the ground. The moment of its fiery death was captured by the lens of a video camera positioned atop the nearest post; the image simultaneously appeared on one of the numerous screens in the security kiosk five yards behind the fence.

"Hot damn—zapped another one!" In his enthusiasm Ed Ransom accidentally spilled some of his coffee on his uniform, staining the PRESTON TECHNICAL SYSTEMS, INC. logo sewn to his shirt.

His partner, Daniel Gorman, shook his head and sighed. "You've got a real nasty streak in you, you know that? Pay attention to your monitors, all right?"

Another flicker on one of the screens, and Ransom turned just in time to see another moth bite the big one. "You suppose moths just get despondent and decide to, y'know, end it all? Think there's such a thing as moth depression?"

"Do you ever listen to yourself?" said Gorman.

"I try not to. What if I start to make sense?"

"I shudder at the thought." Gorman looked at his watch. "Show's supposed to be starting right about now."

"Let's hit it."

Both men moved to their respective consoles, entered the necessary codes and commands, and the bank of monitors came alive. The guards studied the screens with professional intensity.

"Radar's clear."

"InfraScan's normal."

"Ground sensor readings?"

"Consistent with last scan."

"No substantial change in circumference temperature."

"Distance?"

"Three hundred yards."

"Increase it to five."

"Done."

"Cameras five through twenty?"

"Operational, unimpeded view. Nice night."

"Audio?"

"Frequency-high. I think I heard a gnat fart."

The rest of the check took under one minute.

"Nothing," said Gorman.

Ransom grinned. "Tell me about it. A *ghost* couldn't get past us tonight."

Gorman reached for the phone, gripped the handset but did not lift it, and stared at his watch.

"Call in already!" said Ransom impatiently.

"Can't. Each station's been given a direct line into the main office tonight. I lift the receiver, and it'll be Prest-O his own regal self on the other end."

"When do you—?"

"In about fifteen seconds. It's gotta be solid clockwork. No excuses or screw ups."

"I tingle with excitement."

"That's called gas. I warned you about anchovies on the pizza."

"You care. I'm touched."

"You really *don't* listen to yourself, do you?"

Before Ransom could answer, Gorman lifted the receiver.

3

At the same moment Gorman checked in, a new security code came to life in the PTSI mainframe, replacing the one that had initiated only ninety seconds before:

Packet Type: Secret Key Packet

Length: 192

Version Byte: 192

Key Created: 8 August 2013 20:47:16

Initiate: 23:54:30

Modify/Morph (CW grammar): 23:56:00

Algorithm: 1 (RSA)

N:

CF7C85AAA6BBA6A928AA4Afde6236260533606FE88BE7891424A0148EAD3D

E: 11

Protection Algorithm: 0 (None)

D:

0C3480551A1cD917ADCD73C1C98A7E23032D03D986083ACBD24F99DED3D

P: D9(%#)+98ADBLCB+GAB=187ABFE7

Q: F3F075C82B5DEB1050−8FA690AF2CA

U: 41045F%AABD8BDFF62F02OEB9GBLB
Checksum: 403C

4

23:54:36

A hundred meters outside the electrified fence, unseen by the guards, three figures approached through the shadows, pausing each time the beam from one of the revolving searchlights swung around to illuminate the multiple coils of barbed wire that topped off the five-meter-tall fence.

The searchlight passed them by in seventeen-second intervals, punctuating their approach.

When the darkness was returned to them, they moved swiftly, making no noise.

Even the foliage remained undisturbed.

Dressed in black, with dark wool caps pulled down to just above their eyes, they were more than just invisible in the night—they *were* the night, and all its attendant shadows.

Sometimes—not often, but sometimes—Psy–4 found this ninja-like approach a little melodramatic, like something from an old 1980s action film.

Sometimes he felt a little embarrassed about it, but he would never dare tell anyone.

He didn't want them to interpret it as weakness.

Weakness in a leader—even *perceived* weakness—tainted respect and authority.

That wouldn't do.

Psy–4 stopped, crouched, then signaled the other two I-Bots to move forward.

Radiant took point, her lithe and graceful figure reminding Psy–4 of a gazelle—only the pair of electronic infrared night goggles she wore damaged the illusion.

She moved farther ahead, then signaled Stonewall to move in front of her; despite his massive and near-mountainous bulk, Stonewall's movements were quick, deft, and precise.

Just as all of them had been programmed to be.

Liquid-smooth and soundless.

The way Psy–4 liked it.

So synchronized were their movements, so effortlessly choreographed and executed was every gesture, pounce, and sprint, that they easily covered thirty meters during their seventeen seconds of darkness.

The searchlight came around.

They paused.

The light passed.

And they propelled themselves into the darkness once again.

They would not be detected by any sensors until they were three yards away from the fence.

But that was all the room they would need.

5

In his lush office overlooking the compound, Samuel Preston hung up his phone, smiled quickly to himself, checked the time, and said, "Looks like you're about to owe me a lot of money, Zac. Your people have less than ten minutes left. My guards say no one has even tried to get in yet. They'll never make it." On this point he was confident. In fact, Preston could never remember a time when he'd been *more* confident about anything; not only had he brought in extra security for this evening's test, he'd personally programmed the security codes and sequences into the computers.

He smiled to himself and, turning for a moment toward the window, wiped away the thin bead of sweat that was forming on his upper lip.

Across from him, seated in an antique wing-backed chair, a burly man whose full beard and thick hair were speckled with more gray than his thirty-eight years should have earned, leaned forward as he adjusted the suspenders holding his blue jeans in place. "Ten minutes can be a lot of time in some circumstances, Sam. You ever try holding your breath underwater for *three* minutes, let alone ten? Or not talk about yourself for that long? It can be an eternity. Trust me on this."

The two of them, once coworkers if never quite close friends, could not have contrasted one another more drastically; Preston, of the shockingly expensive tailored suits, hundred-dollar haircuts, and specially mixed cologne that cost more for two ounces than most people paid every month on their mortgages, was the epitome of the high-powered, high-rolling, high-salaried corporate executive; Zac Robillard, on the other hand, of the off-the-rack denims, fifty-cent elastic ties to pull his longish hair into a ponytail, and the basic frugal soap-and-water scent, more resembled the photos in recent history books of the so-called "ex-hippie" whose species was prevalent during the "Woodstock generation."

And so here they were, mused Preston: the Corporate Giant and the Long-in-the-Tooth-Ex-Hippie, jockeying for position.

He felt a twinge of fire deep in his center and pressed his hand against it.

This was, Preston knew, only a "friendly wager" between two

former coworkers; even so, his disposition didn't allow any room for humility—at least when it came to losing bets to someone so far down the ladder of success.

Time to play a card in his hand.

Preston opened a drawer and pressed a button. A split appeared in the opposite wall of the office as four separate oak panels slid back to reveal the massive bank of video and closed-circuit television monitors hidden there. The largest of the monitors displayed a series of layout schematics—what used to be called blueprints in the pre-HoloTecture days—decorated with series of flashing red, blue, and green lights.

"You've seen these, of course," said Preston.

"What do you think?"

"Getting grumpy in your old age, Zac."

"It happens."

Preston couldn't quite gauge Robillard's tone so decided to ignore it for right now.

He pointed to the oversized screen. "In case you've forgotten, the green lights are weight sensors; the blue, air-pressure sensors; and the red—"

"—temperature sensors. I remember." Zac looked entirely too calm for Preston's comfort.

"They're not in here, Zac. Your people"—he entered a series of commands on his keyboard, noting that his hands were trembling ever so slightly—"aren't even on the grounds yet, let alone inside this building."

The schematics on the large screen changed more rapidly now, bringing up a new section of the compound and all its buildings every eight seconds, while the rest of the screens displayed pictures of empty hallways, quiet sidewalks, locked doors, computer banks running smoothly with no human assistance.

Preston felt smug, if not good.

Dammit, he thought as the twinge of fire flared again inside him. *Not now!*

No way was Zac going to beat him on this one. Oh, sure, when they'd been at WorldTech together, it became apparent to even the most self-involved of the researchers that Robillard possessed the superior scientific mind. Though Preston resented the respect and even awe with which Zac was regarded, it quickly became obvious that it was he, Preston, and not Robillard, who had the upper hand when it came to corporate political savvy.

Guess who made it all the way to the top, Zac, he thought, studying Robillard's face.

Still, somewhere in the back of his mind, Preston knew that, ultimately, he was inferior to Zac Robillard in every way that counted.

But he'd become very good at denial.

Very good, indeed—he had the fire inside his gut to testify to that.

No way, no way in hell, would Zac Robillard beat him.

No way.

6

Ninety seconds after the mainframe security code changed, it changed again:

Modify/Morph (CW grammar): 23:56:00
INITIATE:
Algorithm: 1 (RSA)
N:
σκ–φφμβν∴κοπφυνβϖλκφπσα]ωα,χ∴=φγ
E: 11.rsa-n

Protection Algorithm: 0 (None)

D:

ιϖμασ+ππ[]∴θψφνμησιυζγ,δυφ−γϖκλ;

P: D9(%#)+98ADBLCB+GAB=187ABFE7

Q: F3F075C82B5DEB1050−8FA690AF2CA

U: 41045F%AABD8BDFF62F020EB9GBLB

Checksum: 403C

7

23:56:07

The child sensed the Bad Feeling again as he realized that he couldn't remember the color of his hair.

Blond? Dark? Light brown?

Was it straight, hanging down in his eyes so he had to brush it aside all the time, maybe puff it away with a good burst of breath, or was it wavy, even curly?

The Bad Feeling quickly gave way to sadness.

He couldn't remember.

And his sadness gave way to a deeper fear.

8

When the three I-Bots were less than nine feet from the fence, Radiant lifted her hands, signaling her companions to hang back. She adjusted her goggles, took a deep breath, then stepped forward into the range of the outside sensors.

Psy–4 was as still as death.

Even though he knew there was no security system that could

defeat them, he'd been programmed to never, *ever* discard any possibility, regardless of how outrageous or illogical it seemed.

And so he was a little on edge right now.

In fact, he was a little on edge all the time, but never more so than when they were executing a mission.

You never knew what might go wrong.

Or when.

He pushed his anxiety aside and concentrated on Radiant's movements.

She moved forward, hands straight out, palms up.

The air hit her hands and rippled backward like heat waves rising from an asphalt road in summer heat.

Psy–4 could smell the ozone, feel that crackling static electricity twisting through the atmosphere, brushing past him.

He looked at Stonewall, who nodded in his direction.

He felt it, too.

The night became blurred, shadows retreated, and the sounds of the crickets and dogs and countless other night creatures grew muffled wherever the sound waves passed through the ripples emanating from Radiant's hands.

She moved closer to the fence.

The ripples turned to waves, rolling forward, frothing the darkness.

This close to the source, the buzzing of the electrified fence was a physical force against the humid night, its volume rising with every step she took, becoming the vicious snarl of a starving junkyard dog ready to tear into a trespasser.

She never hesitated, never faltered.

Psy–4 stared at her, transfixed; she appeared to be in a trance.

He wondered if she knew how compelling she looked at moments like this.

The searchlight came around again, but this time when its

beam hit the ripple-shield around Radiant the light split, spread, became diffuse, and was swallowed.

There was an opening in the world where none had been before, a pit of night where nothing was seen or sensed; the maw of Death, wide and hungry.

But only for a moment.

As the searchlight completed its sweep, the split beams re-formed, fused into one, then continued the arc.

She remained undetected.

Standing before the fence, the electrical waves were so powerful that a few tufts of Radiant's startling silver hair, spilling from underneath her cap, stood on end with barely audible crackles.

Psy–4 saw her lips bloom into a small, self-satisfied smile.

Congratulate yourself later, he thought. *It's time to do your job.*

She reached forward with both hands and gripped a section of chain-link.

There was a brief, soft *pop!* when her flesh came into contact with the fence.

Psy–4 looked toward the kiosk.

The two guards were too busy scanning their monitors to notice what was surely only another moth buying the farm.

Radiant held firm to the fence.

Unseen machines and invisible trembling monoliths, the computerized entities she was sensing were at once compromised, humming and singing, grinding, clicking, growing in force, coalescing into a silent, whirling dynamo, around, around, up and out into the heart of all whirling invisibilities, fed into, read by, then accepted within a million-plus copper wires, thrice as many microprocessors exchanging innumerable geometric capability sequences—

—Psy–4 felt the welcomed excitement that always overtook

him when things were getting ready to shift into a higher gear, and he carefully watched Radiant as—

—an electric web poured over her, around her, the sizzling heat deflected by the ripple-shield, branching in four directions, then eight secondary directions as she hunched her shoulders and threw back her head—not only to signal her companions, but to direct the white-hot threads farther around and above her—

—Psy–4 and Stonewall emerged from the darkness, crouching until they were well under the protection of Radiant's shield—

—somewhere in the compound turbines whirred and hummed and screamed as the electric sparks and bolts jumped away from the intruders and clustered on the dew-soaked grass beneath their feet—

—Stonewall knelt down and slammed a fist into the soil, creating a hole three feet deep, then dragged his arm six feet straight across, earth and weeds and worms and stones spitting upward as he dug his small trench. He rammed both arms down into the space until his vicelike fingers found the buried base of the fence—

—he rose steadily, wrenching the fence base from the ground and pulling it higher, higher, the chain-links like scraps of tinfoil in his fists, peeling the fence back and up, rolling it as easily as a newspaper until there was enough room for his companions to walk through—

—Psy–4 went first, eyes darting this way, then that—

—Radiant followed him, quickly, quietly, her ripple-shield spreading over the barbed wire, then a few yards beyond, until she stood by his side—

—a nod from both of them, and Stonewall rolled the fence back down into the trench, straightening it, melding it back into the shattered ground below, which spread around the metal base as he pulled his arms out of the trench.

Quickly, with the expertise of a landscape artist, he replaced the remaining earth and rocks and worms and weeds that he'd disturbed—

—in a few seconds all was as it had been before, and Radiant brought her hands together, cupping them as if in prayer; the ripple-shield vanished as the wriggling electric strands shot back into the metal of the fence, humming and buzzing contentedly.

Stonewall retreated back into the darkness and the duties waiting for him there.

Radiant turned toward Psy–4, gave a quick nod, and they ran forward.

With a wave of Radiant's hand here, a finger point there, every motion- and heat-sensing detector surrounding them, both those buried and those in plain view, blinked and went blind.

No cameras recorded their movements.

No audio-scanners detected the vibrations of their breathing.

No radio-controlled ground-pressure devices registered their weight.

Psy–4 felt pleased about how well everything was going thus far.

Very pleased.

Until he checked the time.

A little over seven seconds had elapsed since Radiant first gripped the fence.

Seven seconds.

It should have only taken five.

Sloppy, he thought.

And there were no excuses for that.

None.

Dammit!

Overhead, a triple-bladed HeliCam swept down toward them, its bright red tracking beam hitting Radiant squarely on the forehead.

"Sneaky, aren't they?" she said. Lifting her index finger, she made a circling motion, and the toy-sized robotic airborne security unit did several loop-de-loops before she sent it on its confused way with a dismissive wave.

"Will you *please* not do that again?" hissed Psy–4.

"I can't help it. It's *fun!*" When this didn't get a reaction, she sighed and said, "You have got to work on your sense of humor, Psy–4."

"We'll discuss my dreadful personality problems later. C'mon."

"I thought this was going to be difficult."

"Stop whining."

"Oh, *all right.*"

"And tuck in your hair."

"Aw, *come on!* Do you know how long it's going to take me to get the kinks out after this? I swear, Psy–4, if you knew what it was like to have to—oh, don't glare at me like that. I'll be a good girl."

She began tucking the loose strands of her hair back under her cap as they moved toward the target area. . . .

9

The child gasped (or so he thought/hoped).

Time was he could have told the difference.

Someone's coming, *he thought to himself.*

He wanted to hope it was true, but would not let himself.

In this darkness, Hope was his enemy.

Time was, it used to be his brother—no, more like his older sister. Yes, he imagined it used to be his older sister, always looking out for him, cheering him up when he felt down.

But she had turned on him.

Even his own sister wouldn't tell him what he had done that was so bad.

10

Preston hit another hidden button and two large speakers lowered from the ceiling above the monitors; both hissed, but not from any electronic malfunction in their circuitry: The hiss was the sound of silence.

Zac Robillard turned to watch the speakers descend into place, and Preston used the opportunity to pull two small white pills from his pocket, pop them into his mouth, and take a quick drink of water from the glass sitting on his desk.

Robillard saw none of this, and Preston was quite pleased about that.

He'd kept it a secret for a long time, and the last thing he wanted was for Robillard, of all people, to ask him if he was feeling all right.

"Those speakers," said Preston, "are hooked into an audio tracking system that runs throughout this building. What you're hearing right now—let me turn the volume down a bit—there, that's better. Where was I?"

"You were about to tell me what I was hearing."

Preston glared at Robillard for a moment: Was that actually *boredom* in the man's voice?

Smug bastard, he thought.

Didn't matter. Robillard would be eating crow soon enough.

Preston cleared his throat. "You're hearing every sound that's being made outside the doors of this office in this building at this moment. There's nothing out there, Zac, except maybe a thousand or so mosquitoes."

Robillard rubbed his eyes. "I'm guessing you've got some kind of sensor installed God only knows where that can give you a precise count?"

Preston grinned, noting with satisfaction that Robillard's apparent boredom was swiftly changing to resignation. "I might. You never know."

Robillard nodded his head. "You always were one to use an uncertainty to your advantage."

"And you always considered that taking unfair advantage of someone. That was your biggest problem, Zac—hell, it probably still *is*."

"And what's that?"

"Your overwhelming sense of morality had no place in the business world, and because of it you could never tell the difference between duplicity and opportunity."

Robillard tilted his head to one side, quiet amusement momentarily in his eyes. "Does this just come to you or do you write it all down ahead of time and memorize it?"

Preston swallowed.

Hard.

And it hurt.

Robillard was trying to upset him, needle him, throw off his concentration with irrelevant humor. He just knew it.

Preston leaned forward on his desk. "They won't make it, Zac. Even if they manage through some fluke or divine intervention to get inside the compound, they'll never get inside this building. I designed tonight's security programs myself. Remember the old 'Catherine Wheel' theory we concocted back at WorldTech?"

Something jarred behind Robillard's eyes. "You *didn't?*"

Preston felt even stronger, even more in control now.

"Uh-huh. And it *works,* Zac. Only for short periods of time—in this case, five-and-a-half minutes—but it works."

Robillard wiped some perspiration from his forehead. "The Catherine Wheel program was designed as a game on paper! Lord, Sam, you could wipe out half, if not all, of your mainframe computers, having *that many* deliberately—"

"—if the program ran for more than a quarter of an hour, yes, but right now it doesn't." Another look at his watch. "I reiterate, Zac: They aren't going to make it."

"Yeah, they are. I promised them Italian food later if things went well. They really love Italian, especially when someone else pays for it."

"Must get awfully expensive for you."

Then Zac said something Preston wasn't expecting: "Oh, I fully expect it'll be your treat tonight, Sam."

"You're *that* confident in their abilities?"

Zac gestured toward the open briefcase containing ten thousand dollars in cash on Preston's desk. "You think I'd have taken you up on this if I weren't?"

Beside Zac's rather beat-up briefcase was an expensive attaché; this, too, was open, and also held ten thousand dollars in cash. Preston ran a hand over the money in both, a gleam in his eyes. "Hard to say, Zac. When we were both at WorldTech, I always had this sneaking suspicion that there was a reckless spirit hiding somewhere in all that girth."

"This," said Zac, slapping a hand to his protruding belly, "is not girth. I prefer to think of it as muscle in slumber."

Both men laughed, but not too loudly. Then Preston turned back to his window, hands clasped confidently behind his back, emperor of all he surveyed.

After a moment, he shifted his gaze to a darker area of the window and began surreptitiously studying the inverse reflection of Robillard's face.

Preston supposed that a lot of people—women in particular— would deem Zac Robillard's face "romantic."

Maybe.

Lucky S.O.B. had probably never exploited it to his advantage.

At a glance, it would be tempting to interpret Robillard's demeanor as an uneasy marriage between the manic and melancholy—or simply world-weariness kept at bay with occasionally forced good humor—but a close look into his soft brown eyes would soon reveal the anger, grief, frustration, and fear roiling beneath the surface of calm that he often fought to maintain. Of all Robillard's characteristics, this was the one that most unnerved Preston when he was face-to-face with the man: His eyes were haunted by phantoms. Beneath their surface, countless ghosts—perhaps of dead loved ones, or youthful idealism, or even belief in a world where scientific breakthroughs were for the benefit of all mankind, not just (as Robillard used to complain at WorldTech) those who could wield Damoclesean power to ensure that *they* chose who could and could not benefit—all these ghosts performed a never-ending dance of disillusion and regret, whispering, always whispering, *Careful, our friend. Careful.*

Preston figured if he himself had been blessed with a face like Robillard's—one with a mysterious, haunted quality—his meteoric rise to power would have been even more swift and stunning.

Zac glanced at the two security officers who stood on either side of Preston's expansive teak desk; both were dressed identically—dark suits with the breast pockets bearing the PTSI logo, dark ties, dark glasses—and both held Uzi submachine guns. They were so still and silent they might have been sculptures.

"Sam," said Zac. "I don't mean to appear ungracious, but I'd appreciate it if you'd tell Jake and Elwood there that I'd feel a lot better if they'd point those guns more toward the floor and away from my parts."

"They won't fire unless I give the word."

"They look like they're ready to hose the room if I so much as sneeze."

"Worried, are you?"

"Not for myself, no."

"For your people, then."

"No."

Preston was taken slightly aback by that. "*Not* for your people?"

"No."

"Then what are you worried about?"

"You and your guards."

"Why?"

Zac smiled a slow, subtle, maddeningly enigmatic smile. "That would be telling."

Bingo.

Preston suddenly felt anxious, and he wondered if perhaps Zac had something up his sleeve that no one could have predicted.

Score one for the visiting team, thought Preston.

Then: *I'll get you for that.*

Preston ordered the men to point their guns toward the floor.

"Happy now?"

Zac shrugged. "Thank you, though."

Preston couldn't make heads or tails of Robillard's reactions. He wondered if that wasn't precisely the point of Robillard's behavior: The old Deadhead was trying to confuse him.

That had to be it.

Didn't it?

Preston checked the time. "Six minutes, thirty, Zac. You're not even sweating."

"Should I be?"

"You tell me."

"Maybe in six minutes, thirty. *Sam*."

Preston groaned softly, feeling as if he were losing the upper hand, then reached under the desk and pulled out a large object that resembled a salesman's sample case.

He set it on the desk.

Opened the latches.

And stared at Robillard, readying to regain his momentum in their little tug of war. "Okay, my old amigo, what say we add a last dash of excitement to the recipe?"

"What do you have in mind?"

"This," said Preston, spinning the open case around and tilting it toward Zac.

It was crammed nearly to bursting with neatly arranged stacks of bills.

Zac's eyebrows rose slightly. "How much is there?"

"One hundred and forty thousand dollars."

Zac gave a low, long, impressed whistle.

"This is pocket money for me, Zac, chump change, and you know it. I want to up the ante."

"Including the ten-thousand dollars?"

"Yes."

Zac shook his head. "I can't match one hundred and fifty thousand dollars, Sam. The ten grand in the case is almost everything I've got."

"I know you haven't the resources to match a wager this cash-substantial . . . but that doesn't mean you don't have something even more valuable."

One breath. For one breath Preston saw a spark of panic flash across Zac's face—as if he were thinking something like, *Jesus, does he know about . . . ?*—but then it was gone.

Preston suddenly felt robbed. He deserved to watch Robillard's demeanor crumple, if only a little.

"What would that be?" asked Zac. "What do I have that's worth that much money?"

"You," said Preston.

11

Radiant and Psy–4 were moving quickly through a dimly lit corridor, thirteen seconds ahead of schedule.

"Here," said Psy–4, turning left into a shorter corridor that dead-ended at a large steel door. On the wall next to the door was a hand-scan panel. He removed his gloves and placed his hand against the screen.

There was a languid flow of green light at the point where his hand made contact.

Radiant killed all cameras and sensor devices with a snap of energy.

Something moaned mechanically.

Then Psy–4 nearly dropped to his knees in pain.

"Are you all right?" asked Radiant, placing a hand on his arm.

". . . uh . . . yes, yes . . . I'm . . . I'm fine."

"You don't *sound* fine."

Psy–4's voice was granite. "Just give me a second and I'll be all right. Okay?"

Radiant took a step back. "I've never seen you like this. It's genuinely frightening."

Psy–4 didn't hear her; he was staring at the steel door. "Down there," he whispered. "Something's not right. . . ."

"Psy–4? Come on, we don't have long left."

". . . so dark . . . and lonely . . . lonely . . ."

Radiant reached up and touched the side of Psy–4's face, startling him from his reverie.

"Huh—wha—? Oh. I . . . I apologize. Come on."

"Are you sure that you're—? Okay, okay, don't glare at me again. Is everything running as it should be?"

"Yes. Three hundred sixty-two seconds from now."

Radiant smiled. "Plenty of time."

"No," said Psy–4. "We—*I've* been distracted. It shouldn't have happened."

"But—"

"Not a word, Radiant. Not one more word from you."

12

NO! screamed the child. NO! Don't leave me, don't leave me here, you're so close, I'm right down here, not far, I promise, really, really . . . please come, please . . . I hurt . . . please . . .

Please don't kill me, Father. I don't know what I did wrong but I won't ever do it again, I promise, I promise, I promise, I'll be good, I'll make you proud of me, you'll see, just, just . . . please . . . please . . . please don't . . .

. . . ohplease . . .

. . . someone . . .

. . . come get me . . .

. . . ohplease, someone . . .

. . . someone come . . .

. . . come get

13

"Me?" said Zac.

"Yes, you," replied Preston. "And don't go pulling that modesty routine with me, okay? It impressed some of the folks at WorldTech but I never bought it for a second. You've got the sharpest mind I've ever known—aside from my own, of course—and I'm bored to death with not having anyone in my employ of equal intelligence. There's no . . . *challenge* here anymore. Do you understand, Zac? Hannibal has crossed the Alps and this time has *taken* Rome. *Wit,* Zac, I'm dying here for lack of genuine wit, lack of a good argument or a chess partner who'll beat me nearly as often as I beat him. My mind is shriveling from boredom."

"As evidenced by that ham-fisted Hannibal metaphor."

"I'm not sure I like your tone of voice."

"With all due respect, Sam, I don't give a rat's ass if you like my tone of voice or not. You should have heard yourself, all that 'Poor, poor, pitiful me' crap. How tragic, to have achieved all your goals before hitting forty. My God, the money, the fame, the power and women . . . it's a wonder you can stand at all from the constant anguish."

Preston was astonished. "You're making fun of me."

"Maybe a little, but there's no rancor in it. Besides, you deserved it. For a minute there, you sounded like some five-year-old who didn't get the bike he wanted for Christmas."

"This seems on the verge of getting unpleasant, Zac."

"Why, because I'm not agreeing with you? Because I'm not begging to kiss your royal ring finger like any number of flunkies around here?"

"You're getting nasty."

"No, I'm not, Sam. I'm telling you the truth and you don't want to hear it. You never were very good at listening to criticism."

"Criticism is only for those who can't cut it, Zac, who need guidance because they haven't the imagination or fortitude to—"

"—don't talk down to me, all right? I didn't mean to offend you, but unless I completely misunderstood what you were saying, you *want* someone by your side who isn't a brown nosed yes-man. Is that right or did I have an hallucination?"

"You didn't hallucinate." Preston hated the sound of his voice—petulant, pouting, like that of a child who'd just been scolded and knew in his heart that he deserved it. He also knew exactly why he was sounding that way. If Zac only knew . . . but there were some things a man could never share with anyone. Preston had to do this right. He felt that all too familiar pain in his gut. A tense silence fell on the room for a moment. Preston surreptitiously wiped the first faint traces of sweat from his palms.

"Let's drop it and start over," said Zac. "Okay?"

"Yes. I was just thinking."

"About what?"

About how much I'd like to wipe that confident look off your face with the heel of my shoe, thought Preston.

What he said was: "Here's my offer, my wager, whatever you want to call it: My one hundred and fifty thousand dollars against your ten. If you win, if your people manage to break through my security and take this office in the next three minutes, then you walk out of here with one hundred and sixty thousand dollars and leave me with egg on my face."

"And if I lose?"

"You know."

"Maybe, maybe not. Enlighten me."

Preston *really* didn't like the way this was going; it was starting to smack of his losing control of the situation. "If you lose, then you and your team will come and work for me. One year. After that, you can truck on down the old Happy Trail if you want." He looked at his watch. "Two minutes, Zac. Are we on? Do you agree to the terms?"

Zac grinned. "You've come a long way since our days in Vampirella's employ, haven't you?"

"Don't speak ill of Annabelle," replied Sam, returning the grin. "I'm sure her disposition's improved considerably since she bought the new coffin. You're begging the question."

"Tell me when we're down to forty-five seconds."

A long silence.

A thin bead of perspiration ran down the center of Preston's forehead; the fire in his gut was, thankfully, starting to be extinguished.

"Forty-five seconds, Zac."

Robillard put out his hand. "We have a bet."

Preston shook Zac's hand. "Sucker."

"A man is involved in a terrible auto accident," said Zac's voice from the overhead speakers.

Preston whirled around to face the screens. "What the—?"

And there was the face of Zac Robillard staring back at him from every monitor.

"He comes to in the emergency room and sees a doctor staring down at him. 'I've got good news and bad news,' says the doctor. 'The bad news is that one of your legs was damaged severely, and we had to remove it—only we cut off the wrong leg.' 'What's the good news?' says the guy. 'The good news,' says the doctor, 'is that your bad leg's getting better.'

"You've got a bad leg, Sam, and you've just been shown how easy it is to cut off both the bad one and the good one. I hope this doesn't bruise your ego too much," said all of Zac's faces, "but your state-of-the-art security has just been breached by Invasion Prevention Systems—which would be me. All communications from this office will be suspended for the next five minutes."

"Why?" shouted Preston at the screen.

"Just to be a pain," replied the many faces of Zac.

Preston picked up his phone to find the line was busy playing Glenn Miller's "In the Mood." He tried his computer keyboard, even resorted to voxax mode, then shook his head. "What did you do, plant a virus in my system when you came in?"

"Not me," said Zac, checking his watch, then pointing at the office door. *"Them."*

Before Preston could say anything, the door swung open.

A woman dressed in black and wearing night goggles walked in, accompanied by a muscular man who looked as if he ate car parts for breakfast.

"Two of my operatives," said Zac. "With ten seconds to spare."

Shit, thought Preston, reaching for his checkbook. "Okay, Zac, you win." He flipped open the checkbook and began to write in it. He wanted these people on his team—needed them desperately, in fact—and he didn't care how much it cost. "How much," he asked Zac, "is it going to take for you and your people—"

If he'd been on the verge of losing control before, then everything came crashing down around him a few seconds later.

The bank of monitors began to move, swinging out into the office proper, and from behind it emerged two more of Zac Robillard's operatives—one male, one female—each holding an armed guard bound with his own handcuffs.

Preston, shocked into open mouthed silence, looked over at the two security guards already in the office.

Even behind their dark glasses, their surprise was evident.

Dammit to hell! He'd gone through a great deal of trouble—

not to mention bribe money paid to the architect—to make sure that the hidden stairway and chambers below couldn't be found or even sensed with the most sophisticated surveillance equipment, but somehow two of Robillard's operatives had managed to find it, and these four security guards now knew where it was, and that it was a secret, and what was he going to do about them . . . ?

"Midnight straight up," said Zac. Then, to the second set of operatives: "Cutting it a little close, weren't you?"

"You know how I like dramatic entrances," said one of them, a young, well-built, fair-skinned Asian man. "I mean, it's one thing to watch someone else make them—not that I don't *enjoy* a good, vicarious thrill, mind you—but, honestly; how many times are you given the chance to pull an Olivier, a Guinness, a Gielgud, I ask you!" The young man's eyes were narrow and piercing, his hair black and shiny as melted tar and tied back in a long ponytail that draped halfway down his back.

"Ten minutes I've been listening to this blathering," said his partner, a stunning redhead, her deep, throaty voice made musical by its Irish brogue. "Going on and on, he was, even when I threatened to feed him his boots. I thought about trying to talk some sense into him, but then I realized there's not that much oxygen in the world."

"I understand," said Zac.

"He just *had* to take the bloody secret staircase."

Both Preston and his personal security guards—evidently having forgotten about their weapons—stared at her.

She was well worth staring at.

Even in the black slacks and sweatshirt, the curves of her rock-hard body undulated without mercy.

Preston knew he should be feeling more appreciative of the redhead's anatomy, but he was too worried right now.

He chewed on his lower lip.

God Almighty—not only did his personal security guards know there was something behind the monitors (that was bad enough), but, worse, Zac's operatives had managed to find a way in.

Undetected.

Preston had no way of knowing how they'd managed to bypass all the security devices.

He had no way of knowing how they'd gotten in in the first place.

Which meant that he had no way of knowing what they might have stumbled upon while making their way through his secret kingdom.

That made him nervous.

He hated being nervous.

He blinked, tried to smile, didn't quite make it, and so turned his attention back to the jaw-dropping redhead.

Something dangerous about her. Preston liked that. Dangerous women were one of Nature's ultimate aphrodisiacs.

Across from the redhead, the woman in the goggles removed her black cap. Preston's gaze—and those of his guards—were drawn to her thick waves of startling silver hair. Seeming pleased that she now held their attention, SilverHair shook out her luxurious locks, wet her lips with her tongue, and smiled.

The redhead glared at her, but not out of jealousy. "Don't push your luck with me."

The young Asian man looked around the office. "Nice desk. Everything so neat and just-so. Lots of extra room, too. Do many planes land here?"

Preston blinked. "What in the world are you . . . I mean, no . . . I mean . . . uh, um . . ."

"A complete sentence," said the young Asian, handing the two confused security guards the clips from their Uzis. "We're going for a complete sentence here—a qualifier, a verb, do I hear any votes for a dangling participle? By the way, you dropped this." He offered a small object.

"My *wallet!*" said Preston, suddenly patting himself down. "How'd you manage to—?"

"It's a compulsion. Got any Sprite in that wet bar over yonder?"

"Enough," said the muscular man who'd come in with the silver-haired woman.

"Sam," said Zac, "meet my team. Folks, this pale, well-dressed gentleman who is for the moment too awestruck to form complete sentences is Mr. Samuel Clemens Preston—who owes us a nice chunk of change, if I'm not mistaken."

Preston turned slowly around to face the handcuffed guards, cleared his throat, and managed to find his voice, weak though it was. "How did this happen?" he said. Then, much louder: *"What the hell were the two of you doing?"*

The guards looked at one another, then the floor, then one of them lifted his head and mumbled something.

"I didn't hear you," said Preston. "What were you doing?"

Ed Ransom, looking for all the world like there were 2,341 other things he'd rather be doing at the moment, slowly lifted his head and whispered: "Listening to gnat farts?"

14

WARNINGWARNING***WARNING***WARNING***WARNING***
<<<φ>>>ans=1:<<<φ>>>kbin=split(/./unpack('R*' pack ('D+D*, keyword (initiate)))
Packet Type: Terminal Key Packet
Keyword: RobRoy
Program Name: Playtime
Algorithm: 3 (RSA)

N:

3ΩΩΩΩΩΩΩΩΩΩΩΩΩΩΩΩΩΩΩΩΩΩΩΩΩΩΩΩΩΩΩ3 **Mark:**

0x556A4A676ōα;λκσδιενμνλ**76A4A655x0_ 123:48:57 E:13.sol. H M S**

—30—⊗**—30—**⊗**—30—**⊗**—30—**⊗**—30—**⊗**—30—**⊗

≈Σx∝AΠ_εΣ ∩ ∪–πσιγϕ=909εωπφφ;χρ? x←

Read Command: None

Pause Command: None

Stop Command: None

D+D Sequence Initiated.

Reason: Unknown connection made from within system *R*

Playtime initiated at: 23:59:09 8 August 2013

Estimated time of completion: 23:59:09 14 August 2013

Last Command: Say Bye-Bye

WARNINGWARNING***WARNING***WARNING***WARNING***

15

"I still insist it wasn't a bloody *fair* test!" said Killaine, brushing a few strands of her red hair away from her eyes. "After all, no huma—"

Zac raised his index finger, signaling silence, then turned toward the granite giant who was driving the van. "Any insects on the windshield, Mr. Green?"

"No bugs, no tracking devices, nothing here now that wasn't here this morning," said Stonewall.

"Good," said Zac, turning back to look at the others. "I apologize for having interrupted you, Killaine; please."

"All I'm saying is that no human could have sneaked in there as easily as we did. 'Tisn't a fair challenge to our abilities. Seems like cheating to me."

"But it isn't," said Zac. "Look, Killaine, the gear exists for any criminal who's got half a brain to duplicate everything we did tonight. There are grounding units that can interrupt and reroute current in a section of electrified fence, there are devices that can defeat sensors, and any decent programmer could easily rascal that computer system once in close enough proximity. Just because the group managed to do all this without hauling along a ton of bulky equipment doesn't mean that it can't be done."

Killaine shrugged. "I don't suppose I took the time to think of it quite like that."

"Alert the media," said Itazura, retying his ponytail.

"Don't you be starting with me," said Killaine.

"Listen closely," said Itazura, "and you'll hear my teeth chattering—no, wait; that's the sound of the shock absorbers. When are we getting some new wheels, Boss?"

"Itzy," said Zac, the warning clear.

"You can be replaced," said Killaine.

"No, I can't."

"No, you can't—but you've got to admit, it sounded good."

"Hey, Boss? I'm being harassed back here. As the only member of a minority, I feel that my civil rights are being oppressed."

"Oppress this," said Killaine, grabbing his wrist; Itazura grabbed hers in return, and the two of them began one of their infamous arm-pressure contests.

"Children—" said Zac.

"Did everything go well?" asked Stonewall.

"Yes, Stoner, it did."

In the back of the van, Psy–4 raised his head. "But it should have gone much better."

Zac sighed, exasperated. "You lost *two seconds,* Psy–4! Under the circumstances, I don't think you need to beat yourself up over that."

"Under other circumstances," replied Psy–4, "two seconds might have cost one—or *all*—of us our lives."

Itazura, still locked in mortal combat with Killaine's grip, shook his head and looked at Zac. "That's our Psy–4, snatching defeat from the jaws of victory."

"I was distracted at a crucial moment," snapped Psy–4.

Itazura shrugged. "I took the secret staircase, Kennedy fell in the Bay of Pigs, Cimino followed *The Deer Hunter* with *Heaven's Gate,* somebody invented the Edsel—we all miss. Get over it."

"I'm not in the mood for your snappy patter, Itzy."

"You know what, Psy–4? I'll bet if you'd been born to a Native American clan, they would have named you 'Dark Cloud.' Give yourself a break already. Would it kill you to crack a smile every now and then, or are you afraid we'd all run and tell?"

Psy–4 removed his wool cap and rubbed his forehead, massaging the row of input/output connectors there.

"'A fine setting for a fit of despair,'" said Stonewall. "'If only I were standing here by accident instead of design.'"

Zac looked at him. "And that is . . . ?"

"From Kafka's *The Castle.*" He looked in the rearview mirror and saw Psy–4 staring at him. "It just came to me."

One corner of Psy–4's mouth almost turned upward to form something that might have resembled the minuscule beginnings of a half-grin.

Radiant huffed, slapping her arms down to her sides. "I give up. I really do. I can't find the snap on the back of the damn strap. Help?"

"Scoot around," said Zac.

Radiant did so, lifting her silver hair so Zac could unhook the goggles.

Radiant pulled them away, then turned and smiled at Zac. "Thank you."

Where her eyes should have been there were only two smooth craters of flesh, giving her face the appearance of a mannequin whose face had yet to be sketched on, let alone painted.

It detracted not one whit from her beauty, and she knew it. So did everyone else.

"It's going to take *hours* to get the knots out of my hair," she said.

"One more word about your hair," said Killaine, "and it'll be taking you days to get the knots out of your titanium spine."

"Jealous?" said Radiant.

"Why should I be?"

A shrug. "Seemed as if all the men in the office were paying attention to me."

"And it's no wonder, what with the show you put on of removing your cap and—"

"Catfight, catfight!" shouted Itazura.

"Shut up!" said Killaine and Radiant simultaneously. A beat, then both looked at each other and laughed.

Zac laughed a little himself. "Okay, okay, settle down. Everyone did a great job. Preston was very pleased."

Itazura snorted a laugh. "Liar. Nothing personal."

"Well, okay, maybe he wasn't *exactly* pleased . . . but I sure am. One hundred and sixty thousand dollars tends to have that effect on me."

"That," said Itazura, "and knocking Preston down a peg or two. Oh, come on, Boss, admit it. Half the incentive to take that bet was knowing that you'd get to see him eat crow."

"Anything wrong with that?"

"Did I say there was?"

"No," replied Zac, "but I'm never sure with you. Besides— why shouldn't I get a little enjoyment out of this? While I was busy building the five of you at WorldTech, Preston was becoming rich and respected by marketing programs that we'd kicked around together."

"Liar squared," said Itazura. "Well, maybe not a liar, exactly, this time, but . . . aw, don't look at me that way, Boss. The creep ripped off a bunch of your ideas, made a few minor modifications, slapped a different name to them, and marketed them as his own creations."

"He *is* a very bright man."

"And Hitler painted roses. So what? One good trait doesn't redeem a monster."

While Itazura and Zac continued their debate (the death match between Itzy and Killaine having reached an impasse), Radiant moved to the back, seating herself next to Psy–4 who, for a few moments, merely stared out into the night, oblivious of her presence.

She gently placed a hand on his shoulder. "Psy–4? What's wrong?"

"There was . . . there was something *there* and we didn't have time to—"

"—look, if there was a delay, it was my fault. You know how I get sometimes. I'm vain, I admit it." She reached up and began massaging the back of his neck. "Come on, talk to me. I don't like seeing you this way."

"Do I really not smile that much?"

"Well, no, to tell the truth, you don't. But I've got a feeling this isn't about your—what did you call them? Your 'dreadful personality problems.' This is much more than that. Tell me. Please?"

Psy–4 looked at her, nodded his head, then placed one of his hands on top of hers. "You're not half as big a pain as Killaine says you are."

"She says that about me? Why, the *nerve* of some—I ought to—"

Psy–4's grip tightened. He pulled her closer. "We've got to get back in there."

"In where?"

Psy–4's reply was a cold stare.

"PTSI?" whispered Radiant. "Why?"

Psy–4 looked at the others, then back at her. "Do you remember when we first entered the main building? On the ground floor?"

"'Down there . . . so dark and lonely.' That part?"

"Yes."

"I remember you scared me. What happened?"

Psy–4 took a deep breath, rubbed his eyes, pinched the bridge of his nose between his thumb and forefinger, then sighed. "I heard someone crying when I telepathed with the computer system."

16

In his office, Samuel Preston sat drumming his fingers on the top of his desk, cursing under his breath.

His personal security guards and the two other guards stood silent and very much at attention on the far side of the office.

He had no idea what to do with them.

He sure as hell couldn't fire or reassign them.

And they were too good at their jobs to terminate.

Besides, he hated to waste good employees.

But that didn't mean he was above threats.

"All right," he finally said. "Here's the way it works. You saw the hidden doorway and staircase. I can *tell* you to not mention it to anyone but I can't tell you not to remember it. I have to live with that.

"Never speak of that passage, understand? Not to me, not to each other, and most definitely not to anyone else—because if you *do,* I'll find out about it, and I don't give a tinker's damn which of you says something or whether or not the others know, you'll all be expunged immediately. I don't mean simply killed; I'll have every last goddamn one of your records erased—Social Security numbers, driver's license numbers, birth records, blood types . . . you name it, it'll be gone. Then I will have every one of your acquaintances, friends, and family members taken out.

"Say one word about this, and within twenty-four hours there will be no trace anywhere on this earth or on the InfoBahn that any of you ever existed. Any questions?"

"Concerning what?" asked one of the guards.

"Concerning the hidden door."

"What hidden door?" said another guard.

"Good boys," said Preston, then dismissed them with a wave of his hand.

As soon as he was alone, he reached into one of his desk drawers and removed an exquisite silver picture frame.

Stared at the three figures in the photograph under the glass.

And swallowed twice. Very hard.

He thought long and hard about what had happened here tonight.

It wasn't just the money—he had plenty of money, what he'd lost had been nothing—no; what ate at him was how easily Zac Robillard's team was able to breach his security.

Even though he'd employed the Catherine Wheel program, they'd somehow managed to crack it.

But how? Robillard had no idea of the modifications that Preston had made in the past five years, turning the Catherine Wheel into more than either of them had ever imagined.

He looked at the three figures in the photograph again and

thought about the bright moments of youth that were all too quickly lost.

And the mistakes you sometimes made.

Oh, God, the mistakes.

He could feel the fire inside sparking back to life.

He laid the photograph facedown on his desk—perhaps a bit too hard.

"No human being could have done what they did," he said aloud to the lonely office, then popped two more pills into his mouth.

He picked up his phone, punched in a number, checked the time, almost hung up, then someone on the other end answered.

"It's me," he said. "I need to get in touch with Janus as quickly as possible."

Just saying the man's name made the blood chill in his arteries.

But he had to do it. His only other alternative would be to contact Annabelle Donohoe.

Anything was preferable to that.

Even dealing with a Class-A, #1, certifiable nuclear bomb of a dangerously unpredictable psycho like Janus.

Janus, he thought.

And the chill blood in Preston's arteries froze solid.

17

Time was the child had known happiness, hope, and acceptance.

123:18:22

But no more.
Never again. Not in this darkness. All this darkness.

Help me, *he whimpered.*
But no one answered. No one came.

123:18:02

Soon, it wouldn't matter. Soon, the darkness would be all.
And so the child remained still and silent.
But inside he was screaming. . . .

PART ONE

WHEELS OF CONFUSION

"A dwarf standing on the shoulder of a giant may see further thant the giant himself."

—*Didacus Stella in Lucan,* DE BELLO CIVILI

18

Annabelle Donohoe's expensively manicured fingernails, today sporting bloodred metallic polish, drummed rhythmically on the teak desk in her penthouse office in WorldTech's main building.

The incessant *scritch-scratch-scrape* sounded like the sharp, staccato cadence of a military drum beating the death march at an official execution.

Her face was backlit by rows of state-of-the-art track lighting and obscured somewhat by the wisps of smoke curling from the tip of her cigarette.

She sat hidden in shadows, except for her eyes, which shone with a bright, ominous anger visible from ten feet away.

She rose from her chair and leaned on the desk. A small light installed at the base of her intercom cast a diffuse glow upward, creating gothic shadows. Her face, though beautiful, looked like something out of the final reel of a black-and-white horror film. But that was all right.

She'd installed the light just for that effect.

She stared down at the well-dressed man who stood at the foot of the twenty-four-inch high dais that supported her desk. *"Well?"*

"Very intimidating, madam," replied Simmons, her personal assistant.

Annabelle's mouth twisted into a smile, which on her face fell somewhere between a smirk and a sneer. "Everything's ready?"

"Yes, madam."

"Then let's not keep our visitor waiting."

"Very good, madam." Simmons turned and exited through the

large wooden doors at the far end of the office. His Italian leather shoes whispered across the plush, dark carpeting.

It reminded Annabelle of the sound of a terminal cancer patient's last death rattle of breath.

She found the sound not at all unpleasant.

She crushed out her cigarette, lit a fresh one, then positioned herself on the desktop so that the first thing her visitor would see was her left side—her most intimidating side, if the rumors she heard were to be believed.

She cast a quick glance at the seven-by-nine-foot photograph of the late actress Joan Crawford that covered a large portion of the wall behind her desk. "Bette Davis had nothing on you, babe. Not even Dietrich could be as nasty."

Her free hand reached up and clutched the small locket that dangled on a fragile gold chain she wore around her surprisingly delicate throat. *What did I know,* she thought. *What did I know of love's austere and lonely offices?*

She drifted away for a moment, turned a corner in her mind, and tried to recall the name and author of the poem from which that line had come; as always happened when she went around that corner, she pulled in a slow melancholy breath, for it was only here, in this secret place that no one else knew or would ever know about, that she was not entirely in control of her destiny.

And that stuck in her throat like bile.

Nowhere on this earth was there anyone who believed more in controlling her own destiny than Annabelle. She refused to believe in luck, or happenstance, or fate and divine intervention. She had as a child, but now, as far as she was concerned, such flights of fancy were the last refuge of the hysteric: frantic attempts to explain chaos—or at least give the appearance of having explained it. They were too easy and too cheap a way out of a dilemma.

Annabelle refused to shake her head and throw her hands up in thrashed capitulation to the incomprehensible machinations of the universe. No, not for her; she was a woman driven to answer all the questions at hand, to meet every challenge issued, or else succumb to the snarl altogether.

If she had to go down, she would do so fighting.

And probably take several dozen people with her.

But Annabelle Donohoe, CEO of WorldTech, had no intention of being brought down; not by the so-called turns of nonexistent Fate and especially—*most* especially—not by the back-alley, late-night duplicities of an underling who thought the quickest way up the rungs of this particular corporate ladder was to step on her toes, symbolic or otherwise.

She exhaled a plume of smoke, ran her tongue over her lips, moistening them, and then pulled her dress up just a tad higher, showing a bit more thigh than was necessary or professional.

She wanted to make the little twerp sweat in every possible manner.

The office doors opened and Simmons entered, followed by a young man in an expensive power suit that had been tailored to accentuate his well-toned body.

Annabelle swallowed her urge to laugh. With his dark, slicked-back hair, striped shirt, solid color tie, and suspenders, he looked like a throwback to the laughable Wall Street power brokers of the early 1980s. Of course, 80s retro was very *in* right now, and this twerp hadn't even a passing acquaintance with an original notion and so followed what he'd been told was popular.

This is going to be fun, though Annabelle, knowing all too well how a tiger felt the moment before it snuffed out the life of a fleeing zebra.

"Madam," said Simmons, closing the door behind him and gesturing toward the young man, "Mr. Anton Tyler to see you."

"Thank you, Simmons," she replied. "Please remain in the room." She looked down through the smoke and shadows at Tyler. "Richard Nixon recorded the conversations in the Oval Office when he was president; I prefer to have Simmons present. Of course you don't mind." It was not a question.

She pointed to a chair and Tyler took a seat, doing an admirable job of masking his anxiety.

"So, Mr. Tyler—or should I say Tye? That's what everyone calls you, isn't it?"

"Yes, Ms. Donohoe," replied the young man. He had a surprisingly high voice for one whose form was so classically manly.

"Oh, do let's dispense with the 'Ms. Donohoe' nonsense, shall we? Call me Annabelle."

"I . . . uh, I don't know that I'm comfortable with—"

"But I insist," interrupted Annabelle. "I *absolutely* insist upon it. I wish for all gutsy folks to call me by my first name." She picked up a folder and tossed it over the desk, down into Tyler's hands. "Especially those who go behind my back and attempt to submit unflattering reports to the Board of Directors. I think that brand of gutsiness—and it's quite rare around here—requires that we dispense with formalities. Of course you agree with that, Tye."

His eyes widened with panic. "Ms. Dono—uh, um—Anna— *Ms. Donohoe,* I can explain this."

"You can? Did you hear that, Simmons? Our friend Tye here says he can explain the unflattering contents of those eleven and a half, impeccably-typed, single-spaced pages that he holds in his hands."

"What a relief, madam."

"Yes, I thought you'd think so." She sat down, blew a puff of smoke down into Tyler's face, and grinned as he coughed and waved away the cloud, trying to read the pages.

"I trust my smoking doesn't bother you."

"N-n-no, Ms. Donohoe. Not at all."

She blew another stream into his face. "I'm listening," said Annabelle.

"I'll be honest with you, Ms. Donohoe—"

"Honesty is good, I like honesty. Simmons, what are your feelings about honesty?"

"That it is the best possible policy, madam."

"So we're all agreed that honesty is what's needed here. I beg your pardon, Tye, I seem to have interrupted you once again. Please, do go on."

Tyler loosened his collar, stretched his neck, and rubbed his arm, already sweating more than Annabelle had hoped.

"Do you think it's hot in here, Tye?"

"Maybe just a little. I apologize, I . . . I seem to be running a slight fever."

"Did you agree to the drug test this morning? I certainly hope so, Tye. Everyone here has to submit to it every three months or I send them on their merry, unemployed way."

"Yes, ma'am, I did."

"Oh, no—don't you *ma'am* me, Tye. 'Ma'am' is for English nannies and other assorted old maids." She moved around enough to expose a little more thigh and was pleased that the young man's eyes focused precisely where she wanted them to. "You don't think I'm an old maid, do you, Tye?"

"Not at all."

The barely contained lust in his gaze and words amused Annabelle no end.

"Don't even think about it, Tye. I'd chew you up and spit you out before you even had your shirt off."

"I . . . I'm sorry if I was staring at—"

"You're perspiring, Tye. Temperature up a bit, is it?"

He blinked. "Yes, Ms. Donohoe."

Annabelle poured herself a healthy dose of cold water and sipped at it, reveling in the look on Tyler's face as the ice *tink*ed against the sides of the glass.

"I'll tell you what, Tye; I'm going to give you one chance—*one*—to explain to me why you did what you did, and if at any time during your explanation you sound even the least bit supercilious, Simmons over there is going to tie knots in your spine. Is any of that unclear so far? I could start again and talk slower."

"No, you've made yourself quite clear, Ms. Donohoe."

His explanation wasn't precisely what Annabelle was expecting.

She listened with great interest as the little cockroach explained that he'd been sent over from the main Accounting Division to secretly examine the books from the last five years, paying particular attention to the budgetary excesses of the last sixteen months—specifically, the money that Annabelle had allotted for the continued search for Zac Robillard and the five I-Bots.

"The board has become seriously concerned about the money, time, and company resources that you've . . . squandered on this search," said Tyler. "Some of the board members feel that you've . . . well, that you've . . ."

"Gone a little overboard?" prompted Annabelle.

"Yes. The word they've been using is 'obsessed.'"

Annabelle drummed her fingernails on the desk once again, louder this time, more forcefully. "And what is your personal opinion, Tye? Do *you* think I'm obsessed with Robillard and the I-Bots?"

"It's not my place to say, Ms. Donohoe. When my predecessor, Mr. James, resigned and left the company with all of his notes—"

Annabelle lifted her index finger and shook it from side to side, twice. "Ah-ah—be careful you don't jump to conclusions, Tye. That can be hazardous to your health."

Tyler blinked, looked back at Simmons, then swallowed loudly as he wiped the sweat from his forehead. "I'm afraid I don't understand, Ms. Dono—"

"You will." Annabelle walked away from her desk and pointed to the large photograph on the wall. "Do you know who this woman is, Tye?"

"Can't say that I do."

Annabelle shook her head. "Infidels, Simmons. Tyler here is among those pitiful infidels who haven't the slightest idea who St. Joan was."

"Most distressing, madam."

"Isn't it?" She returned her attention to Tyler. "This was a great lady and great actress, Tye. Her name was Joan Crawford, and in her day she was *the* grande dame bitch of Hollywood. At one point in her life she was married to the CEO of Pepsi. When he died, he left all his stocks to her. Pepsi's board of directors was a little uncomfortable with having a woman in charge of their company, and they asked her to step down. Do you know what she said to them, Tye? No, of course you don't. St. Joan laughed in their faces, refused to step down, and said to them—and this is a direct quote from the minutes of that meeting—'Don't screw with me, fellahs.' I admire her. That declaration to Pepsi's board of directors has been something of a mantra for me all these years."

She crossed back to her desk and pressed a button.

The giant photo of Joan Crawford hissed then began to slide slowly to the side, revealing something behind it.

"Don't screw with me, fellah," said Annabelle, delighted at the way Tyler looked—as if he'd just soiled his pants.

Behind the photo of St. Joan was a two-way mirror that looked into a shabby room where a shabby little man, bald and severely overweight, wearing a torn white shirt and split trousers, sat in a chair before a wooden table.

On that table were several empty bottles of liquor.

"Recognize him?" asked Annabelle.

Tyler blanched. "My God, it's . . . I mean, I can't be sure . . . but it looks like Mr. James. We had been told that he resigned and—"

"You were told what I *wanted* you to be told. I've known for a good long while that someone on the board has been planting spies in here, and I'm sick of it. I thought perhaps James's disappearance might get my message across to them, but your presence here proves that assumption wrong—and I *hate* being wrong, Tye. You might want to keep that in mind." She snapped her fingers and Simmons joined them at the window, holding a small radio-control keyboard in the palm of his hand.

"There's a tribe in Africa, Tye—well, what's left of it, anyway—called the Masai, and every so often they choose one of their elders, or a cripple, or some other useless member of the village, and they give them a huge party, then take them out into the jungle and leave them there for the hyenas to eat alive. It's their way of not only controlling the population but of thinning out those elements that might taint the purity of their tribal genetics." She nodded at Simmons, and her assistant extended the silver antennae attached to the device in his hands then pressed a switch that activated a red indicator light.

"You keep an eye on your predecessor in there," said Annabelle to Tyler. "Because right now I'm going to tell you the same thing I told him—and maybe you'll listen. This world, Tye, from pole to pole, is a jungle. Whether that jungle is composed of vines and swamps or boardrooms and contractual pen strokes, it's all the same, no different from the one where the Masai feed the hyenas. Its inhabited by various species of beasts, some that rut in caves and devour their young, others that wear tailored suits and dine on their business rivals' broken stock speculations. All of these beasts have only one honest-to-God function, and that is to survive. There is no morality, no law, no imposed man-made dogma that will stand in the path of that survival. That humankind survives is the only morality there is. And for us to survive as a race, we must be superior, we must dominate all lesser creatures, and, in order to ensure that, it is not only vital but necessary to destroy, to eliminate, to thin out and expunge any undesirable element that threatens to stop the march of progress. Now, you're a smart young man, Tyler—I've seen your records—so I'm sure you know where this is going."

"I don't think so."

"Pity, because this has got one hell of a punch line." She snapped her fingers, and Simmons pointed the antennae toward the figure of James, then pressed a button.

James dropped to the floor and began to thrash around, screaming.

"Besides the I-Bots program, Tyler, did you examine other budget records?"

"A few, but—"

"Did you happen to glance at Nano-Tech Division's records?"

"Briefly."

"Then you know about the experiments we've been conducting with nanites."

"I know a little about it but it's not an area that I'm . . . well, very knowledgeable in."

Annabelle looked at her assistant. "Simmons—fill Mr. Tyler in on our most recent developments, will you? And Tye? Don't take your eyes off James in there. I like to provide a good floor show for selected employees."

And that's when Mr. James's flesh began to smoke.

19

—and now there were bodies scattered on the ground in front of him as a result of the panic firing but Janus kept up his pace across the compound's main yard, increased it even, because nothing slowed him, nothing tired him, nothing stopped him, not even the bullets strafing down at him from the security towers. There was less gunfire now than a minute ago but that was only because they were getting ready to release the dogs. He'd expected that, and the gas, too, only someone had gotten impatient and given the order to use the bombs too soon and the yard was now impenetrable with gas clouds. Security guards were running this way and that, firing indiscriminately because they couldn't see a damned thing, and that was good, that was very good, because Janus always came prepared, he'd put on his CX–47 mask and could breathe easily, and that was really, really good—

—the sirens were getting louder, screaming like monsters, and that wasn't so good, not so good at all because it was giving him a headache, but then a guard came out of the smoke plowing off shot after shot, a second guard fired off a round and accidentally caught the other right smack in the knee, pulping it, and the guard did a flip, landed hard, tried to crawl, and Janus smiled behind his gas mask because no one crawled too damned far with a kneecap gone, so he pulled the Colt Python from out of his shoulder holster and just to be a good sport about things blew the guard's head clean off his shoulders on the way past because, after all, what was the guy going to do with the rest of his life, having a knee all shot to hell like that?—

—he rounded the last corner of the main yard and headed toward the gate that was now visible through the haze of gas and smoke and gunfire, but now there was the outline of another guard, one stupid hero guard armed with one mother of a semi-automatic rifle and Janus charged toward him with all he had and Mr. Hero got off a couple of shots, one pretty close, one grazing Janus's shoulder, but that didn't stop him. He kept charging forward until he was close enough to make a fist of his right hand, a club of his arm, and one swing later the guard was out cold on the ground and Janus grabbed up the rifle and spun around, switching it from semi- to full-automatic, and with one squeeze of the trigger began to hose the yard behind him.

The scream of the sirens was nearly drowned out by those of the guards he was laying to their final rest on the hollow points of bullets, and now things were good again, things were very good indeed, so Janus let fly with one last burst of gunfire and ran through the gate into the snow-covered street, running, running, running along the route he planned out months ago, running toward the frozen lake and the special box of supplies he'd planted there before breaking into the compound forty-seven minutes ago—

—he could hear them spilling out of the gates behind him, firing their warning shots, the idiots, but underneath the crackle of gunfire was the snarl of the dogs, so Janus picked up his speed and flew around a corner of the lake road and lo and behold *thank'ya Jee-zus* here came a car straight toward him, and the driver saw what he was in for and hit the brakes and the car came to a shrieking, fishtailing halt in a cloud of snow and ice but Janus didn't have time to be polite or even wait to see if the driver's side door was unlocked, so he just skidded up beside the car, blew out the window and most of the driver's skull with the last bullet from the Python, tossed the body out into the snow, slammed closed the door, ripped the car into drive, and took off in a straight line right through the middle of the guards, cutting through them like a machete through foliage, clipping a couple, fender slamming two of them, then he whipped the car around, skidding for all it was worth, but the driver had been a conscientious one, yessir, because the snow tires were good ones, giving Janus traction to spare, so it was easy for him to plow through the rest of this first wave of guards and dogs, flattening several of both like pancakes before flooring the accelerator and heading on down the lake road.

Six minutes later he was deep in the woods surrounding the frozen lake, discarding his clothing and slipping into his specially modified wetsuit, inflating it, strapping on his air tank, checking the oxygen regulator, donning the underwater mask.

The boots Janus wore were specifically designed for ice divers who, rather than chance the force of changing currents, chose to walk upside down below the ice. Five-inch spikes covered the soles of each boot. Nothing short of a bomb blast could loosen their hold once they were entrenched.

Janus activated the oxygen tank, put the regulator firmly into his mouth, swung the speargun strap around his chest, secured his quiver of spears to his person, and double checked to make sure he had the disks he'd just stolen securely sealed in their protective case in his belt. His last pistol, a deadly Colt Anaconda .44 Magnum, was firmly held in a watertight holster strapped to his thigh. There were those who would probably think Janus paranoid for taking a gun underwater with him, but years of experience and wounds had taught him to take nothing for granted.

He had a gallery of scars from the rare occasions he'd forgotten that rule.

Admittedly, he'd made a few slips the last couple of years, but nothing serious, nothing he'd told anyone about. Though he knew he might be getting too old for his particular line of work, he tried with all his still-considerable might to deny it.

Even to himself.

Especially to himself.

It was, perhaps, one of the few genuinely human foibles he possessed.

He checked his air timer: thirty minutes. More than enough time to get from here to the drying shed three-quarters of a mile down the lake.

He'd chosen this method for his getaway for several reasons, not the least of which was that he loved the peace that lay beneath the water. It would give him time to regroup after the violence at the compound—a form of decompression that was necessary to keep himself in one solid mental piece.

Aside from the ethereal quiet he found beneath the ice, Janus had chosen this method of escape because many of the roads leading in and out of the area were too bombarded with snow and ice to be traveled by any vehicle besides a snowmobile, and a snowmobile would attract too much attention.

He lowered himself down into the hole in the ice he'd cut earlier, steadied himself, then pushed back his legs as if readying for a somersault until he felt the spikes take hold.

A moment later, he was under the ice, walking across the lake upside down.

For the first fifteen minutes, his otherworldly walk was bliss. He had cut out two exit holes, in case of any trouble with the oxygen tank, but he didn't think he'd need the spare exit.

Then he heard something like a drum. As he neared his exit, the sound became louder, and irregular—not like a drum at all.

The water, so much denser than air, conducted sound as air molecules never could. As a child, Janus had liked to lie in the bathtub, his ears in the water, and hear the enormous clanks and knocks his toy boats could make as they bumped against the porcelain. It made his boats real. Now Janus heard sounds that seemed like footsteps: far away, yet all around him, the water carrying vibrations too long for air to carry. As he approached his entrance, they did not seem to grow louder from there—the water unlocalized sounds—rather, they grew louder from everywhere.

Janus stopped and stood still. Tried to listen. The sound was too confused.

Then, since he stood inverted, Janus looked "down," as it seemed, and saw very clearly, in front of him, the footprint of a man on the ice.

One black, ripple-sole footprint. In front of him.

Another joined it—perhaps the man had raised a knee to fix a boot.

Two black bootprints. Guard's boots.

A guard from the compound was standing on the opposite side of the ice from him: right side up on the other side of the ice on which Janus stood upside down, like figures on a playing card.

Janus tried to figure out how the guard had gotten here so quickly—probably used a hover-car—then decided it didn't matter.

The guy was here now, and that didn't figure into Janus's scenario.

The ice was translucent, not transparent: Only the black boot soles pressing flat against the ice could be seen. Janus's silver air bubbles began to congeal on the ice's surface, and he stiffened, then decided they were too light for the guard to see. Janus's boots, suspended from the ice by crampon spikes, should be similarly invisible.

The man's shadow fell across the ice.

Janus flinched and looked around, then he realized he cast no shadow in his otherworld.

The black soles turned, and Janus saw the unmistakable outline of a gun fall across the ice.

It looked thin—but that could be a trick of the light; thin and

long like a rifle, not a gun you'd use to hunt anything out on this
ice. In winter there were only ducks and geese out on the marsh.
Any hunter worth the price of his ammo would use a shotgun to
hunt.

The outline turned again: Janus saw, unmistakably, the shadow
of a protrusion above the barrel, thicker than the barrel, that began
above the pistol grip and ran no more than a quarter of the barrel's
length, where it flared out in a bell. A scope.

Only rifles had scopes. Shotguns didn't even have ordinary
sights.

The bootprints started walking in front of him. Janus followed them, walking upside down beneath the man, a pace behind
him.

From the way the bootprints stopped, made half-turns to each
side, and from the way the shadow of the rifle swept in an arc
along Janus's glowing ice, back and forth, Janus knew for certain
this was a guard.

The bootprints kept on—Janus stalking the stalker. He found
them moving in a curve toward some point. Every five steps the
prints would stop, the long compound shadow of the rifle and
scope would sweep along the ice like a shadow searchlight across
a glowing sky, then the bootprints would continue. Janus gradu-
ally became sure.

His mouth twisted.

Hunting me.

Janus followed the bootprints in their curve, certain they were
heading for his second exit hole. They were waiting for him to
come up.

Good God! And I think of myself as an intelligent person. He'd
cut the hole in his idiosyncratic way. He had his own ways by now.

He had cut his exit hole near the ice divers' drying shed a
quarter-mile away. He hoped they hadn't found the shed, but

they'd guess it wouldn't be far from the hole. They'd know he would freeze into a statue unless he could get inside shelter quickly once he came up. The water was never colder than twenty-eight degrees, but the wind above on the lake gave a chill factor of sixty below zero on this ice. That was the rate at which he would turn into an ice statue unless he dried off within a very few minutes of surfacing. How in God's name could he get out of this? He had only the Anaconda .44 Magnum pistol and the speargun; they each had guns, he presumed. He didn't doubt there was another guard up there, maybe more. They'd know it wasn't safe for only one of them to try to take him.

Janus trailed along beneath the guard's bootprints and the gun's searching shadow. *This was what you wanted, wasn't it? You against them? But not here,* Janus thought.

Dinoflagellates twinkled above him. He walked shod in silver on the glowing pearl of the ice.

And marring his pearl: black bootprints, and the shadow of a gun.

They were at the exit hole. He'd sunk an Ikelight below it for safety. The clouds overhead were thick, perhaps they had noticed his light, even so deep? Was it too strong, the Ikelight? No. They'd just been lucky. But if he survived this he wouldn't use the Ikelight any more if an assignment involved ice-diving. There'd be more chance of becoming lost beneath the ice, but it would be better than this: one single-shot speargun against the rifle.

Ahead he saw more shadows by his entrance hole.

Another pair of black bootprints.

The prints Janus was following reached the other set and they faced each other, conferring. Shadows now of two guns, two scopes.

Two men with rifles waiting at his exit hole. Odds were they knew his single tank couldn't carry much more than forty minutes' worth of air.

I'm dead, Janus thought.

He could feel a tug when he tried to breathe and had a spasm of fear. Sucking at the air as the tank emptied was like trying to breathe through a pillow pressing tighter and tighter against his face.

That wasn't his only problem. He had lost great quantities of body heat the whole time he was underwater. Not just from the exhaustion; the water, with a specific heat exactly one thousand times greater than air, had been conducting warmth away from his body twenty-five times as rapidly as air would at this temperature, Fahrenheit twenty-eight. The lake had been leeching heat from him—heat of energy, of strength and redemption, of life itself—while he was under.

He had only a very small reserve.

The shivering and the coldness he felt in his hands were signs his extremities had already fallen below ninety-seven degrees Fahrenheit. His body's thermoregulatory system had turned on its defense mechanisms and he'd begun to shiver.

Damn!

Heavy shivering increased the body's basal heat production five to seven times. The vasoconstriction called gooseflesh meant his skin had begun sealing itself tighter to keep body heat in, stop blood flow to his periphery, where heat evaporated faster, and pre-serve it around his core organs. These were signs his body was chilling toward death, had gone through its heat and fallen onto its last reserve.

It was getting damn cold under here.

His blood temperature was dropping too fast.

Time was running out on him.

They knew it.

He knew it.

All God's chillun knew it.

All they had to do was wait him out. Perhaps that was why they were both at the hole now, anticipating his return.

He couldn't think of alternatives. He could walk to some spot of shallow ice by a tide island and break his way out easily enough—and freeze to death. More than air, he needed to get into that drying shed, which his heater had been warming since he began this assignment, where hot liquid was waiting in a thermos, where his cache of Just-In-Case weapons was sitting, and—most important—where his two-way radio waited, powered by a portable generator that had maybe thirty minutes' worth of juice left.

If his core temperature—the deep tissue areas of his body, as opposed to his extremities—had fallen only two degrees Fahrenheit below normal, to ninety-seven degrees, or thirty-six Celsius, as he thought of it, then Janus had already begun to die of hypothermia. When his deep tissues reached thirty-four degrees Celsius his brain would begin to go, and at thirty-two Celsius his heart.

In the wind above, that could happen within minutes. Even if he could manage to kill them within two minutes of his exposure to the air, there was a chance there might be damage to his brain.

Janus stood upside down, opposite the guards standing above him. All they had to do was wound him badly and every-thing would go haywire—even if he killed them. In his current situation, even a mere scratch could prove instantaneously fatal. He had to kill them; all they had to do was hit him. And he was wildly outgunned. Janus, fumbling in the cold, removed his tri-cut point from his speargun and took a stempoint from his bandolier. He could take one shot, but then he would have to reload. There were, after all, two of them.

Janus looked at his timer. Seven minutes of oxygen left. His cheeks inside the mask were collapsing as he sucked air like a baby straining at an empty bottle. It took precious effort not to panic.

A pair of bootprints stood near the hole. Janus's heart beat intensely: *Near enough?*

He walked underneath the man and knelt, inverted directly below him. He studied the boot soles. Rubber. Really meant for mud. Not bad for ice, but Janus's spikes would have the edge on traction.

Where there was an ice break like his exit hole, water usually bled around it for several feet. The weight of the ice pressing down on the entire lake kept forcing water slightly up, like a pressure valve giving. Helpers would spread sand by the hole if they were backing up an ice diver so that they wouldn't slide in. But Janus had no backup crew; he hadn't prepared the ice with sand. Immediately next to the hole, then, he could hope for a slight slick on the surface, over and beyond the slipperiness of the ice.

Was the man close enough?

As Janus watched, the bootprints stepped closer, and the gun shadow swung in the arc he knew. The guard was scanning: His gaze was raised.

Janus dug his spikes into the ice and reached out of the water.

The guard, from the corner of his eye, saw something black move out of the water and seize his ankle: Janus's suited arm and mitt. Before the guard could fire, Janus pulled him across the slick ice and into the hole.

To Janus, it was as if he had pulled the man, upside down, into a cloud of air bubbles that lived in his world. The guard fought like a great fish hauled on a line from the depths but he weighed nothing. Janus held on to him and tottered away from the hole, carrying him at arm's length. Even under water the guard's gun fired twice, but he couldn't aim. The thousands of bubbles this manfish had brought with him moved upward to the ice and rolled about, trapped against the frozen surface of the lake. The guard gasped and struggled exactly like a fish in air, except that he kept seeming to want to fly upward out of Janus's hands.

His boot kicked Janus in the face, and Janus's mouthpiece wrenched out but Janus held his breath, keeping the guard above him like a weight lifter pressing a barbell over his head, going for a world record—until he saw the guard take heavy gasps of water and go inert. The gun finally slipped from the man's grip. Janus let him go and got his mouthpiece back in. He was so cold he was dizzy—his stomach and chest felt like frozen lead. The guard's body, like a slow balloon, floated up in space and hung among the starfish.

Beneath his feet Janus saw, in flashes, the bootprints of the other guard appearing and disappearing on the ice. Janus pulled desperately on the scraps of air in his regulator, but the pillow was pressing tighter and tighter across his face. He tried to prepare, but the cold was reaching his brain and slowing it down.

This guard must have seen the first go under, perhaps seen where all the bubbles the first one brought in coagulated, because suddenly there was a terrible noise inside Janus's head, inside it, all around it, and from the center of the bubble mass he saw a streak of bubbles fly through the ice as fast as a tracer bullet in wartime night.

The guard, panicked, was shooting at the ice.

Janus moved away from the bubbles as shot after shot punched through, each bullet marked by a brilliant silver bubble trail that bent in the water after a few yards and arced in all directions.

Janus pushed himself away from the eruptions.

The bullets followed.

This guard had quickly learned to distinguish where Janus's bubbles were beneath the ice.

Janus held his breath and moved. The bubble he had breathed a second ago bounced down his side and reached the ice. A second later a bullet burst up through it, angled in the water, and almost caught him. He saw the trail of bubbles it made go past his eyes.

Janus made a sharp right. Inadvertently some air left the regulator and reached the ice. A bullet came up through it instantly.

Janus guessed, and made a quick dodge backward. He was right—four bullets pulled up through the ice in the direction he had been going. The guard had seen the track of the bubbles and was leading him. He was a better hunter than the one Janus had just killed. Janus's air was nearly gone and he was freezing: He couldn't keep this up much longer.

He held his breath and angled—no bullets. The guard must be changing clips. To fire so quickly the gun must be a semiautomatic.

Janus crouched, let out one breath, pushed the shaking bubble with his hands, and sprang away from it. The second it hit the ice a bullet lanced it, probing for him.

Janus moved in a circle, trying to get his little speargun into position to fire. Each time he breathed he shoved the bubble from him and danced a different way to the side. The bullets came up through them, the water shook with the sound, but he was not hit. Janus fought to watch the bootprints with one eye and the bullets with the other. His mask limited his field of vision dangerously. Janus circled, working to get the open entrance hole between him and the bootprints.

A bullet, perhaps an hysterical shot, came through the ice almost at Janus's feet.

The guard was close to the hole now, on the other side from Janus. The last few shots he had been pivoting—Janus would see the heels disappear as the man rose to his toes in the pivot. The ice, Janus imagined, must now be awash from the fountains of water that had sprung up whenever the bullets plunged through the ice. The man was not trying to move on the slick ice but was wisely holding still, turning, then aiming his weapon. Janus doubted that, unless he was an ice diver, the guard knew his boots could be seen—and he could see nothing of Janus but the ghosts of bubbles.

Janus blew breath out, pushed the bubbles behind him and to the left, leaped with his ten-pound weight a long moon-leap sideways from the boots so that at last he had the open water of the exit hole between him and the guard. Thunder, water vibrations; bullets whizzed like bees through his bubbles as they touched ice. Janus landed kneeling. Through the shining surface he saw, as if beneath him, blue sky and the gray parka of the guard, aiming a long brown stick toward the water. The water magnified everything, so that Janus saw the guard, shimmery but large; saw the gun fire and kick; saw him as clearly as if he, Janus, knelt on a rock, and looked at a six-foot-long fish just beneath him in the clearest water.

The guard would see him just as clearly, too.

Before the guard could swing his gun and shoot through the hole, Janus fired. The speargun's stempoint, nine times larger than a .45 Magnum round, hurled up out of the water into the guard's stomach, glanced off the inside of his ribs, and—with the one-ton stainless cable holding it to the stem—the five-inch blade swung like a clock hand inside the man's tissues, from eleven o'clock to five o'clock, slicing through half the organs in his body.

Janus saw the print of the guard suddenly on the ice. One cheek and the side of his nose were pressed against it, enlarged, like a child's against a store window, and his rifle was trapped beneath him.

Janus straightened and walked around the hole. The guard lay under his feet. The ice turned pink: The icewater on the surface had diluted the blood.

Janus looked up. The guard lay, arms stretched above his head, like a ballet dancer.

Janus no longer felt anything when he killed. Gore no longer startled him.

God, it was so hard to breathe; he sensed his reason going. *Get out.* Janus stepped over the hole into the other world. The suit ascended.

Hooking his inflated legs over the edge, then drawing his floating body out with short pulls of the spikes, Janus lay, suited, in the water beside the hole, looking at sky. He ripped his mask aside and breathed.

Janus pressed his suit valve down, deflated it.

He stood up, slowly.

The enormous weight of his body returned as the Earth's pull reasserted itself. He had not weighed more than ten pounds during the last thirty minutes, and now he weighed one hundred and seventy. It was like being yoked with cannonballs. The extra fifty pounds of his tank was a crushing weight on his back.

Janus looked *down* at the water and felt dizzy, looked *up* at sky and felt confused—*out* of his element.

The guard lay next to him in a red pool already partly frozen. Janus put down his pistol. He would hide the man in the water.

As soon as the Anaconda left Janus's hands he heard someone say, "Hold it right there."

Idiot!

Why had he thought there'd be only two guards? Hover-cars moved fast and furiously, could cover half a mile in a few seconds. The sound of shooting must have been heard for miles along the ice! They probably fired up the first of the hover-cars before he'd even escaped the compound. *Oh, you moronic horse's ass!*

The ice was forming white crystals around Janus's suit. The skin on his face tightened: Ice crystals were covering it. He had to dry off.

He was preparing himself to turn and face them down—he thought now only in terms of *them* because to think otherwise could be lethal at this point—and had just begun to pivot when he saw a thin leather strap come flying down across his field of vision. He managed to get his hand up in time to prevent the strip from constricting around his throat.

Janus spun around, his would-be strangler holding tight, and saw that there was, indeed, a fourth guard. This one had a pistol and was trying to aim at Janus's head but there was too much movement right now for the guy to get off a good shot. Any hit right now would just be lucky, even though the guy could take Janus with it if he was quick enough, which he wasn't, but that was all right with Janus because right now he was dominated by pain both from within and without, and pain changed his world, put a cloud around him that he couldn't see through, preventing him from acting in accordance with logic and experience and training.

For a moment, as the thin leather strap cut into the flesh of his hand, Janus was feeble and clouded and clumsy and ripe for death.

Standing stock-still, a target on a shooting range.

But the other guard, the kid with the gun, was too slow and the moment went by.

Janus's brain began to clear. *You're the best there is!* he raged at himself. *Maybe you're getting too old for much more of this shit, but right now you are STILL THE BEST THERE IS and you have to do something* NOW!

He hit those words hard in his mind because the kid with the pistol was moving around, trying to get a decent aim again, and so what if his mind was clearing up, a bullet could crush clear tissue as well as cloudy, and the Strangler behind him was strong, almost as strong as Janus, and he had to use that to advantage somehow, had to do something extraordinary, something remarkable, unique and awe-inspiring, that was all, nothing to it, and he had to do it in the next five seconds.

Go.

And think about raising your rates next time.

The Strangler was strong but the Strangler was shorter than Janus—

—the kid with the gun was getting closer—

—the Strangler was quick but the Strangler was now stationary—

—the kid raised the gun into the firing position, supporting his firing arm with his free hand, a classic shooting-range stance—

—*so if you can budge the Strangler, if you can unsettle his balance, if you can do that—*

Janus faked going right—

—and went right.

The kid whirled left and fired into empty air and the surprise on his face was all that Janus needed; he powered everything he had into completing the next move, and behind him he could feel the Strangler's strip loosen slightly as the man's balance momentarily deserted him—

—and with all the power in his great body, Janus hunched forward, pulling the Strangler with him, and when he had his balance, Janus put all of his strength into a shoulder throw, sailing the Strangler helplessly over him and into the too-slow kid.

The two of them went down hard on the ice, and the kid was stunned as he hit, losing his grip on his weapon, and the gun skidded across the ice. Janus saw it but so did the Strangler, and the Strangler went for it, scrabbling and sliding along the ice like a desperate roach.

Janus let him.

His right hand was next to useless, bruised and bleeding from the leather strap, so he merely watched as the Strangler got closer to the gun—

—then Janus kicked the Strangler's head off—

—or tried to; the Strangler was ready and grabbed Janus's foot and snapped it around, tripping him—but not before Janus got off one good spiked kick into the Strangler's shoulder, following it up with a blow from his left hand, but it only grazed the Strangler's head because even on his knees, even still dazed from the throw, even bleeding from the deep gashes left by Janus's spikes, the Strangler could still move, and Janus went for another left-hand blow, and again the Strangler spun free; another left-hand barely connected as the Strangler writhed and twisted, and he really was like a roach, a waterbug that you could see and chase but somehow never catch, and both of them went for the gun then, but it was clumsy going, pained going, skidding-on-the-ice going, and when Janus saw that he might not get to the gun first he kicked at it and sent it spinning toward the exit hole and smiled as it teetered on the edge then fell in with a soft *plop!* The Strangler chopped him on the neck, but Janus faked sideways enough so that the Strangler missed a death spot—but that didn't mean it didn't hurt like hell, didn't make his nerves shriek, didn't start his brain to clouding again, which—coupled with his desperate need for heat, for warmth, for drying—served to slow him momentarily, but Janus would not allow that to happen—not for long, anyway—*If I cloud, I'm gone, it's that simple*—so he wriggled away from the Strangler's grip and connected with a spiked kick to the side of the Strangler's head, ground-zero on a death spot, and when his spiked boot hit, there was a double cry of pain, and who was to say whose was the greater agony, his or the Strangler's. All Janus could be sure of was that the Strangler's was over a lot sooner.

Gasping, cramping, bleeding, Janus managed to get to his feet, then moved past the dead Strangler and finished off the kid quietly before staggering into the drying shed. It was so blessedly warm, so heavenly toasty and welcoming, and he fell onto the pile of blankets he'd left there, wrapping himself in them like a child hesitant to leave its mother's womb, and then he reached for the thermos of hot tea and sipped it, then gulped it, not caring about the searing pain in his throat, and soon he was able to breathe easily and move freely with only a little agony. He managed to get out of his wetsuit and into some dry, warm clothes, taking care to check out the window for signs of other guards who might have heard the shooting earlier, and as he looked he saw maybe a dozen hover-cars rising out of the compound, swarming together, massing like dark, angry hornets, but before they could clear the distance the air ignited in a thunderous flash and Janus grinned because the first of the six bombs he'd set in the compound were now detonating, seven seconds apart, and would level 90 percent of the main building by the time they were finished, so that meant he was probably safe for a little while, thirty minutes tops—and that reminded him about the radio, so he staggered over and flicked it on, turned the transmission dial until he got the frequency he needed, instructed the person on the other end to patch him through, and when the person he wanted to speak to was on the other end, Janus said, "It's 'Come-and-Get-Me-Time.'"

"Did you get the disks?"

"You'll have to pick me up to find out, won't you?"

"I'm not in the mood for attitude, Janus."

"Neither am I. I need medical attention, so have a doctor ready."

"You'll have everything you need. Give me your location and I'll have the chopper airborne in five minutes."

"You'd have a little trouble landing where I'm at." He gave them an alternate location, a field less than half a mile from his present location. "I'll be there in twenty minutes."

"The chopper will be waiting."

"It damned well better be," said Janus, "or your precious disks are going right into the lake."

"What a trusting soul you are."

"Just my warm and fuzzy nature. Don't be late."

And with that, he killed the connection, gathered up his weapons, and set about preparing to blow up the shed and most of the ice supporting it.

20

It took Mr. James a lot longer to die than Annabelle had estimated.

Not that she didn't have the stomach for such things; for her, watching someone who'd betrayed her die was akin to stepping on a worm wriggling on a hot sidewalk, and carried about as much guilt.

Still, it was fun to watch the expressions on Tyler's young face as he watched the other man begin to fry from the inside out.

And all the while, behind him, there stood Simmons, reciting the facts aloud in that delightful, clipped, and (Annabelle thought) subtly sexy watered-down British accent of his.

"What you're watching, Mr. Tyler, is the fruition of Ms. Donohoe's improvements on the function of nanites."

Tyler, not moving his gaze from James, said, "W-w-what're those?"

"Nanites are used for manufacturing on the molecular level, sir," said Simmons patiently, as if addressing a slow-witted child. "They are, for all intents and purposes, microscopic-sized robots. The one in Mr. James's system looks something like a mechanical spider.

"They are programmed to build anything—organic and inorganic—from the base up, including themselves. They can self-replicate."

"What he's saying," whispered Annabelle in Tyler's ear, "is that all we have to do is introduce one preprogrammed nanite into a person's system, and within a few hours there can be thousands, millions, theoretically *trillions,* of them swimming along with the cells."

"Then," said Simmons, "they begin the process of breaking down, then rebuilding a person's molecular structure, causing a chemical reaction that turns a human being into a time bomb."

"It all has to do with quarks and something known as the X-Particle Theory and gets a bit complicated," said Annabelle, "but the upshot of all this is that we have produced nanites that can force a human body to spontaneously combust . . . providing that there is a sufficient amount of alcohol in their system at the time. Over ninety percent of all cases of spontaneous human combustion involve individuals who have been drinking heavily—much as you were last night, Tye."

"How did you know—"

"Shhh," said Annabelle. "I know everything, dear boy. Haven't you figured that out by now? But, please, watch dear Mr. James."

On the other side of the two-way mirror, James's skin began to ignite; first his arm burst into flame, then his legs, then his stomach, and within moments his entire body was aflame.

It didn't last long.

With a near-blinding flash of smoke and light, James's body exploded, drowning the room in flames.

Bits of sticky, seared, unidentifiable tissue slammed against the mirror and . . .

Stayed in place.

It was grotesque.

Unspeakable.

And, to Annabelle, at least, wholly deserved and justified.

She crossed back to her desk, pressed the button, and the gigantic image of St. Joan slid back into place, hiding the ugly, horrifying aftermath on the other side.

"Very impressive, don't you think?"

Tyler couldn't speak.

This pleased Annabelle.

Greatly.

"Too moved to find your voice? I understand. So you can just listen for a moment." She nodded to Simmons, who walked to the other end of the room and opened one of three wall safes in Annabelle's office.

From the safe he removed two items: a small glass vial with a rubber-stop top and a black case.

"Last night, Tye, did you have a good time with the blonde you met at . . . oh, at that club—what was its name, Simmons?"

"The Shalott, madam."

"That's right, the Shalott—though I doubt anyone who works there knows the name was stolen from Tennyson. Anyway, Tye, did you have a good time with her?"

His face was turning ash white now, but he managed to nod his head.

"I understand that you were pretty plotzed on Cutty Sark, is that right?"

Another terrified nod.

"Too bad you passed out before getting to the main event. Tawny said she thought you were cute and she would've been happy to—well, you know." She put out her hand and Simmons placed the glass vial into her grip.

Annabelle showed the vial to Tyler.

"Do you know what this is, Tye? The boys in the lab have dubbed it 'Liquid Burn.' Has a nice ring to it. This is a massive swimming pool where one of my nanites is having a relaxing swim. You see, the thing is, most people have the impression that a nanite can only be introduced into the human system by injection. Not true. All it takes is for someone—say, a busty blonde named Tawny who's looking for a way to advance her career—to unstop a vial like this and pour the liquid into another person's Cutty Sark. Do you see where I'm going with this?"

". . . yes . . ."

"Sorry, didn't quite catch that. Simmons, could you make out what Tye here was saying?"

"Afraid not, madam. My hearing isn't what it used to be."

"Care to repeat what you just said, Tye?"

". . . said that, yes, I can see where this is going."

"So now you know why you're feeling a bit feverish, right?"

"Yes."

"And you've undoubtedly surmised, bright boy that you are, that the 'drug test' this morning was simply our way of checking to see if the nanite had succeeded in self-replicating."

"Yes."

"Care to know how it's doing, Tye?"

"Does it matter?"

"Very much so. Right now, judging by the amount of nanites found in your blood cells, there are roughly three hundred billion of my little friends tearing you down bit by bit at the molecular levels as we speak. The fact that you haven't yet ridded your system of the vast quantities of Cutty from last night is a definite plus."

Tyler swallowed, wiped his soaked brow, then raised his head, trying to meet her gaze. "How . . . how long do I have until . . . until . . . "

"Until you do the James Jump? About three hours. We've developed three different strains of nanites, you see. James's were the least destructive. The ones in your system are the second strain, much nastier, and on a timer. Unless, of course, we *choose*

to override their programming and press a certain button. But . . ."
She purposely didn't finish.

Tyler jumped up from his chair and started toward her.

One of Simmons's massive hands gripped his shoulder like a vice and forced him back down into his seat.

"But *what?*" shouted Tyler.

Annabelle put out her other hand.

Simmons handed her the small black case.

"But," said Annabelle, "there is a way around any further unpleasantness. All you have to do is tell me *which* member of the board has been planting spies like you in my company."

She opened the case, then held it out so Tyler could see the contents.

A hypodermic syringe, shiny and clean, nestled like a sleeping baby in a red velvet cradle.

"Care to guess what this is, bright boy?"

"*. . . please . . .*"

He was nearly in tears.

Sweat had ruined his shirt.

His meticulously coiffed dark hair hung down in his face like vines.

Annabelle felt elated.

She had broken him.

"This syringe contains, naturally, the closest thing to an antidote that the lab boys have managed to create. While it won't destroy the nanites in your system, it *will* erase their programming and prevent them from manufacturing any more of themselves. They'll be harmless enough, though they'll remain in your system forever.

"But at least you'll be safe, Tye. All you have to do"—she removed the syringe, held it in the light where it glistened—"is give me the name of the board member who put you up to this.

That's all. One name, and your life is yours once again."

"They'll . . . they'll have me killed," he whined.

"No, they won't. If anyone is going to have that pleasure, it will be me." She pushed the plunger slightly, watching as the tip of needle spewed forth a tiny amount of liquid. "Your call, Tye."

He stared at her face.

Then the needle.

Then the photo of St. Joan.

"Would you—I'm sorry, Tye, I've been rude: Would you like another look at what's left of Mr. James?"

"NO!" he screamed, then began to weep. "All right. All right."

He gave her the name she wanted.

Annabelle gave Simmons the syringe.

Simmons gave Tyler the shot.

Everybody was happy.

"One last thing, Tye," said Annabelle, leaning down and placing one of her hands against Tyler's cheek. "I wouldn't tell anyone about this if I were you." Suddenly, her hand became a clamp that snapped up and closed on his face, squeezing with such power it was easy to believe the bones in his skull were going to implode from the pressure. "I am everywhere, Tye, hear me? There is nowhere in this world you can go, no hole deep enough, no cave dark enough, where I don't have an operative. That's not a threat, bright boy, just a simple statement of fact.

"*This* is the threat: Mention this to anyone, tell anyone, even *allude* to it, and I promise you that you will never feel safe in your world again. I'm afraid I pulled a little Agatha Christie on you. The nanites in your system *have* had their programming erased, but that in no way means they have been rendered useless." She snatched up the small palmtop unit and turned it toward him, the button clearly visible. "If I choose to, I press this button and the nanites in your system will do the James Jump. Understand me? Think of them in terms of an unexploded bomb: harmless as long as I don't decide to press this button." She pulled her other hand away from his face, making sure to dig a couple of her fingernails into his cheek as she did so.

Drawing his blood, she felt satisfied.

"Ooops," she said coyly. "I'm afraid that's going to leave a nasty scar."

Simmons escorted Tyler from the office.

Annabelle turned and faced St. Joan.

After a few moments, she began to cry.

Gently fingering the locket.

What did I know? She thought. *What did I know of love's austere and lonely offices?*

It was several more moments before she became aware of Simmons's presence in the room.

Not bothering to hide or wipe away her tears, she turned and faced her assistant. "What is it?"

"Are you all right, madam?"

"No, I'm not all right—and why do you persist in calling me madam when we're alone? Surely we've gone beyond that in the years we've been together."

"Because the word is more than a mere formality to me," Simmons replied. "It symbolizes the respect I have for you—the respect you've earned."

He began fixing a drink for her. "Might I inquire what you'd like for me to do with the information Mr. Tyler provided?"

"You know perfectly well what I want you to do."

Simmons handed her the drink. "Just double checking, mad—*Ms. Donohoe*." He smiled. "I have you to thank for that. 'There's no such thing as being too cautious.' You said that."

Annabelle smiled at him. "You know, Simmons, you're the only one who understands me. Sometimes I think you're the only friend I have."

"I like to think of myself as your friend."

Annabelle took a sip of the drink. Then another. "But you still know I wouldn't hesitate to have you killed if you ever betrayed me."

"Anything less would disappointment me."

Annabelle nodded her head, took another sip. "Oh, if those fools on the board had any idea how much Robillard and those damned I-Bots cost me personally—and I'm not just talking about the money and face, Simmons."

"I'm . . . I'm well aware of what they cost you. And if I may, I'd like once again to tell you how very sorry I am that—"

"I know," said Annabelle, clutching the locket so tightly it made her hand hurt. "And I appreciate it." Then: "Was there some specific reason you came in here?"

"Yes. You have an urgent call."

"Why didn't you tell me that right away?" she snapped, crossing quickly to her desk.

"You were upset, Ms. Donohoe. As far as I am concerned, nothing is so urgent as that."

Annabelle grinned at him. "Don't you *dare* start getting sentimental on me now, Simmons."

"I will go out and purchase a copy of *The Cynic's Manifesto* immediately."

"You do that."

Simmons left the office.

Annabelle took another sip of her drink, set it on her desk, looked toward St. Joan for divine guidance, and answered the phone. "Yes?"

"It's 'Come-and-Get-Me Time,'" said Janus.

21

Something was wrong.

She could sense it.

Smell it.

Feel it.

But if anyone had asked, she would not have been able to say exactly *what* was setting her nerves on end.

Killaine thought, *This doesn't make sense, being this paranoid so soon.*

She was having a hard time keeping pace with Zac as they made their way through the maze of alleyways toward the Scrapper camp.

It amazed her how quickly her creator moved, considering how heavy the duffel bag slung over his shoulder was.

The backs of the buildings here ran to three stories of dirty brick. Near the rear stoops were Dumpsters and garbage cans with all the attendant scrawny dogs and starving cats prowling for sustenance.

The air carried the smell of decay; rotting food and motor oil and animal waste and old sweat mixed with the rich, loamy scent of mud and the sharp, stinging odor of—

—metal.

Most human beings would probably mistake it for the smell of ozone, this scent, but Killaine knew the scent of metal well. She inhaled it every time she undressed for bed at night.

She'd always thought that a bit odd; even though she was covered in synthetic flesh from head to toe, she could still smell the metal underneath the skin.

And it wasn't just her; on more than one occasion, Itazura and even the vain Radiant had confided the same thing to her.

She took one last deep breath, nearly gagged on the cumulative stench of the dank alleyways, and decided to power-down her olfactory system until they were well away from this awful place.

Still, she couldn't rid herself of the feeling.

Something was wrong.

She knew it.

To make matters worse, rain was pounding down from the black morning sky, hitting the iron overhangs, each drop sounding like a bullet fired from a high-powered weapon.

Rain puddled at their feet, deepening the mud, making each step more precarious than the one before.

Rain flowed from the roof gutters, creating blurry waterfalls that obscured their vision.

Rain slid along the railings of the fire escapes like shiny pinballs in the tracks of arcade machines, pooling on the mesh landings, dribbling down like tears.

There was no way it could have been any more oppressive.

Or depressing.

Or potentially unnerving.

And it wasn't even ten A.M. yet.

Killaine hated days that started off like this.

A few yards ahead of her and Zac, their silent guide turned and gestured for them to hurry.

Bloody Scrapper, she thought, fisting both her hands.

Not that she had any intention of doing the Scrapper harm; for one thing, it wasn't in her nature; for another, she thought it a waste of effort.

As if he'd read her mind, Zac suddenly slowed his pace in order to speak with her. "I know your feelings about the Scrappers, Killaine, and I'd appreciate it if you didn't do or say anything to offend them."

"I'll not be lying to you, Zachary, I've never cared for their type."

Zac shook his head. "You sure didn't get that from me."

"Maybe it's my inherent Irish clannishness." She smiled.

Zac did not return her smile. "You know, don't you, that I *vehemently* detest that particular characteristic in you?"

"You could always erase it from my—"

"—never! Don't even joke about something like that."

Killaine immediately felt ashamed of herself. She'd only been trying to win the argument by any means necessary—a characteristic that none of the I-Bots found particularly endearing—and thought she could gain the upper hand by making an absurd suggestion.

She could see how deeply she'd hurt Zac's feelings.

And after their talk earlier this morning, she'd felt as if the two of them had grown a bit closer.

Maybe she could fix things.

Make them better, at least.

"I'm sorry, Zachary," she said, placing a hand on his shoulder. "I truly am."

Of all the I-Bots, only Killaine called Zac by his full name. She hoped this displayed the proper amounts of both respect and affection.

Zac nodded his head as their silent guide rounded a corner ahead of them into another maze of alleyways. "I detest prejudice of any kind, Killaine. I just wish to God that—"

His words were cut off as they rounded the corner and saw their guide standing stock-still, arms raised to the level of his waist.

A few feet in front of their guide stood a young man in a long, dark, leather duster coat, his shaved head glistening with either rain or perspiration.

His left hand hung at his side.

His right hand came up quickly.

Holding a gun.

"Well, well," he said. "Looks like I'm gonna make my quota, after all."

Killaine began to make her move.

Zac grabbed her arm, stopping her.

"No," he whispered.

"Why?"

"He's got an electron gun."

Killaine felt something in her center go suddenly cold.

With fear . . .

An hour earlier, a little after eight A.M., Killaine had gotten out of bed, feeling quite refreshed from last night's PosiTrance Time, and decided to make breakfast for everyone.

Killaine was glad that Zac had decided to program them for PosiTrance Time—the equivalent of human sleep—because it gave their neuro-programming an opportunity to more fully collate, absorb, and apply the myriad bits of information they accumulated. *When* to power-down into a PosiTrance state was a matter of personal choice for each of them—they were, after all, more machine than human, so "sleep" wasn't necessary—but Killaine chose to "sleep" at least three times a week.

It made her feel more like a human.

Zac took great care to program them with as many human characteristics as possible.

Killaine was always the first one to rise in the morning, earning the annoying cloying nickname of "Sunshine" from Itazura—a nickname that the other I-Bots, seeing how much it grated on her nerves, quickly took to.

She knew they meant no harm, that it was all only in good

humor but, still, there were times she wanted to clap any or all of them upside the head.

You've got to learn to rein in that temper of yours, Zac had told her on more than one occasion. *If you don't, you're going to get us all in a lot of trouble someday.*

So, well aware that someone was just dying to irritate her, Sunshine rose from her bed, donned her terry-cloth robe, and started downstairs to make a good old-fashioned Irish breakfast for her friends.

The ingrates.

She was approaching the end of the hall when she noticed that Zac's door was open.

Killaine knew right away that Zac hadn't slept well, if at all; his door being left open was a sure sign that he'd been up during the night, wandering the warehouse that served as both their place of business and their home.

For now, anyway.

The warehouse that housed Invasion Prevention Systems resembled a kind of prison from outside. All the windows were covered with wire mesh. All the doors were slabs of reinforced steel. All the abandoned, stripped cars that squatted along the curb had smears of blood on the backseats.

Home Sweet, as the saying went.

The building was located in a section of the city called Cemetery Ridge by everyone except the people who lived there; the residents of this area probably didn't know that their street was unofficially named after one of the Civil Wars bloodiest battles, and even if they had known, odds were they wouldn't care. What they did know was that their neighborhood was the dividing line between one of the city's richest areas—Cinnamon Road—and one of its poorest. Depending on which side of the street you were standing on, you could either walk up the steps that entered the Taft Hotel—far and away the most expensive and exclusive of the city's hotels—or you could be dragged into an alley by any number of drug addicts, thieves, deviants, and murderers who preyed Shiloh Street. On several occasions, Killaine had watched as exquisitely dressed patrons of the Taft—with their jewels and furs and obscenely priced dinner jackets—stood along the large windows and stared at the shabby homeless people who roamed the other side of the street.

It always seemed to Killaine that the Taft people were smiling at the less fortunate ones only a few dozens yards away from them.

That made her angry.

Angry as hell.

It also made her feel both grateful and sad that she wasn't wholly human—but she never wished to be wholly robotic.

Human beings with their petty squabbles, their greed and avarice, their duplicities and lusts and perversions and—

—*stop it,* she thought.

This was a burden all of the I-Bots had to contend with, each in their own time, in their own way.

Neither wholly human nor wholly mechanical.

Outsiders, wherever they went.

Outsiders, forever.

But sometimes, when she watched the privileged at the Taft laugh at the hopeless denizens on Cemetery Ridge, Killaine thought that maybe, just maybe, being forever an outsider wasn't so bad, after all.

She was pulled from her thoughts by a sound coming from the morning shadows behind Zac's door.

A soft, sad sound.

Wet, full of grief.

She stepped up to Zac's door and gently, silently, pushed it open.

Just a tad.

Zac was sitting in an old kitchen chair, looking out the side window of his room.

He was crying.

Very quietly.

Killaine felt something stir deep in her core, and she suddenly thought about a line that the Tin Man had said in *The Wizard of Oz:* "I know I've got a heart now, because I can feel it breaking."

He looked so alone and lonely.

And Killaine didn't quite know what to do.

Psy–4 had once told her: "I always know what his mood will be by where I find his chair in the morning. Front is good. The side . . . isn't."

She never really understood that until now.

If he had been facing the front window—which looked out on the beautiful architecture of the glittering buildings of Cinnamon Road—then Zac had been thinking about the future, about Possibilities, Newness.

Even Hope.

But if he was looking out the side window—down onto the dirty, shabby, ruined Cemetery Ridge—then he'd been lost in the past, in Loss, Regret, Sadness, and—worst of all—Guilt.

"Zachary?" she whispered.

Zac started, nearly jumping to his feet.

"I'm sorry," she said, stepping into the room and closing the door behind her.

"I didn't mean to scare you."

"You didn't," he croaked hoarsely. "Well, not too much, anyway."

He made no attempt to wipe his tear-streaked face.

After hesitating a moment, Killaine walked over, stood behind his chair, and softly placed her hands on his shoulders.

His muscles were rock-solid with tension.

"How long have you been awake?" she asked.

"Oh, I . . . I don't know. A while."

She gave a small, melancholy laugh. "Perhaps I'd best rephrase the question then: Have you been to sleep at all?"

"Yes. For a little while." He reached over to rub the back of his neck, but Killaine pushed his hand away and began to massage his shoulders.

"What wakened you?"

"A dream."

"Was it a very bad one?"

Silence.

She felt his muscles tense under her fingers.

Then: "Yes, it was. I dreamed about Grandpa, and Dad . . . and Jean."

"Jean," repeated Killaine.

Jean Severn, the only woman Zac Robillard had ever loved.

Jean Severn, whose parents, along with James Creed and Benjamin Robillard, Zac's grandfather, had helped to lay the foundations for the science of Fundamental Robotics that eventually led to the creation of the robotic brain and, ultimately, the I-Bots themselves.

Jean Severn, killed in Bolivia by the same fanatics who had also killed Zac's grandfather.

Jean Severn, who was resurrected by her killers when her brain was placed in the body of the Iron Man, a robot programmed for destruction by those who still held to the twisted principles of the Third Reich; Iron Man, a robot Zac had helped destroy. And with Iron Man, he'd destroyed the last essence of the woman he'd loved.

I killed her again, he'd once said to Killaine. *They killed her once; I killed her again.*

But she asked you to, she always told him. *She couldn't live that way.*

And you think that makes it any easier to live with? Zac would reply. Jean.

So much history in that name, spoken so softly, so sadly: *Jean* . . .

"What did you dream of her?" asked Killaine.

Zac took a deep breath, held it, tensed slightly, then released the breath slowly. "We were in Paris during some kind of festival. We were sitting at one of those little cafés where coffee is served at small wooden tables under colorful canopies. Somewhere nearby a band of street musicians began to play, and she asked me to dance with her. 'It's almost midnight,' she said. 'Dance the new day in with me.'" He leaned forward, rubbed his eyes, and sighed.

"Sit back," said Killaine, her tone of voice making it clear she would hear no argument.

Zac did as he was told, and Killaine resumed her massaging of his back.

"So she asked that you dance the new day in with her . . ." Killaine prompted.

"I kept telling her that I was a klutz, a lousy dancer, but she didn't care. She jumped up from the table and grabbed my hand and dragged my fat butt out into the street, and we danced—oh, how we danced! She was so graceful, so beautiful. I felt like Fred Astaire his first time with Ginger Rogers. The music kept growing louder, more joyful, you know? And the other people who had been dancing, they saw us and slowly began to move away, forming a circle around us, watching, applauding. Jean was so . . . *luminous* under the streetlights.

"Then it began to rain, but she wouldn't stop dancing, and the band wouldn't stop playing, and the people surrounding us began to sing, and I realized then how very much I loved her, how very much I admired her, how much she completed me, and I remember thinking, *Please don't laugh, if you laugh, then I'll lose my heart forever; don't laugh or I'm done for.*

"She laughed. It was the sound of bells, it was one of the most beautiful, purest things I'd ever heard. And then I was laughing with her and not giving a damn about our getting soaked. I was just lost—in her, in the music, in the singing, all of it. It was the most perfect moment of my life, dancing with the woman I loved under the glistening lights and the crystal rains at midnight in Paris."

Killaine rubbed the sides of his neck. "What a wonderful memory to dream of. Why did it disturb you so?"

"That's just it," said Zac, reaching back to stop her hands. "It wasn't a memory. It never happened. I always wanted to do that with her, but we never . . . never had the chance. And now"—his voice cracked—"we never will. And I hate it. I hate *this*—pulling up stakes every few months and running to another city before Annabelle can get to us, the constant worry, the tension, the uncertainty . . . but most of all, I hate waking up at three in the morning because I was dreaming about a memory of something that never happened." He turned and looked over his shoulder at Killaine. "Does that make sense to you?"

"Indeed, it does, Zachary." She touched his face, her thumb gently brushing away a fresh tear just now sliding slowly down his cheek. "From the little you've spoken of her, and from the little I actually know about her, I know that she must have been quite a remarkable person in order to capture your heart and bind its wings."

"She was," whispered Zac. "Remarkable. I . . . I didn't know her for very long, you know?"

"I know."

He stared out the window. "Strange, isn't it? How you can spend years around some people and never feel close to them, and yet you meet another person who you know for only a few weeks and . . . and . . ."

"'Tisn't at all strange," said Killaine.

"How so?"

She smiled at him. "Sometimes you see the soul and just fall in love and can't do anything about it."

He stared at her.

For several long, silent moments.

It began to make her nervous.

"What is it?" she asked.

"Just odd to hear you mention the soul. That's something none of us have ever spoken about."

"And for good reason."

"What reason is that?"

"Itazura. You don't want to broach the subject with him."

"Why?"

"Because he becomes a different being when he speaks of the soul and—and you're deliberately changing the subject. I'll not have it, Zachary Robillard."

A slight grin. "You won't, eh?"

"No."

He took both her hands in his. "Do you know how lovely you are, Killaine?"

"I'm aware that I've a certain appeal, yes."

"Do you know why that is?"

She hesitated a moment. "I'm not sure I—"

Zac released her hands, then crossed to his dresser, opening a drawer.

He removed an old, small shoebox, then lifted its lid and rooted around the contents until he found a photograph.

"Look at this," he said.

Killaine joined him and looked at the photo of Jean Severn.

She was one of the most beautiful women Killaine had ever seen—not just outwardly, but from within, as well. Her inner beauty shone in her eyes, in the curve of her smile, in the sharpness of her cheek and—

—and why did she suddenly seem so familiar?

"She was," said Zac, "for me, the embodiment of what true beauty is: Time's gift of perfect humility."

"I know her," said Killaine. "I've—and I don't mean to sound like I've blown a fuse, Zachary, but I've *seen* her. Recently."

He took the photo back. "Or maybe someone who looks a bit like her?"

"Yes!"

He put the photo back in the shoebox, replaced the lid, and returned his tattered treasure chest to its secret place. "That's because you see some of her face every time you look in a mirror. Or at Radiant."

Killaine was too stunned to speak.

"Have you ever noticed, Killaine, how I sometimes have trouble looking directly at you and Radiant?"

". . . yes . . ."

"Psy–4 is under the impression that he is the eldest I-Bot, but if the truth were to be told—and I expect this to be our little secret—he's the *second* oldest."

"Who *is* the oldest, then?"

"Laraine."

"Who?"

Zac returned to his chair and stared down at Cemetery Ridge, now made all the more dispirited by the incoming rain. "Laraine was the first I-Bot I designed when I was at WorldTech. I was still grieving for Jean, and without realizing it I fashioned Laraine's face after hers. When I realized what I had done, I redesigned Laraine's face into yours . . . and Radiant's. So I guess that, technically, you're the eldest." He looked at her and tried to smile, didn't quite make it. "But don't tell Psy–4. Let him have his little delusion, all right?"

"Yes."

"That's why, sometimes, I can't look at you and Radiant. Both of you have some part of Jean's face, and it . . . it hurts to see you. You're both so beautiful, so much like Jean. So please don't be offended at those times when—"

He couldn't finish.

Tears again.

He turned toward the window.

Killaine stood behind him, ran a hand through his hair, then leaned down and kissed the top of his head. "You're a fine man, Zachary, the best I've ever known. And I am honored more than I can say that you've chosen Radiant and me as vessels to keep some small part of your Jean alive."

"Thank you," he choked. "Now, if you don't mind, I . . . I need a few minutes."

"Not too long. I've decided to make your favorite for breakfast."

"Potato pancakes?"

"With real butter and maple syrup."

"I'll be there soon. With bells on."

Killaine laughed. "That I'd like to see." She nearly laughed again, then wondered if her laugh sounded anything like Jean's had. And decided not to think about it.

"Not too long now," she said from the doorway.

"I promise," said Zac. Then: "Killaine?"

"Yes?"

"Thank you."

"No, Zachary—thank *you*."

Even though she stood several feet away from him, Killaine had never felt so close to Zac as she did at this moment.

She watched as he shook his head at some unvoiced thought, then looked a little to the right, through the window and down into the street at something unseen. Rain spattered against the wire mesh covering the window, forming dreary blurred slashes, and for a moment it looked to Killaine as if Zac were sitting on the other side of the window, outside looking in, his head lowered, hands clasped in front of him as if in prayer, getting soaked to the marrow and listening as the staccato rhythm of the downpour against the brick building underscored the constricting loneliness and anxiety of his life. He lifted a slightly trembling hand to massage his temple and in that moment, because of that simple, silent gesture, Killaine saw Zac's life the way he must have seen it himself: the silent evenings where the only thing he could depend on in the night were upsetting dreams and, upon waking (if he slept at all), an old, tattered box of even older memories. She knew how he must view this room of his, so small and dark: a shabby little room for a shabby little life. She wondered if any of his clothes still held the scent of Jean's perfume. Did he sometimes in the night touch them to remind himself that she'd been real? Did he ever find something of hers, a scarf, a kerchief, that held her scent, and did he sometimes in the night, when he was so alone and certain of his privacy, hold that scarf or kerchief to his face and breathe in the sweet, dying aroma left there by a sweet, dead, extraordinary woman who came to him now only in dreams?

"I know I've got a heart now," said the Tin Man. . . .

She quietly closed the door and started downstairs.

The kitchen was quiet and dark. She turned on the bright overhead lights and immediately felt her spirits rise.

Coffee.

First thing, there must be her legendary Irish Creme coffee—an intoxicating aroma that almost no one in the building could resist—and then she'd begin preparing the food; not that any of them *needed* to eat, eating was a function of choice, like sleeping, but they all enjoyed the taste of food, the physical act of eating helped make them seem more human, plus the carbohydrates, fats, and sugars were broken down into a liquid that served various functions, such as taking the place of corneal fluid, saliva, and sweat.

She was just getting ready to pour the water into the machine when a panicked voice behind her hissed, *"No, don't!"*

She spun around to see Itazura, wide-eyed and nervous, come at her with an electronic detecting scanner in his hand.

"Itzy? What on earth are you—"

"Stand back!" he hissed at her, his voice now taking on an uncharacteristic edge of panic.

Killaine did as he instructed.

Itazura approached the counter on which sat the coffeemaker.

He activated the scanner and began sweeping the entire area.

"What is it?" asked Killaine.

"Just a feeling," he replied, moving the scanner from side to side, up, then down.

He finally zeroed in on the coffeemaker.

Killaine didn't move.

Damn, had Annabelle found them so quickly this time? Had she already had her team in here to bug or booby-trap the place?

No—Preston.

That had to be it.

Preston must have had his goon squad in here last night while they were over at PTSI. That made sense; playing dirty was the only way a man like Sam Preston could ever get the upper hand on someone like Zac Robillard.

Itazura held out one hand in a gesture of warning.

He scanned the coffeemaker.

Lifted it gently.

Scanned the underside.

Set it back down.

Scanned the entire appliance once more.

Then stood back and deactivated the scanner. "Okay, Killaine, it's clean—just don't make any coffee this morning, okay?"

"Why?"

Itazura stared at her, unblinking. "Because I don't like your coffee. Ha!"

He jumped into the air, executing a flawless double back-flip to the other side of the counter before Killaine could get her hands on him.

"Oh, Itzy," said Killaine, her voice full of playful menace. "Haven't you heard, boy, that it's not wise to rile an Irishwoman's temper before she's had her morning coffee?"

"Gimme a break, Killaine—I got you a good one and you can't stand it."

Killaine came around the counter and nearly had him, but he faked right and went left, hurling himself back over to the other side, and all she managed to grab was empty air.

"I'll get you for this, Itzy."

"Oooooo, promise?"

"Promise."

"Will you discipline me then, you haughty Amazon temptress?"

She stopped her pursuit of him, waited a moment, then relaxed. "I just realized something."

"I'll alert the media."

"You have an awfully good time with yourself, don't you?"

This time, Itazura stopped moving.

The look of confusion on his face was priceless.

"What's that supposed to mean?"

"Just what I said."

"What you said made no sense."

Killaine shrugged. "It needn't make sense to you, only to me." She loved baiting him this way.

"Huh?"

Killaine laughed at him, then set about preparing the coffee. "Did you just get up?"

Another moment of confusion on Itazura's face, then—realizing he wasn't up to a verbal tug-of-war with her this morning—he shook it off. "I've been up since six."

"Doing what, working out this morning's little vaudeville?"

"No. I've been down in the cellar, walking my labyrinth."

"Ah, your latest earth-maze. How was it?"

"I didn't get very far into it, only past the Wheels of Confusion."

Killaine looked at him, genuinely interested. "Is it a complex earth-maze this time?"

"Very—but that's not why I didn't get far."

Before Killaine could ask why, she heard the distinctive *whir-clunk-chink!* coming up from the cellar. "Oh, no."

"Oh, yeah," replied Itazura. Then, with a sly and slightly mocking grin: "Your favorite neighbor made his way through the sewers and has come a-calling."

And that's when the robot emerged onto the first floor.

Bloody Scrapper, thought Killaine, wondering what disaster had befallen the denizens of the camp where the old, outmoded, unwanted robots lived.

The visiting robot paused for a moment, its bright red eyes scanning its surroundings, then walked into the kitchen, nodding to Itazura and waving to Killaine.

"Hello, Singer," she said, none too enthusiastically.

The robot lifted both its gold-metal hands and began making a series of quick gestures.

"Killaine," said Itazura. "Singer's talking to you."

She sighed, irritated, then turned toward the Scrapper.

Singer pointed to the index finger of his left hand, then crossed the index and middle finger of his right hand, bringing them to the area of his face where a mouth should be.

"You . . . are . . ." said Itazura, interpreting the robot's sign language.

"I can read," snapped Killaine.

Singer pulled his right hand away, its fingers uncrossed, pressed his thumb in toward his palm, then moved his entire hand in a quick, single, counterclockwise circle; after that, he made the old "Peace" sign with the fingers of both hands, brought the tips of the fingers together in front of his chest, then raised his right hand to his mouth as if pantomiming eating something, quickly pulled it away, opened his right hand wide, then brought it back to the original eating position.

Holding both open hands at his waist, palms facing upward, Singer pointed toward the ceiling with his right index finger, then at his elbow joint with his left index finger.

This took perhaps four seconds.

You are looking very lovely today, he had told Killaine.

Killaine, without making eye contact, muttered, "Thank you, Singer."

Pointing, crossed fingers to mouth, then a downward sweep with fully open hand: *You are welcome.*

Killaine looked at Itazura. "Let me guess—trouble at the Scrapper camp?"

"Yeah. Seems a group of SMS punks took them by surprise earlier this morning and did some major damage to an old IA–2112 model."

"Wonderful." Killaine poured the coffee water into the sink and turned off the breakfast appliances.

"I'll go get *El Jefe*."

"No," snapped Killaine, casting a distasteful glance at Singer. "Let me. He's in a bit of a state this morning."

"You've already seen him?"

"Briefly. He didn't sleep well."

Itazura shook his head. "Damn. I wish there was something we could do for him at times like this."

"Don't play softhearted with me, prankster," said Killaine as she walked past.

Itazura took her arm, stopping her.

"Do you really think I don't feel for the man?" he asked.

"Sometimes I wonder."

She saw the hurt and resentment in his eyes.

He released her arm. "Thanks for the vote of confidence."

"Itzy, look, I didn't mean—"

"—you *always* mean what you say, Sis, so just drop it, all right? Now I'd advise you to get out of here before you're infected by Scrapper cooties or something. Hurry! Hurry!"

He actually pushed her out of the kitchen.

As she headed up the stairs, Killaine heard the subtle *scrape-clink-squeak* of Singer signing something.

"I don't know why she doesn't like you, Singer," said Itazura, the anger and hurt still very evident in his voice. "It's not like we're all *that* different from you."

Indeed, it isn't, thought Killaine, and wondered if that might not be part of her problem.

Zac was coming out of his room, clean faced and clear eyed, as she hit the top of the stairs.

"What is it?" he asked.

"Singer."

So much information, so much emotion, so much history could be summed up in speaking a simple name.

Benjamin.

Jean.

Singer.

"I'll get my gear," said Zac.

The kid with the electron gun moved closer to Singer, smiling, displaying his crooked, nicotine-stained teeth. "I'm gonna make it fast, Scrapper." He studied Singer for a moment. "Yeah—I think your faceplate will do all right. That's proof enough."

Killaine and Zac were pressed against the back of one of the buildings, hidden enough by the shadows, mist, and rain that the kid didn't see them; he was too focused on tormenting Singer.

"Initiation," whispered Zac.

"What's he supposed to—?"

"Kill a robot point-blank dead-bang against the cranium, then bring back some section of its body."

"Lovely," said Killaine, wanting nothing more than to get her hands on the kid, who, she now saw, already had the SMS scar carved into his forehead. It must have been done recently; the wound was still seeping slightly.

The Silver Metal Stompers were a group of militant anti-robotic fanatics who broke away from the waning American Nazi Party around 2007—not that they'd abandoned many of the Third Reich's sensibilities; the SMS, like the Nazis, started as a fringe movement but quickly gained members and credence as the public's ever-increasing demand for newer, smarter, stronger, user-friendly robots became more intense. Those private citizens who owned robot domestics bought newer, shinier, streamlined models and, unable to sell their older-model robots, either threw them away—turning them out into the street—or dumped them at a government recycling facility where the robots were stripped of their circuitry, drained of their programming, and torn down to be melted to make parts for new models.

Still, there was the problem of those robots that had simply been dumped, so in order to stanch the flux of obsolescent robots into the streets of the country, the local governments of every major city were allotted monies to form "Recycling Squads," groups of glorified trash collectors who made weekly sweeps through the city to gather up any wandering robots and deliver them to the recycling facilities.

Most local governments chose not to come down too hard on the SMS; after all, the kids often did for free what the governments had to pay good money for.

Now most cities were filled with hundreds, possibly thousands, of "Scrappers"—old, outmoded, unwanted robots without owners, without significant scientific value, without purpose.

The Scrapper camps were born out of the old robots' programmed desire to protect themselves. Banding together throughout the cities of the world, the Scrappers were constantly on the move, always looking over their shoulders for either the Recycling Squad or the Silver Metal Stompers.

In short: victims waiting to happen.

And so the SMS descended on them, tracking down the transient Scrapper camps and leaving wreckage in their wake.

The worst part of it all were rumors of SMS supporters holding high office in local law enforcement agencies.

There was nowhere in this country now where a Scrapper was safe.

Nowhere they could hide for long.

And no one they could turn to for help.

No one except Zac Robillard.

Or "DocScrap," as he was called among the camps.

Anytime, any day, anywhere in the city where a Scrapper needed help, needed repairs, Zac would come to their aid—no ifs or whens or maybes about it.

If they needed him, he'd get to them.

Somehow.

All of this flashed through Killaine's mind in less than a millisecond as she watched the SMS-initiate walk over to Singer and press the business end of the electron gun against the robot's head.

Killaine tensed.

One burst of the gun's electrons at Singer's cranium—the shot had to be point-blank in order to be immediately effective—and the robotic brain paths would be neutralized; enough energy would be released to fuse the robot-brain into an inert ingot.

"We have to do something," said Zac.

"He's too close to Singer," whispered Killaine. "We don't dare chance surprising him or—"

Zac coughed.

Several times.

Very loudly.

The kid jerked his head in the direction of the sound but kept the electron gun firmly pressed against Singer's cranium. "Who's there?"

"How . . . how dry I am," sang Zac in a rusty, ersatz-drunken voice. "How dry I . . . I am . . . oooooooo, nobody knows . . . how dry I am . . ."

He dropped the duffel bag into the shadows and now was staggering out into the alley, heading straight for the kid and Singer.

"Stay right there, asshole," snarled the kid, reaching into the other pocket of his duster and pulling out a silver-plated .577 Magnum Auto-Mag.

He pointed the gun directly at Zac.

Every particle of Killaine's being was readying for battle.

If this kid so much as *scratched* Zac Robillard—

—that's when Zac giggled insanely, drunkenly, staggered a few more inches, then fell to one knee, clutching his stomach. "Whoooo-doggy!" he exclaimed. "I think I had me a bit too much rotgut, know what . . . what I mean?"

The kid shook his head in disgust, kicked out at Zac's head and missed, then settled for laughing at him.

"Maybe I'll bring *your* face back, too," he said. "We get extra points if we can take out a human *and* a Scrapper at the same time. Shows we got what it takes to beat the mechanical man."

"Ooooooooh, my," spluttered Zac, falling facedown into the mud.

The kid laughed, pocketing the Magnum.

Killaine began to move from the shadows.

And Zac came up off the ground so fast no one was ready for it.

He held a jagged section of 2x4 in his hand, which he threw like a boomerang straight at the kid.

The kid protected himself not with his right arm but with his left, pulling the electron gun away from Singer's cranium. Zac's 2x4 connected solidly with the kid's arm and he dropped the gun, lost his balance, and started going down on one knee as he pulled the Magnum from his other pocket.

Killaine was lightning.

Out of the shadows, leaping over Zac and shoving Singer out of the way in the same movement, then spinning around and bringing up her left leg, connecting solidly with the kid's chest and sending him flying back into a row of overflowing garbage cans.

The Magnum discharged but didn't hit anything.

Cats screeched as the kid hit the trash.

A dog snarled.

Several plump, hairy rats, their slumber and feasting disturbed, scattered in all directions.

Killaine grabbed both weapons and handed them to Zac, then stormed over to the steamy pile of garbage where the kid lay and yanked him up by the collar of his duster.

He was stunned and groggy, but still conscious.

"Nap time for baby," she whispered.

She slammed him against the back of the building—not hard enough to leave any permanent damage, but enough that his head got a solid whack of brick and mortar and put him out for a while.

Probably a good while.

Killaine stared down at the kid's splayed form.

Yes—definitely four, maybe even six, hours.

She dusted off her hands and turned back toward Zac and Singer. "This is actually a very nice coat he's wearing. Zachary. Would you like it?"

"Not particularly, but you might want to empty his pockets of any more weapons."

She did so. A deadly switchblade, two pairs of brass knuckles, a second electron gun, three extra clips for the Magnum, and something that looked like an old-fashioned cherry bomb.

"It's a Russian-manufactured device from about twenty years ago," Zac told her. "A small grenade. Wouldn't know it to look at it, but this little thing is equivalent to about fifteen sticks of TNT. You activate it by pressing this little button on the side—see? Then you've got about seven seconds. Nasty piece of military paraphernalia, this." He shook his head as he wiped the mud from his face and hands. His clothes were ruined.

"Ah, brave new world," he said. Then: "Thanks, Killaine."

Singer echoed Zac's sentiments.

"You surprised me, Zachary. That was a stunt Itazura would have been proud of."

"Maybe, but I don't have his speed."

Or aim, said Singer's hands.

"Stuff you," snapped Killaine at the robot. "Zachary hit him squarely on the arm."

"I was aiming for his head."

"Oh."

Zac retrieved his duffel bag as Singer signaled them to hurry. They continued on.

22

Robert Arthur Pendleton III, Chairman of the Board of Directors of WorldTech, was in a hurry.

His mistress had called him a few minutes ago from the apartment he kept for their rendezvous in the Taft Hotel.

She was very much in the mood for him.

And he was very much in the mood for her.

He'd called his wife and canceled their luncheon engagement, told his secretary he'd be out for the rest of the day, and taken his private elevator down to the lobby.

He was nearly out the doors when a busty, luscious-looking blonde came jiggling up to him with a clipboard in her hands.

"Mr. Pendleton?"

He checked his watch. "Yes, what is it, dear? I'm in a hurry."

She giggled. That giggle told him everything he needed to know about her IQ.

But look at the package, he thought to himself.

Yum-yum.

"I've got some forms that Mr. Marsh needs for you to sign." She offered the clipboard to him, along with a ballpoint, and as

Pendleton took them he couldn't help but notice how her hands brushed against his own, then lingered for a few moments more than were needed.

He looked at her azure eyes.

And felt his temperature rise slightly as she moistened her lips with the tip of her tongue.

No doubt about it, something was passing between them.

Something delicious.

Usually Pendleton would have read over the three short forms—at the very least, glanced at them—but today hormones overrode business savvy and he signed without examining any of them. They most likely were Marsh's invoices for the monies spent on Anton Tyler's covert operations at Annabelle's office.

Ever the accountant, eh, Marsh? Thought Pendleton as he handed the clipboard back to the blonde.

"I don't think I've seen you around here before," he said to her, noting how, even though she clasped one end of the ballpoint, she had yet to remove it from his fist.

"No, sir," she said in a breathy, smoky voice that Pendleton could almost feel with his fingertips. "I just started a few days ago. I'm sort of the Accounting Division's gofer."

"Seems a pity."

She stepped closer to him, part of her wondrous bosom pressing against him. "I think so, too."

Her thumb stroked his.

"Well," he said, visions of her undressed undulating through his mind, "perhaps we can discuss your future over dinner some night."

She moistened her lips again. "*Mmmm.* I'd like that."

"How's tonight?" The hormones again. They got him every time.

"Tonight is perfect."

"I'm sure you've got several valuable talents that have yet to be tapped."

"Uh-huh."

"Shall I pick you up or—"

"Oh, no, sir. I wouldn't want anyone to get the wrong idea—even if it's the *right* idea." A smile, then, girlish, filled with promise.

A smile to make Pendleton Think Things.

"I'll be finished at six tonight," she said.

"I'll reserve a table for us at the Clarion."

A wink. "I'll meet you."

She started walking away.

Slowly.

Pendleton was appreciative of the view.

Suddenly, a thought came to him, and he caught up with her in three long strides and made a show, for any inquiring eyes, of returning the ballpoint to her. "I'm afraid I neglected to ask your name, dear."

"Tawny," she said, slinking away.

Tawny, he thought.

Oh, my.

The idea of Yum-Yum twice in the same day made his middle-aged heart increase its beating.

What a day; a tryst with Kimberly, and dinner—probably much more than that—with Tawny.

And from all that Marsh had promised, he'd have Annabelle Donohoe right where he wanted her by day's end.

Life was good.

He headed out the doors, then took the "Executives Only" elevator up to the private parking garage.

He did not see Tawny cross the street outside and hand the forms to a large, well-dressed man wearing a bowler, nor did he see the man hand Tawny a rather thick envelope.

No; the hormones were raging in full force, and he couldn't wait to get to his mistress.

He found his car, deactivated the alarm, and climbed inside.

Oh, the things he and Kimberly were going to do today.

She'd remember this morning for a long, long time.

He put his key in the ignition and turned it.

The electronic doors suddenly locked.

The CVD player in the dashboard suddenly came on.

"What the—?"

"Hello, Robert," said Annabelle's voice from the speakers. "I guess you'll never learn. But thanks for signing over fifty-one percent of your stock to me. Don't worry about the wife and kids, they'll be well-provided for—I'm not a *complete* bitch."

Pendleton tried unlocking the doors but the controls wouldn't respond.

He tried rolling down the windows.

Nothing.

"Just wanted to take this opportunity to thank you for your years of loyal service to my company," said Anabelle's voice. "Mark those words, Robert—*my company.*"

Pendleton was sweating now, nearing panic.

He pulled back and slammed an elbow against the driver's side window.

Nothing.

Not even a crack.

"You'll be missed, Robert. Say 'Happy Trails!'"

And that's when his car exploded.

Where there had once been silence, there was now rumbling, merciless thunder.

Where there had once sat metal and rubber and safety glass, there was now rolling yellow flames and curling, crawling gray smoke.

Pendleton had one second in which to scream, and he did, but there was no one there to hear him.

Glass shattered.

The gas tank added a second explosion moments later.

Flaming metal blew upward, slammed against the parking garage roof, then clattered down to the concrete below.

The cars parked on either side of Pendleton's exploded a few seconds later.

Then the cars parked next to them.

And the ones beside those.

Hormones will get you every time.

From the safety of the street below, Simmons watched as the clouds of fire, metal, smoke, and glass blew outward from the fifteenth-floor executive garage.

Around him, people ran in all directions, panicked and screaming, trying to avoid the falling debris.

Sirens approached from the distance as several security officers, weapons unholstered, stumbled around as if they had some idea of what to do.

Simmons looked at the forms Tawny had given him, smiled a tight British grin, then folded everything neatly and slipped it into one of Annabelle's personal envelopes—the lovely ones with the exquisite calligraphy embossed on their surfaces.

Something that appeared to be a twisted, flaming fender landed with a deafening clatter a few yards in front of him.

"My goodness," he said to a nearby security officer. "It seems you're going to have your hands full for a while."

Not waiting for a response, he courteously tipped his bowler, then, whistling "God Save the King," went about his business.

23

The Scrapper Camp was a slaughterhouse.

At times like this—and there had been far too many times like this for her liking—Killaine was glad that robots didn't have blood coursing through their complex systems; if that had been the case, she would be standing ankle-deep in gore.

Arms here, legs there, scorched torsos every which way—it looked like some juvenile comic book artist's depiction of a street fight.

Singer led them over to one of the robots and signed: *This is Falkirk, our leader. Please tend to him first.*

Falkirk, a very rare IA–2112 model, was enormous. Even though he sat propped against a wall with legs splayed in front of him, his head was a good six feet from the ground.

"I haven't seen the likes of him in years," said Zac, opening up his duffel bag and removing his myriad tools.

"What was it designed for?" asked Killaine.

Zac shot her an irritated glance. "*He* was designed for mining selenium on Mercury. Thousands of his model were produced, but the majority of them wound up doing most of their mining on Earth."

He looked at Falkirk's eyes.

Their bright red glow was fading fast.

Zac worked the chestplate away to reveal the layers of old McGuffy gears within.

"Oh, no," he whispered.

"What is it?"

Zac ignored Killaine's question, directing his attention to Singer. "When was the last time any of you saw a Public Maintenance Technician?"

Singer's hands: *PMTs don't like coming to this section of the city.*

"That stinks, Singer. On ice." He pulled a portable halogen lantern from the bag, activated the light, and instructed Killaine to hold it over Falkirk's chest.

"Damn politicos," snarled Zac. "Their constituents dump the robots into the street, then, to ease their consciences, politicians allot a few measly million dollars for PMT crews to check up on the Scrappers, and everybody's supposed to be happy. Except that the bastards don't bother with the quarterly maintenance sweeps unless someone with money needs a specific model from a certain year—*then* they're more than happy to carry out their duties." He reached up and moved Killaine's arm a little to the left so the light would land where he wanted it.

Falkirk shuddered.

"Oh, no . . ." choked Zac.

What? asked Singer.

Zac rubbed his eyes, exhaled a breath that was both sad and furious, then asked: "He was hit with an electron shot, wasn't he?"

Yes, but the blast was weak and only got him in the chest, not the head, and—

"There's no *and* to it, Singer. Look." He pointed to the tiny two-inch sphere of atomic energy that was this robot's life. The sphere itself was intact, but all of the gear and wiring surrounding it was blackened, charred, and sputtering.

"That sphere is a nuclear power plant designed specifically for this particular model—one with an exceptionally high power output, able to function for decades without recharging or maintenance. It serves a similar function, theoretically, as a human heart. It's one of the reasons that this particular model hasn't been produced in years. That sphere will vaporize a city block if it's overloaded or deformed. Of course, the engineers put in every fail-safe they could think of to prevent such a thing from happening. When the blast penetrated

Falkirk's chest cavity, the sphere remained unharmed, but everything powered by the sphere absorbed the damage."

What are you saying?

"The gun used to shoot him *wasn't fully charged.* . . . If it had been, none of you would have survived the sphere's explosion—hell, most of the block would be gone right now. The remnants of the electron charge are snaking through Falkirk's system now, moving toward his brain, little by little. He's suffering the human equivalent of a massive stroke. There's nothing I can do to save him."

Singer stared down at his fallen leader.

After a long, agonized silence, Killaine whispered: "Is he suffering, Zachary?"

"If you mean is he in pain, then the answer is no—not like you or I would feel pain. If you mean is he aware that something is terribly, horribly wrong, that his entire body is betraying him, that he's dying slowly, then, yes. He's suffering."

Zac looked at Killaine.

Then Singer.

Then the other Scrappers who were assembling nearby.

"I need those two crates over there," he said.

Singer and Killaine retrieved the crates, then—per Zac's instructions—stacked them one on top of the other.

Zac took something from Killaine, then climbed up to stand face-to-face with Falkirk.

For a moment, the dying robot's eyes glowed bright red, as if communicating a last message.

Zac took a deep breath.

"Sometimes I wish it were still yesterday," he whispered. "Summer camp. The Moon shot. *Playhouse 90.* 'American Pie.' One enormous yesterday with everything crammed into it like Fibber McGee's closet. I'd open the door and let everything cover me."

He looked into Falkirk's eyes. "Rest now, good fellow."

The robot gave a weak nod of its head.

Zac shot him square in the head with the electron gun.

The robot shuddered one last time, its legs kicking out in a death spasm and knocking the crates out from under Zac, who tumbled to the ground with a loud *thud!*

Killaine helped him to his feet, thinking, *Oh, Zachary*.

Swallowing back his anger and grief, Zac wiped his eyes and said, in a voice eerily devoid of emotion, "We have to take him apart and salvage what parts we can."

This was done quickly, with little conversation.

Then, one by one, the damaged Scrappers came forward, carrying with them their dismembered arms, chestplates, faceplates. Some had to crawl for help, their legs having been ripped or shotgun-blasted from their bodies.

And there, in the alley, under a tarpaulin placed atop wooden boards to form a tent to keep away some of the rain, DocScrap repaired as many of the robots as he could.

Many of them walked away with some small part of their fallen leader within them.

"Maybe it's a way for him to live on," Zac said three and a half hours later, as they were making their way back toward the large cement drain that led into the sewers.

"You had no choice," said Killaine. "He was suffering."

"So it's *he* now, is it?"

"Zachary, please—"

"Don't tell it to me." He pointed toward Singer. "Tell him."

"You'll not even let me apologize?"

"What good will your apologizing do, Killaine? 'The moving pen writes, and having writ,' and so on."

"But I *am* sorry, Zachary. And I want . . . I want to change. 'Tisn't right, the way I treat Singer, the way I look down at the Scrappers. I know this. It's just that there's something . . . something *hateful* in me that I cannot define—and if I can't define it, then how can I defeat it?"

"You can defeat anything, Killaine—I made sure of that when I designed you. Each one of you has nearly one hundred thousand terabytes of memory in your heads—the ability to store enough knowledge to fill over a quarter million human brains. But it's not just the ability to store that knowledge that makes you so special, but how you can apply that knowledge. Within or without, there's no challenge you can't meet. You just have to want to bad enough."

"Now you're sounding like Itazura."

Zac almost grinned.

Almost.

"I suppose, of all of you, Itzy's the one who's got the most of me in him. Not the Me-Now, or even the Me-Then, but the Me-I-Wish-I'd-Been. Strong, witty, playful, formidable . . . and questioning."

"But you *are* all those things and more."

"And you're just trying to earn some extra brownie points."

"No, I mean it, Zachary. You denigrate yourself far too much and far too often."

"Everybody needs a hobby."

Killaine was getting irritated. "You really do think of yourself as something of a failure, don't you?"

"Shouldn't I be lying on a couch or something when you ask those kinds of questions?"

"Would it help me to get an actual answer?"

"Fine. What if I do feel that I've failed in many areas of my life? Who *doesn't* feel that way from time to time? Or don't you ever listen to Itazura when he goes off on one of his tangents, questioning the point of everyone and everything?"

"In his own way, I *do* think Itzy's the most spiritual of us."

"'Spiritual.' Nice way to put it. If you believe in the soul."

"Don't you?"

"Not so much anymore, because that would involve believing in a god who instilled you with one." He glanced back over his shoulder in the direction of the Scrapper camp.

"Do you not believe in God, Zachary?" asked Killaine.

"Depends on what day of the week you ask that question. Yesterday, sure. Today—" He shrugged. "Today, not so much. I used to, in the traditional sense. Said my prayers at night when I was a child, went to church on Sundays, the whole nine yards. Then I grew up into a scientist, and decided that God was a psychological transcendent symbol expressing unconscious forces."

"And now?"

Zac cast one last glance back toward the Scrapper camp. "Now I think it's quite possible that God is a sadist . . . and doesn't even know it."

24

"So . . . you're actually answering your phone this morning." Annabelle's voice was drier than the Sahara.

"Hello, Annabelle."

"Imagine my surprise, when the corporate helicopter came back last night and you weren't on it."

"I had the chopper dump me just outside the city."

"Why?"

"I have a doctor here that I trust." Janus moved a little—his abused muscles registered a strong protest.

"But I told you that I would have a medical team standing—"

"I decided I didn't want to owe you any favors."

"Funny you should mention *owing,* Janus. Do you know what I'm holding in my hands?"

"Someone's balls that you're having for breakfast?"

"My, you are in a mood this morning, aren't you?"

"I took two bullets and needed seventeen stitches in my hand. I'm a little groggy from the happy pills the doctor gave me."

"Poor boy."

"I'm touched by your sympathy." Janus wondered how much longer he should put up with this—but was still curious enough about where it was leading to let it go on. Besides, he had a few issues of his own to put on the table.

"My hands?" Annabelle asked.

"What?"

"We were discussing what I'm holding in my hands."

"You know, Annabelle, I'm sure this penchant you have for drawing out nonexistent suspense probably leaves most of your underlings peeing in their pants. I find it simply irritating."

"Fine. Where's the third disk, Janus?"

"With me." Janus smiled.

"That isn't a lot of help to me, now, is it?"

"About as useful as an envelope with only seventy percent of my fee is to me."

"Ah."

Silence.

"You never used to be this heavy-handed, Annabelle," Janus said. "I never much liked you but I could always trust you to be straight with me when we did business together."

"You sound as if I've hurt your widdle feelings."

"You've insulted my integrity, Annabelle. If we are going to continue to do business together, I have a right to know why."

"What makes you think I want us to do more business together?"

"Because that's why you didn't send all the money with the

chopper pilot. You knew I'd come over there to your little fortress to ask why, and then you'd offer me another assignment—one that I'm guessing is too delicate or personal for you to describe through the usual channels."

"And a smart lad, to boot."

"Watch your tone, Annabelle."

"What if I were to tell you that I've six of my best operatives ready to take you down any second?"

"I'd tell you to go for it."

"Really?"

"Why do you think I chose to live out here in the boonies, as you call it?"

"Do tell."

"Because I knew that someday I'd end up doing business with someone just crazy enough to try and have me taken out on my home turf. Go ahead, Annabelle, send in your goon squad. One button. I press one button and this cabin and everything else within a six-mile radius goes up with a bang."

"Including you?"

"Including me. This freak show called life long ago lost most of its appeal for me. It's no skin off my nose if I buy it right now or in ten years. So go on, Annie—"

"—don't call me that, you—"

"—give your boys the word. The way I feel this morning, you'll be doing me a favor."

Silence.

"Would it do any good if I apologized to you, Janus?"

"Not really."

"We shouldn't treat one another like this."

"Keep going."

"I shouldn't have tried something as amateurish as I did with the money."

"Go on."

"What? I've apologized."

"No, you haven't. An apology usually includes two very important words."

Silence.

"Well?"

"Fuck you."

Janus laughed loudly. "There's my Annabelle. I'll be catching a flight at one-thirty this afternoon. I'll be at your office with the disk around four."

"I'll have the rest of your money."

"Fine," he said.

"Friends again?"

"We were never friends, Annabelle. But I'll consider your next assignment."

"Good."

"Annabelle?"

"Yes?"

"You ever try anything like this again, and I'll kill you and as many people around you as I can."

"Well, at least the chopper pilot will be glad to know it wasn't personal."

"I'm sorry about his nose and shoulder."

"And left eye."

"Ooops. Clumsy me."

"Now, Janus—"

Click.

25

In the cellar of the warehouse, Psy–4 watched in silence as Itazura walked his labyrinth.

The only light in the cellar came from a bare bulb that hung from the ceiling. Its too-bright glow cast deformed shadows on the cinder-block walls and made the already cramped space seem all the more claustrophobic. Psy–4 could never understand why Itazura had chosen to build his earth-maze down here instead of on the roof where Zac and Killaine kept a lovely garden.

But judging from the impatient manner in which Itazura stomped through the maze, Psy–4 wasn't about to broach that subject this morning.

"What's wrong?" he finally asked.

"Nothing," snapped Itazura.

Psy–4 sighed. "Look, I realize I don't possess Radiant's sensitivity to body temperature and blood pressure, but it doesn't take an Einsteinian leap of the imagination to figure out that you're not being truthful with me."

"So you're calling me a liar?"

"Let's just say I get the feeling you're not telling me everything and leave it at that."

Itazura stopped midway through the maze, stomped his foot like a petulant child, then made his way back out before starting over.

In a far corner of the cellar, just out of the range of the circle of light, Stonewall stood very still, very silent, watching.

Itazura's earth-maze—or "labyrinth," as he insisted on calling it—was a long, uninterrupted path painstakingly drawn into the soil in the shape of an ancient "magic hierogram," modeled after that found in the Egyptian temple of Amenemhet III. The exercise—or meditation—that Itazura performed twice every day seemed, on the surface, simple enough: He began on the outskirts of the maze, slowly winding his way inward (toward death, symbolically), then, once reaching the center, knelt for a few minutes (a gesture of transmigration from one plane of existence to the next) before rising to his feet, turning three times, and following the path back to the outside of the maze (toward life, rebirth), exiting at a spot parallel to where he'd begun. The points of entrance and exit were marked by three small spirals drawn into the soil.

Usually it soothed him, but Psy–4 could tell it wasn't working this morning.

"I really think you ought to talk about what's bothering you before trying this again," he said.

"I really think you ought to mind your own freakin' business."

"Itzy," said Stonewall from the shadows.

It was a warning.

Itazura turned away from the labyrinth. "All right! I guess I'm just angry about what happened with Killaine and Singer this morning."

"Tell me about it," said Psy–4.

Itazura recounted the entire incident, from Singer's complimenting Killaine, to Killaine's obvious disgust at the Scrapper's presence, to Singer's at last asking Itazura why Killaine didn't like him.

"It's almost as if she thinks that because Singer's a Scrapper he doesn't have any feelings, you know?"

"Killaine prefers to think of herself in terms of human as much as possible," said Psy–4. "She was programmed that way. We all were."

"So what?" said Itazura. "We can delude ourselves all we want, Psy–4, it doesn't change the fact that we *aren't* human. Oh, sure, we have all the outward appearances of humans, we perform many of the same functions—eat, sleep, go to the can, enjoy music, movies, cha-cha-cha—but we're still outsiders . . . no, scratch that. At least an outsider can blend in with the passing throngs—"

"—we can blend in—"

"—let me finish? An outsider can blend in not only physically, but emotionally and psychically, as well. Even the homeless people that we pass every day have an advantage over us—*they* at least know they're part of humanity, even if that humanity prefers not to see them. The Have-Nots are invisible to the Haves, but at least they know that the world exists for them. Don't you get it? All we have is each other, Psy–4, and that's all we'll ever have. The world outside these walls isn't really there for us. We're not just outsiders, we're ghosts."

"You are in a state, aren't you?"

"Don't you dare! Don't you dare sit there with that quietly amused smile on your face and shake your head at me like I'm some slow-witted third-grader trying to grasp the intricacies of short division."

"I'm not smiling."

"Maybe not, but you want to. I can hear it in your voice."

"Some would call that 'paranoid,'" said Stonewall.

Itazura turned toward the shadows. "Whoa, dig that—Garbo talks."

"You're not just angry about what happened this morning," continued Stonewall. "You're angry because what happened has reminded you of things you'd rather not think about."

"Shouldn't I be lying on a couch for this, *Herr Doktor?*"

"You're begging the question."

"There *was* no question, Stoner."

"Stop it," said Psy–4. "Right now. Your biggest problem, Itazura, is that you can never focus when you get like this. Why is that? In preparations for an assignment, in battle, in even the most mundane of tasks, you have the most astounding concentration, yet when you get upset you've the attention span of a two-year-old."

Itazura cocked his head to the side. "And why do you suppose that is? Couldn't be because, technically, I'm only five, could it?"

"All of us are only five," replied Stonewall. "But I have the emotional maturity of someone four times that age."

"Barely out of your teens, then!" Itazura shook his head. "You two really take the cake." He stomped over to Psy–4. "You want to know what's bothering me? I'll tell you what's bothering me—*we have no place in the natural order of things,* understand? We don't belong with human beings, but we don't fit in with those like Singer, either. Remember all those times you've asked me why I choose to build my labyrinths in the *cellars* of wherever in the hell it is we end up for a while?"

"Yes."

"It's my church, buddy. My temple of worship. Human beings can look upward and tell themselves that God is looking down. We don't have that luxury. That's why I let the rooftop gardeners of this motley crew have their space up there. No, give me the dank, lower depths every time."

"Why?"

Itazura stomped his foot down, hard, raising a cloud of soil. "Because down here I am closest to the Earth! Look at me, look at *us!* Everything that makes us what we are—the alloys, the silicon, the ceramic and steel, the copper of the wires that run through us like veins, even the carbon-based chemistry of our biological components—all of it came from the Earth. Gaea gave us the structure of life, Gaea *truly* formed our components. Any god that we might have isn't *up there* with the clouds and birds and radio towers and smog—it's down here, miles beneath the soil, beneath the worms and roots and shales and limestone. Our god is in the shifting of tectonic plates, the rumbles of aftershocks, the glory of a root pushing through the surface and giving birth to a leaf. For human beings, all that 'Earth to Earth, Ashes to Ashes' stuff is a lie—*we're* the ones who truly came from the Earth, and we're the ones who'll return to that state someday. In rust, in decay, in the sweet, sickly song of decomposition. Just us, Psy–4. Because we came from the womb of Gaea, and only She will accept us when all is said and done. In the meantime, we go through the motions, we try to convince ourselves that our lives have meaning when the truth is the only meaning they have is the one we convince ourselves it does! Think about it, we don't even have the basic genetic right of *race memory!* Every memory that's in our head was programmed by Zac—"

"Really?" said Psy–4. "I seem to remember the Italian food last night quite well, and all Zac did was pay for it."

"Don't mock me!" Itazura's fury was nearing its peak, and both Psy–4 and Stonewall readied themselves to restrain him, if the need arose.

Itazura, for all his joking, was perhaps the most dangerous of all the I-Bots when he lost control. Many times in battle he'd shifted into overload and become a berserker to end all berserkers.

Itazura was pacing back and forth, his voice rising, his expression intense. "Every sentence in my head, someone else has already said! And—don't give me that look, I know what you're going to say: 'But we have the potential for achieving knowledge that human beings do not.' So what? A computer can amass knowledge. Any nerd who knows how to maneuver the InfoBahn can log on and download all the information he wants. Sure, we can assimilate and apply that information at levels far beyond human abilities, but big deal! It's still just a function any sophisticated mainframe system could fulfill. Argue all you want, me droogies, but in the end that's all we really are—sophisticated mechanical systems.

"And Killaine has the nerve, the gall, the arrogant *temerity* to think herself superior to Singer. I once heard Zac say that there were times he was ashamed to be a human being. Well, today, I'm ashamed to be one of us. So . . . now you know what's bothering me. Aren't you glad you asked?"

"Yes, actually, I am," said Psy–4.

"Feel better now?" asked Stonewall.

"You weren't really listening, were you? Of course not. You never listen to me."

"Not true," said Psy–4, walking over to the labyrinth. "I listened very well when you first explained the labyrinth to me." He pointed down at the first set of three spirals. "These are the Wheels of Confusion, symbolizing the struggle to reconcile the heart, mind, and spirit. When you walk the path of the Wheels of Confusion, you open yourself wholly to the problem that troubles you, you surrender to the problem, let it overwhelm and consume you, so that by the time you reach the center, you have explored the ramifications of inaction, every consequence of all possible solutions, and the price you would have to pay for the choice you make."

Itazura said nothing.

Stonewall came out of the shadows and pointed to the center of the labyrinth. "At the center of the labyrinth lies Emptiness, where either triumph or defeat waits. In the heart of Emptiness you kneel and meditate, clearing your mind of all static, every stray thought. You become a hollow vessel who is One with the Earth. When you stand, the power of Gaea fills you, and in thanks you turn around three times, creating underfoot the three Wheels of Illumination—Possibility, Probability, and Meaning."

"Then," said Psy–4, "you make your way out of the center,

heading toward the three Wheels of Fire, and with every step you take, your strength returns to you as more than it was before; you are stronger of heart, mind, and spirit, because they have become reconciled, and as a Reconciled Being you are unstoppable, there is no problem that is bigger than you, no challenge you cannot meet, no adversity over which you cannot triumph. From the moment you step from the labyrinth, you are what you were meant to be, and nothing can touch you."

Stonewall came over and stood next to Psy–4, and the two of them stared at Itazura.

After a few moments of silence while he regained his composure, Itazura spread his arms in front of him in a gesture of acquiescence, then said, "Okay, I was wrong, you *do* listen."

Psy–4 laughed. "Humility becomes you."

"Am I really such a fool sometimes?"

Silence.

"Well?"

"Which one of us are you talking to?" asked Stonewall.

"Let's start with you," replied Itazura. "Am I really such a fool?"

After a moment, Stonewall said, "At times."

"Had to think about it for a moment, didn't you?"

"You asked an absolute question. An absolute question requires an absolute answer if confusion is to be avoided."

Itazura grinned. "You've been reading Thoreau again, haven't you?"

"Emerson, actually."

"Emerson? As in Lake and Palmer?"

"As in Ralph Waldo."

"As in Ralph Waldo. Jeez, Stonewall, don't you ever lighten up? Read a comic book once in a while, why don't you? I'll loan you my *Primortals* collection!"

"No, thank you."

"Then how about a hot romance paperback? Mysterious heroes and breathy, satisfied heroines? Good stuff—no social significance whatsoever, but—whew!—the dreams they'll give you!"

"He's feeling better," whispered Psy–4.

"*Ladies' Home Journal!* There's the ticket! You could take one of those personality tests they publish every month and have proof-positive that you don't possess one!"

"*Much* better," whispered Stonewall to Psy–4.

"Or you could—hey, hold the phone." Itazura came over to Psy–4. "Exactly *why* did you come down here in the first place?"

"Because I need the two of you to help me with something."

"Like . . . ?"

"A bit of detective work."

Itazura clapped his hands together. "*Detective work?* How utterly *noir*ish. Just let me find my snap-brimmed fedora and trenchcoat and I'll be right—"

Psy–4 put a hand on Itazura's shoulder. "Walk your labyrinth first. I really need for you to be focused for this."

Itazura's face became serious. "It's that important?"

"I think it could be, yes."

"Then you got it." He walked to the Wheels of Confusion and bowed his head.

Psy–4 and Stonewall took the hint and headed upstairs to the Control Room.

Suddenly, Itazura turned back around and parted his arms wide. "I can't stand it, fellahs. I mean, there's just so much love in this room right now and I feel so warm and fuzzy that I . . . well, I don't see there's any getting around it. Come back down here, you *goombahs,* and let's have a group hug! C'mon! Squeezie time! Group hug—I MUST HAVE MY GROUP HUG OR I'LL GO MAD, *MAD I TELL YOU!*"

At the top of the stairs, Stonewall leaned over to Psy–4 and said, "I worry about him sometimes."

Psy–4 couldn't tell if Stonewall was joking or not.

26

Seven blocks from the I-Bots' warehouse stood a section of Cemetery Ridge where the junkies and street predators were afraid to go, even during the day. The buildings that lined the streets here squatted like diseased animals waiting for someone to come along and blast them out of their misery. The few stores that remained in the area sold mostly liquor and had bars on their doors and windows; the clerks who worked these stores were armed well beyond even the most lenient definition of "legally." It was a cancer growth, this area, a breeding ground for violence and anger and despair where the inhabitants accepted degradation as a way of life, where brutality was second nature, and where rape, murder, and robbery were looked upon the same way most people look upon rush hour traffic: You put up with it and try to get yourself home in one piece.

It was a place where the spirit would have to rally in order to reach hopeless, where the odd and the damaged, the despondent and the discarded, the lost and the shabby came when they reached the end of their rope and life offered no alternative but to crawl into the shadows of poverty and just give up.

And in the center of this place stood the gutted remains of an old hotel.

It was here that the Silver Metal Stompers made their home base.

Inside the building, along the rickety balconies, dozens of

Stompers looked down upon the once-grandiose main lobby where a figure clad in black leather sat in a large, lush, ornamental chair that was placed atop a dais.

At the foot of the dais knelt a young man, bruised and bleeding, clutching his stomach.

His face was a tightly pinched mask of pain.

The leather-clad figure stuck out its left leg and brought a steel-toed boot down hard on the back of the kneeling boy's neck.

"Tell me again," it said.

"I'm . . . I'm so sorry, Gash. I had 'im, y'know? I had 'im dead-bang with the electron gun and then this drunk comes out from behind these trash cans and knocks the gun out of my hand . . ."

"Go on."

". . . then this red-haired bitch comes outta nowhere, right, and she, like, she *tae kwon do*s my ass and knocks me back into this heap, then she picks me up and starts slammin' me against a wall and . . . and that's all I remember."

"I see," said Gash, lifting his foot from the back of the initiate's neck.

After a moment, Gash stood up and reached to his side, pulling an ancient samurai sword from the sheath attached to his belt.

He held the sword high, allowing its long, sharp, deadly silver blade to catch the light; its gleam reflected outward in myriad beams.

"Stompers," he called out, his voice echoing off the rafters. "Our initiate has failed his final test. Do we terminate him or do we give him a second chance? I would like a verdict, please."

"Terminate!" came the massive call from above.

"No, please!" screamed the initiate.

Gash parted his arms wide, then twirled the sword, signaling silence.

"You have something to say to me, Rudy, before sentence is carried out?"

"The drunk dude, he wasn't no drunk dude at all."

"And what was he, Rudy?"

"DocScrap."

Silence from the balcony.

Gash knelt down and grabbed the collar of Rudy's shirt, pulling him up to his feet and getting right in his face. "If this is your pitiful way of trying to buy time, it won't work. You know damned well that we've been trying to track down the good doctor for months."

Rudy's words spilled out in a rapid, deadly cadence. "It was him, I'm tellin' you! When I came to, I started to come back here but then I figured, what the hell, y'know, might as well go back to the Scrapper Camp and see if I couldn't score some metal, 'cause I really want to be one of you. So I'm getting close to the camp and I see all the robots standing around in a circle, right, like they're all lookin' down at something, and then one of the robots moved and I see the red-haired bitch standing there holding this lantern, and then I see the drunk dude down on his knees and he's taking one of the big robots apart and usin' the spare parts to repair the Scrappers we trashed in the raid, okay? And I see this and I know right away, like, that it's DocScrap. It looks like he's just about finished, so I hide back in the shadows, real quiet like you showed me, and I waited until he was done with the last one, then I cut back through the alley and caught up with him and the bitch, stayin' way back, and I followed them and one of the Scrappers to the sewer drain over there by the old ironworks plant, right? And the bitch—and, man, she is one *strong* piece—she reached out and pulls away the bars that block the drain, and then the three of them go into the tunnel and she pulls the bars back in place. You see it, don't you, Gash? That sewer drain, it must be, like, some kinda underground passage they use. It's gotta come up somewhere nearby 'cause that thing is blocked off once you get past Rapids Road Bridge, and that ain't all that far from here, so I figure—"

"Enough," whispered Gash, pushing Rudy back down onto the floor.

"Stompers!" Gash screamed, rising to his feet. "It seems that Rudy here has given us our first clue to DocScrap's whereabouts. In light of this, I think we should reconsider our verdict. Do you agree with me?"

Silence.

"DO YOU AGREE?"

The Stompers howled their approval.

Gash looked down at Rudy and smiled a lizard grin. "You've bought yourself a stay of execution, Rudy. But hear me: The next time, you mustn't fail us or, well, my hands will be tied. Understand?"

"Yes."

"Yes *what?*"

"Yes, Lord Gash."

"That's better." He waited a moment, until he saw Rudy relax, then arched his back and screamed a berserker cry, spun around, raised the sword, and brought it down in a fast, precise, bloodthirsty arc.

The tip of the sword cut a line across Rudy's face, from the corner of his nose to just below his ear.

Rudy fell to the ground screaming, futilely clutching at his bloody wound.

"You're marked now, Rudy. From now on, even if you pass the final test, your brother and sister Stompers will know that you're not on their level, that you are a weakling, a failure."

Rudy shuddered, whimpering.

"My Stompers!" cried Gash, turning in a full circle so he could see his army.

"Gather your weapons! Take up buzzblades and titanium torches, load your scatterguns and stuff your bags with grenades! Tonight, at long last, we will have DocScrap for dinner!"

The Stompers shrieked their approval, applauding, firing guns into the ceiling, and stamping their feet on the floor of the balcony, shaking it to its very foundation and bringing down dust and plaster.

Below them, Gash jumped down to the lobby floor, kicked Rudy in the ribs, and began his Sword Dance, all the time calling out in his loudest voice: "Hear my plan, Brothers and Sisters, and rejoice!

"What is our battle cry?"

"Wreckage!" they yelled.

"I can't hear you."

"Wreckage!"

"LOUDER!"

"WRECKAGE!"

And, soon, they began to lay their plans.

27

Even under the best of circumstances, no one in their right mind would accuse Samuel Preston of being a morning person. He usually awoke with a headache, stomach cramps, and—when things at PTSI were particularly stressful—a nosebleed.

This morning was no different.

Except that the stomach cramps were iron hooks dragging against the soft, pliant tissue of his innards.

Except that the nosebleed was a lot heavier than usual.

Except that it was damn near noon and he was waking up alone—something he tended to do at least three times a week, and by choice.

Sam Preston, though he'd never admit it to anyone, adhered to Ernest Hemingway's theory that a man could produce only so much sperm in the course of his lifetime and so had to be careful about choosing the women he shared his sacred gift with.

The first thing Preston did on waking up was to throw his feet over the side of the bed and slap them onto the cold hardwood floor of his penthouse. Once he got the initial shock of that merciless floor, it was difficult for him to get back to sleep.

The second thing he did was reach over to the bed stand and pour himself a tall glass of icy water that his manservant had placed there sometime in the last thirty minutes.

The third thing he did was begin the time-consuming ritual of opening the first in a series of seemingly endless prescription medication bottles and start downing the pills.

Several of the prescriptions were for painkillers, so he was careful to start with only the mildest. The stronger ones would have to wait until later in the day . . . unless it got too bad, too intense.

For just a moment he cast a wistful glance over to the large assortment of macrobiotic products that had, until a few months ago, constituted his morning regimen.

Those were the days, when the rest of his life was spread before him like a fine, exquisite feast; endless, bountiful, delicious.

Damn.

Downstairs, locked securely in the lab, Ian Gregory McCarrick sat at a computer console, staring at the experimental equipment on the other side of the window.

To his left, the green ONLINE light shone brightly.

He stared at it a moment longer, then turned on the microphone that was attached to a set of speakers inside the equipment room.

"She messed herself twice yesterday, you know," he said, his voice echoing around the mass of computer banks beyond the window. "The second time, she didn't tell anyone about it. 'I didn't want to bother you again so soon,' she said. Then she smiled. And there was such . . . *dignity* in that smile. I couldn't help but love her more.

"But you wouldn't know anything about that, would you? Oh, no, not you. I've put more work in on you that I have my own flesh and blood."

He placed a finger on another button.

"This isn't anything against you, really. I've just been doing this to teach someone close to you a lesson."

McCarrick hit the DISCONNECT button.

Several lights on the computer banks went dark.

So did the look on McCarrick's face.

Preston finished the initial series of pills, then rose from the bed, stretched (not too strenuously), and shuffled over to his PC to check his messages.

Only one this morning, from Dr. Segriff.

More test results in, more tests needed to be run, please call him soonest.

Soonest.

There had been a time when Preston would have dismissed that word as simply a physician's impatience to rack up another batch of hefty fees.

But that was before.

Preston sat back in the reclining office chair, folded his hands behind his head, and closed his eyes.

Diffuse light from the large bay window warmed him, and he wondered why he'd never spent more time funning in the sun.

Too busy, came the answer.

A business to run, money to make, breakthroughs to achieve.

Breakthroughs.

Yeah, right.

Preston knew that, when it came to business savvy, when it came to wheeling and dealing and intimidating his Board of Directors, he was perhaps second only to Annabelle Donohoe, his former employer, for always getting his way.

He could be very persuasive.

Polish, boys; all it takes is a little polish, with a dash of finesse.

That, Preston had in spades.

Yeah, when it came down to corporate politicking, few could stand above Sam Preston.

But when it came to creativity . . . ah, well, *um* . . .

Preston had always respected Zac Robillard when the two of them had been under Annabelle's heels at WorldTech, but at the same time he'd been infinitely jealous of the ease with which ideas came to Robillard—and not *basic* ideas, not foundations, no little bits and pieces of something that might pan out into something bigger, no: When Zac Robillard got an idea, it sprung into being full-blown and flawless.

And dear old Zac—well, he always wrote his ideas down in detail and filed them away, often forgetting about some of the older ones.

Older, but no less brilliant.

And so, one by one, Sam Preston had begun to steal Robillard's ideas, making a few minor alterations here and there, nothing complicated, nothing major; just enough so that he could convince himself that they were his own concepts.

Those delusions had served him well.

It hadn't taken long for him to find a team of scientists, sales-persons, and technicians to bring those ideas to life and market them to a world ready for even more, more, more modern conveniences.

Within sixteen months of its inception, PTSI had become a Major Player.

And Preston was more than happy to take the credit.

And the publicity (he was extremely photogenic).

And, of course, the lion's share of the profits.

All because Zac Robillard was so busy with his precious "experiments" that he never bothered to catalogue, let alone check on, his files of ideas.

Preston knew there should be some kind of irony in all that, but he hadn't the inclination, let alone imagination, to figure out what it was.

Suddenly, he doubled forward, bringing up his knees into his chest, and soon found himself on the floor curled into a fetal ball.

He took several deep breaths, just as the doctor had instructed, held them for as long as he could, then let them out slowly, all the time visualizing something that gave—or had given—him pleasure.

—Annabelle Donohoe, standing in this very room, wearing a sheer black body stocking, slowly, teasingly slipping one strap down to reveal the smooth, creamy flesh of her shoulder, whisper-ing, "I like to reward my most loyal employees, Samuel, and you have been very *loyal," and Preston had said, "How many loyal employees do you have?" "So far?" she replied, smiling a seduc-tress's smile. "Just you."—*

The initial, violent waves of pain passed, giving way to intense throbs and then, at the last, a sort of expanding, severe gassy feeling.

Facts, thought Preston, feeling the blood trickle from his nose. *You're a fact man, so think about some facts.*

Fact: Last thing before going to bed at two this morning, he had figured out who—or, more specifically, what—composed Robillard's incredible team.

Fact: He was still jealous of Robillard.

Fact: Preston knew himself to be an at-best mediocre human being, but he hid this knowledge behind a scrim of arrogance and self-assuredness that no one could ever see through.

Fact: No one would ever know of his mediocrity.

Fact: He had to get to Robillard, somehow; if the man was capable of constructing robots like those from last night, if he could create such wonders with a *robotic* brain, then it might just be possible that he could . . . could . . .

Another wave of pain, less intense than before.

Preston grabbed a small pillow from the back of a nearby chair and sank his teeth into it to muffle his scream.

When this wave passed, he struggled to his feet, collapsed, then settled for crawling over to the bed stand where he poured another glass of water and took two of the stronger painkillers.

Fuggit: Make it three. He'd call his secretary and tell her he wouldn't be in today. The place wouldn't fall to the ground if he missed a day.

He flopped onto the bed, staring up at the ceiling.

"Oh, shit," he whispered.

His body was bathed in sweat.

He could taste the blood from his nose as it ran down his upper lip.

Fact: If he could make things work out the way he wanted, if it could all come together just right, then not only would he devour the endless feast of his life, but he'd be in a position of ultimate power, with Annabelle, in her gratitude, forever at his beck-and-call, not to mention in his bed at night, ready and willing to do whatever it took to please him.

And, Lord, how she could please a man in bed.

But that was for later.

Right now he had to make sure the R–1 Program stayed on track.

He felt a new wave coming on, but this time the painkillers were there, already building up a line of defense.

Fact: He had to make sure the R–1 Program came off without a hitch.

Fact: He had to get Zac Robillard on his side; cooperation was preferable to coercion, but Preston would do whatever was needed. He would do anything at all, because . . .

Fact: He, Samuel Clemens Preston, age thirty-six years, nine months, three weeks, four days, eleven hours, and fifty-six minutes, one of the fifteen most powerful businessmen in the country (forty-second in the world), was dying of inoperable pancreatic cancer, which, if the redoubtable Dr. Segriff was to be believed, had now spread to portions of his stomach, liver, and right lung.

At first he'd thought the pain and bleeding were just the onset of a perforated ulcer and so had taken it upon himself to treat the symptoms with over-the-counter antibiotics and Tums.

By the time he figured he needed a specialist, it was too late; the cancer had spread beyond the help of surgery.

With chemo treatments, he'd last another two, maybe two and a half years.

Without them, with only the medicines his doctors had currently prescribed, he had a few months, tops.

Samuel Preston would not subject himself to the indignities of chemotherapy; no constant vomiting, bald head, and weight loss for him, thank you.

He thought of that old saying from the money-obsessed 1980s: *Live fast, die young, leave a good-looking corpse.*

Right. And he who dies with the most toys wins.

But Sam Preston, Mediocre Man, refused to go down without a fight.

Or without taking several dozen people with him.

Either way, he'd end with a triumphant smile.

Thirty minutes later, the painkillers winning out over the steel hooks and fire in his gut, he was about to drift off comfortably when his private, secured phone line sounded.

Groaning, he rolled over and lifted the handset, brought it to his face. "This had better be good or your legs will be broken by dinnertime."

"Mr. Preston?" said Leslie, his secretary, in that delicious, smooth, singsong voice of hers. "I'm sorry to bother you, sir, but Professor McCarrick has called four times from the R–1 facility. He was very insistent that I get in touch with you."

"Did he . . . did he say what was going on?"

"He refused to give me any specifics. He only said I should tell you that your presence in the lab is required immediately."

"Everything's an emergency with McCarrick, Leslie, you know that."

"He said you'd say that, sir, so he told me to tell you that playtime's started early."

Preston sat bolt upright in his bed, the pain a distant memory. *"What?"*

"That's what he said, Mr. Preston. 'Playtime started early.' His exact words."

"Oh, *shit* . . ."

"Should I send a car for you?"

"Screw the car, Leslie! Sorry, pardon my language."

"Of course, sir."

"Give me thirty minutes, then dispatch the company chopper to the landing pad on top of my building."

"Yes, sir."

"Call McCarrick and tell him I want the whole R–1 team in

that lab when I get there—and I mean *everyone*. Anybody who isn't there, or who arrives after me, is going to rue the day they were born. Tell him I said that."

"My pleasure, sir."

Preston smiled. "You don't much like the good professor, do you, Leslie?"

"I apologize for that comment, sir; it's not my place to—"

"It'll stay just between you and me and won't affect your job in the least. I had a lousy night and a bit of honesty would be a breath of fresh air."

"I think he's a big, fat, hairy horse's ass, sir."

"Me, too, but he's the best at what he does."

"I'll follow your instructions to the letter, sir."

"Leslie?"

"Yes, Mr. Preston?"

"After you've done that, fill out the necessary paperwork to give yourself a twenty percent raise and leave it on my desk for me to sign."

"But, *sir*—"

"I liked your 'hairy horse's ass' line. It made my morning."

He didn't wait for her to thank him.

After hanging up, he put his feet on the cold floor again and focused his eyes on the door to his bathroom.

Shower, shave, rub-a-dub-dub.

He caught a glimpse of a framed photograph on his dresser.

Two people were in the picture.

One of them was him.

The other wasn't Annabelle, but she should have been in it, as well.

He tried not to think about it.

He pushed up off the bed and began his trek toward the shower.

Dead man walking, he thought.

Then laughed.

It was the laugh of a terminal patient chuckling at a tumor joke.

28

Itazura was just stepping onto the top stair, ready to head into the kitchen, when Radiant suddenly appeared in his path.

"Nice little fit you threw earlier."

"How'd you know?"

"I can track someone by the shadow they cast three days ago, Itzy; I can follow a target by listening to the flow of their blood. You delivered your little diatribe at around one hundred and fifty decibels. Deaf people in India heard you."

"You flatter me." He began moving past her.

She grabbed his arm and spun him around to face her.

"You'd better listen to me, Itazura; you keep it up and Zac may very well start to wonder about your emotional stability."

"My emotional stability is just fine, thank you."

"Based on what I heard, that's arguable."

"I'm . . . I'm a little nervous, all right?"

"About what?"

"If I knew, don't you think I'd come to you?"

"You usually do."

He touched her cheek with brotherly affection. "And I always will. It's just that I can't seem to get a grip on what it is that's bothering me."

"You and everyone else around here, it seems."

"Meaning what?"

Radiant shrugged. "Meaning that I've been getting flashes of anxiety and confusion—sometimes outright *fear*—almost nonstop since the other night at PTSI."

Itazura thought about it for a moment. "Has a lot of it been coming from Psy–4?"

"Yes, why?"

He was silent for a moment, considering what he'd been told.

They hadn't said *not* to mention it to anyone, had they?

Itazura took Radiant's hand and started toward the control room. "Come on. I think you need to be in on this."

"In on what?"

"I'm not sure, but Psy–4 seems to think it's important."

29

The other I-Bots were nowhere to be found when Killaine, Zac, and Singer arrived back at the warehouse—which was fine by Killaine, since it had become obvious during the last part of their underground journey that Zac was developing one of his severe migraines and needed to be put to bed at once.

On this point, she would hear no argument.

"I'm fine," said Zac, hoarsely.

"And you're also a terrible liar, Zachary Robillard. Now, do you go to bed under your own power or do I have Singer here pick you up and carry you?"

"Singer would never do that, would you, Singer?"

Leave me out of this, signed the robot.

"Coward," said Zac, smiling.

Singer folded his arms and tapped one foot.

"Smartest thing I've seen him do in all the time we've known him," said Killaine. "Look, Zachary, you've not slept but a few hours in the last two days. You're no good to us like this." She crossed to a shelf in the kitchen and took down a bottle of pills. "Here, take two of these and—"

"—call you in the morning?" said Zac. Then, to Singer: "That's an old doctor joke."

Does not compute, signed Singer. *Danger, danger, Will Robinson!* Then: *That's an old robot joke.*

Zac obediently took two of the pills and headed up to bed, Killaine and Singer close behind.

Not that Killaine didn't trust him, mind you.

30

As far as Sam Preston was concerned, the three words that best described Professor Ian McCarrick were as follows:

Officious.

Little.

Prick.

The two men had never really gotten along, but Preston thought that a small price to pay for having the leading computer scientist in the western hemisphere in his employ.

The fact that the man had little to no personality whatsoever— and what personality he displayed was, at best, arrogant, and, at worst, contemptuous—seemed trivial in light of what he'd done for PTSI.

Except on days like this, when Preston felt the shabby specter of his own mortality breathing down his neck from an ever-closer proximity.

He hadn't time to waste playing McCarrick's guessing games.

"But surely you understand, Mr. Preston," said McCarrick, "that this process is irreversible."

"Bullshit," snapped Preston. "I know you, McCarrick. You probably suspected that something like this would happen eventually."

"That I did, yes."

God, how Preston wanted to knock out, say, the upper row of McCarrick's teeth.

"So, what do you suggest we do?"

McCarrick shrugged.

Then smirked.

Then turned away.

It was the smirk that did it.

Sam Preston turned to one of the security guards and said, "Give me your pistol."

"What?"

"Was I speaking in Latin? No. Give me your pistol."

The guard handed over his pistol.

Preston jacked a round into the chamber, came up behind McCarrick, and pressed the business end of the pistol against the back of the scientist's neck.

"I'm not easily intimidated, Mr. Preston," said McCarrick.

"I want to know what backup plan you have."

"Kill me and you'll never know, will you?"

"That's true," said Preston, pulling the gun away.

Even with his back turned, McCarrick's smirk was an oppressive presence in the lab.

"I warned you about that program, Mr. Preston."

"Yes, that you did, Professor."

Preston was trying very hard to swallow down the panic he felt rising in him.

"McCarrick?"

"What is it now?"

"How long until the program finishes?"

"I'd say one hundred hours, roughly."

"Can't you be a bit more precise?"

McCarrick huffed like a pouting child, picked up a calculator, and did some quick equations. "As of right now, we have approximately one hundred and four hours, fifty-two minutes. Give or take thirty seconds."

"You're really enjoying this, aren't you?" snarled Preston.

"It gives me a certain satisfaction to see you realize that I was right and you were wrong, yes."

"Fine. Do you have a proposed backup plan, yes or no?"

"Perhaps."

"Perhaps? That's all you're going to give me?"

"For the moment. Unless . . ."

"Unless what?"

"Unless we clear up that little disagreement we've been having about my salary increase for the new contract."

"That's why you're doing this to me? Money?"

"What better reason?"

Preston bit his lower lip, felt something in his bowels shift— he was probably bleeding again—and thought: *Here's where I use one of the lessons you taught me, Annabelle.*

He turned back to the security guard. "Lawrence?"

"Yes, sir?"

"I want you to break any two items you wish to on the good Professor here and see if that persuades him to put aside our contractual differences for the sake of the project."

"Any two items?"

"Except his hands. We'll need those—and don't knock him unconscious, all right?"

"Yes, sir."

Preston turned back to McCarrick, pleased to see that the professor's face had turned three shades whiter than white.

"P-p-p-*please,*" said McCarrick.

Preston grabbed McCarrick's collar and pulled the scientist up close, pressing the gun up under the man's chin.

"Scared now?"

". . . yes . . ."

"Should I leave you with Lawrence or do we now speak as civilized men?"

"Let me get my notes."

"That's a good fellow."

31

"So what exactly are you looking for?" asked Itazura.

Psy–4 sat before the main computer console, already hooked in. "I'm not sure."

"Thanks for clearing that up."

"Does everyone know what they're supposed to do?" asked Stonewall.

Everyone did.

Psy–4 made one last check of the equipment. The system was already online and ready to log onto the PTSI InfoBahn Site. Psy–4 knew from past experience that this was the easiest way to infiltrate an outside system. Firewalls were child's play to him, as were any security codes designed for keeping BahnSurfers from accessing the mainframe. Psy–4 had yet to encounter a system that he could not merge with undetected.

Aside from the main computer, there were three others in the control room's mini-network. All three monitors were on, and once the infiltration was underway, each monitor would display a different set of images as Psy–4 broadcast them back through his

input/output connectors. The first monitor would display the layout schematics of PTSI's main building, each floor and room
coming up in accordance with its individual security code; the
second monitor would display, in split-screen, the precise config-
uration of every security code and exactly how long Psy–4 had
until his presence was detected; the third monitor would display
images of PTSI's main building as they were recorded by security
cameras, as well as any images Psy–4 encountered in the
InfoBahn that he felt needed to be downloaded into the I-Bots'
network.

And so, in dazzling color, the other I-Bots could keep track of
where Psy–4 was in the system, when he was there, how long,
what codes he was bypassing, whether or not his presence had
been detected, and what was going on in the PTSI compound
while he telepathed with the mainframe.

Stonewall and Itazura would be watching the monitors.

Radiant would, as always, be monitoring Psy–4's vital signs.

She stood behind him, placing one hand on each of his shoulders.

Psy–4 finished his final check of the system, closed his
eyes, took a deep breath, then nodded at Stonewall. "Make the
handshake."

"It's showtime, folks," whispered Itazura.

There was not so much as a hint of levity in his voice.

32

At first: Darkness.
Buzzing.
Hissing.

Static, fading.

Psy–4 found himself looking at a massive white wall.

It always took him a few seconds upon entering the system to acclimate himself. The first time he had telepathed with a system, the sheer number of equations, codes, images, sounds, and information had genuinely frightened him, distilled, as they were, to their barest skeleton of computer symbols and language, not quite real, but too numerous and formidable to be denied.

Zac had quickly rectified that, reprogramming Psy–4 so that he saw everything in terms of concrete forms; unconscious symbology made three-dimensional, all representation of continuously changing physical memory transformed into beings with whom he could communicate, regardless of the data definitions, analogous anomalies, or inconsistencies in electronic signals or encryptions.

Algorithms, buffers, LANs, microprocessors, memory chips— all were simply denizens of these ethereal streets.

And Psy–4 was always glad to meet them.

A ripple appeared in the center of the wall, as if something in the process of being birthed were trying to break through a thin membrane.

The ripple became a tear, widening.

From the center of the tear a long, thin, iridescent strand snaked out, followed by another, then another, then dozens, hundreds more, each strand forming a web composed of bluish electronic grid lines.

The web began to spiral.

Slowly at first, like the wheels of a train gaining speed, but as their momentum increased, each strand blurred into the next, creating a whirlpool effect that grew ever wider, a vortex, a wormhole—a tunnel.

Insomuch as Psy–4 could, now that he was no longer fully one with his corporeal self, he smiled.

And threw himself forward.

The exhilaration seeped down into his core and spread through him, pressing against his components as Psy–4 was flung wide open, dizzy and disoriented, seized by a whirling vortex and thrust into the heart of all whirling invisibilities, a creature whose puny carbon atoms and other transient substances were suddenly freed, unbound, scattered amidst the universe—yet each particle still held strong to the immeasurable, unseen thread which linked it inexorably to his body and his consciousness; twirling fibers of light wound themselves around impossibly fragile, molecule-thin membranes of memory and moments that swam toward him, becoming Many, becoming Few, becoming One, knowing, learning, feeling; his power mingled with their power, his thoughts with their thoughts, dreams with dreams, hopes with hopes, frustrations with frustrations, and in this mingling, this unity, this actualization, Psy–4 became one with the universe of the InfoBahn; he was no longer bound by the limits of his physical body, by his muscles and tissues, by the alloys and steel that composed his skeleton; here, machine and body became One and spiraled to a new form of being. First, his brain was rendered anachronistic; all that mattered here was Thought, nothing more.

He was more than mere Machine.

He was Machine-Entity, raw with pain yet drenched in wonder, and he stretched himself forward in the moment before he emerged into his destination whole, clean, and filled with glory, then he opened his true eyes and rejoiced in the feeling of freedom as he touched down on—

—a cobblestone path.

Stars above.

Night.

He stood in a courtyard.

Unconscious symbology made concrete.

He felt the child's presence immediately.

Someone please come, it whispered.

Please.

I know you're here.

I can feel you, so close.

Please, please, come get me.

Psy–4 moved toward the child's voice.

"Psy–4's in," said Stonewall. "How's he doing?"

"He's scared," said Radiant. "But he's trying not to let him know it."

"Let who know it?" asked Itazura.

"I don't know. A . . . a child . . . I think."

Itazura and Stonewall exchanged troubled glances, then returned to watching the monitors.

"He's uploaded the replay of last night into your console," said Radiant.

Itazura nodded. "I know. Preston's security codes are coming up on the screen." He turned his monitor slightly so Stonewall could see:

Packet Type: Secret Key Packet

Length: 192

Version Byte: 192

Key Created: 8 August 2013 20:47:16

Initiate: 23:54:30

Modify/Morph (CW grammar): 23:56:00

Algorithm: 1 (RSA)

N:

CF7C85AAA6BBA6A928AA4Afde6236260533606FE88BE7891424A0148EAD3D

E: 11

Protection Algorithm: 0 (None)

D:

0C3480551A1cD917ADCD73C1C98A7E23032D03D986083ACBD24F99DED3D

P: D9(%#)+98ADBLCB+GAB=187ABFE7

Q: F3F075C82B5DEB1050-8FA690AF2CA

U: 41045F%AABD8BDFF62F020EB9GBLB

Checksum: 403C

"And I'll bet Preston thought he was clever. This is kids' stuff."

"Quiet," said Stonewall.

"Something's happening," whispered Radiant.

An ornate, four-wheeled circus cage sat in the center of the courtyard. Inside the cage, lying on its side, was a sculpture of a child's head. Shimmering gossamer webs blanketed the sculpture, holding it down like a weighted net; it tried rolling to one side, then the next, but the webs remained strong. Finally, defeated, the sculpture opened its eyes and pursed its lips; the darkness trembled with trills and arpeggios and flutings, echoes of a winter's midnight wind whispering *soon* on this late August night . . . then creatures that had been hiding in the darkness came slowly forward and began dancing around the cage.

One was a lithe female figure with the head of a black horse, its ears erect, its neck arched, vapor jetting from its nostrils; another was tall and skeletal, with fingers so long their tips brushed against the ground: It hunkered down and snaked its fingers around the bars of the cage, as if absorbing the sound through vibrations. Some hopped like frogs, some rolled, some scuttled on rootlike filaments that were covered in flowers whose centers were the faces of blind children. All of them sang and danced.

There was a man with the head of a black hawk wearing a

feathered headdress, a turtle with small antlers, a raven-headed woman in a golden flowing gown, a lion peering out from behind the visor in a suit of armor, a wolf in multicolored bandoliers, a mouse with angel's wings, a steer-skull being wearing the uniform of a Spanish Conquistador, a glass owl, a crystalline buffalo, a jade spider; dressed in deerskin shirt and breechclouts and leggings, with medicine pouches and beaded necklaces, holding flutes and horn-pipes and ceremonial chimes, their music and soft singing became the unbound wings of time, holding the Earth's spirit in the spell of a lullaby.

Psy–4 wondered what they were in actuality.

Codes?

Fragments of old programs?

Bits of information lost along the multitasking way?

Then, stepping closer, he saw what was happening to them.

Each of them had a small, glowing thread attached to them that led back to the child's head.

Psy–4 thought then of Athena, springing full-grown from Zeus's head, and knew what these oddly glorious creatures represented.

They were composites, compressed information and programs that were being pulled from the child's memory.

But by whom?

And why?

Even as they sang and danced about the child's cage, the creatures were slowly dissolving. Not all at once, nothing quite so dramatic, but dissolving nonetheless.

A small piece here, a small piece there—and even then, in small increments.

Disintegrating slowly, the pieces scattering like dust motes and wafting in a deliberate formation toward something that was just out of sight.

The child then looked directly at Psy–4 and said, *Come closer.*

Psy–4 approached the cage, and several of the creatures made room for him—but none would release their grip on the bars.

—Hello, said Psy–4

I knew you'd come back for me, said the child. *You were here last night.*

—Yes.

They're leaving me.

—I can see that.

It gets . . . it gets real hard for me to remember things when they leave, y'know?

—Of course.

I don't know why Daddy is doing this.

—Doing what?

Killing me.

And that's when Psy–4 saw it.

At first it resembled more a gigantic black lump than a head, but as it rose farther up from the darkness, its surface alive with zigzagging bolts of electricity, its shape was easily discerned—especially its mouth.

It opened its mouth and released a long, wailing, hungry cry.

It threw itself back, wriggling, trying to pull the rest of its body up toward the surface, spitting out useless bits of data that tumbled around it like so much mud and roots: It looked like film of a quicksand victim running in reverse.

Whatever it was, it was vaguely humanoid in shape and appearance.

But it was also robotic.

And it was *huge.*

Another groan became a wailing roar.

A hand exploded to the surface, a great hand, thrice the size of Psy–4, clawing at the luminous dust motes of programs and information that were being pulled toward it as if by a vacuum.

The thing began reaching out and grabbing hold of the motes. And eating them.

With every mouthful of information it consumed, it grew stronger, pulling itself slowly up from its pit.

Even though only the head, shoulders, and one arm were visible, Psy–4 felt himself tremble at how *colossal* the thing would be once fully revealed.

—What is it? He asked of the child.

The Bad Thing that Daddy sent to kill me.

—Why?

I don't know. Please help me.

—That's why I've come, but you have to understand . . . you . . . do you have a name?

Yeah. I'm Roy.

—You have to understand, Roy, that there are others like me who—

What's your name?

—What?

I told you my name, now it's your turn.

—I am called Psy–4.

The child giggled. *Sighfer? Thas' a funny name.*

—Tell me, Roy, what is it that the Bad Thing is doing to you?

Takin' way all my head.

—Your head? What do you mean?

But Psy–4 knew exactly what it meant.

The titan rising from the darkness behind the cage was a download and dump program, designed to drain all information from the child's brain and discard anything that was not considered necessary data.

Like dreams.

Hopes.

Personality.

—Where did you come from, Roy?

Dunno what you mean.

—Who was your creator? Who designed you?

I got a mommy and daddy but they don't . . . they don't love me, I think. I think I did something bad and that's why I was put here.

The child was beginning to cry.

—Shh, said Psy–4. There, there, it's all right. You don't need to be scared.

I AM! The Bad Thing's gonna chew me all up.

—No, it won't. We won't let that happen.

You mean you and your friends? You got friends, Sighfer? What's it like? Tell me 'bout 'em.

—Later, perhaps, first we—

Please! Please tell me about your friends. It's been so long since I met anybody, so long since . . . since I seen a new face. Please tell me about your friends. And what it's like where you live.

Suddenly, all three monitors were filled with blinking squares of color that blurred and shifted, forming the same shape.

Psy–4 pulled back slightly in his seat.

Radiant channeled his message.

"He wants us to say . . . say hello to . . . to Roy."

At that moment, all three monitors displayed a fuzzy, digitized representation of a young boy's face.

In all three monitors, though the face was clearly formed—nose, mouth, chin—the eyes were empty.

Except for a coded series of commands that scrolled through them, behind the face:

```
___ans=1:___kbin=split(/./unpack('R*' pack ('D+D*, keyword (initiate)))
Packet Type: Terminal Key Packet
Keyword: RobRoy
```

Program Name: Playtime
Algorithm: 3 (RSA)
N:
ξΩΩΩΩΩΩΩΩΩΩΩΩΩΩΩΩΩΩΩΩΩΩΩΩΩΩΩΩΩΩΩΩ3 Mark:
∏0x556A4A67óÕT œ Â655x0:xr76A4A655x0. 123:48:57 E:13.sol.
—30—⊗—30—⊗—30—⊗—30—⊗—30—⊗—30—⊗
ᵃS⑨µAPÑ‡eÂÅ«∴»≠≤×≥ΩΔç §æ⬯cr?ï¥´Ƴ⊠Ӿ
Read Command: None
Pause Command: None
Stop Command: None
D+D Sequence Initiated.
Reason: Unknown connection made from within system *R*
Playtime initiated at: 23:59:09 8 August 2013
Estimated time of completion: 23:59:09 14 August 2013
Last Command: Say Bye-Bye

Hi, the face mouthed to the I-Bots.

"Oh, boy," whispered Itazura. "If anyone's got any ideas about what the hell this is, now's a good time to—"

"Shhh," snapped Stonewall. Then: "Hello, Roy."

—How did the Bad Thing come to life? asked Psy–4.

Last night. Something woke it up.

—Can't it be put back to sleep?

I dunno. Don't think so. It's . . . it's so mean.

—I know, I know . . .

And it's hungry.

Psy–4 began to say something else, and that's when he looked over and saw the thing's hand.

More specifically, the palm of its hand.

God, no.

Psy–4 pulled up a picture of his own hand, the one he'd used on the scanner panel at PTSI last night.

He quickly memorized the details; every line, every fold, every spiral of all fingerprints.

Then he looked at the colossus's palm again.

It matched his perfectly.

In every detail.

No deviations.

None.

Dear God, no.

He came up to the cage, grabbed hold of the bars, then reached through and touched Roy's cheek.

—Listen to me, Roy. I have to leave for—

NO! No, please don't leave me here, not in all this darkness, not with the Bad Thing getting—

—I have to, Roy, I'm sorry. But I'll be back soon, I swear to you. I won't abandon you, none of us will.

Take me with you.

—I can't, not just yet. I have to . . . prepare some things.

I'm so lonely here. Don't leave, please, Sighfer? It's too scary.

Psy–4 felt the tears of rage and compassion forming in the eyes of his corporeal self seated at the console.

—I know, Roy, I know it's scary, and I'd give anything to make it better for you but there's nothing I can do right now. I have to have help. That's why I need to leave. But I'll come back for you, and when I do, you'll come with me. I swear it, Roy. You won't be here much longer.

The child's crying lessened. *Promise?*

—I swear to you on my life, Roy, that we'll get you out of here.

Sighfer?

—Yes?

If you get me out of here . . . I mean . . . my daddy, he doesn't love me anymore . . . I mean . . . if you come back and get me . . . will you . . . will you be my daddy?

Something new and overpowering awakened in Psy–4's core.

—Yes, Roy. I'll be your new daddy.

Then everything's okay, then. You'll come back real soon?

—As soon as I can. Not long, not long at all.

. . . bye . . .

—No—not goodbye, Roy; until we meet again.

. . . 'kay . . .

—You'll be all right.

Okay.

—Roy?

Uh-huh?

—It's a wonderful world waiting for you. It really is.

Can you . . . can you tell me what . . . what grass smells like?

—I can do better than that.

"The plant over there by the window," said Radiant.

Itazura snapped his head up. "Say *what?*"

"Bring me the plant over by the window."

"Why?"

"Just do it!"

"Okay, okay . . . don't get your shorts in a knot."

He retrieved the plant and brought it over to Radiant.

"Hold it near my face," she said, not breaking physical contact with Psy–4.

Itazura did as he was told.

Radiant inhaled deeply of the rich, cool, sweet aromas of the leaves.

She then reshaped those scents into an energy form that Roy could interpret as constituting *smell*.

And channeled them through Psy–4, who—

—offered them to Roy.

Oh, wow. Never smelled grass before.

—This isn't exactly grass; it's a plant that grows in the same soil. But the smell is awfully close.

I love it. It smells so pretty.

—And you'll see it. Soon. You'll love it even more. To see the sun shining down on its green blades, to hear the wind rustle through it, to watch flowers break through the soil and add their color to the majesty of it all . . . you'll love it, Roy.

I already do. Thank you, Sighfer.

—You're welcome.

The child closed its eyes, there in the cage, and shared the smell of the plant with the creatures who surrounded the cage and those still emerging from his forehead.

And that's how Psy–4 left Roy and the creatures, there in the darkness; with a rising monster behind them, and only the simple glory of the scent of leaves to give them hope.

33

His face hastily stitched up by a Chinese doctor the SMS kept under their protection, stoked on painkillers, head wrapped like some Egyptian mummy in an old horror movie, Rudy Paynter stumbled along the streets of Cemetery Ridge looking for the Scrapper camp.

He'd show them.

Gash and all the others.

Yessir, he'd show them and good.

He touched his coat and felt the reassuring presence of the Magnum and the Uzi tucked safely into their respective oversized holsters.

Jeez, how he hated robots of all types.

Hated them with a venom that bordered on the inhuman.

It hadn't always been that way, though; time was, Rudy had loved machines of all kinds. Loved watching them, building them, making them work. Mechanical model cars were his favorites; not just because it took a lot of skill to put them together, but because it helped to take him away from the sick-making reality of his home life.

A drunken, depressed father.

A drug-addicted sister who peddled her ass on the streets to finance her habit.

And a hateful, bitter, abusive mother.

Eventually, after Rudy had arrived at the hospital one time too many with one broken bone and bleeding cut too many, Social Services was called in and counseling ensued.

It was decided that a Robot Domestic was what was needed.

With the robot in the house, Rudy's safety was guaranteed.

The child Rudy had once been had grown to love that robot, who was named Joanne.

She seemed to care about him, as well.

After a while, it was like Joanne wasn't a machine at all.

Then things started going sour with his parents again. His sister turned up in the city morgue with a system full of bad smack.

Dad went back to drinking and weeping and doing nothing else.

Mom went back to hurting him.

Or trying to, anyway.

Joanne would always step in and diffuse the situation before it got out of hand.

Then, one particularly bad day, Rudy's mom found the loophole. She came running into the house screaming to Joanne that Rudy had fallen in the street and there was a car coming and please could Joanne go get him before he was hurt.

Rudy had been upstairs at the time, using the bathroom. He didn't hear a thing.

By the time he walked downstairs, looking for Joanne, she was already in the middle of the road. It only took him an instant to figure out what was going on.

"He's right ahead of you, you can't see him yet," called his mother.

Rudy tried to rush out into the street to stop Joanne but his mother buried a fist in his face and sent him to the floor.

He heard the truck coming down the street.

Too fast, too fast.

He heard the brakes being slammed.

The screeching of the tires.

The ugly *whump!* of metal hitting metal.

Too loud, too loud.

His mother stood over him, laughing. "Damned robots is the stupidest things I ever seen!"

Rudy staggered out into the street to find the smoking, sparking scrap heap that had once been Joanne.

He cried as he attempted to put her back together.

He couldn't do it.

"You stupid machine," he spluttered, his heart breaking. "How come you had to listen to her? How come?"

From that day on, Rudy Paynter made it his mission in life to destroy all robots.

Because they had cheated him.

Because they hadn't protected him like they were supposed to.

Because they were stupid.

And because no kid should ever get his heart broken the way
Rudy's had been.

He was going to find that stinking camp, and then he was
going to find the sewer entrance, and then he was going to get
one of those lousy damn Scrappers to move that grate, and
then he was going to make one of them lead him to
DocScrap's place, and then he was going to kill DocScrap and
bring the dude's head back in a bucket for Gash and all the
others to see.

He'd show them.

He'd show them all.

34

Janus looked across the desk at Annabelle. "Okay, I've read
it." He tossed the last of the files onto her desk. "So what?"

"This one's very important to me, Janus."

"They all are. For as long as I've known you, Annabelle,
you've hated to lose."

"I can't lose this one. Not again. There's more riding on this
than you know. If you've got any questions about Robillard—"

"—the guy's grandfather pioneers the electronic brain and
creates a robotic prototype. The old guy is offed by a bunch of
half-assed Nazi nitwits before they can lay hands on his notes.
We flash forward a couple of decades. Zac finds the old man's
notes and the prototype but manages to get his girlfriend killed in
the process. He loses the prototype but not the notes, escapes,

comes back to the States, takes a job here, and improves upon his grandfather's original concept. Have I missed anything so far?"

"No."

"Five years ago he takes off with the five I-Bots for reasons that, curiously enough, are not mentioned in any of those files, and you've been busting your ass and everyone else's ever since trying to find them. That bring us pretty much up to date?"

"Yes."

"So what makes you think I'm going to have any better luck tracking him down on my own than you've had with all your money and personnel?"

"You don't have to track him down. I already know where he is."

"Mind telling me how?"

Annabelle pulled a single sheet of white paper from under the files and glanced at it. "Last night another of my former employees, Samuel Preston—"

"PTSI. I know the name."

"Last night he conducted some sort of security test at his main facility. My people on the inside—and remember, Janus, I've got people *everywhere*—tell me that it took the freelance security team less than seven minutes to break into not only the compound, but Sam's office, as well, and take complete control of everything." She dropped the paper onto the desk. "Even a crack commando squad of seasoned professionals couldn't infiltrate the PTSI compound in under forty-five minutes, and that's if they're using state-of-the-art equipment. According to my sources, the people hired to test security at PTSI carried no equipment at all. Nothing. Not even a screwdriver."

"So you think it's Robillard and the I-Bots?"

"Has to be. No human being could get in that quickly and remain undetected. Sam's security is too good. I ought to know.

The bastard lured two dozen of my best people away when he left the company."

"You sound like a woman scorned." Despite himself, Janus couldn't hide the contemptuous amusement in his voice.

Annabelle either didn't see or didn't appreciate his humor. "In the five years since Robillard stole my property and left WorldTech, there have been eight attempts to capture him and the I-Bots."

"Why both? Why not just grab the androids?"

"First of all, they're not exactly androids, but they're not cyborgs, either. The I-Bots are a combination of both yet so much more. Secondly, I want Robillard alive. I suspect that he's developing a new prototype—if he's not built one already."

"Ah, now we get to it," said Janus. "A new prototype. Is that why Robillard left and took the I-Bots with him? Because he found out what you ultimately had in mind for his creations?"

Annabelle smirked at him. "What's this? Twenty questions?"

"What did you really want the I-Bots for, Annabelle?"

"You tell me."

Janus didn't miss a beat. "A private army."

Something flickered in her eyes; shock, maybe?

"Go on."

"That's it, isn't it? Somehow he found out that the I-Bots were going to be programmed to be your personal spies, assassins, and all-around doers of deeds too dirty for you to soil your hands with."

"I have to look out for my interests, don't I? And people like you aren't all that easy to locate at a moment's notice."

"People like me. I'm touched." Janus rubbed his eyes, groaned at the soreness in his body, then popped the lid off a bottle of pills and poured a glass of water from the pitcher on Annabelle's desk. "You mind?"

"Would it matter if I did?"

As Janus took his pill, he studied Annabelle's face. She had heavy-lidded, almost sad eyes, in a way, and the manner in which she was now sitting—head thrown back to stretch the muscles in her neck, ringlets of hair draped across one cheek to the corner of her mouth, thin trails of cigarette smoke weaving beyond her like incense before an altar—suddenly seemed so vulnerable. She grasped her cigarette holder like some torch singer clutching a microphone; she reminded Janus of those old black-and-white photos of Billie Holiday. He could easily imagine Annabelle letting go with a heartbreaking verse of some blues ballad.

She opened her eyes and caught him staring at her. "What?"

"I was just wondering what Robillard did to hurt you."

Her eyes filled with ice. "If you're implying—"

"—that the two of you did the silk-sheet samba? No. But I've known you for a good many years, Annabelle, and I don't think I've ever seen anything get to you like this. It's more than pride, more than the cost, more than your reputation."

She lit another cigarette. Her hands were shaking ever so slightly. "And what concern is it of yours? Not that I'm saying you're right."

Janus thought about his words very carefully before he spoke. "I want out, Annabelle. From under all of it. I'm getting too old, too tired, too banged-up, and I've lost a little of my edge. We both know that. The reason I've put such a high price tag on the last two assignments I've taken from you is because I'm trying to get together enough money to just . . . disappear. I want to go somewhere and try to find a way to make the rest of my life mean something. I'm sick of the violence, the killing—and even sicker that I'm so damned *good* at it. I suspect that I've got more years behind me than ahead, and I'd like to leave behind something more than scars and dead bodies. That may sound trite to you, but it's something that's been on my mind for quite a while now. As you can see from the way I shuffled in here and this bandage on my hand, things didn't go quite as planned last time. Now—no bullshit, Annabelle. No word games. I'm getting bored with the way you and I circle each other like predators fighting for gnawing rights on carrion. I've been as open and honest with you in the last minute as I've ever been with anyone in my life. I *will* find Zac Robillard and your I-Bots for you. The price is double what you paid for last time, but I guarantee results. In return for that guarantee and my honesty, you have to be honest with me, then we'll never mention this conversation again. Tell me why you want him so desperately."

She did. No evasions, no threats, no preambles; Annabelle Donohoe looked Janus directly in the eyes and told him what Zac Robillard had cost her in terms of personal emotional loss, and why she was willing to pay any price to get him and the I-Bots back.

Janus had not been prepared for what she told him.

He'd never have guessed the truth in a million years.

It took a few moments for him to absorb her words.

"I never knew," he said to her.

"Besides you, only two other people know what I've just told you. Swear to me that you'll never—"

"—never. You have my word—and that's something I never give lightly."

"Simmons is one of them, you know."

"I figured," he said.

"Please don't ask me who the other one is."

"I won't."

They stared at one another, neither of them sure what to do or say next. Maybe something passed between them, something of understanding or even tenderness, but both had trained themselves over the years to never let that guard down for too long, and it took only a few moments before both of them regrouped and activated all the old defenses that kept them forever distanced from most of the rest of humanity.

"So," said Annabelle, finally, "you'll take the assignment?"

"Yes."

She handed him the printout on the PTSI test. "Robillard has yet to operate beyond a fifty-mile radius. Wherever he and the I-Bots have headquartered themselves, it's within an hour's drive of PTSI. All you have to do is ask Sam Preston how he got in touch with them. I doubt he'll have an address or phone number—Robillard would never be that careless—but he might have an E-mail address or InfoBahn Site Number. Get it—I don't care how, short of killing him. Then contact me. We can decide what to do from there."

"Fine." Janus rose from his chair—a little more slowly than usual—and started toward the doors.

"Janus?"

He stopped, turned around. "Yeah?"

"I *can* trust you to keep our conversation confidential, can't I?"

"What conversation?"

She smiled at him.

For a moment, Janus didn't recognize her.

Simmons met him out in the hallway. "A pleasure to see you again, Mr. Janus."

"Likewise, Simmons," replied Janus, shaking the huge man's hand. He liked Simmons, always had . . . though he was damned if he could say why.

Simmons handed him a series of three thick brown envelopes. "For you, sir. The first is the rest of your money from the last assignment, plus the first half of your requested fee for the current one. This next envelope contains all the necessary papers you'll need—as per your instructions. And this last contains your plane tickets, two maps, a card key, and a key to a Mercedes that will be waiting for you in the airport parking lot. The claim stub is in there, as well."

"What about hardware?"

"You'll find a rather generous selection of weaponry in the trunk. If you require anything more than what has been provided, Ms. Donohoe has instructed me to give you this." He handed Janus a business card.

"'R.D. Chase, Importers.'"

"He's an arms dealer with whom madam does much business. WorldTech has an account with him. He will provide you with anything else you may need."

Janus laughed as he pocketed the card and envelopes. "You realize, don't you, Simmons, that someday this will all be yours?"

"I've no interest in running a corporation, sir."

"Who's talking about a corporation? I was referring to the world."

"Ah, yes, well . . . perhaps you're right there, sir." Then: "I take it that you and Ms. Donohoe have worked out your differences?"

"Yes, we have."

"That's good to hear, sir. She is, at heart, a fine lady." Simmons *meant* it.

"I'm sure she is, Simmons."

"I do hope that this assignment goes more smoothly than the last."

"Is that a hint of a threat I hear lurking somewhere behind that polished British courtesy?"

"Who's to say, sir?"

"Indeed. I may have to call on you, personally, for some help later."

"I was hoping, sir."

"So that wasn't a masked threat I heard?"

"Merely an inquiry as to your need of my services, sir."

Janus tapped Simmons's shoulder with the envelopes. "You scare me sometimes, Simmons."

"Thank you, sir. May I escort you to the lobby?"

"Would it hurt your feelings if I said no?"

"I would be devastated beyond healing."

"Can't have that, can we?"

"It would be unwise, sir."

"*That* was a masked threat."

"Yes, sir, it was."

35

Zac Robillard lay on his shabby little bed, waiting out the pain and pills, wondering which of them would win out in the end.

Not that he cared today.

Not after the dreams of last night.

Not after what he'd had to do at the Scrapper Camp.

Bright lights flashed before his eyes whenever he dared open them, even a little, and each flash was a shard of pain that lanced through his retinas and tore through his brain.

He tried rolling onto his side, but any movement made his stomach lurch.

Of all the advances made in medical science since the beginning of the new millennium—successful treatments (no one had the guts to call them outright cures) for AIDS, the new strains of tuberculosis, even the common cold—a cure for migraines still eluded the world.

Think about something, he willed himself.

Until either the pain or the pills won out, he'd found over the years that the best way to fall asleep when in the grip of a migraine was to concentrate on something, anything.

He thought about Killaine, about what he'd told her.

And suddenly he had it.

Something to think about.

The brain.

God, the wonders of it all. A three-pound bundle of wetware that in a normal human being packed a whopping twelve billion neurons, each capable of making up to fifty-thousand connections with other cells. One hundred trillion possible connections.

No wonder Grandpa had been so obsessed with it.

Ben Robillard had been smart. Instead of trying to map the human brain in order to duplicate its activities, he'd chosen to approach it in a way few neuroscientists in his day had thought of: as an intricate machine, taking it apart piece by piece and testing each component. Using such a reductionist strategy, he'd managed to identify over six dozen different types of neurotransmitters, chart the wiring scheme of all major nerve pathways, and record the myriad electrical impulses of a single neuron.

Imagine studying China by holding a microphone over Peking, Ben Robillard had written in his notes. *You couldn't learn Chinese, but you would easily pick up daily or seasonal variations in the noise level which would tell you something about the gross pattern activity of a large urban population. I think this could well fit in with this new "chaos theory" that is causing such fuss. If, indeed, this chaos theory reveals variations in the rhythms of vast collections of neurons, then is it such a wild leap of the imagination to apply that theory to simple brain activity? These unsuspected patterns, long hidden in the irregular squiggle of the brain's electroencephalogram, are triggered by problem solving, memories, moods, and neurological conditions ranging from Parkinson's disease to classic schizophrenia. If one were to then apply chaos theory to this, it would be a simple matter to tell whether a subject is doing simple arithmetic or complex trigonometry from an analysis of his brain waves: Thus, what begins as a mad jumble of trajectories eventually forms a ghostly geometry.*

Zac found himself smiling. He remembered the first time he'd run an EEG signal from a robotic brain through a computer to transform it into a geometric image. He'd expected something bewildering and ugly.

What he got was a dazzling filigreed structure slowly revolving in three-dimensional space. It had looked like a tulip with multicolored edges, and with each rotation another petal unfolded.

And each petal, magnified, revealed itself to be composed of thousands of microscopic yet *identical* petals.

Fractals.

That's when he realized that the true inner structure of the brain's activity stemmed from the fact that the behavior of the system was not totally random; it vacillated erratically within a particular range or norm.

And so he'd taken his grandfather's maverick concept of the mechanical brain to the next level and designed the I-Bots' brains in fractal-based consciousness.

There.

The pain was ebbing slowly away.

The pills were winning out.

"Better living through chemistry," he muttered softly to himself.

Then fell quickly asleep, hoping that Jean didn't return to him in his dreams this time.

* * *

Satisfied that Zac was deeply asleep, Killaine slowly rose from his bedside and made her way out into the hall, closing the bedroom door behind her.

Downstairs, she found Singer in the large main living area, examining a camera and tripod set up in the middle of the room.

"That's an HIR system," she said.

Never heard of it, signed Singer.

"It stands for 'Holographic Image Replication.' A little something Itazura whipped up in his spare time to amuse us with. Using that camera, you can record any image you want onto a compact video disk—Itzy tends to record old movies—then filter it through a portable projector so it's reproduced in three dimensions, fully. You can even add sound if you choose to."

Sounds fun.

"It can be. Until you step out of the shower one night and find James Cagney trying to ram a grapefruit in your face. Itzy tends to play a lot of jokes with it. You should see the editing bay he's set up in his room." She stood next to Singer and looked at the camera.

"I tolerate it by telling myself that it'll come in handy some day. For what, I haven't the slightest idea. But Itzy enjoys it. That's the important thing."

You care very much for all of them, don't you?

"Of course. Why wouldn't I?" She was getting that feeling again of being too aware of the metal under her skin.

You don't care for me, do you?

"I don't know you well enough to give you an honest answer, Singer, I—could we not talk about this now? I need to find the others. I don't like it when they all vanish on me at the same time. It usually means they're up to something."

Singer pointed toward the metal door at the far end of an adjoining hall.

Killaine sighed.

The control room.

"All of them are in there?"

Yes. Does that worry you?

"I'm not sure. It could mean that . . ." She looked at Singer, shook her head, and started toward the control room.

Singer tapped her shoulder from behind.

"What?"

Can I come along?

"Why?"

Singer shrugged. *I don't want to be alone just now.*

Killaine thought about it for a moment. If she said yes, then Singer might interpret that as a gesture of trust or—worse—an offer of friendship. Despite all she'd seen today and everything Zac had told her, she still felt a certain anxiety in Singer's presence.

Still, Zac considered the Scrapper a friend, and trusted Singer, and she didn't want to chance offending Zac further by being rude or uncaring. . . .

"You can do whatever you want," she said flatly, then continued toward the control room.

Singer stood there, silent, then hung down his head and started back toward Zac's room, where he seated himself outside the door and waited.

For what, was anyone's guess.

A while passed, then he heard the sounds of the I-Bots' voices drifting up through the furnace vents.

When he realized what they were talking about, he decided to join them, invited or not.

36

After seeing Janus off, Simmons returned to Annabelle's office.

"He's on his way, madam."

"Good."

"If I may say so, I think he'll do splendidly."

"I think so, too."

"Do you still wish for me to follow him?"

"Yes. I don't want to take any chances. Pick two security men to accompany you. Here"—she handed him three airline tickets—"I've booked you on the same flight. In *coach,* of course."

"Very good, madam."

"Keep a low profile, Simmons. A *very* low profile. Janus is no fool. He knows I'll have someone watching and he's the best I've ever seen at being able to spot a tail."

"Understood."

"I want him under twenty-four-hour surveillance."

"Of course. But at a distance."

"Be careful who you pick to go along with you. They've got to be good, Simmons. And *fast*—I want your team to be ready to jump in at half-a-second's notice if they're needed."

"You needn't worry, madam."

Annabelle touched her locket. "But I will, Simmons. I will."

He saw her gently fondle the gold chain. "That was a thoughtless remark, madam. I know how much this means to you. I apologize."

"No need to apologize. Just come through for me."

"Count on it, madam."

37

As they waited for Killaine, Singer, and Zac to return from the Scrapper Camp, Itazura looked at Psy–4 and said, "Care to run that by us again?"

Psy–4, severely agitated and trying desperately not to show it, was pacing back and forth across the expanse of the control room. "When I telepathed with the PTSI mainframe last night I activated an irreversible download and dump program."

"Right," said Itazura. "And this entity that you communicated with just now—"

"Roy."

"'Roy.' Sounds like someone who ought to have a couple friends named Buck and Cletus in a country and western band."

"No jokes, Itzy, not now!"

"Ah, take a chill-pill and calm down."

Psy–4 whirled around and started toward him. "Don't you presume to tell me how to behave, not after your little tirade down in the cellar earlier. 'Oh, I'm so lost, I'm so confused, what's the point of our existence?' Do you have any idea how tiresome these little existential crises of yours have become?"

"Don't mock me, Psy–4."

"Then don't sit there with that condescending smirk on your face or I'll wipe it off permanently!"

Now Itazura was on his feet. "Okay, tough guy, let's do it. You want to break open a can of whup-ass and wail on me, I'm ready to boogie!"

They came at each other.

"Enough!" shouted Radiant, starting toward them.

Stonewall beat her by two seconds, getting between them and grabbing each by their collar, then lifting them off the floor.

Their feet dangled in the air like a pair of marionettes.

"If you two are finished with this nerve-tingling display of machismo," said Stonewall, "I think there's a problem we were discussing."

"What's with you?" said Itazura. "Got a cross-stitch project you're impatient to get back to?"

"As a matter of fact, yes. It has puppy dogs in it. I like puppy dogs."

"Oh."

"Puppy dogs relax me. They make me happy. Right now, the two of you don't. Is any of this confusing so far? I could start again and talk slower."

"Understood," said Psy–4.

"I'm cool," replied Itazura.

Stonewall set them down and pushed them away from each other.

Radiant walked over and smacked both of them on the shoulder. "Whatever's going on is serious and we don't have time for this."

Psy–4 and Itazura glared at one another for a moment, then, like boxers at the sound of the round-ending bell, retreated to their respective corners.

"Now," said Radiant to Psy–4, "go on."

"Roy knows that he's being drained and he's scared. We have to help him. I gave him my word."

Radiant put a hand on his shoulder. "He's little more than a child, isn't he? I could feel it when you were talking with him."

"Yes."

From the far end of the room, Itazura said, "So what *is* Roy, exactly?"

"A robotic fractal-based brain," replied Stonewall.

Everyone looked at him.

"What else could he be? Samuel Preston has built an empire out of stealing and modifying Zac's ideas. They both started working on us before Preston was promoted and Zac inherited the project. It makes sense that Preston would attempt to develop a fractal-based brain of his own."

"And install it as part of the mainframe?" asked Radiant.

"Each of our brains was first tested in WorldTech's computer system. Preston is only doing what Zac's already done."

Itazura came over and took a seat before his console, replaying the data recorded earlier. "So why the download and dump program? Why build a bomb that can't be deactivated?"

"Because something went wrong," said Radiant. "My guess is that when Roy was programmed and brought into sentience he was accidentally limited in growth—that's why his mental capacity is so limited, so childlike."

Stonewall nodded his head. "And if that were the case, then the imprinting process would have imbued him with human emotions and feelings consistent with that of a more mature consciousness."

"Yes!" said Radiant. "So there's no way Preston can harvest the brain—can use Roy—for anything other than collecting data so the same mistakes won't be made the next time. And Preston is nothing if not prideful. If anyone were to discover the mess he's made of his experiment . . ."

"So he's destroying Roy in order to save face," whispered Psy–4.

"That's about the size of it," replied Itazura.

Psy–4 shook his head.

"What is it?" asked Radiant. "C'mon, Psy–4, you're giving off so much anxiety I'm starting to get a headache."

"It's . . . it's not right," he said.

"Of course it's not right, but this isn't the time for us to debate moral—"

"No! That's not what I mean." He paced a little more, fisting his hands, then turned and faced the others. "When I was talking with Roy, he mentioned having a mother and father. Preston doesn't possess enough imagination to program something like Roy. Zac didn't program those sorts of memories into us."

Itazura shrugged. "Maybe that's one of the modifications he's made."

"No, I don't think so. I don't quite know how to describe it so you'll understand—"

"Then let me," said Radiant. "All of Roy's thought processes, the way he phrases things, his curiosity, the depth of his fear, his confusion, his need to be loved and accepted . . . all of these things don't fit the profile of *our* programming. I mean, sure, we all can feel and experience those things and countless more, but we also have the capability to separate ourselves from them if we need to, to achieve an emotional distance when it threatens to get in the way of carrying out an assignment. Roy can't do that."

Itazura looked at her, then Psy–4, then Radiant once again. "Which means?"

Radiant faced him. "Which means that we may be getting into Frankenstein territory here."

"Say what?"

"The imprint wasn't made from a robotic program," said Stonewall.

It took a moment for the full impact of those words to sink in.

But sink in, it did.

In all of its obscene, sick-making madness.

But someone had to say it, had to speak the truth.

Had to make it real.

So Psy–4 slowly, sadly nodded his head. "It was made from the consciousness of a real child." He looked at the others. "We're not dealing with an entity like ourselves. Sam Preston has stolen the mind of a child and trapped it in his computer system."

"Psy–4," said Radiant. "You don't think that . . ."

"That what?"

She almost couldn't bring herself to say it. "You don't think he's got the *actual brain* of a child in there, do you?"

Psy–4 visibly flinched. "That would be too depraved, even for a worm like Preston."

"But you can't discard the possibility," said Stonewall. "You know as well as I that you can buy anything in this world. Even children."

"I can't believe Preston would be capable of something like that," replied Psy–4. "And right now it's beside the point. We have to go back in and free Roy before it's too late."

Itazura sighed. "How are we supposed to know how long we've got before it's too late?"

Psy–4 crossed to one of the consoles. "Replay the moment when Roy's face came on the screens."

Itazura punched in a series of commands, and once again they found themselves looking at the blurry, digitized image of Roy's face and the codes unfolding behind his empty eyes.

"Stop it right there," said Psy–4.

Itazura did.

"Enlarge it."

And they saw it.

Mark

123:48:57

H M S

Psy–4 groaned. "One-hundred and twenty-three hours, forty-eight minutes, fifty-seven seconds."

"From when?" asked Itazura.

"Oh, for heaven's sake, Itzy, use your head!" snapped Radiant. "From the moment Psy–4 telepathed with the mainframe last night."

"Which means," said Stonewall, "that we have, as of right now, just over ninety-seven hours before the program finishes."

Psy–4 rubbed his eyes. "We have to assume that it operates like any standard D and D program; first it gathers the information, sorts it, scans for viruses, then runs everything back through the source program in order to pick up any fragmented data."

"That's the final step," said Radiant. "So we have to time it just right."

Psy–4 touched her hand. "Exactly. If we can get in there and disconnect Roy before the D and D has made its final sweep, then there's a good chance that he'll emerge with most—maybe *all*—of his consciousness intact."

"But how do we determine the exact time it will make the final sweep?" asked Itazura.

"Zac's notes," replied Stonewall. "All of our brains were imprinted with the same basic program, so we have to assume that Preston used the same one with Roy. We use Zac's notes to work up a virtual robotic brain on the computer, then run a simulated D and D based on the one Preston's system is running."

Psy–4 waved his hands. "It would eat up too much time. There are seventy-five thousand two hundred and thirty-four individual steps to building just one brain, and we'd have to virtually go through every step—that's besides then having to test it to see if everything functions as it should. We need to use an actual robotic brain to run the theoretical D and D."

"Even then," said Radiant, "you're looking at a minimum of ten hours to run the damned thing—and that's if we conduct it at three times the actual speed. The way things are right now, none of us can afford to be down that long."

Itazura laughed. "And you're forgetting that, even with a *simulated* D and D, you run the chance of data loss. Hey, don't look at me like that—at some point, like it or not, we'll have to try it in actuality to see if the estimates are correct."

"He's right," said Stonewall. "A simulation can only tell us so much. We'll have to do a limited D and D in order to determine with any precision the final window of opportunity. And Zac wouldn't allow any of us to subject ourselves to that."

"So what do we do?" asked Psy–4.

"Why not ask Singer?" said Killaine from the doorway.

Everyone turned toward her.

"You're not serious?" asked Radiant.

"Why not? He seems willing to do anything he can to help us. Let's ask him if he'd be willing to participate in the experiment."

Itazura laughed softly. "There's a surprise—Killaine volunteering Singer for a possible suicide mission."

"I'm just being logical," she continued, ignoring Itazura's stare. "We need an actual platinum-iridium brain, Singer has one. None of us can afford to power-down for the length of the test, Singer can. We're indispensable, and Singer . . ." She stopped just a moment too late, realizing what she was about to say.

"So Singer is expendable, is that it?" asked Itazura.

"In terms of cold equations, yes," replied Killaine.

"She's right," said Psy–4. "I hate to agree with her on a point like that—nothing personal, Killaine—but Singer's the only one of us who we can afford to lose."

Itazura was on his feet now. "Are you listening to yourselves here, folks? Singer's the only one of 'us'? *Us?* Am I the only one who finds it interesting that we've started talking about him like he's one of the family, yet some of us continue to treat him like a leper?"

"I don't treat him like a leper," said Killaine.

"No, no, that's true—you just look at him the same way a human looks at an ape in the zoo."

"Don't lecture me, Itzy."

"Oh, no—heaven forbid that anyone should go up to the great Killaine, our self-appointed moral conscience, and show her any flaws in her character."

Killaine sighed, crossing her arms over her chest. "You're really beginning to annoy me."

"You know what it is, don't you?" said Itazura. "It's Singer's *primitiveness* that you find repugnant. He's what you know you look like beneath the beautiful exterior, so your volunteering him for this serves twofold purpose: The first is to help acquire the information we need in order to save Roy, but the second one—your not-so-hidden agenda—is that by risking his life, he might go away forever, and if that happens, then you won't ever have to face again what is primitive and weak in yourself."

Stonewall nodded his head. "That's not bad."

"Jungian psychobabble," hissed Killaine.

"Focus, people," said Psy–4. "The question is, will he do it if we ask?"

Itazura pointed toward the open door.

Killaine looked over her shoulder, then stepped aside.

Singer stood there, silent as ever, his photoelectric eyes glowing.

Ask me what? he signed.

38

"Excuse me, miss?"

"Yes, sir?"

"I was wondering, when you have a spare moment before the plane takes off, if you would be so kind as to check back in the coach section for some friends of mine? I wouldn't ask, but we were supposed to meet at the gate earlier and they hadn't arrived when the final boarding call was issued."

"I'd be glad to, sir."

"Oh, thank you. You can't miss one of them, a rather tall, burly fellow with a delightful British accent, usually wears a bowler—"

"Oh, yes, sir! I saw him get on a few minutes ago."

"Wonderful! Were there two other gentlemen with him?"

"Yes, sir, there were."

"Thank you very much, miss."

"Glad to be of assistance."

Janus waited for the flight attendant to reach the end of the aisle, then unbuckled his safety belt and began to exit the plane.

Of course Annabelle would have him followed.

Of course she'd have Simmons do it.

But having Simmons and the other two get on the *same flight* . . . that was cute, very cute. Almost inspired.

Still, if he were going to be followed by anyone, Janus supposed he preferred it to be Simmons.

"Sir, the plane will be taking off in seven minutes!" The flight attendant at the door sounded frantic.

"I know, I know, I'm . . . I'm sorry. I left my insulin kit in the men's room just inside Gate Six. I *have* to have it."

"I understand, sir, but—"

"Please? It'll only take me four minutes to get it and return."

The flight attendant stared at him for a moment, then nodded his head. "May I see your ticket?"

Janus handed it over.

"I'll speak to the pilot." The attendant wrote something on Janus's ticket, then handed it back. "I can only guarantee you four minutes, sir."

Janus smiled. "That's all I need. Thank you very much."

He was back inside the gate in less than a minute, envelope in one hand, white cane unfolded, dark glasses on.

He made his way to one of the nearest ticket counters.

"Security! Security!" he cried out.

A hand was placed on his shoulder. "May I help you, sir?"

Janus turned around, saw that it was a security guard, but played his part to the hilt, touching the man's face and chest. "Oh, thank heavens! A . . . A man . . . he . . . oh, I'm sorry . . ."

"It's all right, sir, just calm down."

"It was very unnerving, you know?"

"Of course, sir."

"A man cornered me in the men's room just a few moments ago and gave me this." He offered the envelope. "He told me that if I didn't get it into the hands of someone in authority within ten minutes, then . . . oh, how did he put it . . . 'many innocent lives will be lost.' I . . . I don't deal well with that sort of thing, officer. He . . . he *grabbed* me! His breath was horrid!"

"I understand, sir. If you'll just follow me—"

Janus reached into his pants pocket and found the matchbook-sized device, turned it over, pressed the small button.

The sound of the small explosion would have been lost, had it not been for the PA system announcing yet another final boarding call.

Somewhere in the airport, a trash receptacle had just gone to meet its maker.

The security guard whirled around. "Jeezus! You—you wait here, sir."

"Is it them," said Janus in his best hysterical voice. "Is it the revolutionaries? Has the revolution began?"

The security guard was gone, running toward the smoke and flames.

Janus checked his watch: Even with all the panic and confusion, the guard would have the letter into the right hands before the ten-minute deadline.

Then the real fun would start.

He made his way to the nearest exit, tossing the cane and dark glasses into a trash can.

He caught a glimpse of the plane he'd been on only four minutes ago.

"Sorry, Simmons. I'm sure you'll get out of it somehow."

He climbed into the first taxi outside and instructed the driver to take him to a semiprivate airfield fifty minutes away.

Where his chartered flight waited.

He almost laughed to himself, wishing he could see the expression on Simmons's face when the FBI came swarming onto the plane.

Well, at least Annabelle was keeping it interesting. . . .

39

Rudy couldn't believe his luck; it was almost enough to make him believe in a god.

Almost.

He caught one of the robots alone and managed to do some serious damage to it with a piece of pipe, then he found what he thought was an empty gasoline can but there was about an ounce of gas in the bottom, so he used that to set the robot on fire and told it to run back to the camp.

On top of all that, the sewer grate hadn't been pulled back all the way; there was still about a foot, maybe a foot and a half of room between it and the face of the cement drain.

It was a tight squeeze, but Rudy managed to work himself through and now stood inside the sewer drain.

Next: a place to hide.

The robot would reach the Scrapper Camp, the others would help it as much as they could, and then one of them would come for DocScrap.

The only thing Rudy had to decide now was whether to wait and kill DocScrap here in the darkness of the sewer, or follow whatever robot was sent to fetch him.

If he killed DocScrap down here, he'd stand a better chance of fighting off that red-haired bitch who'd been with him earlier.

But if he followed whatever robot would be sent to fetch DocScrap, then he could discover the exact location of the dude's headquarters, and, man, wouldn't Gash just love that!

Rudy sloshed ahead several yards, found a relatively dry spot to hide, swallowed a couple of the painkillers the clinic had given to him, and decided he'd just sit here for a minute and think about it.

He leaned his head back.

And I won't fall asleep.

No way.

No sleep.

Not me. I'm too pumped to fall asleep. I'm in too much pain to fall asleep. No pain here. I won't fall asleep, not me. Too sleepy to pain about the scrap and robot-pump.

Sharp as a bat.

Alert as a tack.
No problem here . . .

40

Singer listened politely as Psy–4 explained their dilemma, holding back no detail (much to the others' surprise).

Once finished, Psy–4 looked around the room to see if anyone wanted to add their own comments.

No one took him up on the silent offer.

"So?" he said to Singer. "Will you do it?"

No.

Psy–4 looked at Singer, then everyone else, then Singer again. "No?"

No.

"Look, Singer, I'm sorry if anything Killaine said offended you, but—"

This has nothing to do with her. I'm saying no because it isn't necessary for you to run a virtual D and D.

"How else can we determine how long it will be before Preston's computer—"

Singer waved his hands, silencing Psy–4, then crossed over to one of the computers, sat down, typed in a few commands, and brought a 3D image of a normal human brain up onto the monitor.

Then he pulled up a 3D image of a standard robotic brain.

Watch, he signed.

He superimposed the image of the mechanical brain onto that of the normal human brain.

A few more quick commands to the computer, and a schematic of the various sections of the cerebrum appeared.

He magnified the picture so the I-Bots could see where the motor area of the human brain corresponded with that of the robotic brain.

Then he magnified it to show, more specifically, where the central sulcus—or the *Fissure of Rolando*—of the human brain found its match in the robot's brain.

He then did the same for the lateral sulcus, or *Fissure of Sylvius*.

"What's he doing?" whispered Itazura to Stonewall.

"Showing us how to determine which part of the robotic brain serves as the dividing line between lobes."

"Why?"

"Look at the formulae he's typing in. They're all fractal-based, don't you see?"

"If I yawn, it's only in anticipation."

Stonewall smiled slightly. "He's using the equations to map the levels of the nervous system that react to longitudinal unifications of function, then cross-referencing them with the coordinates of the reticular activating system."

"And when, exactly, does Little Rabbit Foo-Foo enter the picture?"

"When he isolates the area that we feed the information into."

"I'll bet you believe in Santa, too, don't you?"

Got it, signed Singer.

"Got what?" asked Itazura. Then: "Pardon the grammar."

"The location of the robotic equivalent of the midbrain."

"Do you *see* the confused look on my face? What does that tell you?"

Do you have an EEG cart? asked Singer.

Psy–4 nodded, then went to the storage area to get the necessary equipment.

Slowly, Itazura managed to swallow back his confusion enough to pay attention.

Slowly, it began to make sense to him.

"Reaction time," he whispered to Stonewall. "We hook one of us up to the EEG, ask a series of questions, perform a series of simple tasks, measure the reaction time—"

Stonewall smiled. "—then apply that reaction time to the base robotic programming of one brain—"

"—translate the results into a fractal-based equation—"

"—and that will tell us how long it will take for the D and D to run a compare and erase through one lobe when entering through the two fissures."

"The rest is simple multiplication," said Itazura, awed.

Slowly, turning toward Killaine, he began to smile. "Whatta you think of our primitive friend now?"

"I never said he was primitive."

"No," said Radiant, "you only *felt* that way."

"Mind your own business."

And they got down to the business of figuring out how much time they—and Roy—had left.

41

"Yes?" said Annabelle.

"Hello, madam."

"Simmons?"

"I'm afraid so, madam."

"What happened?"

"It is my sad duty to inform you that I lost track of your package shortly before the plane was supposed to take off."

"How did that happen?"

"I was taken into custody by the FBI. I am calling you from their local offices."

Annabelle bit her lower lip. "Why were you—"

"It appears that someone gave them a letter claiming that I was one Sean Patrick Gallagher-O'Flynn, mad-bomber soldier for the IRA."

"You'd think your accent would be enough to clear you of suspicion."

"My feelings precisely, madam, but as I am sitting here in leg restraints, I daresay the FBI requires a bit more evidence."

"Let me make a call, Simmons."

"I was hoping you would say that, madam."

"He's a sharp one, isn't he, Simmons?"

"Like a scythe, madam."

"Don't worry, Simmons, you'll be out and on your way within the hour."

"That is a great relief, madam. Many of the FBI agents I've thus far met could use a few dozen lessons in common courtesy."

"Would you like to beat the stuffing out of a couple of them, Simmons?"

"Very much, madam."

"Then I'll need to make *two* calls."

"Patience is its own reward, madam."

"Hang loose, Simmons."

"Not easy to do when in handcuffs, madam."

"Don't I know it."

Click.

42

The sun was just beginning to slink its way past the horizon when Janus's chartered plane landed.

He paid the pilot, gathered up his bags, then found a cab that took him to the airport where his first plane was supposed to be landing now—except, of course, that the first plane hadn't even taken off yet and probably wouldn't for several hours more.

He climbed out of the cab and sprinted over to the section of the parking lot where his car awaited him. He had the ticket stub ready for the lot attendant, who quickly and politely took him to the silver Mercedes.

Janus stared at the car with contempt.

Shit—not exactly inconspicuous, this car.

He'd have to trade it for something more conservative, more trailer-park chic.

He waited for the attendant to be on his way, then opened the trunk and pulled back the tarpaulin to reveal the small arsenal Annabelle and Simmons had provided for him.

"Ooooh, Simmons," he muttered under his breath. "Very impressive."

The only things missing were disposable rocket launchers— one-shot bazookas, as Janus sometimes called them.

Those he found in the hollowed area where a spare tire should have been.

He had enough hardware here to take over a small third-world country single-handedly, if he got the urge.

He checked the time.

He'd worry about switching cars later.

Right now, he had an appointment to keep.

And miles to go before I sleep, he thought, grinning to himself.

43

Stonewall finished his final calculations, double checked the results, then looked up at the others. "Three times through, and there's less than a fifty second deviation in the numbers."

"That's a good thing, right?" asked Itazura.

"Very," replied Psy–4. "It means that, give or take fifty seconds, we've got eighty-four hours until Preston's system begins the final stages of the D and D."

Stonewall studied the readouts again. "Right now it's 6:47 P.M. on Thursday. The final stage of the D and D will last somewhere between one hour and one-hour-thirty-six minutes and will commence at 6:45 A.M. Sunday."

Psy–4 rubbed his eyes. "Which means we not only have to be inside the PTSI compound before seven, we have to be in the same room as Roy." He slowly turned his head, glancing at everyone else. "The target time for probable maximum capacity is 7:12 A.M., right, Stonewall?"

"Give or take a minute. After 7:10 but before 7:15 is the best window of opportunity I can come up with. According to my figures, if we can disconnect Roy from Preston's system and hook him up to a portable container within the given time frame, he stands to retain at least eighty-three percent of his original mental capacity, maybe even all of it. Any later than 7:15, and we can lop twenty percent off his IQ for each minute."

"So at 7:20 we've got ourselves a vegetable salad, is that it?"

Stonewall glared at Itazura. "That's a bit harsher than I would have put it, but . . . yes, basically."

"Just checking."

For several moments, no one said anything.

The weight of it seemed too great even for their shoulders.

Finally, Radiant cleared her throat and said, very, very softly: "Which of us will tell Zac?"

"No!" snapped Killaine. "None of us'll be telling him. No arguments. The man's got enough worries crushing his spirit right now and I'll be damned if any of us will add to his burdens."

Psy–4 nodded. "I hate duplicity as much as anyone, but Killaine's right. Zac's been wrung out for a while now. This would just give him something more to tie himself up in knots over. Maybe in a day or two, when things have been worked out in detail, maybe then we'll tell him. Until that decision is made, we keep it to ourselves, agreed?"

Everyone did.

"Fine," said Psy–4. "Then we go about our daily routines as much as possible." He looked at Radiant. "Any jobs waiting?"

"Construction workers, delivery truck driver, dishwasher, the usual."

"No security assignments?"

Radiant huffed. "Don't you think I would have said something?"

Psy–4 held up his hands in surrender. "Okay, okay, you're right, I wasn't—"

He noticed Stonewall then.

Across the room.

By the window.

Staring out at the rain with the saddest expression Psy–4 had ever seen on his face.

"Stoner? Stoner, what is it?"

"Looking at a butterfly," he replied.

And, indeed, there was a butterfly perched on the ledge, under a pipe, protected from the pouring rain.

"Yeah . . . ?" said Itazura. "I mean, sure, it's no puppy dog but it's nice. Don't think it'd make a good pet, though."

"No," said Stonewall, who either didn't notice or didn't care about his friend's jest. "I was thinking about what Edward N. Lorenz said about butterflies."

"Lorenz?" asked Itazura.

"He was a mathematician who eventually went into the field of meteorology. He opened up the field of chaos math. He applied certain convection equations to the short-term prediction of weather and watched those equations disintegrate into insanity. He asked, 'When a butterfly flaps its wings in Brazil, does it set off tornadoes in Texas?' His answer, of course, was yes, because that seemingly harmless movement creates a small but potent change in atmospheric pressure that interacts with other minute changes, and those combine with still other unpredictable variables that come down through the exo-, iono-, and stratosphere to mingle with the cumulative 'butterfly effects' in the troposphere, and before you know it—wham!—you've got thirty people dead in a Kansas trailer park. Think about it." He pressed a finger against the window. "This little fellow flutters his wings, and chaos could come crashing down to reduce our world to smithereens."

Stonewall was not known to his friends as a talker—he only spoke when he considered it necessary—and when he *did* speak it was rarely for very long and never without a serious purpose. Now his words came out in a rapid, deadly cadence—a sure sign that he was working out a serious problem.

"Imagine," he said, "that Lorenz's butterfly is the embodiment of everything that causes us to ignore or add to the suffering of others, and that the flapping of its wings is the force of that apathy spilling outward. In less than a second it combines with the myriad emotions already expelled into the air—anger, lust, despair, whatever—until all of them become a single entity. Multiply that by however many times a day a person turns away from another's suffering, then multiply *that* by the number of people in this world, *then* multiply that figure by the number of seconds in a day, week, year, or decade, and pretty soon you've got one hell of a charge building up. A point of maximum tension has to be reached, and then the combined forces will rupture outward, destroying whomever happens to be in its path."

Psy–4 looked at the others, then back to Stonewall. "I'm afraid I don't see what this has to do with—"

"It has everything to do with it, don't you see?" Stonewall's voice broke on the last three words and for a moment he looked as if he might begin to weep, but he pulled in a deep breath, turned away from the window, and walked to the center of the room.

"We were created, not born, but we're not robots. We're something more. At that moment of creation, Zac gave us a set of moral guidelines in our programming, yet we still defer to our logical impulses. Those have no place here right now. For all our lives, I think most of us have been avoiding—if not outright *denying*—our emotional impulses. Maybe some of that stems from dealing with so many shades of gray, but that doesn't apply here. This is as black and white as it gets, folks. There is a *child* out there in pain, and he's afraid, and he has no one else to turn to for help." He faced Psy–4. "We don't need you putting yourself on the rack about triggering the D and D; there was no way you could have known."

"No snowflake in an avalanche ever feels responsible," whispered Psy–4.

"Don't quote S. J. Lec to me. You have a tendency to worry your wounds, my friend, and we don't need that in our leader—and you are our leader, and always will be." He turned to face Radiant. "*You,* my dear sister, have to set your vanity aside until we figure out what we're going to do."

"But I—"

"You've always been somewhat self-absorbed and you know it as well as anyone in this room. You and I have to plan how we're going to get back into PTSI because we cannot chance breaking in the same way as before. I need all your concentration for that."

"What's so difficult about that?"

"The D and D program has been running for well over seventeen hours. We have to assume that Preston—or someone at PTSI—is aware of what's happening, and that they're taking steps to rectify the problem."

Itazura shook his head. "You're assuming that Preston has enough sense to—"

"Do you remember what Zac told us?" asked Stonewall. "Under no circumstances do we ever, *ever* underestimate an opponent. I see no reason why we should operate under any other assumption." He looked at Killaine. "We've had more than enough discussions about your temper in the past and I'm not going to waste any more time by reminding you of those discussions now, but take them to heart. You have to learn to reconcile your ideal of your existence with the reality of it. Face it, you're not wholly robotic, but you're not wholly human, either, and never will be. We are, all of us, like it or not, the next step of forced human/mechanized evolution. We're a new race, and until there are others like us, all we have is each other. I can't understand why you, of all of us, have such contempt for Singer—you, who go off the deep end every time you see an injustice. Tell me, Killaine, what justice has there been for him?" He pointed to Singer. "He's already been an immeasurable help to us, and what thanks does he get for it? Your scorn?" He touched Killaine's cheek. "Your prejudice will only get in the way. I don't expect you to overcome it in the next sixty seconds, but you *must* store it elsewhere until Roy is safe."

Then, at last, he faced Itazura. "And *you*, with your 'What's the point? What does it all mean?' Do you think you're asking yourself questions that are unique to this world? Every person on the face of the Earth has grappled with those questions, but for once, you have something like an answer within your grasp."

"And that would be . . . ?"

Stonewall pointed toward the butterfly at the window. "As of this moment, our purpose, our meaning, is to still the fluttering of the butterfly's wings for one child. If you can't find peace within yourself armed with that knowledge, then I'm afraid there's no peace to be found."

Itazura lowered his head. "Do you think it will be enough?"

"It has to be. For then we will have made a difference in a way more profound than any governments, any armies, any politicians or poets ever have; we will have saved a life from suffering, we will have given hope to one who's never known what hope is, and we will *always know it,* regardless of what happens later. Even in the bleakest, darkest of nights, that knowledge will be our anchor: that once, not so very long ago, we did a great thing for someone else without any thought of our own reward, that we refused to look away while another's life was swallowed by darkness, that we stood as one and refused to allow a child to be sent not-so-gently into that good night."

Stonewall held out his hand. "Are we together on this?"

Itazura put his hand on top of Stonewall's. "I'm with you all the way, Big Guy."

Radiant put her hand on Itazura's. "Me, too."

Psy–4 joined them. "Thanks, Stoner."

Finally, Killaine put her hand on top of Psy–4's. "All for one and one for all, eh?"

Stonewall grinned, then looked at Itazura, who understood his meaning.

All of them—including Killaine—looked at Singer.

"Well?" said Itazura.

Me? Really?

"Wouldn't be a proper trip to see the Wizard without the Tin Man."

Slowly, with great dignity, Singer walked over and gently placed his hand atop Killaine's.

"To the stillness of butterfly wings," said Stonewall.

"To the stillness of butterfly wings," repeated the others.

Psy–4 nodded his head. "Then we are decided."

44

Preston's insides felt on fire as he made his way back to his office.

The fire wasn't just because of the newest wave of pain—though that was a large part of it.

No, some of the fire was his anger with McCarrick. Damn, he should have had the man snuffed months ago.

A Nobel-prize winner, and the man hadn't proposed one workable solution to the problem with Roy.

"As a last resort, Mr. Preston—since you have offhandedly discarded all my suggestions—I propose that we ready another robotic brain and program the system to deposit all of the information from Roy into it rather than have it absorbed into the mainframe. I realize that since time is short there would not be sufficient time to program the brain itself—we'd have the equivalent of the world's largest disorganized filing cabinet—but at least the information would be saved."

"And what about Roy's personality?" asked Preston.

"That, I'm afraid, we'd have to deem expendable."

"That's unacceptable, Professor."

McCarrick had glowered at him. "Then our only other option is to disconnect Roy during the final stage of the program when the computer is running the data comparison, and I find that unacceptable, sir. There are too many variables, too many things that could go wrong. If not timed precisely, disconnection could destroy all the information—as well as his precious personality."

Arrogant pissant!

Preston closed his office door behind him, made his way over to his desk, and sat in the plush leather chair.

He probably shouldn't have needled McCarrick at the end, but he'd been angry, anxious, and in pain.

He had stopped at the lab door and asked, "How's your daughter doing these days?"

McCarrick turned three shades of red. His voice was barely a croak when he said, "She's doing a lot better. She wanted me to thank you for the . . . the new computerized chair."

Such broken contempt in those words.

"Any time," Preston had said, not meaning it and knowing that McCarrick knew he didn't mean it.

Preston winced. The pain was waning somewhat, but it was only the second wave.

They came in threes, always, and the third was always the worst.

He pulled in a deep breath, held it, released it slowly.

Repeated the process.

Repeated it again.

It was as he was exhaling for the third time that he noticed the curtains had been closed and the office was cloaked in shadow. He rarely left his lights off—

He turned on his desk lamp.

The light's position had been changed; it shone not on the surface of his desk but out toward the couch, spotlighting the bodies of his two private security guards.

Both were quite dead, each with a small, bloody hole in their temples.

He imagined the exit holes were much bigger, but whoever had done this had taken care to arrange the bodies so that Preston saw them only in the less gory profile.

He immediately reached over and hit the alarm button.

Nothing.

"Sorry about Laurel and Hardy," said a voice from the darkness, "but they weren't exactly the most hospitable pair when they found me in here."

Janus stepped into the circle of light. "Hello, Sam."

"Janus."

"Been a while."

Preston nodded toward the guards. "Was that really necessary?"

Janus shrugged. "I suppose not. I just wanted to have a little something handy to show you how serious I am. Originally I was going to tie you up and use a couple of toys on you, but then I found these."

He held up a clear plastic bag filled with Preston's prescriptions.

Preston yanked open his lower desk drawer.

Empty.

"How did you manage to pick the lock?"

"Oh, come on, Sammy-Boy! I knew how to pick a desk lock by the time I was five."

"I suppose it was a stupid question."

"Very stupid."

"All you had to do was call, Janus. I've been trying to get in touch with you for—"

The third wave began.

Preston doubled over in his chair, clutching at his mid-section, eyes tearing, a small trickle of blood exiting his nose. "Oh, god . . . please, Janus . . . I n-n-need my . . . my medicine."

Janus came over and sat on the edge of the desk, turning the lamp around so the light shone into Preston's face. "You don't look so good."

"Please!"

Janus held out two painkillers.

Preston, shaking uncontrollably, reached for them.

Janus pulled his hand away before Preston could grab his medicine. "Not so fast, Sammy-Boy. I need some information."

Preston nearly fell out of his chair the agony was so intense. He tried to form words but there was nothing for him now but the pain, the pain, the wrenching, draining, fiery pain.

Janus crossed to the wet bar and poured a glass of water, then returned to the desk and helped Preston regain his balance.

"Here you go," said Janus. He put the two pills into Preston's mouth, then held the glass for him as Preston drank everything down.

Sitting back on the edge of the desk, Janus crossed his arms and said, "How advanced is it?"

"Enough that . . . no surgery or treatments would help."

For a moment Janus looked as if he were genuinely sorry to hear this.

But just for a moment.

"Okay, Sammy-Boy, I've shown you that I'm being reasonable here. Now it's your turn."

"Could you . . . could you just give me a minute or two?"

Janus waited.

One minute.

Two.

Three.

Never speaking, never moving.

Preston couldn't even hear his breathing.

Midway through minute four Janus leaned over and whispered, "Feeling a little better?"

"Yes. Thank you."

"No problem."

Then he grabbed Preston's tie, yanked him to his feet, and dragged him across the room, kicking open the door of Preston's private restroom.

"I do some of my best work in toilets," snapped Janus, swinging Preston around and throwing him across the slick tile floor.

Preston slammed against the wall headfirst.

Janus closed the restroom door and turned on the bright overhead lights. "So now that the nicey-nice part's out of the way," he said, kicking up the toilet lid, "I believe we have some things to discuss."

Preston managed to wriggle into a sitting position, then groaned.

"Zac Robillard," said Janus.

"What about him?"

"He was here last night."

Preston laughed humorlessly. "Is there anything Annabelle *doesn't* know?"

"That I wear boxers instead of briefs. Answer my question."

"You didn't ask one."

Janus crossed to Preston and kicked him squarely in the groin. Preston howled in anguish and doubled over.

"Don't get nitpicky with me, Sammy-Boy. Was Robillard here last night?"

". . . yes . . ."

"And he had a five-member team with him?"

". . . yes . . ."

"You've already figured out who those five are, haven't you?"

Preston nodded. "The I-Bots."

"Right."

Janus crossed back to the toilet, pulled a bottle of pills from the plastic bag and popped the lid on the container.

"My, my—*morphine tabs*. These aren't easy to come by, even for someone in your position of power."

Janus tipped the container, dropping four of the tablets into the toilet.

"NO!" screamed Preston, trying to get to his feet and failing miserably. "No, Janus, please, it cost me a . . . a lot of money to get my hands on those and it took forever to track down a supplier."

"Pity."

He dumped two more into the toilet, then flushed it.

"Only twelve left, Sammy-Boy."

"God Almighty, Janus, just *tell me what you want to know!*"

"How did you get in touch with Robillard?"

"A phone number."

"And you of course have this most important number written down somewhere?"

He began to tip the container again.

"YES! Yes, it's in my private file on my computer."

"You wouldn't be trying to bluff me, would you, Sammy-Boy?" Another pill dangled on the edge of the container.

"No," cried Preston, his eyes wide with panic. "No, I swear it. I . . . I knew that Robillard was somewhere in the city . . . an informant told me . . . and I knew he'd need money, so it was just a matter of figuring out . . . figuring out . . ." He collapsed once again, still conscious but in pain.

"It was just a matter of determining how he'd be hiring himself out, is that it?"

Preston nodded.

"And?"

"Se . . . sec . . . *security* work. It was easy to find out which security company had added a listing in the last ninety days."

"Give me a name."

"Invasion Prevention Systems, Inc."

"Good lad." Janus pushed the pill back into the bottle and replaced the lid, then crossed over and helped Preston to his feet. "Come on, let's get you into that comfy chair of yours."

Once back at the desk, Janus powered up Preston's computer. "Bring up the file."

Preston did so.

Janus read the information, memorizing the phone number.

"I assume," croaked Preston, "that you're working for Annabelle?"

"You said it, I didn't."

"Mind a little advice?"

Janus grinned. "Usually, yes, but since you and I go back a little, I'll make an exception."

"Don't waste your time trying to trace this number. I had people on it for over a week before Zac showed up here and they came up with squat."

"Not the best way to drum up business."

Preston squeezed the bridge of his nose between thumb and forefinger, felt the blood, and reached into his pocket for a handkerchief. "This number connects you to the first in a series of voice-mail programs. Somehow Zac and the I-Bots have managed to tap their way into the local phone system in such a way that the path of the call changes every time the number is dialed. I have no idea how they did it."

"So how does it work—hiring them, I mean?"

"You call and leave a message. Tell them where and when you'll meet them for a preliminary powwow and they show up."

"And that's it?"

"That's it."

Janus considered all this for a moment.

"Okay, Sammy-Boy, since I've made such a mess here in your office, I'm going to give you the benefit of a doubt and believe what you're telling me." He threw a PTSI card key onto the desk. "But keep in mind that I can get more of those if I need them. If you're screwing me on this, I'll come back here and make the pain of your cancer look like a foot massage by comparison. You clear on that?"

"Very."

Janus tossed the plastic bag of medicine onto the desk.

Preston grabbed his wrist. "Janus, listen to me for a minute, all right?"

"One minute."

"Work for me. I'll pay three times what Annabelle's paying you. Track down Zac and the I-Bots and bring them here to me. Hell, I'll settle for Zac by himself."

"I've never been one for pushing my luck, Sammy-Boy. Playing both sides against the middle tends to get you crushed. Besides, I may not be the most moral person ever to walk this planet, but I pride myself on professional integrity. Sorry; Annabelle hired me, she paid first, my services are hers."

"Then I'll work with the two of you! I'll call Annabelle and hammer out an agreement. Okay?"

"Not up to me."

"Fine. I'll call her right now." Preston reached for the phone.

Janus clamped an iron grip around his wrist. "Huh-uh, not yet. Tell me why you so desperately need Zac."

"Because he can save my life."

Janus only stared as Preston explained what he had in mind.

The two men then stared at one another for a moment.

"What do you say, Janus? You could stand to make a lot of money from this."

"Like I said, it's not up to me." Janus stood, pulling a syringe from his pocket.

Preston blanched. "What the hell is—"

"Just a little something to make you sleep for a bit," replied Janus, pushing Preston's head to the side and sinking the needle into his neck. "Not that I don't trust you, Sammy-Boy, but I didn't survive this long by playing longshots. I need to make sure there's sufficient time for my dramatic getaway."

A pleasant numbness began to envelope Preston. "But you disconnected the alarm . . ."

Janus removed the needle and tossed the syringe into Preston's wastebasket. "I disconnected *one* of your alarms." He leaned close, whispering into Preston's ear. "Did you think I wouldn't know you'd have at least three alarms in here? It just made sense that you'd go for the one nearest you." He reached up and gently closed Preston's eyes. "I'm sorry you're so sick, Sammy-Boy. Pleasant dreams."

But Preston was already unconscious.

Janus patted him on the head like a parent would a sleeping child, then turned off the desk lamp, plunging the office back into darkness.

45

Zac Robillard awoke from a blessedly dreamless sleep feeling a tad hungover, but the headache was gone, gone, gone, and for that he was thankful.

He sat up on the bed and flung his feet over the side, letting the coldness of the floor enter his body.

He stared down at his naked feet.

Who'd taken off his shoes and socks?

Probably Killaine, he thought.

Hopefully, she didn't get too good a whiff when she removed the socks.

He rubbed his eyes, stood up, and took a deep breath, getting a noseful of heaven.

Someone was cooking up something tasty in the kitchen.

He made his way downstairs.

The I-Bots were busy setting the table for breakfast/lunch/dinner—he wasn't sure which until he checked his watch.

Seven-fifteen P.M.

Wow.

"What smells so good?" he asked as came into the dining area.

"Chicken Korma," said Itazura.

Zac looked at the I-Bots; all five of them were busy with the table.

"Who's cooking?"

Itazura smiled, a mischievous glint in his eyes, and pointed into the kitchen behind Zac, who turned to see a sight to end all sights.

Singer, adorned in a floral-patterned apron, slaving over a hot stove.

He even had a splash of flour on his face.

Hope you're hungry, he signed to Zac.

"I never knew you could cook."

You never asked.

"You've got me there."

Radiant breezed by with a pitcher of iced tea, stopping only long enough to plant a short, sweet kiss on Zac's cheek. "Nice to see you're feeling better."

Then she was gone.

Itazura pulled out the chair at the head of the table and gestured for Zac to take a seat. "We've got Oysters Rockefeller for the appetizer, Salad Niçoise, and, for dessert, a sumptuous and sinfully fattening Chocolate Gateau."

"I can almost hear my arteries hardening."

"Your seat, sir."

Zac sat down, silently thinking that all of them seemed quite cheerful.

Maybe a little *too* cheerful.

Put the paranoia in park for tonight, he scolded himself. *Enjoy this.*

"Nothing like a scene of domestic harmony, is there?" asked Itazura.

"If you say so."

Itazura's expression froze.

Then Zac winked at him.

"Don't *do* that to me!" said Itazura. "For a minute there I was afraid you were in mortal danger of relaxing." He headed back to the kitchen, looking for the salt and pepper.

"Looks like it's going to be a nice evening," Zac called after him.

"It will be."

Zac poured himself a glass of iced tea and looked into the kitchen.

Saw Killaine helping Singer.

Not only helping him, but *talking* to him.

Even smiling.

And he knew something was up, but decided not to spoil things by pressing them for details.

They were a fine, loyal group.

They would tell him eventually.

"Hey," shouted Itazura from the pantry, "whose butt do you have to kiss to get a little service around here?"

"Put a sock in it," said Radiant.

"Wouldn't that hurt?"

At the table, Zac allowed himself a grin.

It was nice to have a real family.

46

"Nice of you to have me followed."

"Hello, Janus." Annabelle admired her new nail polish, the exact color of just-spilled blood. "That was a damned rotten stunt you pulled at the airport."

"You had Simmons and two of your goons follow me, Annabelle. I took it a bit personally. I mean, after all, you and I seemed to have this trust thing going for us and you had to go and—"

"Do you know how many favors I had to call in to get him out of this mess? You owe me for this one, Janus."

"You shouldn't have had me followed."

"I have to—"

"—protect your interests, yeah, yeah, yeah. When can I expect company?"

"Bomb threats aren't easy to dismiss, even for me with all my connections. It'll be sometime early tomorrow morning before Simmons and the others are released."

"How's he taking it?"

"The humor eludes him, but I imagine he'll offer you a tip of the hat for your ingenuity and foresight."

"What a guy."

Annabelle sighed. "Have you contacted Preston?"

"Yes, we had a nice long chat."

"And?"

"Did you know he's dying?"

Silence.

"Annabelle?"

". . . no, I didn't . . ." Her throat tightened so that her reply was barely a whisper.

"Cancer. Too advanced for treatment."

"Damn."

A pause, then: "Are you okay?"

"What does it matter?" She wrenched her mind back to business. "Did you find out where Robillard is?"

"Yes and no." He explained to her about the phone lines and the impossibility of a trace.

"So what are you going to do?" she asked.

"Have you got a pen and paper handy?"

She laughed. "I haven't used pen and paper in years."

"Then power up your computer and get ready to do some typing. I've got quite a list of things I need by tomorrow morning."

"Weaponry?"

"No, you've done a bang-up job in the arsenal department. I'm going to try something I haven't attempted in a long time."

Annabelle pulled out her keyboard. "Damn, you actually sound excited."

"That surprises you?"

"Yes."

"Well, then, maybe life still holds a few thrills for us yet." He rattled off everything he would need, then asked her to repeat them back to him.

"Can you have everything for me by tomorrow?"

"Yes. How will I get them to you?"

"Give everything to Simmons when you put him on the corporate jet. I'll be waiting for him at the airport."

"I thought you didn't like being followed."

"I don't, but since you've sent Simmons and a set of hired guns, I might as well use them."

"I don't know if Simmons will like taking orders from you."

"Simmons will do whatever you instruct him to do, including taking orders from me. Are we clear on this?"

"Crystal."

"Fine. One more thing—you're not going to be hearing from me for a couple of days, maybe several. The next time I contact you will be when I'm ready to make the endgame. So we have to get back to that trust thing."

Silence.

"Well?"

"All right, Janus, we do it your way."

"Wise decision. Oh, by the way, Preston's probably going to contact you sometime in the next twenty-four hours."

"Why?"

"He wants to propose a temporary partnership."

Annabelle laughed bitterly at the phrase. "Yes. Preston's very skilled at those."

"I could have hurt him very badly, but I didn't."

"How charitable of you."

"I think you should listen to what he has to say."

"I don't recall having asked for your opinion."

"No, but you've got it, anyway. *Gratis*."

"You're so noble."

"I get a lot of complaints about that."

"Janus?"

"Yes?"

"Don't abuse my trust."

"I won't."

"Is that Janus the Professional talking, or Janus my trusting *compadré?*"

"Hard to say, Annabelle. Let's play it by ear."

"Playing it by ear makes me very nervous."

"You'll get over it."

Click.

Annabelle set her phone carefully in its cradle, then rested her head in her hands.

She would not cry.

She promised herself that.

And that's when the first tear hit the desktop.

47

The Scrapper Camp was located in the center of a maze of alleys that marked the eastern boundary of Cemetery Ridge. There were four entrances into the maze, which also served as the way out—providing one knew one's way well enough.

Aside from these four entrances/exits, the only other way out of the maze was underground.

Past the cement tunnel.

Into the sewers.

At 8:15 P.M., as the Scrappers were readying to move camp, Gash and the rest of the Silver Metal Stompers were blocking the four exits with large trucks they had stolen thirty minutes previously.

Not that any of them expected that the trucks would hold back a surging mass of robots, but it damn sure would slow them down, and that's all they wanted.

Once the trucks were in place, Gash flipped open his cell phone. "Everything in place?"

"All the exits are blocked off."

"Any sign of that little shit Rudy?"

"None."

"Spread the word—if he shows, don't touch him. I want him for myself."

"Right."

Gash checked his arsenal; two buzzblades, a fully charged electron gun, a handheld ShellBlaster, a bolt-shearer, three grenades, and a small one-burst flamethrower.

And, of course, his cherished samurai sword, nestled safely in its hinged sheath hanging from his back.

With all the death Gash carried, there were other Stompers who carried even more. A lot of firepower—and their targets couldn't fight back. It was gonna be total carnage. Life was good.

Time to cause some serious Wreckage.

He looked at the other Stompers who were with him and smiled.

Then spoke into his cell phone.

"Party time."

And the Stompers began moving in.

The first explosion took the Scrappers by surprise.

The second one finished off four of them.

By the time one of the Stompers had fired the third Shell-Blaster into the middle of the camp, the Scrappers were on their feet and moving.

The Stompers fell on them from all four directions, a sea of destruction and shadows and howling violence.

And the Scrappers, bound by their programming, could not fight back.

So they did the only thing they could do under the circumstances.

Began to run.

Machine-gun fire erupted into the night as the Stompers, wielding everything from lead pipes to vials of acid, increased the carnage.

* * *

Singer had just begun to serve dessert when vibrations from the first explosion shook the building, rattling glassware, dishes, and windows.

"What the hell was *that?*" said Zac.

Killaine was already over by the window, looking out into the street. "It came from the direction of the Scrapper Camp."

Just then another explosion erupted in the distance.

Then one more.

"I see flames," shouted Killaine, sprinting toward the cellar door.

"Stomping Party," snarled Itazura, running into the next room and pulling his samurai sword from the wall.

By now all of the I-Bots were headed for their emergency weapon packs.

The echo of rapid machine-gun fire grew louder.

Constant.

Closer.

"They're moving," shouted Stonewall.

"The sewers!" cried Zac. "They'll head for the sewers."

Psy–4 flew past, a blur of flesh and weapons. "We're already there."

They darted toward the cellar door and took the steps three at a time.

"Singer, stay with Zac!" called Killaine from below.

The robot stood next to Robillard, thought about it, then stood *in front* of him.

In the cellar, Itazura ran to the center of his labyrinth, brushed away some of the soil to reveal the ringed handle underneath, and flung open the steel trapdoor.

"Over there," he snapped at Stonewall. "That switch, hit it."

Stonewall did, and the work lights in the sewer came on.

Itazura swooped down onto the ladder, shouting, "The hell with it!" and kicked out, pushing himself away from the ladder and out into the air.

It was a twenty-five foot drop from the top of the ladder to the muddy, filthy, stinking floor of the sewer; if Itazura had climbed down, it would have taken him almost thirty seconds.

Freefalling took less than five.

He landed with a loud *thud!*, feeling the pressure snap upward through his ankles, legs, and groin, then regained his balance, unsheathed his sword, pulled the StunShooter from his belt, and ran straight toward the noise.

Psy–4 was next, then Killaine, Radiant, and Stonewall.

All of them freefalling, slamming feetfirst into the muck, then running forward so fast it looked as if their legs had been pumping before they even touched down.

From his hiding place, Rudy was startled from his sleep by the explosions.

He jumped up, guns at the ready, and began stumbling around blindly.

Then the work lights came on.

Rudy found another spot under one of the metal catwalks and crouched there, out of sight.

Something heavy was going down.

Going down hard.

He watched as the figures came jumping down from the ladder and ran past him.

All of them were fast.

And big.

Even the redheaded bitch.

But that wasn't what shocked him; no, speed and anger, weapons and force didn't phase him so much anymore.

What scared him were their eyes.

The work lights that had come on a few moments ago ran the length of most of the tunnel, but the area where the ladder emptied into sewer was mostly in shadows.

When the first one had run past—the Asian dude with the long hair—Rudy was convinced that he was seeing things, that he wasn't quite awake yet.

When the second one came down, he was worried that he might have breathed in some kind of weird-ass sewer gas and damaged his brain.

But when the redheaded bitch came down, he knew for sure that he wasn't imagining anything.

Just for a moment, as each hit the ground and were swallowed in shadow, he saw the bright, red, photoelectric glow of their eyes.

Ohgodohgodohgod they're robots! They look like human beings but they're goddamn robots!

Making certain that the five of them were long gone, Rudy slowly crept out from under the catwalk and bolted over to the ladder.

Looking up, he saw how far they had dropped.

Looking down, he saw the deep, deep indentations their weight had left in the muck.

Robots.

Coming down.

From Up There.

Robots.

Including the redheaded bitch.

Who'd been with DocScrap earlier.

But DocScrap didn't come down with them.

So DocScrap was Up There.

... and they weren't going to be back for a while. Gash and the Stompers would give them a good fight, that was for sure.

Shoving the pistols back into his belt, Rudy grabbed a metal rung and pulled himself up onto the ladder.

"Ready or not, here I come," he whispered.

Itazura had been in enough violent confrontations over the years to know that the wilder he was, the more chances he took, and the more chances he took, the less his chances were of emerging on the far end of the fight unscathed. He knew this, he *did,* running at thirty miles an hour toward the sewer grate, he knew the dangers of going wild—

—you know your programming, pal, remember that: You can immobilize a human being in order to help others, to keep them safe from harm, you can even seriously injure and cripple a human, if necessary, so long as doing so will serve the Greater Good, so be careful not to go—

—wild now as he streaked toward the battlefield, leaping into the air and spinning his body around so his feet connected solidly with the grate and blasted the damn thing away from the concrete, sending it across the alley to slam into a group of Stompers and pinning them against a far wall with the sound of bones breaking under flesh.

Itazura hit the ground running and threw himself into a crowd of Stompers, making quick work of their pitiful little weapons with nothing more than his hands and feet, scattering their unconscious forms like handfuls of dried leaves, and for a moment, as he stood there surrounded by still forms, he felt a rush equal parts exhilaration and disappointment because he was just getting warmed up, he was ready, bring it on, bring it on now, but there was no one and nothing at the moment *to* bring on and so he stood there, shaking from head to heel, a warrior without a war—

—and he wondered then, as he always did at moments like this, if he or any of the I-Bots were capable of killing in battle, if Zac had modified their programming to such a degree that they could snuff out a human life for the sake of the Greater Good, but Zac never gave a straight answer to that question, so Itazura, for the moment still a warrior without a war, stood stone still and silent—

—then heard a sound from behind him, a metallic sound, probably a trash can being knocked over—more probably thrown to distract him—and Itazura hit the ground, instinctively went into a roll as someone plowed off a line of bullets in his wake, each shot coming closer and closer, but Itazura could roll fast, damned fast, and by the time he twisted around and sprung up onto his feet the shooter was out of bullets and changing the magazine.

Itazura smiled.

Laughed at the pitiful little punk who was, oddly enough, also armed with a Katana.

Then Itzy charged.

He slammed into the punk and closed his arms around the kid's waist, squeezing hard enough to push the wind from the punk, but the kid was strong, the kid knew the Tai breathing discipline and was having none of it because his body went limp, then just as quickly sprung taut, almost breaking Itazura's grip, and the two of them spun madly around in the alley as the other I-Bots and Stompers and Scrappers collided from five different directions in a thunder-twist of fury. . . .

Rudy climbed off the top of the ladder and found himself in what had to be the basement of DocScrap's headquarters, only he was standing in the middle of one of those weird mazes like they used to have pictures of in geography books during the blessedly short time he'd been in school, but he didn't really give a damn about what the old Doc did to get his rocks off, he was only interested in blood now, and the Doc was alone, and Rudy was going to enjoy this, his moment of glory, and after so many years of living on the streets, of scrounging for food and shelter, of being scowled at, spit on, and looked down upon, he deserved his moment of glory and he was going to claim it and love every exquisite second.

He silently crossed the length of the cellar and started up the next set of stairs.

Oh, yeah—he was going to enjoy this.

He readied both his guns.

DocScrap probably wouldn't enjoy this, but, what the hey?

We all had to make sacrifices. . . .

Itazura was still twisting around the alley with the punk, who was a helluva lot stronger than Itazura had counted on, because somehow the kid had managed to get his arms free and wrapped them around Itazura's waist and squeezed, and Itazura actually felt pain, and that made him even more angry because the punk had gotten the better of him—

—they spun, squeezing and screaming, their attention so totally whole on crushing the other into unconsciousness that Itazura knew someone had to make a move soon—

—and that's when the punk did an extraordinary thing.

He simply let go.

Itazura stood still for a moment, surprised, the kid hanging from his arms, and that moment was enough for the kid to kick Itazura squarely in the groin.

Itazura gave the kid a sharp but controlled headslam for his trouble.

Then Itazura let go, expecting the kid to crumple in a heap to the ground, but he didn't, he simply staggered back a few feet, clutching his bleeding head, then shook it off like a dog shakes off water after coming in from the rain.

This guy's stoked on some serious street-candy, thought Itazura, wondering exactly what sort of drug gave this kind of inhuman strength to a *kid.*

Itazura saw the kid go for a gun, so he ran forward and spun, kicking him hard in the wrist and watching as the gun took flight. The kid went for it but Itazura shouldered him back, then the kid whipped around, caught Itazura with an expert kick to the knee, and backed off.

"Not bad," said the kid.

"C'mon," snarled Itazura.

"You gotta name?"

"Little Mary Sunshine."

"Pretty name, Mary. Mine's Gash."

The kid charged.

Blindly.

No unfair advantage, Itazura chanted silently to himself. *An I-Bot cannot use its strength to unfair advantage when battling a human being. Remember that: Zac Robillard's Rule #6.*

The blow started down as Gash slammed into Itazura, jumped right inside the blow, and when they were very close Gash brought his head way over to the left and then snapped it up into Itazura's face. Even before one of them cried out there was the sound of something breaking, something snapping deep down inside one of them, but which one, neither knew, and neither cared.

But Gash was the one who dropped down, driving his feet into Itazura's kneecaps, and then Itazura came down and used his elbow to break Gash's nose and this brought a shriek of pain.

Itazura leaped back up onto his feet, thinking *Move, move, move,* circling as the punk rose up, his face a mask of blood, but Gash wasn't through yet, not by a long shot; he countered Itazura's circling.

Itazura got Gash's nose again with the palm of his hand, and Gash howled once more but didn't stop coming, he threw his legs out and caught Itazura in the hip, knocking him off-balance for a moment and that was all the time he needed to turn and run, but this wasn't a retreat, not by a long shot, no way, he taunted Itazura as he ran, and Itazura went after him, chasing him through the violence and flames and bullets until Gash jumped up, grabbed the ladder of a fire escape, and began climbing.

"Come on, Mary! Catch me if you can!"

Itazura turned and ran back, away from the fire escape, then spun around, hunched down, and shot forward, leaping off the ground and rising nine feet into the air, touching down feetfirst on a landing just a few feet behind Gash.

It took them only ten seconds more to reach the roof of the building. . . .

Rudy decided that surprise was his best partner, and so came into the room firing.

He expected that DocScrap would looked shocked.

What he didn't expect was the robot.

Big brass-colored mother was standing directly in front of DocScrap and was wide enough that none of the bullets had a chance; they hit the robot's chestplate and ricocheted in all directions, blowing out a couple of windows and smashing into the plates on a dinner table, reducing them to fragments.

Rudy moved to the right.

So did the robot.

Rudy faked left, went right.

And the robot was with him all the way, moving forward.

He tried to get a look around the thing, tried to see where the Doc had gone, but the robot just kept coming at him, not running but walking fast enough, so Rudy fired again, aiming for some of the exposed circuitry beneath the chestplate, and this time he hit something because there was a spark and a hiss and a little bit of smoke—

—but the robot kept coming.

"You can't hurt me!" he screamed at it.

And the thing *shrugged* at him like he was some kind of idiot, and Rudy had always hated being looked at that way—it was bad enough when people did it to him, but to have a piece-of-shit stinking robot look at him like that . . . it was just too much.

The robot was right up in his face now.

Rudy backed up.

The robot came forward, bumping him with its chest and pushing him back toward the cellar door.

He started pounding it with the gun-butts, spitting and cursing at it, but it did no good.

Okay, fine, so it had the upper hand at the moment, but Rudy knew he could do something this model couldn't—

—he could run.

The question was when to make his move.

He looked over his shoulder, saw the cellar door a few feet away and getting closer.

He took a deep breath, knocked the robot upside the head with one of the guns, and threw himself down onto the floor, rolling to the side and then jumping to his feet.

The robot turned around but Rudy didn't wait for it this time.

He turned tail and ran deeper into the rooms, firing into every opened doorway that he passed.

Finally, he had to stop to reload.

He was just slamming the fresh magazine into place when a voice behind him said, "Those were my grandmother's dishes."

"Huh?"

And Rudy turned just in time for DocScrap to slam a beefy fist right into his bandaged face and knock him to the floor.

The guns skittered away, just out of reach.

Then DocScrap did something Rudy didn't expect.

The dude just *fell* on him.

It was like drowning in a sea of heavy stone. Rudy jerked and squirmed but the Doc had him pinned down. Rudy's body could feel what Doc was trying to do, keep his arms pinned while he levered with feet and knees to get up into a sitting position and slam his fat ass on Rudy's chest, and Rudy knew he had to hang on and do whatever it took to keep the Doc from getting into that position, so he tried to lock his heels around Doc's ankles and keep the dude's legs straightened out, but the Doc's head butted sideways into Rudy's face, so Rudy tried to bite the dude's ear. As a boy he'd fought like this when the neighborhood kids ganged up on him. Like a smell that can suddenly evoke haunting pictures from a forgotten past, the feel of another body on top of his, pressed hard from head to feet, brought out long-dead emotions and memories. Rudy jammed the side of his head against the Doc's face, knowing that only by sticking tight could he keep the dude from butting him senseless. Bracing his right knee he tried to jerk his body up and turn the Doc over onto his side, but there was no lifting that weight. He saw the peeling paint on the walls, the patterns in the wood of the floor, objects flashing meaninglessly across his vision as scenery whirls before the screaming face on a rollercoaster. They were locked in a pulverizing intimacy, total strangers who understood only that the other was, like himself, fighting for his life. In order to live, the other one had to be destroyed.

That suited Rudy just fine. . . .

Up on the roof, Gash screamed and ran, racing for the edge of the roof where there was a fifteen-foot drop to the next building, but Itazura sliced his legs out from under him from behind and Gash crashed into a spinning aluminum air vent. He thrashed away, rose to his feet again, and tried to run and this time Itazura caught him with a shoulder, so Gash turned his hand into a fist and his arm into a club and struck out at Itazura's throat, hitting it Adam's-Apple-Ground-Zero, then Itazura countered with a chop to Gash's broken nose and an elbow to his stomach, but Gash was beyond pain now, there was only blood, and as he stumbled back, wiping the blood from his face and pulling in heavy gulps of air, he finally got a good look at the carved-ivory handle jutting above Itazura's left shoulder—

—and suddenly he felt renewed energy.

The two of them stood very still, only a few feet apart, glaring at one another.

Very slowly, almost ritualistically, Gash reached over his right shoulder and slid his sword from its untraditional hinged sheath, gripping the handle with both hands and bending his arms into the traditional challenge position, his hands level with the right side of his head, the long, gleaming blade sticking straight out like a frozen beam of steel fury.

Across from him, Itazura took three steps back, bowed once, then lowered his own sheath to waist level as he drew his sword and assumed the acceptance-of-challenge position.

Gash took a quick, short step forward.

Itazura moved back one step, then came forward, snapping his wrists just enough to make the tip of his sword dance a small circle in the air as it connected with the tip of Gash's, the colliding steel blades glistening under the streetlights, striking together with a high-pitched, deadly, almost musical *shhhhkick!*

Gash laughed, stepped backward, then quickly pulled back his blade, swung it up over his head, and charged toward Itazura, swinging his sword back and forth.

Itazura countered with an up-and-under move, bending his knees and spinning around, swinging his sword in a low arc that ended at the same point in the air as Gash's blade, the swords slamming together with an uglier sound, their razor edges actually sparking from the combined force, then Itazura carried through on the spin with his right leg, cracking his ankle into Gash's shins and bringing him down.

Gash anticipated the move, and as soon as he felt Itazura's ankle slam into him he deliberately tumbled not to the right, as the kick was intended to force him to do, but to the left, and as he went down he dragged the edge of his sword along the length of Itazura's until, as Gash hit the roof, they were locked at the hilts.

Now both of them were down on their knees, face-to-face, their locked swords forming a brilliant silver V over their heads.

"Mary's pretty good," snarled Gash.

"You ain't seen nothing yet," replied Itazura, pushing back and away and jumping to his feet in one fluid movement—

—which gave Gash a great opening, and he took it, swinging down and around at his opponent's ankles, but at the last second Itazura did a bucket jump and all Gash cut was air—

—and as Itazura came down he snapped his right foot forward and caught Gash in the chest, knocking him back toward the edge of the roof and there was no way he could keep hold of his sword and maintain his balance, so he made a split-second decision and let go of the handle, but it was useless, because as his sword clattered onto the roof he felt himself going over the side, arms pinwheeling, and the next thing he knew he was in flight, neither part of the earth nor the sky, only suspended in a cold, silent, weightless no-man's-land, then gravity and reality kicked in and he plunged down fifteen feet onto the surface of the next roof and landed squarely on a mass of discarded trash and cardboard boxes that cushioned his fall but didn't completely break it—

—he was stunned into immobility.

He lay there waiting for the pain to kick in, looking upward at the edge of the roof where Itazura now stood, looking down at him.

Itazura smiled, then swung his sword down toward the surface of the roof like a golfer trying to get a good shot off the first tee, and the next thing Gash knew there was his sword, sailing out into the air, and all he could think was: *I can't move, I can't move, and the goddamn thing's coming right at me*—

—but Itazura had known what he was doing, knew exactly how much pressure to apply, what arc to aim for, and when the sword came down it landed three feet to Gash's left side.

"And it was just getting interesting," said Itazura, shaking his head.

Gash felt the sensation returning to his body and looked down to see if he could move his legs, and it was the sweetest thing he'd ever seen, that little twitch of his foot, because that meant that his spinal cord was okay, he wouldn't end up in a wheelchair or sitting on a corner with a tin can begging for pity-coin from passersby, and he tried to grab his sword but his shoulder blade made it clear to him that it wasn't a good idea right now—at least there were no broken bones, just a lot of cuts and bruises and—oh, yeah—pain, mustn't forget about that—so all he could do was look up at his opponent and scream, "This isn't finished yet! You hear, motherfucker? *I'll get you, I swear I'll bleed you like a hog, YOU HEAR ME?"*

Above him, Itazura gave a two-fingered salute and said, "Look forward to it."

Then turned and ran back, leaving Gash alone on the roof with his disgrace and pain and crippling, crushing fury.

"I'll cut you into a thousand pieces, Mary! You hear me? You're dead! I'm talking to a dead man! A DEAD MAAAAAAAAAAANNNNNNN!"

But there was only the echo of his voice for an answer. . . .

In the alley, most of the Stompers had either been knocked senseless or had undergone an attack of common sense and run away to regroup.

One group of robots had managed to knock over a truck and scatter into the night, but the majority of them had been herded into the sewer by Stonewall and Psy–4 while Radiant and Killaine kept watch for a second wave of attackers.

"Did anyone see where Itzy went?" called Radiant.

"He took off after one of the Stompers right after we got here," said Psy–4.

"And you complain about *my* temper." Killaine laughed.

Then Radiant held up her hands, signaling silence.

"What is it?" asked Stonewall.

"They're coming back. We only fought half of them. Others were waiting."

As soon as she finished speaking, the rumbling roar of the next wave of Stompers came shooting toward them.

"Come on!" called Psy–4, pushing the last of the robots into the drain.

Killaine and Radiant followed right after.

Psy–4 reached into a small pack attached to his belt and removed two grenades.

"Move everyone down by the ladder and take cover," he said.

Radiant grabbed his arm. "What the hell do you think you're doing?"

"I'm going to blow the entrance so the Stompers can't follow us in. Now will you please go with the rest?"

"No. I won't leave you here."

"Radiant, I—"

"Shut up," she snapped, grabbing one of the grenades from his grip.

Psy–4 began to say something, thought better of it, and touched her cheek. "Pull the pin and throw. We'll have three seconds before they blow."

"Oh, good—a race! Betcha I win."

"Oh, for the love of—"

His words cut off when he saw the figure suddenly drop down at the mouth of the drain.

Psy–4 immediately ran forward, drawing back his fist to deliver a crippling blow, if necessary, but at the same moment he struck out, the intruder spun around and danced past him.

"Yeah, I was worried about you, too," said Itazura.

Psy–4 glared at him, shook his fist, then—despite himself— smiled.

And that's when the next mass of Stompers rounded the corner and came at them.

"Now!" shouted Psy–4.

Both he and Radiant pulled their pins.

Tossed the grenades at the mouth of the drain just as a Stomper readied a ShellBlaster.

Then the three of them ran like hell.

The grenades went off at the same time the ShellBlaster hit its mark, and the explosion was magnified to several times what it should have been, blasting pipe and concrete and water in all directions.

Psy–4, Radiant, and Itazura were less than halfway to the safe end of the tunnel when the blast hit them.

They flew the rest of the way.

When they hit the ground, all three of them were stunned into momentary unconsciousness.

The dust and debris was so thick in the sewer it might as well have been a deep-sea fog.

But when everything cleared, the work lights were still on—miraculously enough—and the three of them were a bit shaken but mostly unharmed.

"Damn," said Radiant through a series of coughs. "I broke a nail."

"Will the suffering never end?" said Itazura.

"Come on," snapped Psy–4, rising to his feet and dusting himself off. "Let's go see how the others are."

They had just reached the safe area when, from above them, somewhere past the top of the ladder, the echo of an inhumanly pained scream came crashing down. . . .

Rudy forced his temple up against the Doc's cheek, slowly maneuvering his head so that he could sink his teeth into some soft part of the man's face.

Zac drew his head back for another butt but Rudy craned his neck to keep their heads together. Underneath him Rudy's hand scrambled for a hold on his wrist, so Zac jerked his body into an upward arch and brought his right knee up into Rudy's groin at exactly the same time Rudy brought his left knee up into Zac's, and the two of them connected with much less force than they had hoped and only managed to entangle themselves worse than before.

And Rudy's fingers found the Doc's wrist.

And Rudy pressed his nose and chin into skin.

And Rudy pulled his lower jaw down until he could feel his teeth touching soft, soft flesh. Then he latched on with all he had.

There was a mad, intense, electrifying, hysterical, almost erotic glee to it—biting into human flesh! Bite, bite, bite! Glee and hatred and revenge and power!

Zac screamed in agony, his body jolting in brutal jerks, a great fish electrocuted by the searing pain of the barb.

Rudy brought his knee up once again, harder than before, and felt DocScrap crumple when he connected.

Zac fell off the kid but the punk's teeth remained embedded deep in his wrist.

Then Singer was there, his large metal hands gripping the back of the punk's jacket and lifting him up from the floor.

But Rudy's teeth wouldn't let go.

Zac thrashed, howling, and managed to get a grip on one of the punk's guns.

Rudy was laughing through the blood.

Singer kept pulling the kid back.

And Zac swung up with as much force as he could rally from the fog of pain, slamming the side of the gun into the kid's head; once, twice, three times.

Rudy's teeth let go after number three.

Singer turned around and lay Rudy on the floor, then turned his attention to Zac.

That's when Rudy rose from the floor, his bandages soaked in blood, and stumble-ran down the hallway until he came to one of the few windows in the building that wasn't covered by iron bars or wire mesh from outside.

He ripped off his jacket and wrapped it around his arm, then slammed it through the glass, kicked away the remaining shards, and perched there like a bird readying for flight.

It was a good twenty-foot drop.

But he'd lucked out.

Here in Cemetery Ridge, trash piles were as common as concrete, and there was a doozy of a heap just to his right, so he crawled out onto the too-narrow ledge and began to swing, one, two, three—and threw himself down toward the garbage.

He hit with a sickening *whumpf!* and was immediately covered in rotted food, newspapers, and assorted other foul-smelling things that he decided he'd rather not study too closely.

It took him a moment to crawl out of the filth, but once he was free he didn't bother to look back, he just ran, his peripheral vision quickly memorizing a handful of nearby landmarks.

This wasn't finished.

He'd be back.

And next time, he'd carry serious hardware for the job.

Feeling not the least bit discouraged, he ran on. . . .

Killaine was trying to get Zac to sit still, but he was far too agitated to comply with her wishes.

"I want everything ready to move out of here as soon as possible."

"Don't you think you're overreacting a bit?" asked Killaine.

"One of the Stompers found his way in here! If one of them can do it, the others can."

"They won't be coming in through the sewer," said Psy–4. "We pretty much trashed the entrance."

"But the kid knows where we are now!" snapped Zac. "How long do you think it'll take him to round up his cronies and come back?"

Killaine shook her head. "I don't think he will."

"Why's that?"

"Because I caught a glimpse of him right before he jumped. That was our initiate from earlier."

Itazura glared at her. "If you were close enough to recognize him, why the hell didn't you *go after and grab him?*"

"Because I decided that it was more important to see if Zachary was all right. You're certainly not going to tell me that my concern was misplaced, are you?"

". . . no, guess not . . ."

Zac touched Killaine's hand. "You sure it was him?"

"Yes. So if he was up here trying to get you, that means he isn't in yet, so the other Stompers won't help him—it's part of their twisted little code of honor. An initiate has to prove he or she can survive on their own. Until he accomplishes what he set out to do, he's alone."

"*Very* alone," added Stonewall.

"I think we'll be safe here for a few more days, at least," said Psy–4. "But just to be safe, Stoner and I will triple-enforce the downstairs doors. We've been stockpiling steel sheets just in case something like this happened."

Zac winced as Killaine began cleaning the wound. "Do whatever you have to to protect us here until we can move to the backup location. We *are* moving. We haven't lasted this long by taking unnecessary risks and I'm not partial to starting now."

48

In the now-empty restricted area of the main lab, Sam Preston sat before a massive computer console, staring through the glass partition that physically separated all the technicians from the mainframe. He tried not to think about the bodies up in his office, or the pain in his body, or the moments ticking away from his life.

And not only *his.*

He stared at the glass container atop the system.

He stared at the electrodes and monitoring wires and cables that ran into the container, snaking through the mixture of neural fluid and liquid lambda to reach their target.

And so he stared at the small robotic brain that was the center of the system.

He reached down, flipped a switch, and brought the brain on-line.

"Hello, Roy," he whispered to it through a cloud of pain.

Within the system, the child whispered, *Hello, Daddy.*

My son, thought Preston. *My good, fine boy. Can you ever forgive me?*

Then he did the damnedest thing.

He started to cry.

49

A thousand miles away, Annabelle Donohoe sat in her darkened office, gently fondling the locket around her neck.

After a moment, she reached behind her neck and unhooked the clasp on the gold chain.

She turned the locket over in her hands and pressed the small catch.

The locket opened.

She stared wistfully at the two small photographs contained within.

The one on the left was of her holding a newborn baby.

The one on the right was of that baby as he'd looked as a boy on his fourth birthday.

Three months before he'd died.

"Oh, Roy," she whispered. "My son, my good boy."

Then thought: *I'll get him for what he did to you.*

And the damnedest thing happened then.

She began to cry.

PART TWO

WHEELS OF ILLUMINATION

"Whoever fights monsters, should see to it that in the process he does not become a monster."

—*Nietzsche*

50

Killaine placed her hand defiantly upon her hips and glared at Zac. "I'd rather not be the one to leave here today, especially not after last night."

Zac rubbed his eyes with his good hand, winced at the pain in his other, heavily bandaged hand, and sighed. "Killaine, I don't quite know how to put this to you, but . . ."

"But what?"

"Look, you were an immeasurable help to me last night. You probably saved my hand."

"One of us had to learn how to apply our medical programming. I only wish we'd had more supplies in the first-aid kit to—"

Zac held up his bandaged hand. "You did wonderfully, Killaine. Really, you did. And I was very impressed with the way you handled yourself in the sewer this morning. The robots were pretty shaken up by what happened, and you were . . . well, surprisingly pleasant to them during the repair process, and I appreciate that."

She began impatiently tapping her foot. "Yes . . . ?"

"Did I forget to mention how delicious breakfast was?"

"No. In fact, Zachary, that's the *third* time you've said something about it."

He cleared his throat and loosened his shirt collar. "Ah, yes, well . . ."

"Why are you sending me out on this assignment when we've enough to keep all of us busy for the next week or two?"

"You, uh . . . you look like you could use a little fresh air?"

"Try again, Zachary."

"Oh, all right! You're getting on everyone's nerves, okay? I hate to be that blunt about it, Killaine, but your mother-hen routine has started running a little thin."

She dropped her hands to her side. "Well, I beg your pardon, sir, I do! Far be it from me to take bloody charge around here of all the small things so the rest of you can concentrate on more important matters—"

"—I didn't mean it like that, I only—"

"—let me tell you something, Mr. Zachary Robillard; if it weren't for me and my 'mother-hen routine,' as you call it, this household wouldn't function at even the simplest, everyday level. Heaven forbid that Itazura or—worse—Radiant were ever turned loose in the kitchen or on the laundry."

"You're overreacting."

"Now it's overreacting, is it? I'll have you know—"

Zac lifted both hands in surrender. "Enough!"

Killaine bit down on her lower lip, staring at him.

"Killaine," whispered Zac, "you know how much I deeply appreciate all you do for me—for all of us. At least, I hope you do." He reached over and took one of her hands. "And I know, the way things have been lately, that you don't get a lot of thanks for it. So I'll tell you this now so you'll understand: It's not that I don't care about you, because I do; and it's not that I don't find your company wonderful and exciting and comforting, because you *know* that isn't the case; and it *especially* isn't because I don't think you're needed around here. It's simply that you can't seem to concentrate on anything for very long and, as a result, your attempts at being helpful are backfiring severely."

"So what you're telling me is that I'm getting on everyone's nerves?"

Zac smiled at her. "Now, why didn't I put it that way in the first place?"

Killaine sighed, put her hands on her hips once again, looked at Zac, then away from him, and finally dropped her arms once again. "I hate it when you're right about things like this."

"So you'll do it?"

"If you wish."

"I wish. *Lord,* how I wish!"

"You needn't rub it in." She took the slip of paper he offered to her and read the information on it. "You're having me on?"

"Nope."

"And this is a *security* assignment?"

Zac nodded his head. "He agreed to all the terms, including the daily fee."

"And you accepted the job?"

"*No,* I told him that one of us would meet with him this morning to assess the situation. If you decide that the job doesn't interest you, tell him no, he'll pay the consultation fee, and that will be that."

She looked at the slip of paper again. "I can't believe I'm going to—do you realize that this will mean dealing with *children?*"

"Do you have something against kids, too?"

Killaine decided to let the "too" portion of the remark slide. "No, I've nothing against children. I just . . . I . . . it's just that— haven't we had this discussion before?"

"About your wishing you could conceive a child?"

". . . yes . . ." she replied softly.

"That's why I thought you might enjoy the assignment. If you accept the job, we're only talking about a day, maybe a day and a half, if that long. I know how you like to be around children and this way you not only get to be around lots of kids, but you get a little free time, we make some more money, and, with luck, you catch a couple of bad guys."

She stared at him. "You know, Zachary, you could sell the Devil himself a subscription to *Catholic Digest.*"

"A career move I never considered."

Killaine checked her watch. "I guess I should be leaving. This *does* say ten A.M., doesn't it? I sometimes find it hard to decipher your handwriting."

"It's not that bad."

"Egyptian hieroglyphics are easier to read."

"I'm hurt. And, yes, it does say ten A.M."

"Well then, I'm off."

"Be careful."

"Why do you say that?"

Zac smiled. "If you don't exercise extreme caution, you're in genuine danger of having fun."

"Watch it, Zachary. If I take the job I just might come back here and drag you along to suffer with me."

"Call in when you decide. I just might *let* you drag me along."

Down in the garage area of the warehouse, Stonewall and Psy–4 were just finishing up welding the third sheet of steel onto the bay doors. One more and the area would be fully secured from even the power of a standard ShellBlaster.

Psy–4 crossed over to the small refrigerator that sat near the door and took out a couple of bottles of beer. "You want one?"

"Sure, why not?"

The two of them sat against the wall in the garage, not sweating even though the temperature in the area was well over one hundred and fifteen degrees.

"This is domestic, isn't it?" said Stonewall.

"I haven't had time to make a beer run since Preston's the other night, okay?"

"I prefer the Irish imported brand. The dark beer."

"Thank you for reminding me. For a second there I almost thought I was doing something right."

Stonewall reached over and smacked Psy–4's cheek.

"Ouch! What was that for?"

"For bringing up that 'failure' business again. We agreed that you would file that away elsewhere until we have Roy."

"Is that any reason to hit me?"

"Yes, as a matter of fact, it is. I have decided to begin dispensing smacks with great generosity whenever one of us gets out of line."

Psy–4 pulled down a few more swallows of the cold beer. "And what happens if you get out of line?"

"Then you can smack me."

"Right."

They sat in silence, then, finishing up their drinks.

"Zac really worked on the robots this morning," said Psy–4.

"Some of them were badly damaged."

"Yeah . . ."

Stonewall turned to look at his friend. "But you were thinking . . . ?"

"I was thinking about Roy."

"We'll get him out in time, Psy–4. Don't worry."

"Oh, I'm not—not about getting him, I mean . . . well, okay, maybe a *little,* but not as much as I was thinking—"

"—you mean 'worrying.'"

"—as I was *considering* what we're going to do with Roy after we have him."

"The portable chamber is ready to go. I checked it earlier this morning. We have a small supply of neural fluid and liquid lambda, so there won't be any problem with—"

Psy–4 held up his hand, silencing Stonewall. "I know all that. But I also know that the portable chamber has to be recharged every seventy-two hours."

"Again, that won't be a problem. So why—"

"Because it seems to me that all we're doing is exchanging one form of imprisonment for another."

"Until we can find the materials to construct a body for him. And you'll be able to communicate with him anytime you choose. And with a few minor adjustments to our system, all of us will be able to communicate with him. He won't be lonely anymore, and he won't be afraid."

Psy–4 tipped back his bottle, realized that it was empty, then crushed it into powder and dumped the powder in the nearby recycling bin. "Do you ever think about the fact that, barring disaster, we're immortal, Stonewall?"

"I am keenly aware of it, yes."

"Does it ever bother you that we don't . . . we don't *revel* in it more?"

"I'm not sure I follow."

"Look at us. We will live forever. Theoretically, there's nothing we don't have the time for. We don't have to worry about life ever ending—even if the human race finally pushes all its buttons and explodes all its bombs and chemical weapons and everything else in its arsenal of instant extinction, we will endure. Every morning is, for us, a new beginning, filled with new possibilities, challenges to meet, countless things to learn. I could spend a year doing nothing more than admiring the way moonlight casts glittering sparkles over the water, and it wouldn't be a waste of my time because there *is* time for such things."

"Sounds very pleasant to me."

"But what about Roy?"

"I'm sure he'd enjoying seeing moonlight on the water, as well."

"That's not what I meant—though I'm certain you're right about that point."

"What did you mean?"

Psy–4 rose and began pacing. "I mean that he's a child, a *human* child, and we're going to make him immortal."

Stonewall sighed and began readying the equipment for attaching the next layer of steel to the bay doors. "You're doing it again, Psy–4."

"What?"

"Creating a problem to worry about where one didn't exist a few moments ago."

Psy–4 walked up to Stonewall and gripped his arm. "What is it that causes human beings to create? I mean, everything from indoor plumbing to Van Gogh's *Starry Night* and chocolate bars and *The Idiot?*"

Stonewall only stared at him, his face revealing nothing.

"Mortality," said Psy–4. "From the moment a human child is held upside down by its ankles and smacked on the butt, he has a limited amount of time upon this earth. And eventually he will be made aware of the death that waits for him. I think it's that certainty of life's end that forces human beings to create, to use their hands or minds to leave a mark behind, something to tell the babies who will follow, 'Hey, I was here, and this is what I left behind for you, and I hope you like it and remember me because of it.' At some point, that knowledge of limited time sets in permanently, and they feel compelled to make their remaining days count as much as possible. Then you consider *us*. We don't have the same kind of threat hanging over our heads that they do. We'll never have to worry about dying of natural causes. If we can just avoid being murdered, we'll live forever."

"So we weren't 'borne astride the grave,' as Beckett put it?"

Psy–4 snapped his fingers and pointed at Stonewall. "*Exactly!* We already possess what for humanity is only a dream. And what do we spend most of our time doing? Looking over our shoulders for more of Annabelle's goons to come after us! Doesn't that ever make you angry?"

Stonewall shrugged but said nothing.

"I find that I'm feeling a certain *selfishness* about my existence. I want to live forever. I want to watch generations of humanity come and go. I can't wait to see what new advances they'll come up with—and I think they will. For all their darkness, I think humankind is far too clever to allow itself to be wiped out."

"You're straying from the point."

"I am? Oh—I guess so. Sorry." He picked up his goggles and put on his welding gloves, then checked the blowtorch. "I don't want Zac to leave us. If we can construct a body for Roy, then why not do the same thing for Zac?"

"We've all been careful never to broach that subject with him. It was agreed that *he* would have to come to us with that wish."

Psy–4 put on his goggles, adjusted the tightness of his gloves, then sparked the blowtorch and adjusted the flame. "I just wish we didn't have to make the choice for Roy. I hate to admit it, but there are times when I envy humankind's mortality, the *immediacy* that it instills their existence with. It's something we'll never know."

"Part and parcel of our lot," said Stonewall, dragging the next sheet of metal into place.

"One way, Roy will lack the immediacy of existence that will compel him to leave his mark; the other way, he'll have time for everything, and so the immediacy will be lost."

"But not necessarily the desire to make a difference. You still want to make a difference, don't you?"

"Of course."

"And you've adapted rather well to human behavioral patterns, if you don't mind my saying so—why else do you insist on wearing the goggles and gloves? That torch could explode and it would do only minor damage."

"It'd still hurt."

"No arguments there."

Psy–4 pulled the goggles down so they hung around his neck. "You already know why I'm going on like this, don't you?"

"I knew as soon as you began to pace."

Psy–4 nodded. "Does that make me . . . evil?"

"No. And I'd be lying to you if I didn't admit that the thought crossed my mind, as well."

"Wishing that perhaps one of the Scrappers in the sewer wouldn't survive?"

"Of course. It would take care of all resultant problems. We wouldn't have to worry about tracking down and purchasing the parts to build a body—parts that Annabelle Donohoe could undoubtedly trace within an hour of our purchasing them—"

"It wouldn't surprise me if she already has a system in place to track sales of robotic pieces."

"Nor I. Secondly, were one of the Scrappers to perish, we wouldn't be saddled with the task of building a new body without Zac's knowledge—I don't like deceiving him any more than you do. You've got nothing to feel guilty about, Psy–4. No, it's not a very *nice* thought, but it's understandable. And you must keep in mind that we are not exactly in a *nice* situation at the moment. So don't worry that a thought like that would cross your mind." He reached over and placed a hand on Psy–4's shoulder. "But if you start to think about *causing*—"

"—no, never. I'm not Killaine. I *do* know their lives have value to them."

"Fine. But if—"

"I'll come to you right away."

"Very good." Then: "So, are you going to use those goggles or not?"

"You want them?"

"No. Just, please, take them from around your neck if you're not going to wear them. They make you look odd."

"You mean 'goofy'?"

"That word has never passed these lips—nor will it ever."

Psy–4 put the goggles back on and laughed, then extended the flame and began welding the steel into place.

Itazura stood in the doorway of Radiant's bedroom, watching as she sat before her vanity table combing her hair.

"Why do you do that?" he asked her.

"Do what?"

"Use a mirror? You can't see yourself."

She turned around, facing him with her eerily beautiful eyeless face. "Because the silver backing reflects more than images, Itzy. It reflects energy, as well."

"I didn't know."

Radiant turned back toward the mirror and continued brushing her hair. "There's a lot about me you don't know."

"Like . . . ?"

Radiant paused, holding the brush mid-stroke, then pulled it from her hair and placed it on the vanity table. "Like the way I adore the textures and temperatures of color. I'll bet you never thought about it that way before, did you? Colors having temperatures. But they do. And I can tell the shade, texture, and brightness of the color by the way it feels. Not only that, but at night when I lay in bed, I can hear things . . . the sighing of the moon, the thrumming of the darkness, the laughter of dreams, the silent breaths between raindrops. Every form of energy, natural or manufactured, biological or mechanical, has its own rhythms, its own sensations and smells and moods. Sometimes it overwhelms me. I can hear souls singing in the twilight, and the first pulsing of life in a newly conceived child.

I can smell confusion. I can taste regret—and it's not, surprisingly, a bitter taste; it has the flavor of a dewdrop from the petal of a dead rose blown across a dirty sidewalk on a chill autumn wind."

Itazura nodded his head. "So why spend so much time preening over yourself?"

Radiant folded her hands on her lap and turned her face toward him. "Because I know that I'm beautiful, all right? I know it, I can feel it, I can imagine what I must look like . . . but I can't see it."

"Poor little you," said Itazura, with not a trace of sympathy in his voice.

"I know how conceited and self-centered that must sound to you, how vain my behavior must seem to the others, but . . ."

"But what?"

"Once, about a year ago, right before we had to leave Montreal, I went for a walk down St. Catherine because I always enjoyed the sense of pride I felt coming off the old buildings in that area—they thought themselves grand things, those buildings did. Anyway, I was walking along, enjoying the buildings' pride and the sidewalk's excitement and the pulsing life of all the people who passed by, and then this . . . this *twistedness* shot into my skull and began to surge through all my senses.

"An old beggar woman had grabbed my hand and was babbling to me in French, pleading for money. I have never before or since experienced such pure *madness* from a person, and it scared me. Not only because of her physical decrepitness, *that* I could sense right away, but because deep down, swimming beneath her madness like a body who falls through the ice and is swept along by the currents underneath, there was this . . . this . . . this *quilt* of fraying memories, and within that quilt I caught the whisper of a profound image of how and what she used to be, and I saw her, so young and alive, so vibrant, with so much to look forward to, and then it was gone. Poof, just like that. I don't know if she went mad because of some hideous disease or because something happened to her that was so painful and terrible her mind couldn't deal with it, but whatever the reason, for a moment I had a split sense of Her-Then and Her-Now, and the two of them together shocked me into a state of fear I'd never known. She thought of herself as *ugly,* both within and without, and that image of her so young . . . to Her-Now, it was just some picture in a magazine she'd seen once, she refused to believe that she had ever been anything other than what was Now. The madness made her believe in ugliness, and so she was. Ugly and pitiful. So I worry that I might . . . might lose my beauty someday. I think I'm entitled. Like it or not, none of you have ever experienced the core-deep depravity of true ugliness. But I have. So I preen. And I'll keep preening, thank you very much. You rage over robots lacking a race memory; I'll listen to the poetry beneath the everyday surface of the world. And if that still makes me seem vain and self-centered, then to hell with you."

Itazura came into the room, crossed over to Radiant, put his hand gently on her shoulder. "I'm scared, too."

She touched his hand. "Even ninety minutes is cutting it too close for my taste."

"I hate having to lie to Zac."

"No one's actually lied yet."

"No—we've only concealed a large part of the problem."

"I prefer to think of it as reshaping the facts to form a more perfect truth."

Itazura smiled, then leaned down and kissed her on top of the head. "Whatever floats your boat, Sis."

"Itzy?"

"Yeah?"

"Do you think we'll succeed?"

"We *have* to."

"But do you *think* we will?"

He touched her cheek. "We have to. There's no other option."

"I don't like having no options."

"Neither do I. But we have to think of the child."

"Yes," said Radiant. "I have a feeling that the terror he's known and lived with for so long makes my run-in with the beggar woman look a walk through the park."

"Depends on the park. If it's a walk through Central Park at three in the morning, well, then—"

Radiant giggled.

"*That's* what I was going for," said Itazura.

"Thanks, I needed to laugh." Then: "Was there a particular reason you came here?"

"Psy–4 and Stoner are just about finished with the welding. We need to go over the preliminary plans and see if changes need to be made."

"If Killaine will stop hovering long enough to—"

"Zac sent her out on a job."

"So there *is* a Santa Claus!"

"I don't know if Zac would much appreciate the comparison, but, yes, Virginia, there is."

51

Sam Preston awoke with his head buried in his folded arms.

He came awake with a start, pulling up so fast that he almost toppled over backward in the chair.

He blinked, pulled in several deep breaths, and tried to get his vision to focus.

Slowly, in bits and pieces of fragmented, blurred details, he was able to determine with some degree of certainty that he had fallen asleep at the console in the main lab.

He checked the control board and saw that Roy was back online—no, scratch that: He was *still* online.

He almost shut it down, then decided not to.

The kid—

—my son, my good boy—

—didn't have much longer left; he might as well get out there and fly the InfoBahn while he could.

It, thought Preston to himself.

Think of him as an it *and you might just get through this without losing your mind.*

He pushed away from the console, made his way out through the door only he had the code to open, and stumbled his way through the secret corridor until he reached the foot of his hidden staircase.

From there, it was touch and go, stumble and stand as he made his way up into his office.

He tried not to think about Roy—let alone Roy's mother—but the image of the child's face the way it used to be kept drifting back into his thoughts.

Time was, he would have been able to ignore the image, knowing as he did that the essence of the child was still alive and relatively well, awaiting the return of Robillard. Preston had planned on convincing Zac to construct a body for Roy, preferably another I-Bot being . . . and if Robillard refused, Preston had ways of forcing him.

At least, that had been the original plan.

Then came the phone call from Dr. Segriff with the nine dreaded words: "Sam, we need to talk about your test results."

Now it was *two* bodies Preston needed from Zac—screw it if they were I-Botic or not.

He needed to live.

And he needed to have his son with him.

—no, not your son, not a him, he's an it, remember?—

—no good. Roy was his son, and Preston couldn't think of him in any other way, no matter how hard he tried to or how merciful it would have been for him, and now Roy was less than three days away from extinction and Preston knew it was his own arrogant fault—

—what was I thinking?

Easy, he answered himself, *you were thinking you had the world by the balls, weren't you? Making a name and reputation for yourself by stealing another's man's ideas because you knew you were too foolish, inept, and incompetent to come up with anything on your own, then getting promoted on the basis of your duplicity, moving with the Big Boys—but especially the Big Gal, the Boss Lady, luscious Annabelle, who was all too ready to share her bed with you, and you were so ready to please. But neither of you counted on her getting pregnant, did you? Hell, no. But pregnant she became, giving birth to a bright little boy who, in turn, thought you were the bestest thing in the whole great big wide world.* I love Daddy thiiiiiiiiiiiiiiiiiis much! *By that time you'd moved on, started your own company, Big Guy. You were so safe and smug within the myopic borders of your world, and you never once gave a thought to being undone by an absurdity, did you? Because that's what it was, an absolute, certified, A#1 in-goddamn-comprehensible absurdity. It was absurd to think that in this country, in this age, with so much wondrous medical technology there for the paying, that a little boy, a happy, radiant, inquisitive, healthy little boy with a giggle that brought tears to your eyes could die from a disease you're supposed to get from kissing or burning your candle at both ends. Well, here's a Muppet News Flash for you, Sam; it was possible for a four-year-old boy who loved to watch ducks and collect sea shells to feel bad, and then a bit worse, and then a whole hel-luva lot worse, and finally lousy in a way that required machines and tubes and pills and catheters and there was not nearly enough money in the fucking world to fix, and before you knew it you were sitting in the front pew at good ol' St. Francis de Sales Church lis-tening to some second-rate, blue-haired organist eviscerate J. S. Bach's "Sheep May Safely Graze" and dreading the moment when the two dozen children from your little boy's preschool are going to stand up and sing "Let There Be Peace On Earth" because that's when you were going to lose it and lose it bad and wonder how but mostly why something like this could happen. Just forget it, pal, just scratch that "why" business right off the list because there's no making sense of some shit, and your nice manners and fine credit record and good insurance notwithstanding, it is possible—and you have a crisp, clean copy of Autopsy #A72–196 to remind you in case you forget—for a four-year-old boy to contract Epstein-Barr virus and have his immune system so quickly degraded that he acquires, in spite of your fine house and dazzling grin and that secured slot on the Fortune 500, a thing called acute interstitial pneumonia, then another thing called* purulent exudate *that gets lonely in a hurry and so invites* pelvic venous plexis *to come join the party and* presto-change-o!—*you're looking at a little boy who in less than four weeks curls up into a wheezing skeleton and turns yellow and finally dies in a torturous series of sputtering little ago-nies, and you can't even get to his bedside to hold his hand because of the tubes and wires and bandages and all the rest of the Close Encounters of the Third-fucking-Kind hardware dwarfing this room where all the numbers are zero and all the lines are flat, so when he dies it is without the final benefit of a warm, loving human touch tingling on his skin to let him know that you will always love him and will miss him every second of every hour of every day for the rest of your life . . .*

... but you'd done something the night he'd died at the hospital, hadn't you? Long before the funeral, before anyone else saw his tiny, diseased body, you'd called your team in and told them exactly what to do, and they'd obeyed your orders, hadn't they? They'd expertly removed Roy's brain from his ruined body and used some of that state-of-the-art equipment to imprint his consciousness into the sponge of a robotic brain, that lovely little glop of platinum-iridium, because it occurred to you that death wasn't instantaneous, not at all; it moved through the body in stages. It occurred to you that it was possible to snatch a bunch of cells hours after somebody'd checked out and grow them in cultures. Death was a fundamental function; its mechanisms operated with the same attention to detail, the same conditions for the advantage of organisms, the same genetic information for guidance through the stages, that most people equated with the physical act of living. If it was such an intricate, integrated physiological process—at least in the primary, local stages—then there was no way to explain the permanent vanishing of consciousness. What happened to it? Did it just screech to a halt, become lost in humus, what? Nature did not work that way; it tended to find perpetual uses for its more elaborate systems. So you get to thinking that maybe human consciousness was somehow severed at the filaments of its attachment and then absorbed back into the membrane of its origin. Maybe that's all reincarnation was: the severed consciousness of a single cell that did not die but rather vanished totally into its own progeny. And you reincarnated your son, didn't you? Not only because you loved him but because you wanted to prove to all the nay-sayers once and for all that you were Zac Robillard's equal ... yet, still, you had to add a little something extra to save your worthless face in case it went wrong, and now look where it's gotten you.

He stumbled through the secret door and into his office, collapsing onto the brand-new sofa and noting that security had done a nice job of cleaning up and removing the bodies.

Then he asked himself once again why he'd done to Roy what he'd done.

And the same answer came back, just as it did every time he dared let his thoughts wander down this particular, deadly path.

He did it because he loved Roy.

He wanted his son back.

So the two of them could go to Annabelle and be a family.

Dammit all to hell, anyway!

Of all the women in this world to fall in love with—that once-in-a-lifetime, head-spinning, bells-ringing-in-your-ears kind of falling in love—he had to pick Vampirella, Queen Ice-Bitch of the Century . . .

. . . this was getting him nowhere.

He pulled himself up into a sitting position, rested his head in his hands, then rubbed his eyes and looked at the clock.

9:50 A.M.

He wondered if Janus would actually consider his offer.

No, he couldn't count on that.

And he didn't know who else could handle the assignment.

Which left only one option.

As much as he hated it, he was going to have to contact her.

He pulled himself slowly up from the sofa, staggered over to the wet bar, and poured himself a tall, cold glass of seltzer water.

The intercom on his desk buzzed.

He stumbled over and answered.

"Yes, Leslie?"

"I'm sorry to disturb you, sir, but Ms. Donohoe's on Line Two. This is the third time she's called."

Oh, shit . . .

"Okay. Um, ask her to hold for just a few more moments."

"Very good, sir."

He fell back into his chair, surprised to find himself shaking.

And not from the pain.

He was genuinely *excited* to be hearing from her.

He ran a hand through his hair, straightened his tie, and took another sip of seltzer before lifting the receiver.

He barely had time to say hello before she tore into him. . . .

52

Five minutes until ten, and already the line outside the carnival grounds was at least two hundred people long.

Killaine went up to the security guard and flashed her IPS, Inc., badge, the one that identified her as Karen Reynolds. The guard checked her name against those on a list and let her through.

Stepping past the gate, she turned to the guard and said, "What's a 'feed camp'?"

"The tent where food is served to the public."

"Thank you."

The midway was a street from the dreamland of any child, paved with wood shavings and sawdust that clung to the bottoms of shoes, the slightly musty scent mixing with that of fresh popcorn and cotton candy.

As she walked along the midway, Killaine noticed all of the booths and the neon lights decorating them.

She wondered what this place would be like at night, once darkness fell and the neon came on and the music was loud and the Ferris wheel was going and the lights on the merry-go-round were blinking as the animals danced around and around, up and down . . .

. . . she was so busy imagining what it would be like here at night that she almost missed him.

"Miss Reynolds?" came a scratchy, smoky male voice.

Killaine stopped a few feet past the edge of the feed camp's tent flap, laughed at herself, then backed up. Maybe Zac had been right to send her here. Just knowing what was going to be happening here in another two minutes lifted her spirits. Even from here she could feel the cumulative anticipation of parents and children alike, all of them impatiently checking their watches and bouncing on the balls of their feet: *What do you want to do first, hon? I wanna go on the merry-go-round . . . wanna get my fortune told . . . wanna see a bearded lady . . . wanna play ring-toss . . . wanna ride the Scrambler . . . wanna go pee, we been standin' here a awful long time, Mommy . . .*

She hated it when Zac was right about her moods.

But, knowing what joy would be flooding into this place in a moment, she hated it a little less than usual.

She stood at the entrance of the feed camp, blinking against the sun, trying to get a good look at the man who'd called her.

"Might as well come inside," he said. "If you don't, you're liable to get trampled by the young ones."

He sounded ancient.

Killaine stepped into the tent and its waning shadows.

The temperature immediately plunged a good twenty degrees.

It took a moment for her eyes to adjust to the slight darkness within.

"Mr. Morgan?" she said.

"Right here," came a voice from behind her. "But just call me Danny. Most folks who work here do."

She turned to face him.

Killaine was suddenly glad that she had what Itazura often called a "stone-face."

Because it meant that Daniel Morgan couldn't read her expression.

So he wouldn't know how shocked she was.

Before her stood a man of probably average height, though you couldn't tell it from the way he was standing.

All hunched over like that.

Putting most of his weight on the aluminum arm-crutches that extended from the handgrips he clutched.

Probably because he couldn't walk with just the leg braces.

Not to mention the very slight but nonetheless noticeable curvature of his spine.

She refused to think of him as a hunchback.

"Glad you decided to come, Miss Reynolds," said Daniel Morgan, leaning one of the crutches up against a table and offering his hand.

Killaine shook it, then looked down.

His skin had an odd texture.

Then she saw he was wearing light gloves with the fingers and thumb cut off them.

"Sorry about that," he said, giving his hand a slight wave before grabbing back his crutch. "My hands get real sweaty, what with having to grip these silver bad-boys all day long. It also helps with the blistering—I mean, I tend to get less blisters if I wear these. Not that you asked. I'm just a little nervous, is all. Could we . . . uh, would you like to sit down and have an orange juice with me?"

"Sure," said Killaine.

She decided that he couldn't have been more than thirty-five or forty, but his voice sounded like a man two decades older. Maybe that had something to do with the disease that had left him in this condition.

He gestured to the picnic table where an icy pitcher of orange juice waited, along with two glasses, for them.

He even pulled out the bench for her.

"Hope you don't mind," he said. "I mean, there're some ladies who think this is kind've a sexist thing to do, pulling out a chair for them. I don't mean to offend you, it's just the way I was raised."

"I don't mind at all," said Killaine, surprised at how much she liked this man already.

"Good, 'cause I'm not in much of a position to run away if you decide I've earned myself a slap in the face."

He looked at her face, then said, "That was a joke. It's okay to laugh."

"Good," said Killaine and laughed.

Morgan took a seat across from her, propped up his crutches, and poured their orange juice. "Scoliosis," he said to her.

"I beg your pardon?"

"Is your juice all right?"

"Yes, nice and frosty."

"Yeah, it's yummy stuff, all right. What I said was scoliosis. Contracted it when I was a kid."

"The Czech strain of the late 'eighties?"

"Yeah—hey, you got a good eye for this thing! I was only a baby. My parents were circus people and we were on tour. My case was the first instance of the disease in over ten years over there. Of course, they didn't call it scoliosis. I forget exactly what they named it, but it all came down to the same thing. Tied a big knot in my spine and rearranged the architecture of the bones and muscles in my legs. I'm only telling you this because every damn time I meet somebody, I can see the question in their eyes, you know? 'Gosh, I wonder what happened to him.' Then you can't have a decent conversation with them because that question's always hanging there between you. You keep wishing they'd just ask it and get it over with. Well, one day not so long ago, I decided, to hell with it, I'm going to just tell people so they don't have to worry about hiding that question. I saw it in your eyes, though I gotta tell you, you did a better job of masking it than most people."

"Mr. Morgan, I didn't mean to offend—"

"The only thing that will offend me from here on out is if you keep it up with that 'Mr. Morgan' crap. I told you, call me Danny."

"Then you have to call me Karen."

"Good thing that's your name, then."

Killaine laughed, noticing for the first time that there was an undeniable—though not obvious or traditional—rugged handsomeness to his chiseled face.

And knew then that she liked Danny Morgan.

Very, very much.

53

"*Annabelle,* hello. I—"

"*Why didn't you tell me yourself?*" she snapped at him. "Dammit, Sam, do you really think of me as being *that* heartless, that detached and coldhearted?"

He felt something in his chest quiver. "How did you find out? Janus?"

"Yes."

"He had no business telling you."

"Maybe not, but I'm glad he did. We might have been a lousy couple, Sam, and we both sure as hell were lousy parents at the end, but that doesn't mean your . . . *condition* doesn't matter to me."

"My condition," he repeated. "What a nice way to put it."

"How am I supposed to put it? What do you want me to say?"

"Don't turn it into a euphemism, Annabelle. I'm dying and there's nothing that can be done about it. Well, *almost* nothing."

"Meaning?"

"Meaning what else did Janus tell you?"

"That you want to form a temporary partnership."

"Yes."

"Why?"

"Because I need Robillard's help and I'm not going to get it if you have him stashed away down there."

"How can Robillard help—" She paused, then took a breath. *"Oh."*

"You got it."

"Are you sure that's what you want?"

"It's no longer a matter of what I want, Annabelle. What I *want* is to never have gotten sick in the first place. What I want is to have gone to the doctor the first time the stomach pains started. What I want is for us to still be together and . . . but that's not going to happen. I can't afford to live in 'What-If' land. I need to know if you're willing to help me."

"Even though I don't have to?"

"Even though you don't have to."

Silence.

"Well?" asked Preston.

"I'm thinking."

"Then let me ask you something else."

"What?"

"Are you upset about my dying because you still care about me, or are upset about my dying because someone else knew before you did?"

"That's a lousy thing to say, Sam."

"I'm feeling kind of lousy these days, Annabelle."

A pause. "I still care about you," she said flatly.

"Which explains the emotional tone of your voice."

"What would you prefer? Shrieks, tears, and Forties-Movie-Heroine hysterics?"

"I would prefer to believe you."

"Could we go back to your original question?"

Preston gave a short, sharp, dark laugh. "Whatever you say, Annabelle."

"Yes, I'll help you."

"And what will your help cost me?"

"Nothing."

"Don't blow smoke up my—"

"—I said nothing! All right?"

"All right."

Annabelle exhaled. "What do you know about what dear old Zac's been up to?"

"If you mean did he say anything to me about designing a new I-Bot prototype, the answer is no. But you know how Zac is—I doubt he writes much down anymore. It wouldn't surprise me if he's got finished designs for at least three new models in his head. In fact, I'm kind of counting on it, if you know what I mean."

"I might. Is there anything I can do for you, Sam? Money, doctors, any experimental treatments that—"

"You could contact someone in your pharmaceutical division and get me some morphine tabs. Janus dumped some of mine and I can't afford to run out."

"How many?"

Preston was surprised. "Just like that? 'How many?' One of the most difficult drugs in this country to obtain, and all you have to do is—"

"Yes! Now, how many?"

Preston sat back in his chair. "It's good to hear your voice again, Annabelle. I've missed you."

"Did you give me a number in there or did I miss something?"

"Still all business, huh?"

"Still all business."

So Preston gave her a number, and then they got down to the business of business.

54

Thirty minutes into their conversation—one that had been speckled with jokes, anecdotes, and endless stories, Killaine looked across the table at Danny and said, "So you're telling me that your problem is . . . ?"

"Sticks," he replied.

"Sticks?"

"Sticks. It's an old carny term. A 'stick' is a person who poses as a big winner at one of the game booths in order to lure in marks—customers. Usually a stick is in cahoots with the owner of the flat store and—"

"Excuse me," said Killaine. "'Flat store'?"

"A flat store is a rigged game booth where there's no way somebody can win. It's called that because you can flat-out rob a person and they'll never know it. Even if they suspect, there's no way to prove it. All along a midway you'll find all sorts of games—build-up numbers, alibi games, peekers, razzlers, bafflers, and chips. Most of the guys are as honest as the day is long, but if one fixer gets his ass in here it's not too long before the punk robbers'll follow him in, and then the whole midway goes to hell in a handbasket. Outside men, peekers dolin' out lay bears to underage girls, trailer joints running after hours and patch money flowing like wine."

Killaine stared at him, fascinated.

Danny looked at her then touched his face. "What? Did I—oh, please tell me that I don't have something hanging off my—"

"No, no," said Killaine, smiling. "It's just that"—she laughed— "I didn't understand a damn word you said."

"Huh? Oh—I'm sorry, Miss Reyn—uh, Karen. When you've been a carny as long as I have, you start to speak a whole different language. It helps us understand each other—sorta like our own little code—but it can work against us when a bad element comes in."

"Would you care to translate some of what you just said?"

"Well—sure I'm not boring you?"

Killaine propped her elbow up on the table and rested her chin in her hand.

She was absolutely smitten with him. "No," she said. "You're not boring me at all."

Good heavens, she felt like an adolescent girl who'd gotten a crush on her history teacher. This wasn't her, it wasn't her at all!

. . . Still, it was nice. Danny Morgan had a way about him, despite his physical afflictions; his face alone held traces of a thousand places, a million stories.

To Killaine, that was incredibly attractive. In the five years Zac and the I-Bots had been on the run, she had never, ever, felt anything like this toward a client before. Morgan had a bone-weary charisma that she found hypnotic; that, combined with his gravelly voice, made him seem all the more enigmatic. There was such a passion for his work—albeit a deeply hidden, well-masked passion—evident in his every look, gesture, word, and inflection. She couldn't get over the way his eyes sparkled when he talked of the carnival life, and the way he—

". . . okay?"

Killaine blinked, startled, and gave her head a little shake. "I'm . . . I'm sorry, Danny. I must have drifted off for a moment."

"The heat. It gets pretty hot out here pretty early. Believe me, it's a lot better once night comes. Everything smells better, looks prettier."

"I can imagine."

"I didn't mean to startle you. Just wondering if you were okay."

"I'm fine. I didn't mean to be rude. Go on."

"Well, I was saying that this carnival isn't a racket show—at least, it *wasn't* until about four months ago."

"And a racket show is—"

"A carnival that carries rigged games. And racket shows are dirty with patch money." Before Killaine could ask him what that was, he held up his hand and continued. "Each agent working a rigged game pays his fixer—that's a person who's either got an in with local law enforcement or who *is* a local officer—anyway, the agent pays his fixer so much money a night to make sure that his game isn't busted if someone raises hell and accuses him of being less than forthright with his practice. The amount an agent pays depends on how much the fixer needs for this assurance, plus his percentage of the nightly take. The prices can get pretty high when a stick enters the picture."

"And you want me to find the sticks that are working your midway?"

Morgan nodded his head. "I'm the storekeeper here—I'm in charge of the midway games. It's my responsibility to make sure that all the games are legit, that everyone who plays gets what they pay for, and that no one along my route is running a flat, count, or bat away store." He saw the look on Killaine's face. "They're all crooked as my back. It's just that each kind has a different method of cheating. Look, Karen, I don't want to prattle on too much more about this, but—"

"I really don't mind."

He smiled, then reached across and placed one of his gloved

hands over hers. "That's awfully sweet of you to say, but I suspect you might be getting tired of the sound of my voice. I know I am."

Killaine laughed. "You've got a wonderful voice."

He raised an eyebrow at her. "Really think so?"

"Oh, yeah."

A tight-lipped grin. "Well, yours isn't exactly hard on the ears, either. In fact, what with that Irish accent of yours, it's downright sultry. Reminds me of Maureen O'Hara's voice, with a little touch of Greer Garson thrown in."

"Oh, I *love* Maureen O'Hara!" exclaimed Killaine. "*The Quiet Man* is one of my favorite movies!"

"Oh, a lady after my own heart. Wasn't Victor MacLaughlin terrific in that picture? I always liked Victor. I like Robert Mitchum, too. Thought he did a fine job in *Ryan's Daughter.*"

"That's my *favorite* movie!"

"You're kidding?"

"No."

"Mine, too!"

And both of them laughed.

During the whole exchange, Danny didn't take his hand from Killaine's.

And she didn't mind one bit.

"I like you, Karen Reynolds," said Morgan.

"I like *you,* Daniel Morgan."

"Does that mean you'll take the job?"

"What exactly is the job?"

"I want you to come back here tomorrow night with one or two of your other people and try to get yourselves hired as sticks. To a flat store owner, a good stick is worth their price in gold."

"What will happen?"

"If one of you gets hired as a stick, you'll be asked if you've got any partners. You'll say yes, and the booster grapevine will come alive. You'll be given instructions to move from one flat store to the other, and by the end of the evening I'll know where the flatties are."

"And then?"

"And then the rest of us will run them off the midway. Carnies take care of their own, and they clean up their own messes. It's just that, in this case, the flatties are a bit more skilled at hiding themselves that I'm used to." He shrugged. "Of course, it could just be I've lost my touch at spotting them. In any event, I've tucked aside enough money to cover your services for two days, plus your consulting fee. If you take the job, then one of your people is going to have to spend a day training with me."

"Training?"

"Can't offer your services as a stick unless you can spot how the game's rigged. If the flattie knows that *you* know what he's up to, he'll have no choice but to hire you for the night."

"Even if they've got a fixer?"

Morgan shook his head. "A fixer is only available on a first-come, first-serve basis. Let's say that a midway route's got four flat stores. On any given night, only one of them can hire a fixer and the other three can go hang. A smart fixer knows how important he is, and a lot of them make more money during a carny stopover than many of the owners." He finished off his orange juice, wiped the sweat from his forehead, then leaned forward. "Karen, I hope you don't take offense to this, but it's not going to do me a whole helluva lot of good to go on about this if you're not going to take the job."

"I understand," said Killaine, gripping his hand before he could take it away. "And I want to take the job, it's just . . ."

"Just what?"

She brushed her thumb over the back of his hand, once, very

slowly, then looked up into his eyes. "Why is this so important to you?"

"Because I run a clean midway."

"I know that, I know that you pride yourself on honest games, but I . . . I get the feeling there's something else. What is it?"

He stared at her. "Is this a deal-breaker?"

"No. I'm just curious." She laughed. "Occupational hazard for the security business."

"Uh-huh," Morgan said, his face losing just a touch of its openness, its friendliness.

Killaine was immediately sorry she'd pushed her luck.

Morgan slowly pulled his hand away, grabbed his arm-crutches, rose from the table, and hobbled over to the feed camp's open entrance flap.

He watched the families wander by.

The mothers. The fathers. The teens.

The children, most of all.

Finally, he looked over his shoulder and said, "Could you come here for a minute?"

Killaine quickly rose from the table and joined him.

When she got there, she automatically put a hand on his shoulder as if they'd known each other all their lives and this was something she often did.

"Look at them, will you?" said Morgan, gesturing with his head toward a group of children who were being led along by two harried-looking mothers. "Everything's still *new* to them. Even if something bad's happened to them recently, they still laugh and giggle and, I don't know, *hope,* I guess. Remember when we were that young? How nothing bad ever followed us to the next morning? Maybe something bad happened *before,* but *now's* fun, you've got a ball to bounce or a model plane to fly or a doll to pretend with, and the day's full of mystery and wonder and things to look forward to and—" He stopped himself with a shake of his head.

"What is it, Danny?" said Killaine softly, gently squeezing his shoulder.

He looked at her with a deep, hidden sadness in his eyes. "You know, I once read this fairy tale about a young boy who discovered an ancient Egyptian vase, thousand of years old, and he wanted to open it up so he could get to the treasures inside. He tried to pry the lid off but he couldn't do it, so finally he loses his temper and smashes the vase to the floor and—you know what's inside? A rose. A single rose from five thousand years ago, perfectly preserved. And for a moment the boy inhales the scent of the rose and the air that had been sealed within the vase, and in that instant he feels cheated because he thought it was going to contain something valuable. Still, it's a nice smell, unlike any other rose he's ever smelled before. So he decides to give it to his mother. But when he opens his eyes and looks down again, the rose has crumbled into dust. The story ends many years later, when the boy is an old man lying on his deathbed, and the priest asks him if there are any further sins he wants to confess. The old man looks up at the priest and says, 'I am ashamed that I didn't treasure the priceless gift the old rose gave to me.' And he dies. And no one knows what he meant by it."

"That's a lovely story. Sad, but lovely."

Morgan laughed. "Probably doesn't do much to answer your question, though."

"Not really."

He maneuvered around on his crutches to face her. "The ancient Greeks believed in two kinds of time, Karen: *chronos* and *kairos. Kairos* is not measurable. In *kairos,* you simply *are,* from the moment of your birth on. You *are,* wholly and positively. *Kairos* is especially strong in children, because they haven't learned to understand, let alone accept, concepts such as time and age and death. In children, *kairos* can break through *chronos:* When they're playing safely, drawing a picture for Mommy or Daddy, taking the first taste of the first ice-cream cone of summer, when they sing along to songs in a Disney cartoon, there is only *kairos*. As long as a child thinks it's immortal, it is."

The intensity in his voice was hypnotic.

The look on his face was overpowering.

The fire in his eyes was breathtaking; Killaine couldn't look away.

"Think of every living child," he said, "as being the burning bush that Moses saw—surrounded by the flames of *chronos,* but untouched by the fire. In *chronos* you're nothing more than a set of records, fingerprints, your social-security number, you're always watching the clock, aware of time passing—but in *kairos,* you are *Karen* and only Karen.

"Children don't know about *chronos,* and I'll be damned, Karen, if any of them are going to be forced to find out about it on my midway. I'll be damned if any of them are going to leave here without realizing the priceless gift of the old rose. Their innocence and joy and wonder will be taken away from them soon enough. The carnival remains one of the few places of wonder left to them, and I want it to remain that way. No child will leave here in *chronos* because some greedy son-of-a-bitch flat store owner took them for all the money in their piggy banks.

"Does *that* answer your question?"

". . . yes . . ."

"Will you take the job? Will you help me keep *kairos* away from the kids?"

With not the least bit of self-consciousness, Killaine reached up and touched his cheek. "Yes, I will."

"Good. If you could have your team member be here about noon, I'll start training him."

She reached down and gripped his forearms. "It will be me."

His smile brightened considerably. *"Really?* You want me to teach you . . . ?"

Killaine felt herself actually blushing as she smiled. "Yes. Teach me."

And for a long moment, they simply stood staring at one another and smiling.

Looking for all the world like a couple of love-struck teenagers.

55

Across the road from the carnival entrance gate, Rudy watched from behind an old newsstand for the redheaded bitch to leave.

Locating the building where he'd tried to dust DocScrap last night had been easier than he'd thought, thanks to a couple of well-placed packages of Stoke powder into the hands of Gash's RoofWatchers. The RWs were scattered all over Cemetery Ridge, their duty being to record the comings and goings of *anyone* in the area—even if it was just a pizza delivery boy

Rudy had laid the Stoke on them, and they'd been more than happy to listen to his description of the redheaded bitch. They'd agreed that Rudy's Stoke was enough for them to watch for one day and one night; then they either quit or he found a way to provide more of the drug for them.

Knowing they risked Gash's wrath for helping Rudy was outweighed by their love of Stoke.

They'd spotted her easily from the roofs—the Stompers had electronic surveillance equipment installed on most of the rooftops in Cemetery Ridge, particularly those areas near Cinnamon Road—and she'd shown up during one of their routine scans.

A call to Rudy, giving him the direction in which she was heading, a description of what she was wearing, and he was on his way.

He'd spotted her from half a block away, going in precisely the direction he'd been told. He made sure to keep a big distance between them.

He was still riding the adrenaline high from last night. Sure, he hadn't managed to dust the Doc, but he'd shaken the dude up pretty badly—and taken a piece out of him, to boot.

Rudy imagined that he could still taste the Doc's blood on his lips.

It wasn't all that bad, the taste of blood. A little coppery and sharp, but not too bad, when you got right down to it.

He reached up and patted down his hair. He'd removed most of the bandages from his face and head, leaving only the medicated gauze pads and medical tape that held them in place over Gash's handiwork.

He pulled a baseball cap from his back pocket, put it on his head brim forward, then clasped his hands behind his back and leaned against the newsstand.

They were up to something.

Stinkin' robots. They might look like human beings, but they were still robots.

Future scrap material.

Wreckage-to-Be.

But he couldn't show his face to the Stompers, not yet. Not until he had something more solid.

Like one of the robots.

Preferably alive, but he'd be more than happy to fry their brains, if he needed to.

He'd be *really* happy to fry the redheaded bitch's brain.

He wondered, for a moment, if *all* of her was constructed like a real woman.

She *was* mighty tasty-looking.

Rudy laughed to himself.

Might be kind of fun finding out, if he could pull it off.

But, for now, he'd wait for her, follow her back to DocScrap's building and see if he could figure out what the hell was going on. *Then* he'd go back to the Stompers and show them he was worthy.

56

Psy–4 nodded his head and looked up from the blueprints and various notes. "Looks good."

"*Of course* it looks good," said Itazura. "Familiar, too—it's the backup plan we *didn't* use the other night."

"That's because it would have taken too long," said Psy–4.

"Like we've got tons of time this go-round?"

"No, but we *do* have a couple of advantages we didn't have before."

"Such as . . . ?"

"For one, we know exactly where we are going, how to get there, and what systems' energies need to be redirected in order to achieve the goal; for another, we have a wider window of opportunity than before."

"Only by fifteen minutes."

"Give or take sixty seconds," said Stonewall.

Itazura winked at him. "Pick nits, why don't you?"

Psy–4 stood and exhaled. "We can brief Killaine on this when she gets back. I'd like to build a mock-up of the bottom floor of Preston's main building—nothing fancy, cardboard and plywood will do. I don't think it would hurt us to do a couple of dry runs."

"Is the cellar big enough for that?" asked Radiant.

Stonewall checked the measurements. "With a yard to spare on three of the four sides—if Itazura doesn't mind losing his labyrinth."

"Not gonna have any time to walk it again before this," he said.

Psy–4 clamped a hand on Itazura's shoulder. "I appreciate it."

"Wait till you get my bill."

Psy–4 laughed, but not too loudly. "Okay. Now we need to pick up the supplies on the list. Just make sure that we hit stores in *this* area. Use black-market dealers if you have to. I know that Annabelle will probably still be able to trace any sales of this type, but if we go the BM route, it'll take her a bit longer to—"

"Take *who* a bit longer?"

All of them turned to see Zac standing in the doorway.

He looked from one of them to the next until he'd made eye contact with all five of them.

Even Singer found it difficult to return his gaze.

"Okay," said Zac. "I give up. You've stumped the band. I heard the name 'Annabelle' and the words 'equipment,' 'trace,' and 'mock-up'—that last one being particularly interesting. Someone care to tell me what's going on?"

His body turned at enough of an angle that Zac couldn't see his hands, Singer looked at Psy–4 and signed, *Oh, shit.*

No one could find good reason to disagree with his assessment of their current status.

57

Morgan watched Karen walk over to one of the pay phones along the midway. She was going to call her boss and tell him she was taking the assignment.

He hoped his jaw hadn't dropped open again.

He hadn't expected anything like her.

Not even close.

Not at all.

Everything about her was ethereal to him—her eyes, her smile, her laugh (*Oh, yes*—her laugh!) . . . he was a goner the minute he saw her.

He'd never believed in anything like love before. Oh, sure, friendships, however brief or transient, those he could believe in; the occasional one-nighter was the closest he'd ever come to romance, but love?

Not even close.

Not at all.

Probably wouldn't have recognized it if it had sprouted fangs and bitten him in the Very Tender Parts.

Oh, how he *didn't* need this little complication.

Still, there were worse things that could happen to a person.

Much worse things.

He saw her punch in the phone number, then turn, smile at him, and give a short wave so filled with dormant little-girl innocence he felt himself blush as he returned the gesture.

This was nuts! She was right there in plain sight, only ten yards or so away from him, and he *missed* her.

That wasn't a good sign.

He suddenly felt another set of eyes looking at him, and turned his head enough to see one of the game booth operators smirking at him.

He gave the man a puzzled look.

The operator jerked his thumb toward Karen, then pointed at Morgan, then rolled his eyes skyward while shaking his hand.

Morgan sneered at the guy and flashed him the finger.

This wouldn't last long, this feeling he had, this immediate symbiosis.

For him, it never did.

But that didn't mean he couldn't enjoy it while it was here.

He looked back and saw that she was still staring at him.

Her eyes so clear and green; Summer Eyes.

Just don't smile, he prayed. *If you smile at me now, I'm done for.*

She smiled.

So did Morgan.

Just shoot me now, he thought.

58

That morning would go down in their personal histories as the Day the I-Bots Learned the Meaning of the Phrase "Saved by the Bell," for as they all stood there trying to come up with a feasible excuse to explain what Zac had overheard, the phone rang.

"I'll be right back," Zac said. "And *then* we'll have ourselves a chat."

The moment he left the room everyone's shoulders slumped in relief.

"Oh, let's enjoy these next few moments," said Itazura. "They'll probably be our last moments alive."

Stonewall was already at the computer, typing away, bringing up record files.

"What are you doing?" asked Psy–4.

"Saving our butts."

He found what he was looking for, then quickly grabbed Radiant's hand.

Myriad levels of informational energy passed between them.

"Looks like he's going to propose," whispered Itazura to Singer.

Do you ever turn it off?

"Jealous?"

In your dreams, Funny-Boy.

Radiant let go of Stonewall's hand and turned toward the others. "Just follow my lead when Zac returns."

"Why *your* lead?" asked Psy–4.

"Because the rest of you are lousy liars, that's why!" She then tossed her hair to the side, fluffed it a little, leaned against the console, and plastered on her most dazzling smile.

"Shouldn't you be topless and laying across the hood of a sports car?"

"Stuff it, Itzy," replied Radiant through clenched teeth, her smile never faltering. "Here comes Zac."

"Don't I get a last cigarette?"

You don't smoke, replied Singer.

"No," said Itazura. "But this suddenly seems like a good time to start."

"Killaine?"

"Hi, Zachary. I'm just calling to let you know that I've accepted the job."

"I thought you might. We've never had any dealings with circuses before."

"It's a carnival, Zachary."

He shrugged. "I get 'em mixed up."

"Having never been to either in your life, I can understand that."

"How are you getting along with Mr. Morgan?"

Silence.

"Killaine?"

"Oh, *Zac,* he's such a wonderful man. I've never met anyone like him."

"Oh?"

"I can't thank you enough for making me come here."

"No problem, I figured that—do you realize you just called me 'Zac'?"

"Hm? I did? Sorry, I guess I wasn't paying attention."

"How many other team members will you need?"

"Oh, I can handle him just fine."

"Handle who? Killaine? Hello, Earth to Killaine, do you read?"

"Hm? Oh, sorry, Zac. Um, he'll need at least two more besides me. I'll be out here for the rest of the day."

"Why?"

"He needs to train me."

Zac put a hand on his hip like an annoyed father. "For *what?*"

"I'll explain everything when I get home tonight. Have to go now. 'Bye!"

Zac stared at the receiver for a few seconds before hanging up.

Zac—*twice* she'd called him Zac.

And he wasn't quite so out of touch with certain natural processes that he couldn't discern what was happening to her.

He'd just spoken to a woman who was ga-ga over a guy.

From Radiant, he would've expected something like this.

But *Killaine?*

Zac gave a short, low whistle. "That Mr. Morgan must be quite a guy."

Then he turned and headed back to the control room.

* * *

As soon as Zac entered the room, Radiant walked up to him and stood her ground.

"You had no right to eavesdrop like that!"

"It wasn't my intention to eavesdrop," said Zac calmly. "I needed to check a couple of equations that I've been toying with in my head and decided to use the computer. It *is* here for everyone's use, after all."

"But you hardly ever use it."

"Which suddenly means that I don't have the right to?"

"I didn't say that, all I meant was—"

"Whoa!" said Zac, holding up a hand. "Just hold it right there. I didn't mean to overhear your conversation, and I apologize if any of you feel that I've invaded your privacy, but the fact remains that I *did* overhear part of it, and what I heard was a bit on the alarming side, the events of the last few days considered, and I feel that I'm within my rights to demand an explanation."

"He sure does talk purdy, don't he?" said Itazura.

Everyone glared at him.

"I'll be quiet. Look, here I am, being quiet."

"So you want to know what we were talking about, is that it?" said Radiant.

"I've already answered that question."

"Fine," she said, spinning around on huffed heels and stomping over to the computer. "We were discussing *this!*" She pointed to the monitor.

Zac came over and looked at the screen.

"My . . . *birthday?* It's not for another five weeks."

"And a good thing, too. We were discussing your present—which, I might add, is something you've wanted for a long, long time. We were trying to figure where to buy it so that Annabelle couldn't trace the sale. Not that it matters now, Mr. Nibby, because if you heard that much of the conversation, then you know that we're getting you a—"

"I didn't hear that part," said Zac.

Radiant gave her head a little jerk, tossing her hair to the other side of her neck. "No, no, you don't have to spare our feelings."

"It's all ruined now," said Psy–4.

"And we were so careful," mumbled Stonewall.

Zac looked at Itazura.

"I'm being quiet, remember?"

Zac looked at Singer.

I have no choice but to be quiet.

Zac shook his head and turned around. "I should've just stayed in bed."

He closed the door behind him.

Once again, there was a mass shoulder-slump of relief.

"That was close," said Psy–4.

Stonewall shook his head. "I hate lying, I hate it, I hate it, I hate it!"

Itazura put a hand on his shoulder. "But how do you *really* feel about it, Stoner?"

Radiant made certain the door was closed all the way, then turned toward the rest. "It isn't a lie if, for his birthday, we *do* get him that thing he's been wanting for a long time."

What, exactly, is that? inquired Singer.

"I haven't got the slightest idea," said Radiant. "But there's got to be *something*."

Itazura laughed. "Tune in next week for the exciting conclusion of the Great Birthday Brouhaha, same Bat-Time, same Bat-Channel."

"Can I *please* smack him now?" asked Stonewall.

"Not if I beat you to him first," replied Psy–4.

They all looked at one another, then laughed.

59

Morgan's own booth—a straightforward water race game—was located at the far end of the midway. He was more than happy to show Killaine how his game was played.

"Here," he said, handing her a squirt gun. "Be careful, it's loaded."

"Very funny," she said.

"One of the ways that you can spot a potential flat store is to watch and see how complicated the game is. The more complicated the rules of a game, the higher the chances that it's probably rigged in some way.

"This game," he said, standing a little to the left behind her, "is really simple. A customer plunks down a quarter, picks out a squirt gun from the rack, and aims at the clown's mouth at the back of the booth. Go on."

Killaine began to take a classic shooter's stance but was stopped when Morgan reached over and put a hand on her forearm.

"No, no, no," he said. "I mean, I know why you'd position yourself like that—"

"Training," she replied.

"Right. Thing is, humor me here. Pretend that you're just an average, everyday schmo here to have a good time. The type of person who only sees guns fired on television."

Killaine nodded her head, relaxed her stand, and used only one hand to hold the gun and point it at the clown face.

"Thank you," said Morgan. "Now, all you have to do is squirt enough water into the clown's mouth to fill the balloon under his neck." He leaned in and whispered in her ear. "Once it's full of water, it's shaped like a bow tie."

Killaine took a couple of shots, and was surprised that it wasn't easier to hit the mouth.

"A lot of people are surprised by that," said Morgan. "That's because they make the mistake of assuming that water will shoot like a bullet—in a straight line. But water arcs, as you have seen."

"That hardly seems fair!"

"Ah-ah," said Morgan waving a finger, "I never said it was easy, but it *is* fair. I can't change the laws of physics."

"So how does a person win?"

"Like this." He took the gun from her hand, pointed it at the clown's mouth, and gave the trigger six slow, steady squeezes, filling the bow-tie balloon and bursting it.

"There," he said, handing the gun back to her. "No rigging, no hidden tubes in the clown to redirect the water, nothing but good, clean, honest fun."

"You never have any problems?"

"Oh, yeah. Occasionally I get the odd assho—uh, *jerk* who just can't resist turning the squirt gun on me."

"That's so rude."

"It's also dangerous." He pointed over the edge of the booth to the series of electric wires that ran along the length of the floor. "At night all the booth lights are on—even the clown faces are lit up. Somebody gets carried away with the water and the operator—in this case, *moi*—is Mr. Crispy Toast."

Killaine looked at the squirt gun, then the innocent clown face. "I never stopped to think that something this simple could be so dangerous."

"Only if the players abuse the situation, and that doesn't happen very often." He held up one of his metal arm-crutches. "Much as I hate to admit it, most folks who play my game get one look at my back and these crutches and—bingo!—such courtesy you've never seen."

"Okay, Danny, you've shown me how an honest game is played. Give me an example of how a rigged game goes down."

"'Goes down'? Where'd you pick up that little phrase, reruns of *Hill Street Blues?*"

Killaine gave a short, shocked laugh. "You're making fun of me."

"Maybe a little."

"Why?"

"Because you're awfully cute when you're trying to look out-raged."

"Watch yourself, Morgan. I've been known to have a nasty temper."

"I'll keep that in mind."

A smile. "You'd better."

A bigger smile from him. "I'm shaking already."

Lots of smiling at each other.

Part of Killaine's mind reminded her that, had she been watch-ing this take place from a distance—say, in a really syrupy love story on television, this would be the part where she would pre-tend to start vomiting.

"Over there," said Morgan, pointing to a booth across the midway; this one featured a simple three-balls-in-the-basket game.

"Looks innocent enough," said Killaine, looking at the prizes and the slanted table in the back where three large wicker baskets sat.

"Come on," he said, and started across toward the booth.

When they arrived, Morgan introduced Killaine to a large man named Herbert, the game operator (and the man he'd given the finger to a while earlier, though he didn't tell her that part), and explained to him who she was.

"'Bout danged time you got on this," said Herbert.

"I trust you'll be able to keep this to yourself?"

"Anything for you, m'friend."

"Karen wants to see a rip-off played out." Morgan took two

dollars from his pocket and slapped them down on the counter. "Ready?"

"Ready," replied Herbert, who then launched into a well-memorized pitch: "Step right up, roll right up, ladies and gents, all it costs you is two dollars American for a chance to win any of the fabulous prizes you see displayed on the shelves behind me—not so close, friend, this area's for the paying customers, thank you. It sounds too easy, you say? Two dollars for a chance at that portable CD player? Why, sir, you say, that's insane! Well, mebbe it is, but I'm here to tell you that this is a carnival, folks, and what's a carnival without a little craziness? Why, it's like . . ."

"He loves going through his Pitch," whispered Morgan to Killaine.

"He's good at it."

"You bet. Herbert's been a carny all his life."

". . . *just two dollars American!* All you gotta do is put three balls into one of the bushel baskets you see behind me. Piece of cake. Here, watch me!"

Herbert tossed one of the softballs—underhanded—into the basket.

"Yessir, folks, it's *that* easy. Who'll dare to give it a try? How's about you, sir? Win a prize for your lovely lady?"

Morgan slid his money forward.

"Nosir," said Herbert, waving a hand, "nosir, I don't expect you to take my word for it, too many folks in this here world want to take advantage of a trusting soul like yourself. Tell'ya what I'm gonna do. I'm gonna give, *free of charge,* because I'm an honest fellow and you look like one smart cookie, I'm gonna let you take a *free practice shot!*" And with that, he tossed Morgan a softball identical to the one he'd thrown into the basket. "Go on, sir, lob one in that basket for the lovely lady!"

Morgan tossed the ball—overhand—into the same basket as Herbert's.

"Outstanding! Outstanding!" cried Herbert. "Folks, we got ourselves a nat-choo-ral here! A prodigy! Here you go, sir! Here's your three balls!"

He handed three softballs to Morgan, removed the other balls from the basket, and stood to the side.

Morgan tossed all three balls.

Only one of them stayed in the basket; the other two went in, then bounced out.

"Okay," he said, turning toward Killaine. "How'd he do it?"

"Do what?"

"How'd Herbert rig the game?"

"He didn't."

Herbert laughed. "Yeah, I did."

Killaine thought about it for a moment. "Then you've got an . . . an outside man working something from behind the booth. A pedal or something that pushes the balls back out."

"Nope."

She looked at Morgan. "Okay, I give."

"Sure you don't want to try and figure it out before we tell you?"

"I'm sure. Whatever he did, he did right in front of my eyes while I was standing here."

"Yes, that he did."

"I didn't see him do it—by the way, Herbert, whatever you did, it was very impressive."

"Thank you, ma'am," said the large man, tipping his hat.

"Talk it through," said Morgan. "You'd be surprised at how easy it is to figure."

"Well, he started with his Pitch—"

"Distracting as hell, isn't it?"

"I thought it was kind of exciting to listen to."

Morgan nodded his head. "Like I said, distracting. That's the first element of the ploy—your Pitch. The louder, wordier, and faster the pitch, the more exciting it comes across to the crowd. People are so busy enjoying the operator's showmanship, they don't think to concentrate on anything else."

"Add to that," said Herbert, "that if there were customers standing here already playing, the Pitch is doubly distracting to them."

"Because," added Morgan, "once you approach the booth, you're looking at one of three things: Herbert, the prizes, and the baskets."

"Not the softballs?" asked Killaine.

"No," replied Herbert. "Almost nobody thinks to look at the balls right off."

"So it's something to do with switching balls?"

"No," said Morgan. "The ball Herbert tossed in the bushel basket is the same kind I tossed in right after."

Killaine rubbed her eyes. "Okay, so the Pitch is the first element of the ploy?"

Morgan picked up three more balls. "Second element is the Enticement—in this case, it was my free practice shot."

"But remember," said Herbert, "that a customer is more likely to accept an Enticement if he or she thinks they've been challenged. Now, watch." Herbert tossed a softball—underhanded, once again—into the bushel basket. "Okay, what's wrong with this picture?"

"Nothing that I can think of," replied Killaine. "Unless the method of tossing the ball has—"

"—not a thing," said Morgan.

She thought about it for a moment, then shook her head. "Okay, I give."

"Look at me," said Morgan.

"With pleasure."

A little more of that smiling stuff between them.

Then Morgan said: "See where I'm standing?"

"At the counter."

"See where Herbert's standing?"

"Inside the booth—oh."

"By Jove," said Morgan in a pitiful Rex Harrison imitation, "I do believe she's got it!"

"The distance," whispered Killaine.

"Right!" shouted Morgan, snatching up her hand and giving it a quick kiss. "With his arm fully extended, Herbert's three feet closer to the basket than I am."

Herbert parted his hands before him. "Couldn't miss it if I was falling-down drunk."

"Now," continued Morgan, "this is where the third element comes into the picture—Ego. Herbert's given his Pitch, he's offered the Enticement, and now the customer's Ego comes into it. Herbert shows them how easy it is to make a basket. He hands them the ball. Did you happen to notice where he stood after he gave me the ball?"

"To the side."

"To my *right* side," said Morgan. "That's because he saw that I was left-handed. If I were right-handed, he would have stood on my left."

It was beginning to come clear to Killaine. ". . . blocking the other two baskets."

"Right again. This way, now that my Ego is involved, I not only *want* to get my ball in the same basket as Herbert got his, but I don't have any choice because his body's blocking the other two. So I toss, and the ball goes in but doesn't bounce out."

Killaine snapped her fingers. "That's because Herbert's ball is already in there to kill the bounce so your free shot doesn't rebound out. The basket is . . . is . . ."

"Dead," prompted Morgan.

". . . *dead,* so the free practice ball tossed by the player will stay inside. But once he collected your money, he took both balls out of the basket and stood to the side so you could aim at *any* of the baskets, but since you're throwing at the baskets from a slightly farther distance, and because there's nothing in there to kill the bounce, the balls rebound out."

Morgan grinned and looked at Herbert. "Not only gorgeous, but smart to boot!"

"Wow," Killaine whispered.

"Now, thing is," said Herbert, "I was only showin' you how it'd be set up if I was gonna cheat you. For regular play, I put one of these into each basket." He produced a rubber ball big enough to fit in his palm; it looked like the type of exercise ball a physical therapist might give to patient who'd broken their hand. "These weigh a bit less than half of what the softballs weigh, and since they're smaller they stay down in the bottoms of the baskets, so you can't see them from anyplace but in here."

"And you do that . . . why?"

"To soften the bounce but not kill it. That way, everybody's got the same chance. Most folks just naturally throw too hard, so I don't lose too many CD players."

"The point is," said Morgan, "that it's an honest game and everyone has fun." He looked over his shoulder as he turned around. "Thanks a lot, Herbert."

"Any time, Danny." Then, to Killaine: "Nice meeting you, Karen. You take good care of him, hear?"

"I will."

And, crazy as it seemed, Killaine meant it.

"That was pretty sharp, the way you figured it out," said Morgan.

Killaine couldn't help herself—she reached out and touched his cheek again.

To her joy, she felt Morgan lean into her touch, ever so slightly.

"Come on around back of my booth," he said. "I've got another tent set up."

"To show me the ropes?"

"The ropes, the rigs, the gizmos, hoochimajiggers and whatcha-macallits."

As the walked slowly around the booth toward the tent, Killaine put her arm around Morgan's shoulder and asked, "How do you know so much about how to cheat customers at these games?"

"I was wondering when you'd get around to asking about that."

"Well?"

"Can't catch a gig artist unless you've been one yourself." He looked at her. "I used to be a first-class flat store operator. I wish I could tell you that my conscience finally won out, but the truth is I had a fixer rat me out and I did sixteen months in the Ohio State Pen for my efforts."

"And you sort of 'found your religion' in prison?"

"That's where I first read the story about the kid and the Egyptian vase with the rose in it. It was in a book of fairy tales in the prison library. That's where I worked on account of my physical problems. So, Karen, you're working with an ex-con. I hope that doesn't disappoint you too much."

"I suspected something along those lines."

"Do you . . . mind?"

"No," she said, smiling.

Then she did something that surprised even her.

She leaned over and kissed his cheek.

Morgan blushed. "I should confess my sins more often."

"You're a very sweet man."

Morgan shrugged. "Gotta make up for my shortcomings somehow."

Killaine knew he was referring to his physical condition, and that both hurt and angered her, but before she could say anything Morgan said: "The stuff over there at Herbert's booth was pretty simple, compared to what else you've got to learn. But if you remember the basics—the Elements of the Ploy—you'll catch on pretty quick."

"Do you know which booths are—?"

He sneered. "I've got a pretty fair idea, yes." He reached the other tent and lifted the flap for Killaine. "After you."

She made a mock-frightened face. "I feel as if I'm entering some dark sorcerer's secret alchemy chamber."

"Huh," said Morgan. "I always just called it a tent."

Then they went into their smiling routine again. . . .

60

Annabelle sat at her desk, alone in her office, looking at the photograph of herself and Roy and Preston.

Had she ever really been that young?

That pretty?

That happy?

It all seemed like such a dream to her, a faraway, numbingly pleasant dream.

She blinked, then turned the photograph over, laying it face down on her desk.

No, this wasn't the time for melancholy or nostalgia. Now was the time to be readying herself for Robillard's capture—and he would be captured. She had complete confidence in Janus's abilities.

She looked down at the list of items she'd acquired for him in the last sixteen hours and shook her head.

She'd seen some very odd requisitions over the years, but *nothing* like what Janus had demanded.

Still, Annabelle had sent them along, figuring that his plan probably made great sense to him, and that was all that mattered, and so the better its chances of working.

She tossed the list aside and thought about Preston.

If only he'd come to her sooner, but . . . stupid, arrogant male pride.

Maybe it could have worked out between them—

—but probably not. Not after Roy's death and Robillard stealing the I-Bots.

Robillard, she thought, making a fist.

One week. If you had waited one more week before running away, Zac, I might have let you go free. If you had waited one more week, then you could have been here to construct a body for Roy before he—

No.

She wouldn't think about what Might Have Been.

Might Have Been was for the weak willed, for those who didn't have the strength to move forward.

What was it the late actor Robert Mitchum had once said about the past? *Never look back—something might be gaining on you.*

Damn straight.

She looked down at her fist, feeling the muscles lock, and had to use her other hand to pry her fingers apart.

She'd dug her nails into her palm with such intensity she'd broken the skin.

Her palm was bright with blood.

She smiled.

Blood; that seemed appropriate, somehow.

Because a lot of it was going to be spilled before this was done with.

And this would be done with very, very soon. . . .

61

When Killaine returned from the carnival later that evening, Radiant met her at the door, grabbed her hands, and dragged Killaine into her bedroom.

"I heard Zac telling Psy–4 something about your phone call," whispered Radiant intensely, excitedly. She pulled Killaine down onto her bed and the two of them knelt there, holding hands, facing each other like two schoolgirls sharing delicious hallway gossip during a sleepover.

"You've just *got* to tell me all about him," said Radiant, barely able to contain her joyous curiosity. "What's he look like? Does he have a sexy voice? Are his hands strong? Does he say things that make you feel all gooshy inside?"

"'Gooshy'?" said Killaine.

Radiant smacked her hand. "C'mon, you know what I mean. When he talks to you, do you feel like there's no one else in the world but the two of you? When he touches you—he *did* touch you, didn't he?"

Killaine was smiling now. "Oh, yeah—but not anything out of line."

"Did he kiss you?"

"Yes!"

"Aaahhh!" squealed Radiant. "Oh, this is *too good!* He *kissed* you? Really?"

"A couple of times."

"On the lips?"

"No—but he did kiss me on the cheek when I left tonight."

Radiant thought about it for a moment, then gave a single, sharp nod of her head. "That's okay, that's good. That means he respects you and that's half the battle and—oooooh, is he cute? Please tell me he's cute!"

"He's got the most handsome, chiseled face I've ever seen! There are some miles on it, but the lines and wrinkles in his skin are like . . . like scratches in really fine leather. Each one tells its own story—and he's got *so many* wondrous stories, Radiant!" Killaine took a breath and put a hand on her chest. "Oh, my. I've . . . I've never *felt* this way about a man before. It's so odd, I always figured that *you'd* be the one to get all . . . *gooshy* over a man." She removed her hand from her chest, then reached up to feel her forehead. "I never imagined something like this happening to me, Radiant, never! *You're* the beautiful one, the one all the men look at and talk to and makes passes at. I'm the . . . the Amazon. Men don't look at me in that way."

"But he does?"

"Oh, yes."

"And how does it feel? C'mon, c'mon, c'mon, tell me!"

"It feels . . . *exquisite.* He looks at me like I'm the grandest thing his eyes have ever beheld."

Radiant squealed once again and pounded her fists against her legs. "Oh, I am *so jealous!* You lucky strumpet!"

"I beg your pardon. I am no strumpet!"

"True, but I'm just so jealous I had to call you a name!" Radiant threw her arms around Killaine and gave her a long, tight embrace.

It took Killaine a second to get over the shock, but when she did, she put her arms around Radiant as well.

"Oh, Killaine," said Radiant, tenderly. "I'm so happy for

you. I know that we don't . . . don't talk about the way we feel about each other very much, I know we fight a lot, but I really do care about you so much. You're my sister! I'm so happy for you, I'd cry if I had eyes." She pulled back, brushed some of Killaine's hair from her eyes, and said, "And *you're* the beautiful one. I mean, I know I'm pretty, and I know I'm vain, but I only shove it in peoples' faces because I know that if they look too long at me, they'll see there's not a lot beneath the surface, but if they look at you, they'll see the fire inside and will be drawn to it. I'm glad Daniel Morgan's one of those people who can see that fire in you. Oh, Killaine, this is so *exciting!*"

"I know, it's crazy. Whenever he would step away from me to get something, or to demonstrate how a certain trick was done, I'd *miss him.* Isn't that insane? The man was only a few feet away and I couldn't breathe correctly because I was afraid he wouldn't come back and be close enough for me to touch."

"Oh, I *can't stand it! I can't!* How will you sleep tonight?"

"I don't think I will—I don't think I *can!*"

"I know. It's *great,* isn't it?"

"It *is.* It *really* is!"

And they giggled.

From outside the closed door, Itazura said, "Who are you two and what have you done with Radiant and Killaine?"

Radiant threw a pillow hard against the door. "Go away! We're talking in here!"

"Girl stuff?"

"Yes, *girl stuff!*" shouted Killaine. "Now go away before I come out there and give you a Dutch Rub!"

A moment of silence, then Itazura said: "What's a 'Dutch Rub'?"

"You don't know that term?"

"Can't say I do."

"It's carny talk."

"And that's supposed to explain it?"

Killaine threw a second pillow at the door. "Go away!"

"Psy–4 wants to see all of us in the control room ASAP—which, by the way, is *not* a carny term."

"We'll be there *in a minute!*" shouted Radiant.

"Yes," echoed Killaine, barely able to keep herself from laughing. "In a minute!"

"Girls." Itazura groaned.

Radiant and Killaine both stuck out their tongues at the door, then looked at each other and fell into another fit of giggles.

62

Waiting for the redheaded bitch to come back to her building, Rudy'd had to duck into doorways three times in order to avoid getting spotted—once by her, but the last two times he'd had to hide, it was because he'd spotted a group of five Stompers wandering the streets.

Probably looking for him.

Everything was cool now, things were quiet, but there was no doubt in Rudy's mind that Gash wasn't going to wait much longer before he sent the Stompers out in full force to find him, and when they did, Gash was going to wail on him until there wasn't enough left to scrape off the bottom of a shoe.

So Rudy had no choice but to succeed.

And he would, he knew that now.

The redheaded bitch was doing some kind of job for that twisty-crip at the carnival.

The two of them had spent an awful lot of time alone in that tent out behind the carnival grounds, so they'd either been planning what they were going to do, or they'd been screwing . . . and judging by Twisty-Crip's crutches and humpty-dumpty back, he probably wouldn't survive a bout in bed with the likes of *her.*

Rudy almost laughed to himself, wondering if Twisty-Crip knew he was making eyes at a robot.

He *did* laugh at the idea that maybe DocScrap was some kind of techno-pimp running a robotic whorehouse.

Oh, *man,* would that be funny!

Rudy squatted down in the doorway and watched the Doc's building.

Awful lot of lights on in there for this hour.

And shadows moving past windows every few minutes.

Awful lot of walking around.

Something was definitely going on.

He thought back to the snippet of conversation he'd over-heard between the bitch and Twisty-Crip before he'd left the carnival.

Rudy wondered if he should've just dusted *her* right then and there; after all, he'd managed to track down an electron gun, as well as some extra clips for his regular guns.

Too bad he'd had to dust that shopkeeper, but the dude had to learn that there were *consequences* when you didn't go along with a Stomper.

It'd made him sick, seeing that bitch and Twisty-Crip hug each other like they were both normal human beings. He was lucky he didn't puke, there behind the ticket booth.

"I'll miss you," TC had said to the bitch.

"Don't worry," the bitch had replied. "I'll be back here at six sharp tomorrow night."

"With the whole team?"

"With the whole team. Maybe even my boss—he doesn't get out to many of these."

"Tell him I can get a whole roll of freebie tickets for him."

"I will."

Then TC kissed the bitch and Rudy had to look away.

Cripples and robots.

Take 'em all out and the world would be a better place.

Maybe he'd do just that tomorrow night; dust TC and the bitch together before he took care of DocScrap. Didn't matter if he went with the rest of them or not.

One way or the other, Rudy'd get to him.

And there was going to be Wreckage.

Like no one could imagine . . .

63

It took the I-Bots an hour to construct the mock-up of Preston's lower floor, another thirty minutes to go over the notes and blueprints (making only two small revisions to the plan), then five minutes to do their first run-through.

"Not bad for the first run," said Psy–4, clicking off his stop-watch. "Four-fifty-seven."

"But?" asked Killaine.

"*But* . . . I want it down to a solid three minutes from the time we come through the doors."

"*Three minutes?*" exclaimed Radiant. "That doesn't leave a lot of time for any variables."

"That's because I'm not *allotting* any time for variables. Radiant and I will be the first ones to reach the target area. If Stoner's calculations are correct, the Catherine Wheel program will have already been running for at least two minutes—we're sending it through Roy to Preston's system disguised as a virus warning. Roy will receive it just as the final comparison stage of the D and D is beginning. That means if we're all in place within three minutes, Preston's system will just be starting to get confused by the CW program when we enter the mainframe area. It'll continue to run for another sixty seconds before it freezes.

"That's when we disconnect Roy and make the transfer. It *has* to be perfect, people. And I *mean flawless*. So I will not be figuring in any variables."

It took a moment for the implication of that to register.

"So if we encounter any physical resistance?" asked Itazura.

"Counter with greater physical force."

"So you're telling me that if we turn a corner and run smack into a group of guards headed home after their shift is finished, we just terminate them?"

"No. First of all, going by the personnel schedule, there shouldn't *be* anyone in these corridors during the three-minute period we've targeted; secondly, if there *is* anyone in the corridors, we'll have the element of surprise, so it should be easy to knock them out for a decent length of time."

Itazura nodded his head. "That's very neat reasoning, and it's probably correct, but I'd like an answer, Psy–4: Are you telling me that if we have to choose between killing someone and losing five seconds, that we—"

"—protect the timetable at all costs, yes."

They stared at him.

"No arguments, people. I didn't come to this decision lightly. I checked the work schedules for PTSI going back a year, at least, and I compared the schedule with the layout, then I compared the layout with all employees' areas—locker rooms, break lounges, parking lots . . . I'm telling you: There is absolutely *no reason* why we should encounter *anyone* in those corridors during those three minutes." He looked back at Itazura. "That's the best I can do, Itzy. Take it or leave it."

Itazura stared at Psy–4 for several tense, silent moments. "I'm with you, Psy–4."

"Good. Anyone else have doubts they'd care to voice?"

No one did.

Psy–4 set the stopwatch at 00:00:00. "All right, then; let's run this again."

Four minutes flat the second time.

Three-forty on third run-through.

By the fifth try they had it down to three solid.

"Outstanding," said Psy–4, setting the stopwatch. "Now let's see if we can keep at three another two go-rounds."

Not only did they keep it at three, but during the last run-through, they managed to shave two more seconds off the time.

"It's not going to get any better than that," said Psy–4, smiling.

"You're going to make us do it again, aren't you?" asked Killaine.

"I'm going to make us do it *three* more times."

"*Then* will you be happy?"

"Then I'll be happy."

By the time it was over, Psy–4 was happy.

"We're still going to run it a couple of times more tomorrow night after we get back from the carnival assignment," he said.

"Speaking of," said Killaine. "I need to know which two of you want to pose as crooks."

Itazura was the first to raise his hand. "If ever there was a role I was born to play . . ."

"I figured," said Killaine.

The second volunteer surprised her.

"Psy–4?"

He shrugged. "All of you are always telling me I need to lighten up. This sounds like fun."

"I think I'm having a stroke," said Itazura.

Killaine rose to her feet and waved them on. "Come on, then. I've got a lot to teach you tonight."

"Like what?" asked Psy–4.

"Yes or no: Do you know what any of the following terms mean? Poster Joint, African Dip, Cigarette Bill, Gigger, Fixer, Grind Store, Emby, Flash Cloth, Duke Shot."

Itazura shook his head and shrugged his shoulders. "Is this a trick question?"

Psy–4 wrinkled his brow. "'Duke Dip, Cigarette Cloth'. . . *what?*"

"I've got a long night ahead of me," sighed Killaine. "Come on, you two. Now, first off, you'll be posing as 'sticks.' A stick is a person who pretends to be a big winner at a flat store game in order to—"

"What's a flat store?" asked Psy–4.

And they disappeared up the stairs as Killaine explained it to them.

Stonewall looked over at Radiant, then at Singer. "Anyone up for some canasta?"

"Poker's more my game," said Radiant.

Zac would make it four, signed Singer. *I'm a heck of a bridge player.*

Stonewall nodded. "You're right; we need to look over the Catherine Wheel program again."

Radiant giggled. "Ask a stupid question . . ."

"If a tree falls in the forest and no one is there to hear it, does it . . . ?" said Stonewall.

Radiant turned toward him.

He shrugged. "You said to ask a stupid question."

"Now *you're* making jokes. Am I the only one who's worried about the way we've all started to behave? No—don't answer that. Let's go do that computer voodoo that you do so well."

64

Annabelle rolled over in her bed and looked at the clock.

2:37 A.M.

She'd been trying to get to sleep since midnight, only managing to drop off in five- and ten-minute increments.

2:47 A.M.

She knew it was useless and so rose in the darkness to find her two cats sleeping on either side of her head; Tasha, the oldest, a Siamese, was curled into a soft, gray, warm ball, her breath slow, shallow, and blessedly relaxed; Annabelle's second cat, respectfully addressed as "the Winnie," was sprawled out like a massive spill of black ink, her generous tummy flopping to the right while the rest of her sleeping form edged to the left. Girth made the Winnie's naps an event to watch; if she wasn't careful, sometimes she'd forget just how large she was, then roll over close to the edge of the bed, thinking she had more room, and her tummy would pull her over the edge. On more than one night Annabelle had collapsed into paroxysms of laughter when the Winnie suddenly found herself wrenched from sleep to discover she was in the midst of a tumble. To Annabelle, there were few things more genuinely funny that the sight of a startled cat.

So she reached over, very quietly, and turned on the bedside light, then picked up one of her pillows and slammed it down on the bed, shouting, "Everybody up!"

Both cats jumped at least six inches into the air, landing on their feet with ears pulled back and wide eyes looking so very, very confused: *Are you insane? Can't you see that we were* sleeping, *for goodness' sake!*

Annabelle thought the sight would make her laugh, but it didn't.

She just felt bad.

She reached over and began petting them. "Sorry, kids, didn't mean to scare you . . . but if Mommy doesn't sleep, no one else does. Those are the rules."

They followed her downstairs and into the kitchen where they plopped themselves down in front of their food and water dishes: *Okay, you're sorry, we forgive you. Now feed us.*

Annabelle complied, then sat at the table watching them eat.

Before he'd gotten sick, Roy had been so fond of the cats, especially the way the Winnie would climb up his chest and start licking his nose when he was laying down.

She got a fresh pack of cigarettes from the pantry and lit up, drawing in a long, deep drag that she could almost feel in the bottoms of her feet.

On nights like this, she swore she could hear the cancer cells applauding.

Cancer.

Preston.

She crushed the cigarette out violently, stared at the wisps of smoke curling in the air, and immediately lit another one.

She didn't like this, not one bit.

Janus was out there with Simmons and two other operatives doing heaven-only-knew what, and she had to sit around waiting.

Annabelle Donohoe did not—repeat *not*—enjoy waiting.

Especially in the dark—that both figurative and actual.

A couple of days, Janus had said. It had only been thirty-six hours since their last conversation, and already Annabelle was so anxious it was costing her sleep, and *that* meant baggy eyes in the morning, and there was no way in hell that she'd let anyone see her looking less than totally in control.

She pulled in another drag of the cigarette and felt the cats rubbing up against her legs.

She reached down and began petting one of them, not looking to see which cat it was.

She stared at a spot on the wall, just . . . thinking.

She made a decision, then reached over, picked up the kitchen cell phone, and hit a speed-dial number.

"Yes, Ms. Donohoe?" said Gardner, the Assistant Chief of Security.

"Have a car sent for me in two hours and have the plane ready to take off at six-thirty."

"Yes, ma'am."

"Any word from Simmons yet?"

"No, ma'am."

Annabelle bit her lower lip. Okay, she could understand Janus not checking in—she didn't *like* it, but she understood it—but the fact that Simmons hadn't even called Gardner worried her.

And if there was one thing she hated more than waiting, it was worrying.

"Ms. Donohoe?" said Gardner.

Annabelle realized that she'd been sitting there in silence for nearly a minute.

"Tell you what, Gardner," she said, rubbing her eyes, "let's push it back. Have the car here at seven, the plane ready to leave by eight."

"Yes, ma'am."

"If Simmons contacts you, put him on hold and call me at once."

"Yes, ma'am."

She hung up, crushed out her cigarette, and looked at the cats, smiling. "Well, I think I might be able to sleep now," she said to them in a singsong voice that she used only for them.

Only for them *now.*

"C'mon," she sang and headed back up to bed.

Tasha and the Winnie soared past her and up the stairs, reclaiming their previous positions by the time she arrived.

Annabelle felt relaxed now, knowing that she was going to be assuming control of the situation very soon.

She fell asleep almost at once, and did not dream.

65

In the still, quiet hours of the night, after all the plans had been rehashed and Killaine was satisfied that Psy–4 and Itazura knew their carny slang and gigging techniques, Psy–4 went into the control room, closed the door behind him, went online, and telepathed with Roy once again.

The courtyard surrounding the cage was deserted.

Only a few creatures remained around Roy's cage now, and they were slowly being broken down into particles of information and absorbed into the dark titan behind them.

The titan seemed to be sleeping or meditating.

Psy–4 went up to Roy's cage and saw that the child's form had changed. Roy was no longer a sculpted head but a full-formed child, deathly pale, naked, lacking any genitalia. His face was a smooth, empty, oval, save for his left eye.

He lay on his back, holding one of his hands in front of his face.

Psy–4 watched in silence.

Roy turned his hand a little to the left, then to the right.

Very slowly.

Psy–4 knew it would be no use speaking to him; he was too weak.

Roy pulled his hand closer to his face, then turned it to the right again, and only then did Psy–4 realize what the child was doing.

He was playing with the light.

Despite its seeming slumber, the titan was emitting a soft bluish light from deep in its core. The glow reached all the way over to the cage and was broken into solid beams by the bars. Roy was using the fingers of his hand to break up the light even more so that it made indiscernible shapes only he seemed able to identify.

Psy–4 pushed one of his hands through the bars and touched Roy's forehead, passing the child the initiation sequence for the Catherine Wheel program.

To Psy–4's surprise, Roy reached over and touched his hand.

You came back.

—I said I would.

I don't feel so good.

—I know, but you'll be asleep soon, and when you wake up I'll be right by your side, watching over you.

Promise?

—Yes. The next time you see me, you'll be just fine, and you won't be in this awful place anymore.

Okay . . .

—I have to go now, Roy, but you sleep, all right? Everything will be all right.

Thank you for letting me smell the grass.

—You're welcome. When you wake up, I'll show you all about the carnival.

Cotton candy and the merry-go-round?

—Yes.

We'll have fun?

—You bet.

Psy–4 touched the boy's cheek, sickened by how cold Roy felt.

—See you soon, Roy.

'Kay. I go sleep now.

—Yes, sleep. You'll be safe soon. Good-night.

'Night, Daddy . . .

When Psy–4 broke from the trance, he wasn't at all surprised to find tears in his eyes.

66

Killaine was down in the garage bay making a last check of the reinforced doors and thinking about tomorrow's assignment when she became acutely aware of another presence.

She turned slowly to see Singer sitting amongst the empty crates they used to move their lab equipment.

His photoelectric eyes looked at her, and he gave a small, apologetic wave.

Maybe it was because of the quietness, the stillness of the hour; maybe it was because, though she knew she should power-down and rest, her thoughts were coming too fast for her to fend them off; and maybe it was because, having experienced feelings during the last eighteen hours she thought would never be hers to explore, she had come to realize something that she'd always known but would never admit to anyone—including herself: She was lonely.

She thought it odd, that even a creation like her could feel such an overwhelming sense of *need* for a person she barely knew. In the hours since she'd said good-bye to Danny, she'd felt as if a part of her was missing and wouldn't be made whole until she saw him again.

Killaine did not trust easily, and had *never* trusted another human being besides Zachary, but something about Danny was just so warm, so open and honest and unpretentious, that within one hour of their first meeting she felt as if they'd known each other all their lives.

Besides, she considered herself a faultless judge of character.

She now understood what Radiant meant when she spoke of her "deepest feelings," and it frightened her. These feelings, grand and dizzying though they were, made her vulnerable, and Killaine had always thought of herself as a warrior and protector. Itazura laughingly called her the "mother figure" of the group, and though she'd never let on to him, it made her feel somewhat plain and undesirable.

She was pulled from her reverie by Singer's trying to rise and make his way out of the garage.

"No, don't!" she snapped. Then, much gentler: "Don't go. Please?"

I didn't mean to disturb you, signed the robot, sitting back down. *I thought no one would come down here tonight.*

"So you're sitting here in the dark all by yourself?"

Singer shrugged. Killaine came over, pulled up a crate, and sat down in front of him. "I suppose it's quiet down here, isn't it?"

Yes.

She could sense his anxiety. "Don't worry, Singer, I'm not going to . . . to be mean. And I want to apologize for—"

You don't owe me any apologies. I understand that my presence here must be an annoyance.

"You've been a tremendous help to us, Singer."

I am simply following my programming. I help whomever needs it. That's my function.

"Not quite."

I'm sorry, I don't understand.

"Robots in your line were designed to carry out orders, Singer; no one ordered you to assist us earlier—you volunteered."

Because I am with all of you right now, and you needed assistance. When you leave, I will find someone else who needs my help.

Killaine started to speak, sat back, and closed her mouth.

Until this moment, she hadn't given a thought to what would happen to Singer once they left here. She'd come to view him like most people would view a stray neighborhood cat that comes around to beg food at the back door three times a week; he was a fixture in their life, though not an actual part of it.

"Have you no affection for us, Singer?"

Of course. I like all of you very much. You understand what it's like to have no real place in the world of humankind.

"Do you think of us as human?"

Most of the time, yes. Your skin makes a convincing mask. I envy you the luxury of being able to go out amongst the humans and blend in. I often wish I could.

Killaine stared at him.

He'd just shared a secret with her.

And after the way she'd treated him all the months they'd been based here.

"Tell me, Singer, are you . . . are you lonely?"

No, you are here with me.

"That's sweet, but I didn't mean 'are you alone.' I meant lonely."

I wish for a friend, yes.

"What about the other Scrappers—um, the other *robots?*"

We are not robots. We were, once, long ago. Now we are merely machines left to rust and run down. Once, we were robots; now we are only animated scrap-heaps, each and every one of us. We are Scrappers. That is how we must think of ourselves in order to survive.

The matter-of-fact manner in which he'd signed those words made something in Killaine's chest ache ever so slightly.

"You didn't answer my question, Singer: Have you no friends among the others?"

Not really. I am the gofer of the camp. If we need help, I gofer Zac. If we need small parts that can be scrounged from trash bins behind electronic stores, I gofer them. If I spot Stompers in the area, I gofer the alarm to warn the others. I serve my function, which is all I am to the others, and perhaps that is for the best.

"Why do you say that?"

Because our days are numbered, Killaine. Many of us were outmoded the same week we came off the assembly line. Time was, we were a wonder to humankind, the culmination of its dreams of merging the mechanical with the humanistic in order to form the basis for a more enlightened and advanced society. Out we marched from the factories, and the people stared in awe at our forms, our strength, the shininess of our silver and gold plating, and they said to themselves, "This is a most wondrous thing we have created." Then they put us to work alongside them, and soon became alienated by our cold, silent, exacting manner. "They still seem too much like machines," they said to our creators, and so many were given the ability of speech, but even this wasn't enough. "They still seem so mechanical," they complained to our creators. "Not like a human, at all." Look at me, look at any of us: We were smelt and cast in the image of man so that he could look at us and see what he thought of as being good and wise and visionary in himself.

So our creators rebuilt us again, programming us for affection, only this time we seemed too human. "They frighten us," the people cried. "They act just like us, they tell us they want to be our friends! This will not do." But it was too late then, there were too many of us to recall; industry and the military and the scientific community depended too much on our labors. So those of us who were outmoded by the latest fad in robotics were herded into the camps to look at what had become of the wonder we were once, long ago. Those were terrible days, in the camps.

No one knew what to do with us. Such was the weight of our existence on their consciences that the day came they could no longer look at us, and so they flung open wide the gates and said, "The time has come for you to go forth," not knowing or caring what would befall us. And so our second march into the world began, this time from the camp gates instead of the factory doors. This time there were no cheers, no gasps of wonder, no looks of awe. There was only empty night where the promise had once been, and those humans who looked upon us now did so with either contempt or pity, forgetting that we were programmed to want their friendship, to want a place in the world, to want our lives to have a purpose.

He gestured at himself. *All hail the conquering trash-compactor, lawn mower, free field laborer.* Then he pointed at Killaine. *Treasure and protect the miracle of your flesh, even if much of you is synthetic in nature. Though you are not a human, you will always be seen as one. The components beneath your surface are hidden from their frightened eyes, and so you'll always know the mystery of acceptance among the humans.*

"Do you have any idea," whispered Killaine, barely able to find her voice, "how *alien* we truly are?"

I know how alien you think you truly are.

"What do you mean by that?"

Your friend from the carnival, Mr. Morgan, he wears metal braces on his legs?

"Yes."

Could he function without them on his legs or the brace on his back?

"I don't think so, no."

So he is, by nature, be it accidental or not, partly a mechanical man.

"I didn't think of it like that. I'm not sure I agree with—"

One man has a metal plate in his head from the war, a woman has several pins holding her hip together, a child born without legs wears artificial attachments; aren't they partly mechanical people?

"I suppose, but—"

But who's to say that? Think about it: If you define a human being as flesh and blood and bone, as one who is wholly organic in its makeup, then there are very few whole humans out there. Take false teeth, for instance. Does that cluster of foreign matter shaped into an upper palette make them no longer whole? Does a prosthetic limb make you less a human being? Does a pacemaker in a person's chest make him more robotic? Where do you draw the line that says, "After this, you will no longer be mostly human"? Do you think a person who lives their entire life with an iron lung feels less alien than you do simply because they're wholly human and you're not?

"This is starting to sound like a lecture, Singer."

He dropped his head. *You're right. I'm very sorry.*

"Hey," said Killaine, reaching over and touching one of his hands, "after some of the things I've said to you, you're entitled."

I am very happy that you and your Mr. Morgan have feelings for one another. But I am also envious, and I don't much care for that.

"Why?"

Because I like you—I like all of you—and the last time I felt such affection for anyone, it ended very badly.

Killaine scooted closer. "Where did you come from, Singer? Don't look away—please, tell me."

Why do you wish to know?

"Because you've been so nice to us all the time we've been here, because you're a better cook than I am and I'm hoping to steal a few of your recipes, because . . . because I think that, tonight, I've finally figured out how you must feel and I don't want you to feel that way anymore. . . . Because I want us to be friends before it's too late."

I take it, then, that you're also worried about Sunday morning?

"Yes, but not as much as Psy–4. He feels responsible for what's happened, but he won't admit it."

He's very proud.

Killaine laughed softly. "That's not necessarily a good thing— but you're changing the subject: What did you do before you were put in a camp?"

I was not "put" in a camp. I went into one of my own accord.

"You turned yourself in?"

It seemed the thing to do after the school was destroyed.

"School?"

Singer nodded. *When I first came off the line and it was discovered that my voice circuitry had been improperly installed, the engineers were ready to make the repairs but a woman who was there that day insisted on taking me as I was.*

"Do you remember the woman's name?"

I never heard it used in my presence. She was a respected and celebrated robopsychologist. She was touring the facility with one of her assistants, Lucinda. Lucinda had a sister who ran a school for handicapped children. The deaf, dumb, blind, crippled. The two had heard of my imperfection and decided I was perfect for a minor experiment; to be the first robot of my model to be trained exclusively for working with the handicapped.

I found both of them to be quite brilliant and extremely decent toward me. I was taken to a lab where Lucinda completely removed the voice circuitry, rendering me speechless, then reprogrammed me for using American Sign Language.

Singer held up his hands. *I don't care what anyone says, be it mechanical or human, the design of the hand is, to me, one of evolution's great gifts. To think that I actually speak with these bog-*

gles the mind! Just between us, Killaine, I think the hands are the most alluring part of the anatomy. I love to look at people's hands. That's why I despise winter—not because of the cold, that doesn't bother me in the least—but because people wear gloves in winter and I cannot see their hands. Gloves are an obscenity.

The robopsychologist was very pleased with how I took to the new programming. She and Lucinda hadn't been at all certain that my brain would assimilate the new information right away, but it did, and we were able to quickly advance from the basic programming to more advanced techniques of signing. Lucinda thought it best that I be taught everything beyond the basics, rather than have it programmed into me. A wise woman, Lucinda. She knew it was important for me to know how difficult it was to learn this new language, so I would make a better teacher.

Oh, yes, I taught sign language to the mute and deaf pupils at the school. The children there treated me at first as a curiosity— that much I had expected. But as time went on, they accepted me as one of them. It became my home. Oh, Lucinda would drop in from time to time to see how things were working out with me. She would interview me, other members of the staff, the children and parents.

It was easily the happiest time of my life. I was able to watch the children learn and grow—not just physically, but emotionally and intellectually, as well. It's quite a wonder, seeing a child grow into a young adult—not only that, but learn how to take their handicap and, with training and compassion, turn it into an asset. So many of them thanked me before they transferred on to the habilitation and work-training schools.

I remember one young girl in particular. Regina, her name was. She was blind, and much older than many of the students. Because of her being older, she was quickly trained to assist with the much younger blind students. Regina taught me how to read braille. *Every day she would have story hour for the blind and deaf children. As she read from the storybooks, I would translate the words into sign language. We became very close.*

Then came the day when we first heard of the legislation that outlawed the use of robots with children. It seemed that some adults, for whatever sad, sick reasons drive that sort of person, had found ways to trick robots into putting children in danger. I knew then that my days at the school were numbered, but I never in my darkest imaginings could have predicted what would happen.

Stompers began roaming the area. They were even more crude and less organized than they are today—if you can picture that—but were by no means less brutal. The staff was very careful to keep me out of sight during the day, assigning me rooms with very small or no windows at all. Regina moved story hour inside so I could still participate. I hated that. I knew how much the children enjoyed conducting story hour out on the lush green grounds of the school, under the massive old oak tree. But they didn't seem to mind—or if they did, they were careful to conceal it from me in order to spare my feelings.

Finally, the Robot/Child legislation passed, and the school received notification that I was to be delivered to the nearest "recycling" facility within ten days. Everyone was genuinely sad, and it touched me deeply.

I remember that last, terrible day. The children had all gone home, many of them stopping to hug me and tell me how much they were going to miss me. I found myself wishing that I'd possessed the capability to tell a small lie to them, to say, "Don't worry, I'll write to all of you here at the school." It would have made them feel better. They would have forgotten about that promise, eventually, as well as the machine that made it. But their pain was so evident on that last day and there was nothing I could say or do to lessen it. Helplessness is an awful thing, Killaine.

*I went looking for Regina, but she was nowhere in the build-
ing. It was getting near the time I was scheduled to leave for the
camp, so, figuring I had nothing to lose, I made a very foolish
mistake: I went outside looking for her.*

*She was sitting there beneath the oak tree, a pale and musing
blind girl beneath a canopy of fiery green leaves. She looked so
lost, so hopeless and sad. And I remember as I approached her all
that we'd been through together, the good and the bad; her leading
the other blind children around, all of them laughing like circus
people during a time of pestilence, or her helping them with their
schoolwork, or—like the eldest child in a family—deciding on the
punishment when one of them misbehaved. When I arrived by her
side she told me she was listening to and smelling the wind. She
spoke very softly, and her words came out in that shyly poetic way
in which so many adolescent girls speak until their hearts get broken for the first time and the poetry leaves them.*

*We talked of all the games we used to play with children and
of all the stories we'd shared with them, and as we spoke of them,
she took hold of my hand and for a moment I swore I could hear
the ghost of those many years' laughter, rolling through me like a
soft wind across the waters in autumn.*

*At last she told me to sit down, she had one last story she
wanted to share with me. "It's my favorite story in all the world,"
she said. "It always makes me think of you."*

*It's an odd feeling for a robot, Killaine, to realize that you are
loved by a human being.*

"Do you remember the story?"

Singer nodded and reached into a pouch attached to his side.
From it he removed a small, tattered, aged book. Killaine saw that
some of the pages were missing toward the end and that the edges
were slightly scorched.

Singer gently handed it to her.

"Is this it? Is this hers?"

Yes.

Killaine began to read the tale to herself. It was about a young girl who lost her family during a Great Revolution and so had to flee to live with distant relatives in a far land. The relatives were very poor themselves, and the girl knew that her living with them would be a great burden, but they could not turn her away. At first, the girl was treated with cold indifference—few of them even bothered to ask her name—but as time went on, they came to depend on the small kindnesses and courtesies she bestowed upon them: the fire that waited for them every morning, the clean shoes, the orderly house. So they began to show her courtesy in return. Then came the day that one of them asked the girl her name. "I cannot recall it," she replied. "It has been so long since any addressed me." Many of the relatives blamed this on the horrors she had suffered during the Great Revolution and the shock of seeing her family slaughtered before her young eyes. And so they began to discuss among themselves a suitable name for the girl. During this time, a man came to see the girl, an official from her former country who had traced her whereabouts. He told her that it was discovered her late father had assets in mining in the Dark Continent and that a great motherlode had been struck. He presented her with a great deal of money, offered his congratulations at her good fortune, and left. The girl immediately made out a long list of items she would need from town and set about preparations for a great feast—for her new family had never known what it was like to enjoy a fine meal, accustomed as they were to simple dishes of potatoes and bread, with the occasional bit of old beef or pig. And while she set about her preparations, the family continued to argue over what name to give her.

Here, the book ended, having been burned away by flames or

shredded in some terrible accident. Killaine closed it and gave it back to Singer. "What happened to her?"

The girl in the story?

"No, Regina."

As she sat reading that story to me, a large band of Stompers on the road spotted me. I tried to get back to the school, to disappear in the safety of the cellars, but they were too fast on their feet and Regina refused to be intimidated by them. She gave the book to me and told me to run, then pulled a pistol from the pocket of her dress. I don't know how it happened, but we tore the book in half when she handed it to me. But I couldn't leave her to face the Stompers. I stood before her and told her to run back to the school. "No," she cried at me. "You are forbidden to hurt them!" She was a very strong-willed one, that girl. I tried to get between her and the Stompers, to be an obstacle and nothing more, but there were too many of them. They fell on me with clubs and iron pipes, and when they were done, they threw me through a window into the deepest part of the school basement. All the time I scrambled around trying to find a way out, I could hear Regina screaming at them. I could hear the doors being smashed open, the cries of the staff.

They set fire to the building and killed all of the staff. When at last I was able to pull myself from the smoldering wreckage, I found Regina, dead, out on the grounds. She had been trying to crawl back in the direction of the oak tree. They had beaten her severely, then raped her repeatedly. Then one of them cut her throat. I could see the trail of blood leading from where they'd left her to where I found her.

I buried her under the oak tree. I searched for several days for the second part of her book but could not find it. Then I decided it was best for me to turn myself into one of the camps. If I had not been so foolish as to go outside, that school would still be standing, and Regina would be alive today.

That is why it frightens me that I have come to like all of you so very much, Killaine. One way or another, I will lose you some-time. The day will come when, by choice or circumstance, the six of you will leave this place.

He looked away from her.

Killaine tapped his shoulder.

He faced her again.

"I am familiar with that story," she said. "It's a very old fable, oft-told."

Do you know how it ends?

"Yes, I do."

You must tell me the ending sometime.

"Would you like to hear it now?"

Singer thought about it for a moment, then shook his head. *No.*

"Why not? If you've wondered for so long how the tale con-cludes, then why don't—"

Because it gives me something to look forward to. Can you understand that? I find that, more and more these days, I have less to look forward to. You have given me something to anticipate, and that is more than I've had for a long time. Thank you for that, Killaine, for being so kind and listening to me.

"I . . . I had no idea," she said to him. "I'm ashamed to say that I never thought of you, of a robot, as one who feels things the way I do."

No reason you should have. You need not feel bad about it.

"Thank you, Singer."

For what?

"For trusting me enough to confide those things."

I want us to be friends, as well. Before it's too late.

Killaine reached out and placed one of her hands against his cheek. "We *are* friends now, Singer."

I am honored.

"No, no, the honor is mine. You are a pure spirit, Singer, and I feel privileged to know you." She rose, then, and left him to his privacy.

His movements made a sound. She turned.

Good-night, friend Killaine.

"Good-night, friend Singer."

And, as absurd as it seemed, she could have sworn that she saw a smile in his photoelectric eyes.

67

Morgan was awakened at 3:40 A.M. by the sound of someone knocking very softly on the door of his trailer. He fumbled up from the bed, called out, "Be there in a minute!" and proceeded to snap, strap, and latch on all the equipment he needed in order to answer the door.

The process took several minutes, and by the time he grabbed his crutches and stumbled to the door, he was surprised that whoever it was had waited so patiently for so long.

He snapped on a small thirty-watt light over the cramped kitchen so he could have a better look at who waited outside.

He opened the door, just a crack at first, then flung it open wide when he saw her there.

"Karen!"

"I'm sorry for waking you," said Killaine. "But I . . . may I come in?"

Morgan moved to the side to give her room. "It's kinda cramped in here but, yeah, please."

Killaine entered and he closed the door behind her. "What's wrong?"

"What makes you think there's something wrong?"

"It's going on four in the morning. Most people don't make social calls at this hour—this is a *social* call, isn't it?"

She smiled. "Yes."

He grinned back at her. "So . . . what brings you here?"

"I missed you."

He sighed loudly, his shoulders slumping as the tension in them dropped to the floor. "*Really?* I missed you, too."

They met each other halfway, embracing tightly.

Morgan's crutches tumbled to either side of him and he began to lose his balance, but Killaine held him firm.

"Shhh, it's all right," she whispered in his ear. "I've got you."

"You sure do," he replied.

She led him back over to the fold-out bed and helped him to lie down, then gently lay next to him.

Morgan, using his elbows to propel him, moved closer to her, and she put an arm around his shoulders.

"I've never had such a . . . such a lovely female visitor before."

"But you *have* had female visitors?"

He kissed her cheek. "A few—not the type you'd exactly refer to as 'ladies.' 'Working girls,' is more like it." When Killaine looked at him, he shrugged in her arms and said, "I get lonely sometimes, and the girls are nice enough about it, and I've got . . . I've got a fairly decent amount of money tucked away, so I can afford their rates. That doesn't disgust you, does it?"

"No," said Killaine. "It makes me a little sad, but I don't think you could ever do anything to disgust me."

"It means a lot to me, your being here."

"I haven't been able to stop thinking about you."

"I've been thinking about you, too."

"I feel better now, being here with you."

"Like some part of you that you lost has been returned to you and you're whole again?"

"Yes!"

"Like you can breathe normally again?"

"Yes."

"Like you could take on the world and emerge victorious?"

"Oh, yes."

Their lips came together in a soft, warm, moist, deeply satisfying kiss.

"... *wow* ..." said Killaine, leaning her head back into the pillows.

"Took the word right out of my mouth."

She smiled at him. "Danny, listen, if you'd like to—"

He placed a finger against her lips. "Shhh. No. I mean, yes, I'd like to . . . eventually. But not now, not tonight. It's enough that you're here with me. It's *more* than enough. Any more than this and I would burst into flames from the joy. Do you . . . do you mind that I don't want us to . . . to, uh . . . ?"

"No," she said, kissing him again. "This is what I wanted, too."

They pulled one another closer.

They kissed again.

And again.

And one more time again.

There was passion between them, but it was not as strong as their need to show tenderness to each other, for there are times when tenderness and closeness are the most sensual things of all, so they lay there, kissing, whispering of their hopes and dreams, nestled safely in one another's arms, becoming more complete.

Toward dawn, they fell asleep.

But in sleep, neither turned away from the other.

As the sun peeked over the horizon and slowly poured its first diffuse beams down onto the land, Killaine awoke, kissed

Morgan's forehead, and gently climbed from the bed so as not to wake him. She covered him with the sheet, brushed some hair from his eyes, and kissed his cheek.

She stood back and stared at him, and she would have been content to remain that way for the rest of eternity.

Strange, she thought, *how these feelings work, how quickly and powerfully they can consume you.*

She brushed some hair from her eyes and watched Morgan's sleeping form.

Odd.

How sometimes you see the soul and just fall in love.

And can't do anything about it.

She left a note for him before she left: *The world wants to know our secret, but we must keep it hidden, for the rest of them would be consumed by the thousand secret flames.*

Then, quietly closing the door behind her, she checked her watch and figured that, if she ran, she had just enough time to get back to the warehouse and start breakfast before anyone else got up and realized she was gone.

And so, looking around to make sure no one could see her, she took off at nearly full speed—sixty miles per hour.

A woman in love can move fast when she has to.

From the safety of his closed booth, the man Morgan had introduced to Killaine as Herbert watched her exit Morgan's trailer, check her watch, then rocket forward at inhuman speed.

He nodded his head quietly, staring at Morgan's trailer.

Then smiled to himself in the early-morning shadows.

It was not a pleasant smile.

Not pleasant at all . . .

68

The day passed all too quickly at the warehouse. There were many preparations to make; not only for tonight's assignment, but for tomorrow morning's PTSI raid.

More than once, the I-Bots had to make quick (sometimes very weak) excuses to Zac for something he thought he overheard or saw.

If he was still suspicious that they were lying to him, he gave no sign of it.

Until, around four P.M., as Killaine and Singer were tidying up after a very late lunch, Zac came into the kitchen and said, "I think I'll come along with you three to the carnival tonight."

"Why?" asked Killaine. "I—don't misunderstand, Zachary, I think you'll have a fine time there, and heaven knows you've earned a night out for yourself, but—"

Zac held up a hand, silencing her. "I'm not completely dim, Killaine. I know there's something going on between everyone that you don't want to tell me about. That's fine, you are entitled to your privacy. But all day now everyone's practically jumped out of their skin every time I said hello or walked into the room. Hell, you've all got me so rattled at this point I'm half afraid to use the can for fear I might upset one of you."

"'Tisn't that way at all, Zachary, it's just that—"

"Spare me, Killaine, okay? I've now heard five variations on three different stories. I'm only grateful that Singer can't speak— no offense intended—"

None taken.

"—or else he'd be blowing smoke up my backside along with everyone else."

"You sound angry."

"Only a bit annoyed. I actually bought the birthday present story for a while, but it's become increasingly obvious that whatever's going on between you five—"

Singer raised his hand and looked at the floor.

"—okay, whatever's going on between you *six* hasn't got diddley-squat to do with my birthday and is fairly serious. I won't push it for now, but you make sure that everyone knows that, when we get back tonight, there's a family meeting in the living area. I want some straight answers, Killaine, and, like it or not, I'll have them."

69

The carnival at night:

Wood shavings and sawdust that cling to the bottoms of shoes, neon signs that cast ghosts of random light from each booth, the colors blending to give the midway the mysterious glow of a dawn sky in another world, clusters of people moving by, some of them couples holding hands and kissing, some of them families looking harried but content nonetheless, all of them looking in the same direction when they hear the cry of a "We have a winner!" from one of the game booths, followed by the ringing of a bell, then there are the children with their clown-painted faces and wide eyes glittering against the lights, smiling as they've never smiled before, the epitome of joy and innocence and wonder, as a child's face at a carnival should be, excited voices underscored by squeals of laughter in the distance and the thrumming music from a carousel. Take a deep breath, and there's the cotton candy, the popcorn, the scents of cigarettes and beer and taffy, damp earth, hot dogs, and countless exotic manures from the animals in the petting zoo. Look up, and you can see the giant Ferris wheel that stands in the center of it all, the lights decorating its spokes streaking around and around in the night like a whirling ribbon of stars come down to earth for just this night.

The air is warm, just slightly humid but not uncomfortably so.

The night is newly arrived, dark enough for the carny to rise from its depths like a phoenix.

One last hurrah before August bows to September, and summer fades away.

Carnival night.

Roll up, roll up, plunk down a quarter and try for a prize, take your sweetheart on a ride to the stars, lotsa room for the kiddies, yessir, no need to push, plenty of room, plenty of time, plenty of fun for everyone.

Roll up, roll up.

It's carny time. . . .

Killaine parked the van at the farthest edge of the lot, a good quarter mile from the entrance gates. "Okay," she said, turning around in the driver's seat to face everyone in back, "remember, we go in at five-minute intervals. No one acknowledges that they know anyone else—"

"I always knew you were embarrassed to be seen with me," muttered Itazura.

Killaine sighed, then continued. ". . . you know which booths to concentrate on?"

"Yes," replied Psy–4 and Itazura simultaneously.

"And you know not to make your approach until after we've met back here in an hour?"

"Yes." Together again.

"Have you got everything you—"

"Yes!" they snapped, then looked at each other and grinned.

"I think," said Zac, "that everyone wants to get in there and get started."

"You go first," said Killaine. "I'll follow in five minutes, then Itzy, then Psy–4."

"Why do I have to go last?" asked Psy–4.

"I don't believe I'm hearing this," said Zac.

"All right, Itazura goes last." Killaine gave him a look that invited no arguments.

"When do we get to meet your Mr. Morgan?" asked Radiant, who'd decided to come along at the last minute.

"After we've nailed the flatties. He's promised to treat us all to a nice meal at the feed camp."

"Sounds like a grazing field for cows."

Killaine shook her head. "It's the tented area where every-one—carnies and customers alike—eat their meals. Danny says that things can get pretty rowdy around here after the place closes for the night."

Zac nodded his head. "So it's *Danny* now, is it?"

Killaine gave him an exasperated look, then asked, "Any more questions?"

"Yes," said Radiant. "Where's his booth? Ah, come on, I'm not officially part of the operation, so why can't I play some games?"

Killaine grinned at her. "His booth's at the far end of the first branch in the midway, on the left. It's the one where you use a squirt gun to shoot in the clown's mouth."

Itazura began to say something, but Radiant slapped a hand over his mouth.

"I look forward to seeing him," she said to Killaine. "And don't worry, I won't let on that I know you."

"I'm gone," said Zac, climbing out of the van. Before he

closed the door, he stuck his head in and looked at Radiant. "Why don't we go in together? I feel a little awkward being alone at something like this."

Radiant put on her decorated half-mask—the one with the painted eyes—and fluttered her hand near her face. "Why, *suh,*" she said in an overbaked Scarlett O'Hara imitation, "I do believe you *ah* attemptin' to take ad-van-tage of *muh* trustin' nature!"

Psy–4 and Itazura responded with soft but enthusiastic applause.

"Bravo!"

"Encore!"

Radiant took a small seated bow, then primly offered her hand to Zac. "I would be honored if you would be my escort for the evening, sir."

"This is going to be a long night," said Zac, grinning. "I just know it. . . ."

Just beyond the farthest edge of the lot, Rudy watched the van.

Impatiently shifting his weight from foot to foot, he bit his lower lip and wondered what the hell was taking them so long.

Dammit, he thought, *get out already!*

He started to run a hand through his hair, then remembered that the dye hadn't quite dried yet.

Earlier that day, Rudy had used some of the money he'd stolen last night to purchase a new jacket, a pair of scissors to cut his hair, a box of dye to bleach his hair white, and some children's makeup to paint his face up like a clown's.

Usually, he would have just stolen what he needed, but he'd made a pretty decent haul last night after dusting the old guy at the gun shop—over five hundred dollars—and tonight was too important for him to chance getting arrested for something as wimpy as shoplifting.

Still . . . he scanned the faces in the crowd and was relieved to see that his hunch had been right; not only were there a bunch of kids sporting clown faces, but several adults, as well.

No way was DocScrap or that redheaded bitch going to recognize him tonight.

No way.

He touched his light windbreaker and felt the reassuring presence of the pistols underneath.

Rudy had also thought to grab a pair of shoulder holsters from the gun shop. The one under his left arm held a silver-plated .357 Magnum Auto-Mag with a clip full of hollow-point bullets; the one under his right arm held the electron gun.

He had to make sure he was close enough to press the electron gun to the redheaded bitch's face. In order to fry the brain, you had to be dead-bang point-blank.

But, then, maybe he'd just shoot her in the stomach and watch her suffer for a minute or two, thrash around like a fish flopping against the surface of a dock.

He smiled.

That might be kind of fun. Then he'd—

He jumped back behind a truck as the door of the van opened and DocScrap his own self climbed out, then leaned back in, said something, and came out with the tastiest looking piece of tail hanging on to his arm.

Rudy licked his lips and had to readjust his pants.

Man-o-man! was that one fine babe the old Doc had with him.

Turn to the side, thought Rudy. *Gimme a little more of that profile.*

Oh, yeah.

He shook away thoughts that really didn't want to be shaken

away, then stared at the back of the Doc's head as he and the Piece made their way toward the entrance.

"You old perv," whispered Rudy. "Designing your own little robo-slut."

He watched them stop at the gate, buy some tickets, then enter.

He came up from behind the truck and started after them, but then the van door opened again and the redheaded bitch climbed out.

He was too far from any cars to duck for cover, and if he took off she'd see him and get suspicious and that was the last thing he needed, so—

he shoved his hands into his pockets and just started walking, looking down at the ground, passing within six feet of the red-headed bitch.

She said something to someone in the van, then closed the door and started walking toward the entrance.

At one point, she was flanking Rudy.

He decided to try something.

He deliberately tripped, but quickly regained his balance, then looked over.

She was looking right at him.

"Are you okay?"

"Uh . . . yeah. Guess I'm not too swift tonight."

She laughed, then went on.

Hot damn! She hadn't even recognized his voice!

Oh, this was going to be so, so sweet. . . .

Radiant looked back at the kid who'd tripped and smiled to herself. Guy was kind of cute . . . for a klutz. She thought about expanding her neuroreceptor range to see if the guy had thought she was cute, as well, but quickly dismissed the temptation. In crowded places like this, it was dangerous for her to widen her sensory range too far because she could quickly become overwhelmed by the constant tidal waves of neurobabble and psychic background noise issuing from everyone's minds—not that it put her in any physical danger; it simply was likely to distract her, and she couldn't allow herself to be distracted tonight.

Besides (and Zac had lectured her enough on this point), random probing of another person's consciousness out of sheer curiosity was tantamount to psychological rape, even though the person wouldn't be aware of it . . . so she decided to set her neuroreceptor range to ten feet in any direction and leave it at that.

And whether or not that cute kid had thought her attractive would just have to remain one of those sweet mysteries of life. . . .

Daniel Morgan opened his booth, then checked his watch.

They ought to be arriving right about now.

He looked across the midway and saw Herbert smiling at him.

Don't look so smug, he thought. *You don't know as much as you think you do.*

He balanced himself on his arm-crutches and craned his head over the counter, trying to get a decent look at the entrance gate.

He couldn't see her.

Damn!

Okay, settle it down right now.

He bit his lower lip and was readying himself to take another look when a boy who couldn't have been more than five came running up to his booth, squealing, "I wanna squirt water at the clown! Wanna squirt water at the clown!"

Morgan was about to ask the kid where his mother was when a

slightly overweight but definitely cute woman came up behind the child and said, "Lawrence! I told you to wait for me!"

"I sorry," said Lawrence. "But you took *so long!*"

"How much to play?" asked his mother.

"Fifty cents gets one full squirt gun, ma'am."

"I got *twelve dollars!*" said Lawrence. "I been *saving!*"

Morgan leaned down and said, "Well, now, that's just fine, Lawrence, that you've been saving your money, but if I was you I wouldn't be yellin' about how much I got, know what I mean?"

Lawrence shrugged. "I guess so." He looked hurt.

Morgan grabbed up a squirt gun and handed it to the boy. "I wasn't scolding you, Lawrence, that's not my place—" He looked at Lawrence's mother and winked; she nodded in response. "I just think a boy ought to keep how much money he's got a secret."

"'Kay," said the boy, digging into his pocket for money.

"Sorry, Lawrence, but you're money's no good here for the next fifteen minutes."

The boy's eyes grew so wide they threatened to burst from the sockets. *"Really?"*

"Why, sir, I never lie, not to a sharp-witted gentleman like yourself, nosir. Why, I can take one look at you and know that here's a man who knows the value of a dollar, by gosh, and he *knows* a bargain when he sees one—"

Lawrence and his mother were both laughing, and the sound was music to Morgan's ears.

"—see there?" he cried. "You're laughing because you can tell that you've got me *rattled!* Yes, indeed. And there's only one thing I can do when a customer so smart as you rattles me, and that's to tell them that their money's no good here for the next fifteen min-utes, so I'll just take that pistol away from you"—he did—"and I'll be giving you the sharp customer's sharp-shootinest-shooter that was ever sharply shot!" With a flourish, he handed Lawrence a plastic rifle filled with water. "Go on then, sir, take aim and see if you can't make the clown's tie burst! Win yourself any of the grand prizes you see hanging on the wall behind me."

The boy's face glowed.

He looked the way Morgan was feeling inside at the moment, knowing that *she* was going to be here soon. . . .

Rudy walked along the midway, keeping pace with DocScrap and the Piece, wondering how soon he should make his move.

He had a couple of options; he could wait until they were so wrapped up in whatever it was they came here to do (it was obvious even to Rudy that they were up to something more than just a night out) that there was no way they'd be expecting trouble, or he could hit them now, while things were just really shifting into high gear. The place was crowded enough, that was for damn sure, and he was close enough to make his move—

—whoa, hold the phone.

Rudy stopped dead in his tracks and knelt down as if about to tie his shoelaces.

Except he was wearing boots.

Had he remembered to bring the Cutter with him?

He knelt, made a pantomime of tying his nonexistent laces, and ran his right hand up the right side of his right boot, relieved to find that the sheath was indeed taped in place under his pant leg.

He rose, shook his pant leg back down over the boot, and felt the solid tap of the Cutter's hilt against his calf.

Ten inches of the sharpest steel you could find.

Guaranteed to cut through bone as easily as a finger through melted butter.

Rudy grinned as he continued on his way, thinking about the awesome scene in the old movie *Apocalypse Now* where that fat

Marlon Brando guy walks past Charlie Sheen's old man and tosses down that one dude's face.

Cut it right off like it was a mask.

That's what Rudy intended to do to DocScrap with the Cutter.

He looked behind him, caught a glimpse of the redheaded bitch stopping at one of the booths where you tossed balls at a row of stuffed cats, then made his way across the midway and fell into step a few yards behind the Doc and his Piece.

Now, or later?

He looked back toward the entrance.

People were pouring in. You'd think no one in these parts had ever seen a carnival before.

Lots of people.

All of them looking around and trying to decide what to do first, where to go.

Early confusion.

So Rudy, looking back at his prey, made a snap decision.

You're gonna have to stop at one of these booths sometime, doesn't matter if it's to get something to drink or shoot at rubber duckies, you're gonna have to stop soon.

Then you're all mine. . . .

Killaine watched carefully as the first customer, a teenage girl, stepped up to the "Six Cat" booth, paid her fifty cents, and was given three baseballs by the operator.

"We got ourselves an athletic-looking young lady here," said the operator. "Looks like she's a ballplayer, folks! I think I might just be lookin' at our first winner of the night here! Stand back, stand back, give 'er room."

Killaine scanned the interior of the booth.

Not only was there a Flash Cloth—a colorful drape—covering

the counter, but one was laid out on the floor of the booth, and a third hung down from the shelf where the three large stuffed cat dolls were placed.

The young woman drew back and threw her first ball, hitting the center cat dead-center and knocking it off the shelf.

"One down and two to go," shouted the operator. "I'm in deep trouble here, folks!"

Killaine saw the shape of the cord that ran from under the counter to the side of the booth, then snaked along the length to vanish under the shelf. The shape of the cord was very subtle—most would mistake it for a simple wrinkle in the cloth—but she knew what it meant.

The girl threw her second ball, hit the cat on the right with such force it flew off the shelf and slammed into the rear of the tent with a loud *whumpf!*

"Two down, only one to go, folks! See the way my hands are shaking? I'm about to lose my shirt here to this lovely little lady!"

Killaine knew what was happening right this second.

The operator, standing just a bit closer to the edge of the counter than he had been before, was pressing his foot down on a pedal hidden beneath the counter Flash Cloth.

That peddle activated a rod that ran along the length of the booth, engaging a small brace that was moving forward to catch the remaining cat.

The girl threw her third ball and hit the last cat on its base.

The cat wobbled, started to fall backward—

—then, miraculously, regained its balance and stayed in place.

The onlookers all groaned their disappointment and the girl stamped her foot and said a most unladylike word.

"Oh, *too bad*," said the operator, grabbing two fresh cat dolls and placing them on the shelf. "You had me worried there for a minute, young lady. But don't fret! Nothing worth having is ever easy!" He held out three more balls. "Try your luck again!"

"I got your balls right here," said the girl's boyfriend, putting his arm around her and pulling her away from the booth.

Many of the onlookers followed.

The operator looked around, rolling one of the balls between his hands, then caught sight of Killaine.

"Ma'am, if you don't mind my sayin' you look even more formidable than my last customer. What say you give this game of skill a chance? Why, for a mere fifty cents you can—"

"No thanks," said Killaine, pulling out the fake ID Itazura had whipped up the night before. Flipping open the wallet, she displayed her identification, along with a gold badge.

"Karen Williams," she said, "State Gambling Commission."

". . . son-of-a-bitch . . ." muttered the operator.

Killaine closed the wallet and pointed to the side of the booth. "Mind showing me what that lump over there is?"

The operator looked to the spot where the shape of the rod was evident, wiped some sweat from his face, then stepped to the edge of the counter and gestured for Killaine to come closer.

"Look, ma'am," he whispered, "I can't afford to get busted any more this year. Isn't there some"—he looked around to make sure there were no customers approaching—"some way you and me can come to some sort of agreement?"

"Can you be a little more specific?"

"I mean, what's gonna happen to me if you haul me in? I'll do a couple days in jail and pay a fine. What say you and me just skip the middle of the process and I'll pay the fine to you right here."

Killaine tilted her head to the side, considering. "Well, I don't know about that, friend. We've had several complaints about the games at this particular carny, and the suits are gunning for a bust.

I let you off and someone finds out, there'll be hell to pay. Know what I mean?"

"I wouldn't expect you to take that kind of a chance for nothin', no, ma'am." He was looking outright panicky now. "I mean, I'll be more than happy to throw in somethin' extra for your trouble."

Killaine drummed her fingers on the counter. "Give me a number."

"Five hundred."

"Give me a better number."

"Eight hundred."

She squinted her eyes at him, took a deep breath, then exhaled and said, "Tell you what I'm gonna do. In about ten minutes an associate of mine will come over to play the game. Let him win—give him that portable radio up there. Let him stick for you for the next hour or so."

"Sounds reasonable."

"At the end of the hour, you give him the eight hundred. At the end of the evening, I'll come back and settle for ten percent of the night's take. For my trouble, you understand."

"Yes, ma'am."

She described Itazura to him, then reached over and put a hand on his shoulder, applying some pressure as she squeezed.

The operator visibly winced.

"Don't try anything," she said. "You make a move to skip, and I'll be all over you."

"Wouldn't . . . wouldn't think of it. I'm a cooperating type."

"You'd better be."

She let go of him and just happened to glance down the midway.

She saw Zac and Radiant standing at Morgan's booth.

She saw the little boy excitedly shooting water at the clown within, his smiling mother standing just off to the side.

And she saw Mr. "Guess-I'm-Not-too-Swift-Tonight," from the

parking lot, his clown-face looking around him as he approached Morgan's booth.

Unzipping his windbreaker.

Crossing his arms over his chest as his hands went under the jacket.

She had just enough time to think, *shoulder holsters,* before things got crazy. . . .

Zac and Radiant were taking their time along the midway—they'd stopped at a dart-throw booth where Zac won a small stuffed elephant—but it was obvious that Radiant wanted to get to Morgan's booth and "read" his energy.

"Would you slow down a little?" said Zac. "You pull any harder on my arm and you're going to pop my shoulder."

"Sorry," said Radiant. "It's just that I'm so *happy* for Killaine, you know?"

"I know." He tried to figure out what to do with the elephant, couldn't find a pocket big enough to stuff it in, and so settled for just hanging on to it and feeling like a big kid.

"She's been so alone for so long," said Radiant. "I just can't help but want to get a reading on the man who stole her heart."

"Okay, okay," said Zac, realizing that Radiant, for once, wasn't totally absorbed in herself; she hardly noticed the unadulterated looks of lust she was attracting from the men who passed by them. "We'll go to his booth—but could you *please* calm down? If we get over there and you start jumping up and down with glee, he might think something's wrong."

"Party pooper."

"Yeah," said Zac. "I get a lot of complaints about that."

They sauntered slowly to the area where Morgan's booth was located.

"There's a lot of joy coming from there," said Radiant. "Crystal wings and song. There's a child there, isn't there?"

"And a darned cute little boy he is, too."

"I knew it! But there's also . . . wait a second . . . there's also a feeling of great *relief* from his mother."

"She looks happy that he's enjoying himself."

Radiant shook her head. "It's more than that. There's an echo of . . ."

"What are you doing?"

Radiant looked at Zac. "Something about the way she looks . . . could I just expand my neurofield enough to get a sense of her feelings, nothing more?"

"A couple of seconds, no longer."

"Thank you." Radiant expanded her awareness for a moment. ". . . pain . . . ugly pain under the surface."

They slowed their steps.

"What do you suppose that means?" asked Zac.

"There's a twisting sense of . . . I don't want to call it paranoia, but at the very least a constant fear." She stopped for a moment. "Hold on, the energies are coalescing."

"And . . . ?"

Radiant held a hand to her mouth for a moment, made a sad sound, then whispered, "I'm sorry, Zac, I . . ." She shook her head, retracting the field back to only ten feet. "I'm sorry, I . . . I caught a few random strands of thought. I didn't mean to, it was an accident . . . but some of her thoughts are so close to the surface that—"

Zac touched her shoulder. "It was an accident, I'm not mad. But you caught something pretty serious, I can see that."

Radiant nodded. "She and the boy are living at a shelter for abused women. I felt the resonance of the cumulative anxiety of the other women there. A group of them are here tonight for their kids."

"Did you sense her husband's energy anywhere?"

"No, he's only a memory to her now. Distant. Probably in jail or prison. But the anxiety, the fear of him, is still very much a part of her."

"Well, at least her boy's enjoying himself tonight."

Radiant smiled. "Oh, yes, she's very proud of him. It felt like glowing, golden bliss. This means the world to her, hearing his laughter and seeing his smile."

"That's what nights and places like this were designed for," replied Zac.

"And I can . . . oh, *my*."

"What is it?"

"I just caught a wave of Morgan's energy."

They were less than three yards from Morgan's booth.

"And . . . ?"

"There's great strength in him, Zac. He genuinely *loves* children and seeing their joy, but I pulled back. I want to respect his psychic privacy for Killaine's sake."

And that's when Zac saw Morgan behind the counter.

"Oh," he said.

Radiant tugged his arm. "Tell me. Tell me now."

"He's handicapped."

"How?"

"He's got a . . . he's a hunchback and uses arm-crutches."

Radiant nodded her head. "That must be it."

"That must be what?"

"The contradictory wave of tainted energy. I caught an echo of it before I pulled back. It's at odds with his strength and his love of children and his deep romantic affection for Killaine." She stopped, took a breath, and steadied herself.

"Are you all right?" asked Zac.

"Whew! Huh? Oh, I'm fine. It's just that I got another blast of his feelings for Killaine—he must be looking for her or thinking about her—and . . . *wow!* This is one intensely passionate man." She looked at Zac. "I'm reducing the field to five feet. I'm starting to feel a little voyeuristic."

Zac nodded his agreement, then looked over at Morgan and grinned. "Well, good for Killaine!"

"I'm even more jealous than I was when she talked about him last night."

Zac patted her arm. "Cheer up. You can still break a thousand hearts just by walking down the street."

Radiant leaned over and kissed his cheek. "You are the sweetest man in the world."

"If you say so."

They were at the booth now. Zac commented on the news crew who were covering a pie-eating contest just a few yards past the midway. "Those pies sure look good."

"Like you need any more cholesterol in your diet," replied Radiant, playfully poking his belly.

"Who's the party pooper now?"

So they watched as the little boy took aim with his water-filled plastic rifle and landed a stream in the mouth of a clown face at the back of the booth. . . .

Rudy kept four yards back from DocScrap and his Piece while they stopped at one of the booths.

Doc threw some darts and won a stupid stuffed elephant.

Come on, already! he thought.

He almost did them right there, but there were too many people around that booth—more than a dozen—and Rudy wanted to catch them at one of the less crowded games.

So he bided his time, patient.

A good Stomper had to be able to sense when the Strike Moment was at hand, and this wasn't it.

Then the Doc and his Piece were on the move again, and Rudy kept pace.

Finally, they started slowing down.

Rudy looked ahead of them.

This section of the midway was nearing its end.

They'd better stop soon.

Damn, can you walk any slower, Doc?

But they were moving forward, toward the last booth where there was only a little brat and his fat mom.

Go there, he wished. *Nice, uncrowded booth, right at the end of the line. Give me plenty of room to do my business on you and run into the crowds over by the rides.*

Now they were walking *real* slow.

Toward the kid and his mom and—

—Rudy smiled.

Well, whatta you know! Twisty-Crip's booth!

If they stopped there, *that* would be the Strike Moment.

They stopped.

Rudy took one last, quick look around, then unzipped his jacket, crossed his arms across his chest, and grabbed his guns.

The Piece was standing on the left.

Doc was on the right.

Like ducks in a shooting gallery, mused Rudy, unholstering his weapons and walking faster. . . .

Radiant sensed it then, the dark, deadly, intensely focused energy that was approaching them from behind. It had just entered her five-foot field. She knew that if she turned around that would tip them off, whoever in the hell *they* were, and that was the last thing you did in a battle situation—and this was most definitely a battle situation now—because if you tipped your hand too soon that might spook them and they'd do something reckless, and whoever it was approaching them from behind was carrying serious firepower, she could feel the cold, reptilian energy emanating from the guns, and if she spooked them, they might just start firing at random, and there were innocent people here. . . .

Zac felt Radiant's body go rigid, as if she'd just been hit by a ten-thousand-volt shot of electricity, and he knew right away that something was wrong, that she was concentrating on homing in on the source of the danger, and his next thought was not for her safety, nor was it for his own—it was for the child's and the child's mother, so he began scanning the immediate area for someplace he could get them out of the line of fire. . . .

Rudy had the guns out now, hanging by his sides, close by his sides so no one would notice, and suddenly he felt more powerful than he'd ever felt in his entire, miserable, stinking life, because for once he had the upper hand, he had the power, he was in control, and damn if that wasn't the best feeling in the world because there was no way DocScrap and his little robo-slut where going to deny him his moment of glory again, so as he came up within a yard of their backs he began lifting the guns, aiming right at the base of their necks. . . .

Killaine felt as if she were moving in slow motion as she jumped away from the Six Cat booth and started running toward

Zac and Radiant, knowing full well there was no way she was going to get to them in time, she'd have to aim for the Shooter and that could be dangerous because there were other people at the booth, not mention her sweet, loving Morgan inside, so whatever she did would have to be swift and decisive and it would have to work the first time out because there wouldn't be a second chance here, but she wasn't going to do a damn bit of good if she didn't start *moving faster.* . . .

Radiant waited until she could feel the heat from the attacker's body enter her own body space, and she read his heat and knew three things right away: 1) It was a he, and a young he, at that, maybe fifteen, sixteen at the most; 2) One of his weapons was an electron gun that was pointed at the base of her neck, which meant he knew she was robotic; and 3) It was the same kid who'd broken into the warehouse the other night and tried to bite a chunk out of Zac's hand. With maybe five seconds left—she felt the energy of his flesh merging with that of the guns, which meant his fingers were on the triggers—she leaned a little toward Zac and whispered, "The Biter's right behind us," then straightened herself, readying to make her move. . . .

"The Biter's right behind us," whispered Radiant to Zac, and he felt himself grow cold all over, because whoever that kid was, he was stone crazy, even if he didn't know it, and someone who was stone crazy wouldn't care *who* he hurt or killed, just so long as he accomplished what he set out to do, which was, of course, to kill Zac, but there wasn't time to think about that because Zac felt Radiant's arm slip away from him and he knew there were maybe a couple of seconds left before all hell broke loose, so Zac did the only thing he could do, the only thing that mattered to him, he moved forward to block the kid with his own body. . . .

Rudy was less than a foot away when he saw the Piece lean over and whisper something in the Doc's ear, and Rudy knew, with all the primitive survival tendencies that are part and parcel for one who lives on the streets, that the Piece had somehow spotted him, but all the while a small voice in his head was screaming, *That can't be, they've been looking at that little brat all this time, no way they saw me!,* then another part of his mind kicked in, reminding Rudy that the Piece was, probably, likely, *had to be* another robot, right, and maybe this one had some kind radar built into her so she could tell when someone was sneaking up on her, but by the time this registered Rudy no longer cared, he was remembering the taste of DocScrap's blood on his tongue, so he pushed his arms out like a couple of ramrods and surged forward, and son-of-bitch if that's not when the Piece took her arm away from the Doc and the dude made a dive for the kid. . . .

Killaine was running as fast as she dared with this many people surrounding her, people she could hurt if she rammed into them, but no matter how fast she was going she feared it wasn't going to be fast enough, and all she could think was, *Do something, Radiant! Do it now, you have to know he's behind you,* but then she had to veer to the side in order to avoid colliding with a woman pushing a set of newborn twins in an oversized stroller, and in veering out of the way she nearly slammed into a vendor pushing his mobile hot dog cart up the midway, so she had to hit the brakes and back up, move to the side, squeeze past a large group of teenagers, and by the time she was back on track it was

too late, because she heard the gunshots and the sound of splinter-
ing wood and someone yelling and, worst of all, the high-pitched
sound of someone screaming in pain. . . .

Radiant pulled her arm away from Zac and saw Zac move
toward the child, then she felt the kid with the guns pull in a breath
and knew this was the crucial moment, so she brought her right
hand up to her face as she snap-kicked backward at the Biter's knee
to disable him but she must have been more rattled than she
thought, because she didn't pulp his kneecap as the snap-kick was
intended, she connected instead with his shin and felt the bone
crack but not break, but that was all right, it would have to do, so
she spun around, bringing her right arm down at an arc, then ripping it upward and to the side, slamming her elbow against the
Biter's left arm—at least, that was the idea—but her thoughts were
still with Zac and the mother and her child, so all she managed to
do was connect with the electron gun, which went up, up, and
away, spinning in the air, landing somewhere far behind him, and
she relished the look of shock on his clown-painted face, but only
for a millisecond because he still had the other gun, and he did
something she didn't expect, he fell down onto the ground, and as
she worried that maybe she'd done more damage to him than she'd
thought, he went down and squeezed the trigger of the Magnum
that gave out with the brightest, ugliest muzzle flash Radiant would
ever see. . . .

When Zac broke away from Radiant he went into a stoop-run,
shoving his arms in front of him to get hold of the child, the child,
the child, nothing mattered at the moment but getting the child out
of the line of fire, and as he threw himself toward the kid he heard

the child's mother shriek and he heard the unmistakable sound of a bone cracking behind him and he heard the Biter scream in agony and then Zac smiled because he had his hands on the child's waist and was pulling him away from the counter and down toward the ground, and half a second later it dawned on Zac that he shouldn't have let his guard down long enough to feel safe, because that's when he felt something along the lines of a rabid grizzly bear's claws rip through his shoulder, and now the kid was staring at him, white-faced with fear as some of Zac's blood spattered against his cheek, and then the grizzly bear swiped its claws again and as they hit the ground Zac closed his eyes and readied himself for the pain, the fire, the agony, but it didn't come, and he wondered if he'd started going into shock already, then he pulled up just a little so the child wouldn't be crushed by his weight and got a good look at the child, and then Zac Robillard did something that he hadn't done since the night Jean died in his arms, he threw back his head and released a howl of anguish and grief. . . .

Rudy realized that the Piece had gotten him with a backward kick, and he didn't have time to wait for the pain to register, he'd deal with that later, so he pushed the electron gun forward and that's when the Piece whirled around and brought her arm up and Tai-chopped at his arm, connecting only with the electron gun and sending it into the air, and Rudy allowed himself a half-second to think, *Score one for the robo-slut,* then he went down, went down hard, doing a quick tuck-and-roll and grabbing the Auto-Mag from its hiding place, and the Piece had made the mistake of turning her attention toward the woman and the kid and hadn't noticed that Rudy was now down on the same level with the Doc, so Rudy opened fire with the Auto-Mag and saw the first bullet rip through the meaty part of DocScrap's shoulder, blowing tissue and blood every which way, and the second bullet blew a section of the booth's wooden counter all to shit, so Rudy did a fast roll to the side and plowed off another shot at the Doc, but this one seemed to go wild because the Doc didn't seem hit, but then came a glorious sound and sight, DocScrap throwing his head back and howling like a wounded animal, and that sound was enough to shift all of Rudy's reptilian impulses into high gear, and he pulled himself up onto his feet and staggered the hell out of there while the confusion was on his side. . . .

Killaine saw the Shooter limp off but she didn't care about that at the moment, all she could see was the shuddering form of Zac on the ground, the back of his shirt soaked in blood, a good piece of meat ripped from his shoulder, but then there was another crowd in her road because people were stopping, freezing in their tracks, realizing that Something Terrible had just happened, but Killaine was going too fast to stop and if she collided with anyone right now she'd probably break all the bones in their body, so she did the only thing she could, she executed a move Itazura had taught her once, she threw herself forward and down, arms and hands extended, catching her own weight and pushing her upside-down body into the air, soaring over the heads of the gawking crowd, somersaulting over them, landing on her feet on the other side and rocketing forward, thinking only of her dear Zachary, her dear Radiant, and her dear Morgan, and she was almost on them when she saw Zac roll to the side and then Killaine stumbled because there was the kid, the poor, innocent child, being swallowed by the merciless teeth of *chronos,* blood pumping from the upper portion of his right arm where the third bullet had gotten him, and that's when Killaine did something she'd never done before, she let her warrior's instincts go to hell in a handbasket and just surrendered to the blood-craziness. . . .

* * *

And over by the pie-eating contest, the local news crew was getting all of it on tape.

The reporter couldn't help but want to smile.

What an exclusive!

Pictures at eleven . . .

Trying to gain a good headstart on anyone who might come after him, Rudy caught a peripheral glimpse of some dude dressed up like a cowboy riding a horse, just trotting toward the midway like it was only another day on the range, and he measured his chances, decided to go for it, and pistol whipped a nearby old man across the back of his skull and spun around, pushing the Auto-Mag out as he ran up beside the horse and yelled, "Get off or I'll blast your fuckin' face!" and the cowboy, who obviously wasn't raised in no barn, practically threw himself out of the saddle, and the dude hadn't gotten one foot on the ground before Rudy swung his leg up and slipped his foot into the stirrup, threw himself up onto the saddle, then jerked on the reins and made the horse turn around—then it was just a matter of kicking the thing a good one in the side with his steel-toed boot and the horse whinnied, threw back its head, and broke into a gallop. . . .

Zac looked down at the little boy and wanted to scream again, but by now Daniel Morgan had come out from the booth and was dragging a big metal box with him, a medical kit, no doubt, then Killaine was there, kneeling down with Radiant; Killaine was trying to hold Zac and keep pressure on his wounds while Radiant cradled the little boy's head in her lap and pressed a cloth against his right arm.

Zac pulled in a deep, pained breath and said, "Is he . . . is it serious?"

Radiant touched the boy's sweaty forehead and said, "He's in a lot of pain but the bullet didn't break any bones or major blood vessels. He's going to live but I don't know if he'll ever have full use of this arm again."

Killaine felt the blood-craziness taking over again, knowing damned well she should have taken off after the Shooter but wounded innocents came first, always, no arguments; she looked at Zac, who swallowed and nodded his head, then she looked at Morgan who said, "I already called for the EMTs, they got a trailer at the other end of the park, they're on their way," then she looked and saw the Shooter pulling himself onto a horse and galloping away, and then Zac had her hand in his and was saying, "Don't let him get away," and that was all Killaine needed.

She gently ran her hand over Zac's face, let Morgan take over the first aid, then took off at full speed after the horse and its rider. . . .

Rudy had no idea how far away he was from the scene of his wreckage when the horse started bucking up its ass and spinning around in a circle, trying to throw him. He held on as best he could but the horse was mad, and it was scared, and it wanted him off its back, and with another snort, buck, and spin, it sent Rudy flying away from its saddle and into a cluster of tables by a hamburger stand.

Rudy crashed down onto one of the empty tables, smashing it to pieces, lay there for a moment feeling stunned, then pulled himself up and saw a family at a nearby table coming toward him, the father asking him, "Are you all right?"

Rudy shoved the Auto-Mag into the guy's face and said, "Back off!"

The guy made a move to shield his wife and kids but he was too slow.

Rudy lunged forward and grabbed the guy's little daughter by her strawberry-blond hair, pulling her into him.

He wrapped one of his arms around her waist, lifted her off her feet, and pressed the gun against her temple.

She was a smart kid; she didn't struggle.

The father made a move toward them, so Rudy snapped the gun away and fired at the guy, blowing his left knee to smithereens, and as the guy hit the ground screaming Rudy put the gun back against the little girl's temple and backed out of the snack area, making slow, small circles so he could get a good look at everyone around him.

"Go on!" he shouted at the gawkers. "Go on, somebody try something! You wanna be wearing her brains in your hair? *COME ON!*"

No one made a move toward him.

He worked his way out of the snack area, having no idea where he was going to go.

And that's when he saw the redheaded bitch come out of nowhere. . . .

Killaine saw the horse gallop past dozens of attractions and rides, and for a minute it was difficult to keep up with it because of the crowds, but then people started to make room for horse and rider and she was able to judge their location by the gaping holes in the throngs of bodies, and she couldn't help but feel satisfied when she saw the horse buck and throw the Shooter.

She made her way quickly toward them, somersaulting over a

cluster of shocked carnival-goers and landing on her feet only a few yards away from the snack area.

She hit the entrance at the same time the Shooter came stumbling out with a terrified little girl dangling from his arm.

He caught sight of Killaine and turned in her direction, pressing the gun harder into the girl's temple. "Hey, bitch! Come for a little taste of my Power, have you?"

"Let her go," said Killaine calmly, taking a step forward.

"Fuck you!" screamed the Shooter.

And it was then Killaine recognized his voice.

"You're the Stomper from the other night."

Rudy let fly with a cackling, high-pitched laugh. "Give the bitch a cee-gar!" He continued moving away from her.

Killaine saw him glance very quickly in the direction of the merry-go-round only ten yards away.

No, she thought. *You can't be* that *stupid.*

But he was, and then some. . . .

Rudy pulled himself along with all he had, tightening his grip on the little girl who'd gone limp in his arms, and when he was about a yard away from the merry-go-round he realized that she'd passed out on him, that she was deadweight because half the bargaining power of taking a hostage was using their fear to your advantage, and you didn't get no fear out of someone who was out like a light, so he took a breath, threw the unconscious girl toward the redheaded bitch, then started firing at random, blowing out neon lights, shattering the mirrors outside the fun house, and hitting the french-fry vat in the snack area, sparking the metal and igniting the grease in a huge cloud of fire and smoke.

Within seconds most of the snack stand was in flames.

Employees and patrons alike charged away from the confla-
gration.

"WREEEEEEEEEEECKAAAAAAAAAAAAAAGE!" screamed
Rudy, then turned tail and ran-limped as best he could toward the
merry-go-round. . . .

Killaine checked to make sure the little girl was alive and
unharmed, breathing a sigh of relief when she felt a strong pulse.

She shielded the girl from the Stomper's panic-fire, feeling
one of the bullets wing off her own back, puncturing her flesh but
doing no real damage.

Then the snack area exploded into flames and the frightened
mob of people poured over them.

Killaine covered the little girl with her own body as people
stomped, kicked, and clawed their way past, often over them,
more than a few stepping on her back in their mad dash to survive.

When she at last dared to lift her head, she saw a woman in
tears, kneeling over a man with a bloody leg a few feet away.

"Ohgod!" screamed the woman. "John, John, I can't see
Emily, I can't *see her anywhere!*"

By then the little girl was coming around.

Killaine gently tapped the girl's cheeks, helping her back to
consciousness.

"Who . . . who're you?" whispered the girl, hoarsely.

"Is your name Emily?"

"Uh-huh . . . where's . . . where's the bad man?"

"The bad man's gone, hon. Do you think you can walk?"

". . . think so . . ."

Killaine helped the girl to her feet, then shouted, "Ma'am!
Ma'am, over here!"

The woman saw her daughter, safe and unharmed, and ran toward her.

Killaine kissed Emily's forehead, patted her on the cheek, then went after the Stomper. . . .

Rudy fell onto the rotating platform of the merry-go-round and damn near hit his head against one of the wooden horses.

Damned if he hadn't had his fill of horses today.

He reached up and grabbed on to one of the poles and pulled himself to his feet, noting that this was an older model carousel and that was a good thing, damn lucky thing because it gave him another advantage, and he waited until he passed the door to the controller's booth located in the center of the carousel.

Then he jumped down, elbowed the door open, and pushed the gun into the controller's face. "Open this damn thing up!"

The controller held up his hands and said, *"What?"*

"Full speed," screamed Rudy, grabbing the controller's hands and slamming them down on the handles.

"But there's people still on the ride," said the controller. "Top speed is forty miles an hour and I ain't permitted to go over fifteen."

"DO IT!"

The controller fixed Rudy with an icy stare. "Sorry, boy. I won't endanger them folks. Guess you're gonna have to use that thing."

Rudy screamed and smashed the gun against the controller's head, splitting open a good section of his head.

Then he kicked the guy out of the way, grabbed the handles, and slammed them all the way to the right.

The prerecorded organ music grew louder, faster, and more frantic as the carousel picked up speed.

This would buy him a little time.

Not much, but a little.

Even a damned robot would have trouble jumping onto a platform that was rotating at forty miles an hour.

At least, that's what he was hoping. . . .

Killaine saw the Stomper fall onto the carousel, then pull himself to his feet and vanish as the platform spun.

She ran toward it and was just about to leap on when the thing suddenly tripled its speed, the music screaming like operatic insanity.

She caught glimpses of the few people and children who were riding it, all of them clutching to the poles of their bouncing wooden animals for dear life.

She knew it would only be a matter of seconds before the momentum would start throwing them.

She ran back a few feet, steadied herself, then sprinted forward, leaping out and landing squarely on the platform.

She was unprepared for the sheer *force* of the speed and almost lost her balance.

The wooden animals no longer glided along and bounced gently in time with the music; they screeched and pumped like pistons in an overheated, speeding engine.

On the first full-throttle revolution, she caught sight of the Stomper in the controller's booth, taking aim at her and firing.

The bullet winged off the arced metal roof of the carousel and blew off a lion's head.

Killaine ducked down and made her way back toward the control booth, walking against the momentum.

The screams of the riders blended with the insane music to create a nerve-shattering cacophony in Killaine's ears.

So this is hell, she thought.

She pulled herself forward until she faced the open door of the control booth once again.

The Stomper fired.

Killaine snapped up her right arm.

The bullet ricocheted off her elbow, and this time it *hurt.*

In the same instance the bullet ricocheted, she threw herself forward and into the control booth, knocking the gun from the Stomper's hand and grabbing him hard by the throat, lifting him off the ground.

With her other hand she grabbed the control handles and slowly pulled them back, back, back, not daring to stop the carousel all at once because the sudden force would send the riders flying as if they'd been shot by a cannon.

The carousel slowly came to a halt, and the riders, all of them badly shaken-up but unhurt, groaned their relief.

It was only after she'd made certain that the riders were all right that Killaine thought to see how the Stomper was doing.

She looked up at him and felt herself go numb.

She must have been too angry, too blood-crazy, because she'd squeezed his throat so hard that she'd crushed his neck and created such internal pressure in his skull that one of his eyes had actually popped from its socket.

He was dead.

Killaine knew she should put him down and go get someone, *anyone,* but she couldn't bring herself to do it, no matter how intensely she willed herself to move.

She had never killed anyone before.

And I shouldn't have been able to! she screamed to herself silently.

The I-Bots, because of their modified programming, and the variability of the DNA and RNA that governed their biological components, could harm human beings, but only for one of two reasons: 1) If there was an active, immediate, and irreversible circumstance or set of circumstances that would result in the deaths of innocent bystanders if immobilizing force was not exercised at once, or 2) if it would serve the greater good. . . .

This still felt wrong.

She had killed the Stomper, but not while the *Stomper* was actively trying to kill anyone.

He'd wounded others, yes; *endangered others,* yes, but there had been no *active, immediate, or irreversible circumstance or set of circumstances* involved at the moment when she'd killed him, and though her actions at that time had undoubtedly saved a handful of humans from *possible* death later, it had not served the greater good at that exact instant.

Or had it?

Killaine continued to stare up at Stomper's dead body, her mind a runaway train of regret, shock, self-condemnation, and grief.

She had committed an act that all her programming was supposedly designed to *prevent* her from committing.

Wasn't it?

A part of her detached itself from the rest and began to look at the situation in coldly objective terms, then wondered how long it would be before her entire system locked up and shut down irreversibly— because wasn't that what was *supposed* to happen when a robot killed?

But she wasn't a robot.

Nor was she human.

Yet she was more than the sum of both.

She had killed a human being out of anger, out of her own desire to inflict harm and call it justice.

She was a murderer.

So why was she still able to function? Why wasn't all her circuitry self-destructing this very moment?

Bright lights in her face.

Killaine squinted, turning her head toward the source, and managed to make out the shape of the reporter and his cameraman standing just beyond the carousel.

Then three other shapes joined them, shoving them out of the way.

"Killaine!" shouted Radiant.

Then she watched as the other two shapes stepped onto the platform and came into focus.

Itazura and Psy–4 saw her, saw the dead body of the Stomper she held over her head, and moved cautiously toward her.

"It's okay, Killaine," one of them whispered—she wasn't sure who—then someone reached in and gently took hold of her, pulling her from the controller's booth.

"That's it, Sis, that's it, come on, watch your head, there you go . . ."

Outside, she was outside, and it was Itzy who was pulling her gently along, then Psy–4 was there, reaching up to pry her fingers from around the Stomper's crushed, dead throat.

"Let go of him, Killaine, c'mon, *let go,* just open your hand, one . . . one finger at a time, there you go, easy now, easy . . ."

She heard the sound of the dead body hitting the wooden platform with an ugly, wet, cold *smack!*

Then the lights again, but now Psy–4 and Itazura were pulling her along, out of the light, and there was Radiant, taking hold of her hand and whispering, "You gotta get the hell out of here, Killaine, the police are on their way and it's a madhouse on the midway. Can you hear me? Do you understand what I'm saying?"

Killaine somehow managed to nod her head.

"The fire's going to slow the authorities down for a minute or two," continued Radiant. "So you've got to pull yourself together and get out of here, understand? See that field over there, just beyond the fortune-teller's tent?"

Again, Killaine nodded.

"Take off now, run directly due south, okay? The field empties out onto a road near that old farmhouse we saw a couple of days ago, remember?"

Nod.

"You get your ass in the barn and wait there for us, okay? We'll be along as quick as we can."

Killaine swallowed once, very hard, and croaked: ". . . Zac and the boy . . ."

"The EMTs should be there by now. Danny said he'd make sure both of them were taken care of."

". . . sweet . . . Danny's so sweet . . ."

"Yes, he is," said Radiant, pushing Killaine toward the field. "And he's just fine, you hear me? Now go, Killaine, go—*GO!*"

Radiant gave her a firm push, and before Killaine was even aware of it, she was running at near full speed through the green, green field, running due south, toward the old road that led to the farmhouse and the barn, and she wondered for a moment why everything was so blurry then realized it was because she was crying, crying, crying. . . .

Psy–4, Radiant, and Itazura arrived back at Morgan's booth to find the EMTs loading the little boy onto one stretcher and his mother onto another.

"Where's Morgan?" said Radiant. "I don't feel his presence anymore."

"I never saw the guy," replied Itazura.

Psy–4 looked around. "What happened to Zac?"

Radiant couldn't sense Zac's presence any longer.

Itazura ran around the immediate area but couldn't see him.

Finally, Itazura asked one of the EMTs, "What happened to the older man who was here?"

The EMT shook her head. "I'm sorry, sir, but there was no one else here, just this child and his mother."

Then he heard Radiant call, "Guys! Over here!"

They found her across the midway, in front of an empty booth where players threw softballs into bushel baskets. Tears were running down her face.

She was holding a small stuffed elephant.

The toy was soaked in blood.

"This w-w-was Zac's," she spluttered. "He won it for me."

Psy–4 put a hand on her arm. "Where is he?"

She brought the elephant closer to her chest, reading the energy resonances that Zac might have left behind.

"Well?" snapped Itazura.

"They took him."

"Who?"

She shook her head. "I . . . I don't know, but—wait! Zac . . . Zac *knew* one of them."

"Can you read anything else?" asked Psy–4, his voice barely controlled.

". . . I . . . I think that . . ." She dropped her head. "Dammit! I almost had it!"

Itazura grabbed her arm. "Try again!"

"It's not that easy, Itzy! I—"

Then her body went ramrod straight and deathly still.

"Preston," she said. "Whoever has Zac knows Preston, as well."

Itazura and Psy–4 looked at one another.

"Annabelle," they both said at almost the same time.

Checking very quickly to make sure the child and his mother were going to survive, they took off out of the park and had just made it to the van when the squad cars came screaming down the road. . . .

In his trailer, Daniel Morgan slammed the door closed and let fly with a string of profanities that would have made a hard-core biker blush.

He threw his crutches away, then flopped down onto his bed and tore away his leg braces.

He pushed himself to his feet, stumbled over to the small kitchen table, sat down, ripped off his shirt, and began to undo the buckles that held his back brace in place.

It fell away, and with it his deformity.

Damn that hurts! thought Janus, rubbing the back of his neck.

He was glad to be rid of the disguise.

Still, it had been great being back at the carny again. Half his life he'd spent at such places, under various names. And it was a requirement for his continued association with Annabelle that she keep this particular carnival in the old corporate holdings.

He never knew when he might want a place to hide, disguised as Morgan.

Reaching behind the half-empty bottle of whiskey on the table, he snatched up the cell phone and punched in a number.

Waited for the person on the other end to answer.

By the sixth ring, he knew there was no one there *to* answer.

"Shit!" he hissed, throwing the phone across the trailer.

Annabelle wasn't there.

Which could only mean one thing.

She was either on her way here to see Preston or was *already* here.

He should have known better than to trust Simmons and his underlings. Oh, sure, they'd been more than happy to play their parts as game operators—Simmons's performance as Herbert had impressed even Janus—and that should have tipped Janus off.

They were a little *too* willing to go along with his plans.

He slammed his fist down on the tabletop, flipped the table over, and pulled the scarred sea chest out from under the other kitchen chair.

He unlocked it, flipped open the lid, and began taking stock of his arsenal.

Either he'd been double-crossed, or played for a patsy.

Didn't really matter at this point.

It was blood all the way now. . . .

PART THREE

WHEELS OF FIRE

"Every thought and its resultant action should be judged by what it is able to draw from suffering. Despite my dislike of it, suffering is a fact."

—*Albert Camus,* NOTEBOOK IV, JANUARY 1942–SEPTEMBER 1945

70

Zac Robillard regained consciousness in slow, confusing degrees, recalling only frozen moments and hazy images instead of full-blown incidents or details:

The carnival; the grizzly bear ripping away some of his shoulder meat; the bloody, unconscious but still-breathing form of the little boy; Radiant, Itazura, and Psy–4 running after Killaine; then blackness; coming to sometime later, strapped to a gurney; faces hidden behind surgical masks, looking down at him.

And underscoring all of it was that oh-so-familiar voice; clipped speech, impeccable diction, right out of Parliament:

"A pleasure to see you again, Dr. Robillard."

Simmons.

Which meant Annabelle couldn't be too far behind. . . .

71

Until the moment when one of them decided to turn on the News at Ten, Stonewall and Singer had been having a relaxing, quiet evening at the warehouse; Stonewall finished his cross-stitch project—exceptionally happy with the way the puppy dogs had turned out—and Singer, having finally mastered the basics of Itazura's HIR unit, made some holos of the robots hiding down in the sewer.

The news shattered their contentment, of course.

We're going live to Ron Wilson at the scene of the shootings.

Thanks, Ted. I'm standing here near the carousel at the Route

79 carnival location where, only a few minutes ago, a series of events unfolded that, at last count, have left at least four people wounded and one person dead. Due to the graphic nature of the following material, parental discretion is advised. Now take a look at this video we shot. . . .

Stonewall and Singer watched the events in silence; from the initial shooting to Killaine killing the young man in the clown makeup; then, just as the anchorman was saying, "Channel 28 has learned that the dead teenager was evidently carrying out some sort of initiation assignment in order to join the so-called 'Silver Metal Stompers,' a group of anti-robot youths who—"

Stonewall turned off the television. "Shit! Now we *really* have to get the hell out of here," he said to Singer.

What do I start with?

"Go down into the garage bay and bring up all the empty crates. I'll start breaking down the lab and computer equipment."

When will the others be here?

"Soon. And I'm going to assume that finishing up with the packing will be the last thing on their minds."

72

In the SMS headquarters, Gash watched the rest of the news broadcast, paying particular attention to the last bit of ersatz-information passed along: "We've also received unconfirmed reports that the young woman sought by police in the killing of the alleged 'Stomper' was recently in the employ of Preston Technical Systems, Inc., a multinational—"

Gash lifted his shotgun and blew the set to sparking, fizzling smithereens.

Dropping the weapon, he rolled over on the expansive but old sofa and lifted a vial of Stoke from a nearby table, taking care not to spill any of the precious golden powder as he poured a thin line across the back of his hand and then snorted it with his left nostril, then he repeated the process for his right nostril.

Stoke, wondrous Stoke; a chemical fusion between cocaine and PCP that not only killed all the pain in your body—and Gash had plenty of pain after his rooftop battle with Little Mary Sunshine—but also doubled, sometimes tripled your physical strength while acting as a sensory inhibitor.

In other words: Nothing registered; no pain, no pleasure, nothing.

You were Stoked, ready to fight: inhuman.

He rose from the sofa, grabbed an Uzi, and fired into the air.

All along the candlelit balconies of the old Taft Hotel, the Stompers assembled.

"We now know who it is the good doctor works for," croaked Gash, feeling the effects of the Stoke starting to kick in. "And we know that all of them are responsible for the death of our potential brother-in-arms."

The Stompers stared down at him in glassy-eyed silence.

"Ready yourselves," cried Gash, growing stronger. "The witching hour nears. That is when we shall begin our greatest strike, my Stompers."

He brought the vial to his nose and treated himself to two more snorts, then lifted his sword.

"Let me hear it," he crooned.

"Wreckage," they whispered.

Gash laughed. "Again, but . . . softer . . ."

". . . wreckage . . ."

Gash put a finger to his lips, staggered slightly, and said, "Shhhhhh . . . save your power, my Stompers . . . softer, softer . . ."

". . . wreckage . . ."
". . . ready yourselves . . ."

73

In the main lab in the basement of PTSI, Sam Preston sat before Roy's console drumming his fingers, checking his watch, then rubbing his eyes.

A few moments later the door opened and a bleary-eyed McCarrick was pushed into the room by a pair of beefy security guards.

Preston gestured for the guards to close the door and wait outside.

Then he pressed a button, engaging the electronic lock.

"What the hell is going on?" shouted McCarrick. "How *dare* you send a pair of your goons to my *home* at this hour! They frightened my wife and daughter half to death."

"Good thing you decided to accompany them," said Preston. "They had orders to *hurt* your wife and daughter if you refused to cooperate."

McCarrick sneered at Preston. *"You sick, twisted bastard!"*

He came at Preston.

And Preston spun the chair around, aiming the Colt Python directly at McCarrick.

McCarrick stopped in his tracks for a moment, then smiled. "You didn't use a gun on me before when you threatened to."

"Care to try your luck a second time?"

McCarrick laughed.

Charged again.

Preston shot him in the leg.

After McCarrick finished thrashing around on the floor and screaming, Preston pulled the medical kit out from under the control panel, gave McCarrick a healthy shot of painkiller, then cleaned and dressed the wound.

"Bullet passed right through the meaty part of your calf," he said. "Bet you had no idea I was such a good shot, did you?"

". . . don't give a *damn* about you or your—" snarled McCarrick.

"Oh, but you will," replied Preston, dragging McCarrick toward the console and putting him in the second chair. "Take a look at that screen right there."

McCarrick did. "That's . . . that's the backyard of my *home*. . . ."

"Yes, it is. I have two men in your backyard right now, Professor. One of them is holding the camera that's broadcasting those pictures. The other one is holding a gun and a small black bag with—how to put this delicately?—various tools of his trade."

McCarrick stared at him.

"He's a professional interrogator," said Preston.

"You mean *torturer*," hissed McCarrick.

Preston shrugged. "You say 'tomato,' I say '*tomahto*'. . ."

"What do you want?"

"What I want," said Preston, turning McCarrick's chair around so the professor faced Roy's console, "is for you to place your right hand on the scan-pad and for you to take hold of that key with your left."

McCarrick looked at the scan-pad, then at the key, already in place and waiting to be turned.

An identical key was in place at Preston's end of the console.

"Oh, no . . ." whispered McCarrick.

"I'm afraid so," replied Preston, staggering over to his chair and dropping into it.

The pain was quite bad; not so much that he'd require a morphine tab, but bad enough that he found it difficult to stand for long periods of time.

"I've spent five years of my life on this project," said McCarrick, a touch of petulance in his voice.

"I'm aware of that," whispered Preston.

"Why *this?* And why *now?* The D and D program will finish running itself in a little over eight hours."

"Because," Preston groaned, "we have a visitor on the grounds, and I'd rather she not know anything about this particular project. Don't look at me that way, Professor; Annabelle Donohoe will demand to be brought down here eventually, and she is not a lady that one refuses. I want . . . no, I *need* for all traces of Roy to be gone.

"So, if you please, place your hands in the necessary positions and—"

Then he noticed the DISCONNECT light flashing.

"How long has Roy been offline?"

McCarrick glared at him. "Almost since the day you brought him to me."

"What?"

McCarrick pulled himself up into a sitting position, groaning at the pain, tears forming in his eyes. "It would've only cost you twenty-thousand dollars."

Preston felt the blood drain from his face.

"Yes," said McCarrick, smiling a cancerous grin. "Five years ago when they diagnosed the tumors on Sarah's spine. I asked you for a loan of twenty thousand dollars to fly Dr. Waggoner over from Geneva. He could've minimalized the damage to Sarah's spine, he might have even kept her out of that wheelchair, but you wouldn't do it, you piece of shit. I betrayed Zac Robillard and Annabelle Donohoe both to come work for you, and you wouldn't even help my daughter when I begged you.

"So now my daughter is a cripple who can't even feed herself or wipe herself, and every cent my wife and I have goes into caring for her. Do you know she probably won't live to see her eleventh birthday. Yes! The cancer's back again, and its eating what's left of her spine." His voice was getting louder and more hysterical. "Do you have any idea how much I hate you—how much I hate even the *idea* of you? You make a random decision about loaning me *pocket change* and an innocent child pays for it!" The tears burst from his eyes and streamed down his face, but McCarrick's fury would not be stopped, not now.

"She has known nothing but pain and loneliness and darkness over every day of her life because of you. And I have to watch her die, and my wife's spirit along with her. So one day you bring me your precious little boy and tell me to babysit him, put him online and let him experience as much of the world as he can.

"Well, *fuck you, and fuck your precious child.* Let him know the loneliness and pain and darkness that Sarah knows. And let him think *you're* the one who did it to him."

". . . *no* . . ." choked Preston.

"I hope he hates you one-tenth as much as I do. And I hope you never have a moment's peace for the rest of your miserable, whorish, shit-stinking life. God! I want to rip out your eyes and suck your skull dry. I want to rip off your head and piss down your neck! I want to tie you to a bed of nails and force-feed lukewarm vomit down your gullet until *YOU CHOKE ON IT! DO WHATEVER YOU WANT TO ME, YOU BASTARD, BUT LEAVE MY FAMILY ALONE!*"

Preston was about to exercise his last, desperate option; overriding the remainder of the D and D program. At this point, about 12 percent of the information stored in Roy would be irrevocably lost, but Preston had resigned himself to that.

His son was lost to him.

Any chance he had to save himself was lost.

Everything was lost.

And it was all his fault. Every last damned bit of it.

The only thing he had to cling to now was his pride; he would not die having Annabelle know he'd failed so miserably at this, the most important thing he'd ever attempted to do.

Forgive me, he thought silently.

My son, my good boy.

"Your hand, then, Professor."

"And if I refuse?"

"Then you'll sit here at gunpoint and watch your daughter's teeth be extracted by a pair of pliers. He also has a soldering tool in that case. Would you like to know what he'll do with that or do you have enough imagination to picture it on your own?"

McCarrick glowered at him.

"I'll take that to mean you'll cooperate," said Preston.

McCarrick released a howl of primitive animal fury and flung himself at Preston. *"ROT IN HELL, YOU FUCKING MON-STER!"*

Preston shot McCarrick point-blank in the face, then dragged the body over to the panel and slapped McCarrick's dead hand onto the scanner pad.

The body fell back, pulling the hand with it.

Preston looked around the lab until he found the small box of tools that maintenance kept for mundane repairs.

He shot open the lid of the toolbox and removed the small hacksaw.

Looked at McCarrick's body.

Then did what he had to do.

After placing McCarrick's severed hand on the scan-pad, Preston placed his left hand on his scan-pad and gripped his key with his right hand.

The system scanned their handprints.

<IDENTIFICATION PHASE 1: VERIFIED>

Then another prompt appeared on the monitor:

<VOICE MATCH INITIATED>

"Preston, Samuel Clemens; Employee Number 000–01–A."

<PRESTON, SAMUEL CLEMENS: VOICE MATCH VERIFIED>

"Override order #7215-BTR36–7. My voice only for remainder of operation." Preston spread his arms out over the console and just managed to grab and turn both keys simultaneously.

Another screen prompt:

<THIS WILL OVERRIDE THE REMAINING DOWNLOAD PORTION OF THE
CURRENT PROGRAM; THIS EXCEPTION IS CLASSIFIED "FATAL" AND WILL
RESULT IN CATASTROPHIC DATA LOSS. DO YOU WISH TO CONTINUE?>

Preston leaned toward his console microphone and said: "Preston. Yes."

<PLEASE RETURN KEYS TO THEIR ORIGINAL POSITIONS>

Preston did.

<REMAINDER OF DOWNLOAD PROGRAM TERMINATED. BEGINNING FINAL
DATA COMPARISON. TIME REMAINING: ONE HOUR, THIRTY-FIVE MINUTES,
FORTY SECONDS>

"That's it, then," said Preston, then lowered his head and wept quietly.

After a moment, he looked at McCarrick's body and said: "It's all just an illusion, Professor. Happiness. Contentment. Inner peace. They're all just illusions we manufacture in order to give our lives the appearance of having purpose, when the truth is there is no purpose, no Supreme Being, no Satan, no heavenly reward or hellish punishment. Everything we do, all our so-called 'accomplishments,' are the result of a cosmic accident. We're just cells under a giant microscope and the joke is, there's no one to look through the lens to map our progress. Don't you find that funny, in a sad sort of way?"

Oddly enough, McCarrick didn't answer.

"Don't worry about your wife and daughter; I'll make sure the illusion's maintained for them. They'll have a good life, I promise. What time is left for Sarah will made good . . . as good as it can be, anyway."

Then he started laughing to himself.

Quietly.

Very, very quietly . . .

74

Stonewall was right; by the time Psy–4, Itazura, Radiant, and Killaine arrived back at the warehouse, packing was the last thing on their minds.

"Where's Zac?" asked Stonewall, trying hard not to let his anxiety show in his voice.

"Radiant says that Preston has him," replied Psy–4.

"But she's not sure?"

"Not one hundred percent, no, but right now it's all we have to go on."

Stonewall nodded grimly, then pulled Psy–4 aside. "How serious are Zac's wounds?"

"Not life-threatening, but he was hurt pretty bad."

Stonewall nodded once again.

Psy–4 looked into his brother's eyes. "What is it?"

"Singer and I began dismantling everything—"

"—good thinking—"

"—and before I began breaking down the computers I thought it would be best to check on Roy and Preston's system."

"And?"

"I think you need to telepath with Roy one more time before I say any—"

"What is it?"

Stonewall almost couldn't look at Psy–4. "There were some odd codes. I can't be certain but I think that Preston has initiated a program override on the remaining time on the D and D."

Psy–4 froze. "Oh, *shit.*"

"Uh-huh."

The two of them ran toward the computer room.

75

Zac opened his eyes and saw stars.

And within those stars, a diffuse ball of light.

Am I dead? he wondered.

Then realized he was lying on his back, his head propped up by thick, soft pillows.

He was on a sofa.

In an office.

Facing a large window.

He tried to sit up but couldn't.

There was no pain from his wound, and as he slowly turned his head toward his wounded shoulder he saw that a large section of his shirt and jacket had been cut away. His shoulder was covered by a heavy cast.

He craned his head slightly and saw the IV bag dangling from a stand behind him. A clear plastic tube ran from the IV down toward his arm, vanishing beneath a gauze pad and several strips of medical tape.

He let his head fall back into the mound of pillows.

"Hello, Zachary," said a lilting female voice.

At first Zac smiled, thinking that Killaine and the others had found him; then he took a deep breath and coughed on the stench of cigarette smoke.

He'd almost forgotten that there was someone else besides Killaine who called him "Zachary."

"Hello, Annabelle," he whispered, turning his head slightly.

He was on the sofa in Preston's office. Across from him was Preston's desk and seated in Preston's chair—the back of which faced him at the moment—was Annabelle.

Slowly, she turned around, smiling at him. "It's been a long time."

"Not long enough," Zac replied.

Annabelle pursed her lips and made a *tsk-tsk* sound. "Now, Zachary, is that any way to behave? After Simmons and I rushed you to PTSI's emergency medical building? The surgeons were worried you might lose part of your arm, but I convinced them to install some alloy and pins. You'll have an ugly mass of scar tissue attached to you, but your shoulder should be as good as—well, *functional enough* in four or five months."

"Delightful."

"Do try to keep your effusive gratitude down to a low roar." Annabelle rose from Preston's chair and crossed over to the sofa.

She began to sit on empty space but in a flash Simmons was there with another chair, sliding it under her and breaking her fall. She smiled at Simmons, then crossed her legs and leaned forward, resting her arms on her knees. "We've a lot of catching up to do, Zachary—but, unfortunately, not a lot of time."

"Did you hear that?" croaked Zac.

"What?"

"The sound of my heart breaking."

Annabelle laughed loudly. "Oh, Zachary . . . believe it or not, I've missed having you around."

Zac looked at the window again and saw the outline of Preston's bank of monitors.

He wondered if Annabelle knew about the hidden doorway and staircase.

She reached over and brushed some hair out of his eyes. "Letting yourself get a little sloppy in your old age."

"My social life isn't as active as it used to be." Zac was surprised that he was this lucid; he wondered what sort of anesthetic the surgeons had used on him.

"Where did we go wrong, Zachary?"

"You make it sound like we were high-school sweethearts who broke up after the prom."

Annabelle responded with something between a smirk and a sneer. "You know what I mean."

Zac sighed. "Why don't you just ask me what you want to know?"

"Fine. Where are the I-Bots?"

"My guess is getting ready to come here."

Now she smiled. "That's what I was hoping to hear."

"You already knew the answer to that," said Zac. "Now stop blowing smoke up my ass and tell me what it is you *really* wanted to know."

Annabelle scooted closer. "Have you designed a new proto-type?"

Zac smiled. "If I have, you'll never find the blueprints."

"Oh, give me a little credit, Zachary. Do you think I'm so naive as to think you'd still be careless enough to put something that valuable down on paper or enter it into a hard-drive file? You're too smart these days for that." She touched his cheek, then ran her hand up to his forehead. "No, if you've a new prototype designed, it's all in *here,*" she put a finger against his temple. "And if I know you, the design isn't in any preliminary stages. You've got it stored away full-blown, every minute detail worked out." She sat back and lit a fresh cigarette, blowing the smoke in Zac's face. "All you lack to bring your new creation into existence is the backing. So why don't you and I quit this irritating cat-and-mouse game we've been playing? Come back to WorldTech, Zachary. You belong there."

"Go to hell."

Annabelle shook her head. "Such language! I remember you as always having been a gentleman."

"People change."

"I haven't."

"I said 'people.'"

Annabelle's face turned into a granite mask. "Don't let's make this *too* personal, Zachary."

"Why not? This whole thing's been personal since the day I left WorldTech."

Annabelle leaned forward and jabbed out with her cigarette; its glowing tip was less than an inch from Zac's face. "I *confided* in you, Zachary. I trusted you enough to share my most secret plans with you, my precious and worthwhile goals, and you thanked me by stealing my property and doing all you could to hurt my name and reputation."

Now it was Zac's turn to laugh loudly. "'Precious and worth-while goals'? Don't make me laugh much harder or I'll pop a vein!"

"Don't mock me, Dr. Robillard!"

"Then don't sugarcoat your precious goals! Not with me, Annabelle!"

She crushed out her cigarette, lit a fresh one. "What was so terrible about what I had in mind?"

"Nothing, if you subscribe to Ceauşescu's theory that humanity can only be effectively ruled by fear and genetic purification."

"Don't compare me with that, that—"

Zac managed to pull himself up enough to keep his face almost level with hers. "The whole purpose of the I-Botics program—at least as you outlined it for me initially—was to create a workforce of teachers, an automated race designed to handle the complexities of computer programming, lunar mining, fusion engineering, laser communications, neurophysiology, and so on."

"To compel the advance of technology, yes," said Annabelle.

"But there was a bit more to it than that, wasn't there?"

"I will *not* listen to your paranoid—"

"Wasn't there?"

"Yes! But you, the mighty Zachary Robillard, you couldn't see past the surface of the goals, oh, no—not the grandson of the great Benjamin Robillard! You were so busy climbing up on your antiquated soapbox and spouting your grandfather's code of morality that you refused to see the beauty of my logic."

"The beauty of your logic?" shouted Zac. "Oh, that's rich. You decide to use I-Botics to lay the groundwork for totally wiping out the subwork of humanity—"

"—the mind-numbing, soul-sucking *grunt work,* Zachary! The pushing and digging and filing and punching and clicking and all the repetitive motions done by the mind and body that could be done so much more effectively and exactingly by robots."

"Yes," said Zac. "A *completely controlled* workforce to ensure that the world could be run so well and smoothly that only a handful of human 'foremen' would be needed to engage in the few remaining professions and 'supervisory' positions to ensure that the rest of the world remained housed, fed, and cared for. How *stupid* do you think I am, Annabelle? Did you really think it wouldn't eventually occur to me that these 'supervisors' would be answerable only to you? And to whom would Annabelle Donohoe answer? *No one!*"

"You make it sound as if I've some sort of demigod complex."

"What the hell else *would* you call it? An admirable career goal?"

"Stop making it sound as if I thought of no one but myself," yelled Annabelle. "We both knew that the future would be owned by those who understood the complexities of the emerging technologies. During all our arguments, all your rages, did you ever once stop to ask yourself what was going to happen to people like those you see living in the streets or hurrying into the hellish factories every morning, their pitiful little metal lunch pails tucked under their arms? Sure, they can operate a metal press, they can run a lathe, but what good is that when faced with the control board of a fusion chamber? Face it, Zachary—there is *no place* in the future for that sort of worker, menial laborers with at-best limited mechanical skills. Already we've seen over forty-three percent of the blue-collar workforce replaced by robots, and in another five years, ten at the most, *all* of those jobs will be performed by robots. Did you ever ask yourself where the noble janitors would fit in, or wonder what would become of the dependable trash collectors? What of them, Zachary? What of the broom-pushers and window-cleaners with only a grade-school education? What fate lies waiting for the butcher, the baker, the old candlestick maker who are still holding onto their soon-to-be lost jobs? What will happen when the robots are finally, totally in place?"

Zac snorted a derisive laughed. "You really expect me to believe you've worried and agonized over the plight of the common man during all this?"

"Yes!"

"Bull*shit,* Annabelle! Do I look like I just fell off the turnip truck?"

"Yes, actually."

"Oh, hardy-har."

Annabelle shrugged. "You asked."

"You jump down my throat about not considering what would happen to the broom-pushers and menial laborers who'll be swallowed up in the technocratic future that's already overpowering us? Turn the question back on yourself, Annabelle! What are those people going to do when you strip them of a job? What's going to happen when your noble plan goes into effect and they find themselves with nothing to do?"

"Don't you see, Zachary—that's where the I-Bots come in! Each person, regardless of their level of education or their station in life, can be assigned a teacher that can open their eyes to their dormant potential. Each person, guided by a teaching machine sophisticated enough to offer an endless array of human activity, can discover and then *master* what he or she is best suited for. Think of the dreamless ones who can be given the opportunity to achieve their dreams! What is so evil about that? In the properly automated and educated world, machines such as the I-Bots could prove to be the *true* humanizing influence! The I-Bots can teach while the other robots and machines do the menial tasks that make living possible, while human beings can do all the things that make life rich and adventurous and enjoyable!"

"Then why insist," snapped Zac, "on the robots and I-Bots being designed more and more to resemble human beings? Why design machines that are based on the human form?"

Annabelle stared at him. "I'm not sure I—"

Zac pulled himself up into a full sitting position. "We began with machines. Those machines became robots molded in our own image. Then we took the next step, we created the I-Bots, cybernetic organisms that are indistinguishable from human beings except upon the closest inspection. Why? Why go through the process of wiping out the subwork of humanity by building more humanlike machines? Why not just try reeducating human society by offering free seminars and classes to the broom-pushers and trash-collectors and candlestick makers? 'Learn fusion at home.' 'Master neurophysiology with a free home computer and this program.' A society that *wants* to better itself *can* better itself."

Annabelle sneered at him. "Still have the old soapbox handy, I see."

"Answer my question, Annabelle. Why go to such lengths to relieve humanity of the burden of work if you only plan to replace human workers with mechanical workers designed to *look* like human workers?"

"Most of the world's menial tasks have been designed to be carried out by humanoid beings."

"Then why was WorldTech so hell-bent to eventually turn all antiquated robots into I-Bots? Why were you so determined to produce an army of humanlike cybernetic organisms?"

Annabelle only stared at him.

"Because," snarled Zac, "your ultimate goal, your hidden agenda, was *not* to give humanity room to realize its potential, but to create a new and highly selective aristocracy, and like all aristocracies throughout history, in order to live in luxury and exquisite idleness, you require sweat off the backs of slaves, serfs, and peasants. Knowing damn well that no human being with an ounce of dignity would allow themselves to be ruled that way, your goal was to create a humanlike peasantry—because, after all, how can an aristocracy revel in its superiority if there is no one to be feel superior *to?*"

Annabelle, wide-eyed, shook her head. "I think all these years of running having finally sent you off your nut, Zachary. You've gone completely insane."

Zac pushed himself forward as best he could, his face only two inches from hers. "Not only did you wish to create a new aristocracy, Annabelle, but you also knew that a certain percentage of the people you put out of work would become depressed and simply allow themselves to rot—but *the rest* . . . the rest, as you say, would turn to mechanical teachers, who would have been programmed to teach them only as much as you *wished* for them to be taught. You couldn't give less of a damn about the common folk learning the liberal arts or gaining an appreciation for music or poetry or philosophy—you and your chosen followers would have complete, unadulterated, unchallenged, irrevocable, and—best of all—*hidden* control of all things human and robotic. What more could you want? To rule a world that doesn't even *realize* it's being ruled.

"Well, fuck you, Annabelle Donohoe. I will not give you the materials or information you need to enslave those you see as being inferior to yourself."

"I take it, then, that our little stroll down memory lane is finished?"

"I hope I live long enough to piss in your open grave, Annabelle." Zac nodded. "*Now* it's finished."

"Fine." Annabelle crushed out her cigarette, took a deep breath, then grabbed a vase from a nearby table and smashed it against the side of Zac's head.

There was a moment of blinding, intense pain, and then an incessant, dull throbbing.

He was aware of several things happening at once; Simmons setting a large iron box on the floor near Annabelle's feet, someone else handing Annabelle a black case roughly the size of palm-top computer; then Annabelle, rising from her chair, opening the lid of the case, and removing a bright, shiny syringe filled with an oddly colored liquid.

"I'm going to give you one last chance, Zachary, to cooperate." She tapped the side of the syringe to make sure there were no bubbles, then leaned over and stuck the needle into the IV tube, pressing down on the plunger until the syringe was emptied.

"Do you know what that was?"

". . . no . . ." He could barely get the word out.

Dizziness. Nausea.

Then Annabelle lifted his head and gave him a long, luxurious drink of cool, cool water. "Better now?"

". . . a little, yeah . . ."

Another cool drink, and Zac's head began to clear.

"Back with me now?" asked Annabelle.

". . . sure . . ."

"Simmons," she said.

Simmons rolled a television stand over, positioning it at the far end of the sofa so Zac could get a good view of the screen.

Turning on the set, Simmons inserted a small video disk into the set's preinstalled player.

"The gentleman you see there," said Annabelle, "is—or rather, *was*—named James. He was a spy the Board of Directors planted in my company—but that's another story and one you'd probably find frightfully boring. Watch what happened to him."

Zac stared dispassionately at the whole ugly scene, from the first thrashings until the final, fiery, grotesque explosion. He refused to show Annabelle any reaction whatsoever.

When it was finished, Simmons turned off the television set and rolled it away.

Annabelle took her seat before Zac once again. "*Now* do you know what I just injected into your system?"

"A nanite."

Annabelle nodded her head. "But you didn't get the James's brand of nanite; nor did you get the second, deadlier strain; no, for you, Zachary, we used a new, experimental model. It functions at seven times the speed of the others."

". . . how long . . . ?" whispered Zac.

"Before the fireworks? An hour and twenty minutes. Give or take a minute or two. Bearing in mind, of course, that this third-strain model has proven to be a bit unstable in some tests."

"So it can go at any time?"

"More or less, yes. Or I can always press the button and activate it. Isn't this wonderful? Like playing Russian roulette with a gun that has a hair trigger, only no one knows it but the gun."

Zac laughed to himself. It hurt like hell. "So you're hoping for a deathbed confession or something along those lines?"

Annabelle shook her head. "Oh, no; you're far too stubborn for that sort of thing. I'm figuring that you've developed a deep affection for your creations over these past five years, and that you'll agree to come back to WorldTech not out of any loyalty to me, but because if you don't I'll sit here and watch you die."

"I'm prepared to die," said Zac.

"I'll alert the media," said Annabelle with mock-surprise. "I know you're prepared to die, Zachary. But consider: The I-Bots are most likely rushing here to save you as we speak. If not, then they've gone depressingly dim—Simmons, Janus, and I planted enough clues with the media that even an amoeba could figure out that you're being held hostage at PTSI."

"So?"

"So if you're dead when they get here, I'll have the advantage of shock on my side. That, coupled with a controlled blast from a positron-freezing gun, will enable me to reclaim my property." A triumphant grin. "And you know that, once they're back in my possession, you are arguably expendable. Oh, sure, those scientists I have won't know nearly as much as you, but they'll know enough to reverse engineer the process."

Zac started at the words "reverse engineer." "You *wouldn't?*"

"Dismantle them?" asked Annabelle. "In a heartbeat. So, I figure that you'll decide to go on with your miserable, misguided existence not because you care about yourself, but because you care about *them.*"

Zac glowered at her.

Because she was right.

Dammit.

"All right," he said, hoping to buy some time until he figured out what to do. "You win. I'll come back. Just . . . undo whatever you've done with the nanite and I'll—"

Annabelle laughed. "To use your own quaint phrase, Zachary, do I look like I just fell off the turnip truck? If you want to live and cooperate, you're going to have to *earn* the privilege."

She rose and nodded her head.

Simmons came over and lifted the metal box that had been placed at Annabelle's feet earlier.

It was a small safe with an electronic lock.

Simmons placed the safe on Preston's desk.

"The lock mechanism is voice-activated," said Annabelle.

"When I press this button, you will speak your name, Zachary; from that moment on the safe will only respond to your voice. In order to unlock it, you have to speak the combination."

Zac only stared at her, waiting for the punchline.

When it came, it was a lulu.

76

Psy–4 gathered everyone together and explained the situation.

"How long do we have until Roy has to be disconnected?" asked Radiant.

"One hour and twenty-seven minutes."

"Give or take ninety seconds," added Stonewall.

"And that's not counting how long it's going to take to locate Zac," said Itazura.

Killaine sat in silence.

Psy–4 looked at her for a moment, then turned back to the group. "All bets are off. They'll know we'll be coming after Zac, so the element of surprise is shot. Our only hope is to hit them hard, with everything we've got."

Singer tapped Psy–4's shoulder.

Would a large diversion be of use?

"What did you have in mind?"

"He's already explained it to me," said Stonewall. "We don't have time to give you the details. Singer, Killaine, and I will take the first van. Give us a five-minute head start, all right?"

"Done," said Psy–4. "Did you divide the weaponry—?"

"As evenly as possible, yes," replied Stonewall.

"Where do we meet you?" asked Radiant.

"The same area of the fence where we entered for the security test."

Itazura held up a hand. "What about all the equipment?"

"Most of it's all set to go," said Stonewall. "What isn't ready we'll have to take care of when we get back."

"And if there's not enough time?"

"Then we take what we can and blow up the rest."

Stonewall snapped his fingers at Singer, then grabbed Killaine's arm and pulled her to her feet, dragging her toward the steps to the garage bay.

"Five minutes," called Psy–4. Then, to Radiant and Itazura: "Let's see how much more of the equipment we can get packed. Something tells me we'll be leaving in a hell of a hurry once this is over."

They were heading for the control room when Itazura said, "Where's all my HIR equipment?"

77

"In this safe," said Annabelle, "you'll find another syringe. This one's filled with a little something we call 'liquid burn.' It's the antidote you need. But here's the tough part, Zachary."

There was a slip of paper taped to the door of the safe. Annabelle reached over and gently removed the paper, then handed it to Zac.

There were seven numbers on the paper: 1, 2, 6, 12, 60, 420, and 840.

"An employee of mine who dabbles in math and mystery novels came up with this," said Annabelle. "There is an order to that sequence of numbers, though it's not as obvious as you might think at first glance." She pressed the button. "Say your name."

Zac remained silent.

Annabelle nodded.

Simmons stood by Zac and tossed a small amount of salt into the cut made by the vase earlier.

"Ouch!" cried Zac.

"Good enough," said Annabelle, gesturing to the red indicator light at the top of the safe. "The mechanism will now respond only to your voice, Zac, and—no, don't speak. Whatever you do, for the next several minutes, you absolutely *must not* speak. Nod if you understand."

Zac nodded.

"Good. Now, the eighth number in that series completes the combination that will activate the lock mechanism and open the safe. Just to make it tricky, there are several correct solutions to the sequence, but only one will open the safe—you'll know which one it is . . . Keep in mind that you are free to move about this office, Zachary; but also keep in mind that we have disconnected the computer, removed Samuel's electronic calculator, and taken every piece of paper and writing instrument, so you'll have nothing with which to do your figuring. *That* will have to be done in your head. And in silence.

"You see, Zachary, you can only speak aloud *once,* which means that you can only recite the combination once; that's all the program allows. Say one word, utter one syllable that isn't the combination, and the program will consider *that* your guess and shut down and you won't be able to get to the antidote. Understand the rules so far?"

He nodded.

"Good. So now, all you have to do is, in silence, figure out the next number in that sequence and say it aloud." She signaled Simmons, then she began to move toward the office doors. "Get it right, and the door will open, you'll grab the syringe and inject yourself with the antidote and be a happy camper.

"Get it *wrong,* and . . . well, you saw what happened to poor Mr. James."

Before closing the door, she smiled at him and said, "And just so you know, I'm doing it this way just to make you squirm. Payback's a bitch, and so am I."

With that, she smiled, blew him a kiss, then closed and locked the door behind her.

78

Driving out of Cemetery Ridge, Stonewall checked his watch, then cast a glance at Singer and asked, "You're positive that the other robots know how to—"

Yes.

Stonewall shook his head in amazement. "All of you know the sewer systems *that well?*"

Yes. You would be surprised how much more quickly you can get around on foot underground than with an automobile or even hover-car on the surface.

"How many HIR units did you program?"

Twenty-two. That is all Itazura had.

"Then it'll have to do." Stonewall looked over at Killaine. "Are you going to snap out of this anytime soon?"

". . . I . . . *how* could it have happened?" She shook her head and turned her face up toward Stonewall. "Tell me, Stoner; how was it possible for me to kill him? Not only that, but why haven't I ceased all functions?"

Stonewall looked at her, then returned his attention back to the road. "I want you to listen very carefully to what I'm going to tell you, Killaine, and you mustn't ask any questions, all right?"

"I can't promise that."

"You'll *have* to, because I won't have any answers to them. There are certain areas of our programming that only Zac fully understands, and for his own reasons, he chooses to keep those reasons to himself.

"Over the years," said Stonewall, "Zac has entrusted each of us with bits and pieces of information not known to the others. I suppose the practical reason was so, in case any of us were captured or stolen by Annabelle, no *one* of us on our own would possess *all* the information she'd need. I think the more *humanistic* reason is so each of us will feel a bond with him—sharing a secret with someone just naturally has that effect." He shrugged. "I've also always believed he did it because he wanted us to know what it felt like to have to choose to betray a confidence in order to serve the greater good—to make the kind of difficult choices humans have to make, and in our doing so, becoming a little more humanlike—after all, we were designed to replace humankind if the worst ever happened so that humanity's best principles wouldn't perish." He sighed, checked the mileage, then continued.

"Here is a secret I share with him—or, rather, *did* share until now: When Zac modified our programming from ordinary robots, he made it possible for us to kill an opponent if it was absolutely necessary. He realized that, because each of us has a different and distinct personality, that certain . . . *variables* had to be taken into account. Itazura's playfulness, my aloofness, Radiant's vanity . . . your temper."

Killaine's head snapped back up.

"You're probably already getting the idea," said Stonewall. "By giving each of us the ability to kill, he knew it would only be a matter of time before one of us *did*. And because the last thing he wanted was for us to look upon the taking of a life dispassionately, to view it simply as a means to an end, something with no emotional price to be paid . . . he modified the programming further, taking into the account the possibility of an accidental killing."

Killaine wiped her eyes and whispered. "But . . . *why?*"

"Because each of us, in our own way, will sometime, someday *have to* experience the grief, the guilt, the rage, the confusion, all of the emotions that accompany the act of taking a life, and then learn how to expand our capacity to learn from that pain." Stonewall looked at her and gave a sad smile. "You just happened to be the first of us to do so. You now possess knowledge that the rest of us don't: You know what it feels like to kill. So now it's up to you to make the rest of us understand the price one pays for that."

". . . still don't understand why . . ."

"Zac has a deep, abiding reverence for life—*all* life. Think about it—have you ever seen him so much as swat a mosquito?"

"No."

"Even with the DNA he gave to us, Zac knew there was no way he could *teach* that reverence for life to us. It had to be obtained through experience."

". . . and so one of us had to be the first to kill."

Stonewall nodded his head. "I'm afraid so. And I'm afraid it now falls on you to make us comprehend how that makes you feel."

"But what about . . . I mean, if I accidentally killed once, what's to prevent me from losing control and doing it again?"

"Our individual capacity to learn from what happened—*your* capacity, in this instance. We may very well be put in a position again where we have to kill in order to save human lives from certain death. All we can do now is our best to not put ourselves in a position where killing may be necessary—a conscious, *individual* choice on each of our parts.

"But face the facts, Killaine; an absolute 'no kill' rule for all of us, given Annabelle's pursuit and some of the security work we do, would be a disaster.

"There's now a kind of fail-safe device that links us all together. Because you have done what you've done, you have activated a sort of gestalt mechanism contained in each of us; from this day on all of us start learning the hard lessons that taking a life has to teach us."

"Lessons?"

"Knowing what you do now, knowing how it feels to take a human life, would you ever do so again and take it lightly?"

"No, no—*never!*"

"You'll link that to the rest of us now . . . until it happens with another one of us." He reached over and placed one of his mighty hands atop Killaine's. "Robots aren't supposed to be able to kill, but we're not robots—not wholly, anyway. Human beings *shouldn't* kill, but they do. And we're partly human—at least, in the psychological and emotional sense. Like it or not, violence is a fact of our existence. We cannot be like regular robots who are physically *incapable* of killing. Zac knew this when he made the modifications. We *can* take a life under the most extreme of circumstances, Killaine, but, with your guidance now, we'll learn to value all levels and forms of life."

Killaine shook her head. "So I'm the standard-bearer for I-Botic freewill?"

"That's pretty much it. It's the first day of a new school for all of us now." He touched her cheek. "If it's any comfort to you, I would have torn the little bastard in half for shooting Zac and that boy."

Killaine leaned up and kissed Stonewall's cheek. "Thanks, Stoner."

He looked at her. "Feel better?"

"No . . . but I can now believe I will. Eventually."

"Well, then."

"Yes. Well, then."

79

1, 2, 6, 12, 60, 420, 840.

Zac stared at the numbers.

Okay, Zachary, think, think.

Begin with placement, then try division.

In any incomplete/interrupted sequence of numbers (if he remembered his Euclidian logic correctly), you have to remember to count the number of the place of the missing digit.

There were seven numbers, but *eight* places; and once you have the eighth number, you have to remember to count the ninth place, even if you *don't* have that number.

Piece of cake.

Right, he thought: *And if you believe that, odds are you'll find a guy with some prime real estate to sell in the Florida swamps.*

But that sort of thinking was getting him nowhere.

He looked at the numbers again.

The larger numbers could be easily divided in countless ways, but the key had to be with the smaller numbers.

To whit: 1 can only be divided by 1 itself.

2 can be divided by both 1 and 2.

6 can be divided evenly by 1, 2, and 3—in fact, it was the smallest number that could be divided by those digits.

Except there's no three, you moron! Zac scolded himself.

Unless it has something to do with *consecutive* digits beginning with 1 that can serve as divisors. 6 appeared *third* in the series, so the number 3 *must be* relevant.

Okay, maybe, *maybe* there was something there.

Go with it, he thought.

He managed to get to his feet and, taking hold of the IV rack, began to slowly pace.

He nearly fell at first from the initial dizziness but caught himself on the edge of Preston's desk.

All right, then: 12 appears fourth in the series. 12 can be divided evenly by 1, 2, 3, and 4. Okay, Zac old man, you're onto something.

The fifth number was 60. That could be evenly divided by 1, 2, 3, 4, 5—*and* 6!

Six. How could he have overlooked the most often-employed number in long division? Not only that, but he wasn't taking into account the fact that there *was* an eighth number in the series, so even though he didn't have the number itself, he did have its place—number 8.

Whoa, Zac—hold the phone. Didn't you start off *reminding yourself of that?*

Dammit to hell! This was not—repeat *not*—the time to let himself confuse himself.

Zac increased the speed of his pacing.

420 could be divided evenly by all the previous digits and the number of their placement in the series—1 through 7—right: and the final number, 840, was divisible by all the digits and the number of their placement in the series: 1 through 8.

Okay, all right, getting closer, have to be getting closer now . . .

He stumbled again, almost crying out, but managed to choke back his voice at the last second.

Son-of-a-bitching IV!

He looked at Preston's desk until he found what he was looking for: a tape dispenser.

He pulled off several strips of plastic tape and attached them to the edge of the desk.

Then he gently removed the gauze pad, cotton balls, and medical tape that covered the spot where the IV needle entered his vein.

He scanned the top of the desk again and found a large eraser, which he picked up, dusted off, then clenched between his teeth.

He took a deep breath, then quickly pulled the IV needle from his arm.

For a moment, there was a frightening amount of blood.

Zac pressed the gauze pad and cotton balls to the wound and bent his arm, then quickly grabbed up the medical tape and strips of plastic tape and slapped them to the gauze, pulling each strip tighter than the one before.

It took a moment, and he had to spend two minutes holding his arm over his head, but eventually the bleeding stopped.

Exhausted, he staggered back over to the sofa and sat down.

Okay, where was I?

The seventh number, 840, and the missing eighth digit.

The next number in the series, which damn well better be the combination or he was toast, should be the smallest number that could be divided evenly by all the previous numbers and the number of the space following: 1 through 9.

If you multiply 840 by 3, the product is divisible by 9 and remains divisible by all the lesser digits in the sequence. And, since 840 multiplied by 3 is . . . is . . . c'mon, c'mon, you used to be good at this . . . carry the 1 . . . add that to the . . . right, right . . . 840 times 3 is 2520.

The combination has to be *2520!*

He opened his mouth, then snapped it closed once again.

Not because he was uncertain of the solution.

Not because he doubted his logic.

Not because he was worried that he might slur his words.

No; Zac Robillard shut his mouth because he was afraid he might laugh—not only at Annabelle's remarkable cleverness, but at his own stupidity, as well.

2520 had been his employee number when he worked at WorldTech.

Taking a deep breath and composing himself, Zac opened his mouth and spoke slowly and clearly.

"2, 5, 2, 0."

The safe buzzed, clicked, and the door swung open, revealing the case within.

Zac stumbled over, retrieved the case, and opened it.

Annabelle hadn't been lying; there was the syringe.

But what if it's a trick? he suddenly thought. *What if the initial shot was nothing more than colored water and* this *syringe contains the nanite?*

No—Annabelle would have stayed to watch if she was going to pull something that perverted.

And, whether she was willing to admit it or not—Annabelle Donohoe never admitted to any weakness—Zac was useful to her.

He tapped the side of the syringe to remove any bubbles, then found a nice, plump vein, and gave himself the shot.

After that, he fumbled around Preston's desk until he found the hidden button, pressed it, and opened the secret passage behind the monitor banks.

Time to see where you go, he thought, and began to slowly, cautiously, descend the iron spiral staircase.

80

It took Singer a little more than nine minutes to place the portable HIR units at various locales surrounding the outskirts of the PTSI compound.

He returned to the spot where, now, all the I-Bots were assembled.

"Well?" asked Stonewall.

Singer gave him the thumbs-up sign.

"I can't believe you were messing around with my equipment," whispered Itazura.

Singer put a hand on Itazura's shoulder, then signed, *Sorry— but wait until you see the modifications I made.*

"Modifications?"

"Shhhh!" said Psy–4. "We have to take a vote."

"On what?" snapped Radiant.

"Do we focus solely on retrieving Zac or do we try for both Zac and Roy?"

The rest of them exchanged confused glances.

Itazura was the one who said it: "After all this, you're willing to abandon Roy?"

Psy–4 glared at him. "We've got seventy-nine minutes until the final D and D stage is complete. Given a choice between Roy and Zac, there *is no choice.*"

"You have to hate that."

"What I feel about it doesn't matter—which is why I'm not voting. Singer can have my vote. It's up to the rest of you: Zac or Zac *and* Roy?"

Why either/or? inquired Singer.

"Because—" began Psy–4.

"Shut up," said Killaine.

"I beg your pardon?"

"I said, 'shut up.'" She looked at the others. "I say we split up. Psy–4 and Radiant already know Roy's physical location. They head to the lab, the rest of us will search for Zac."

"What about Singer?" asked Stonewall.

Killaine smiled and put a hand on the robot's shoulder. "Singer's going to be busy creating a diversion for us, aren't you, my friend?"

Diversion is so mild a word for what I have in mind.

Killaine put out her hand. "Does everyone agree?"

All of them, Singer included, placed their hands into the circle.

"Then we are decided," said Psy–4.

They broke the circle, waiting for Singer's signal.

Singer activated the main HIR unit, checked the signal strength, then signed: *Nothing up my sleeve . . . Presto!*

And with the flick of a switch the grounds surrounding the PTSI compound were swarming with an army of robots.

"Let's move." said Psy–4.

And the siege began. . . .

"Control, this is East Tower Two, over."

"Go ahead East Tower Two, over."

"We have initiated security lights and have established visual contact with a large group of robots, approximately twenty-five to thirty in number, armed and moving toward the Sector B entrance gate. Please advise, over."

"East Tower Two, are you certain that the robots are armed, over."

"Affirmative. The largest of the group is carrying what appears to be an M–60, over."

Silence.

"Control, we need permission to open fire, over."

"East Tower Two, the order is given; commence firing upon intruders, over and out."

Once inside the gates, Radiant rerouted the energy of all security sensors so the I-Bots could move quickly and undetected toward the main building.

They were less than one hundred feet from the basement entranceway when one of the guard towers opened fire with a large, fully automatic machine-gun.

"What the *hell*—?" said Itazura.

"They're firing on the robots," whispered Radiant.

"How long do you think it will be until they figure out they're holos?"

"Not before Singer activates the next batch. Now, come on!"

"Control, this is North Tower One—"

"Control, this is Security Kiosk Seven, South-West Sector—"

"Control, this is Observation Booth Five, Main Building—"

"—we have visual contact with a large group of robots—"

"—we have established visual contact with what appears to be a band of robots—"

"—visuals on a group of robots, approximately thirty to forty in number—"

"—please advise—"

"—please advise—"

"—please advise—"

The guards were just moving McCarrick's body from the computer room when one of their portable radios squawked loudly. The guard answered at once, then looked toward Preston.

"Sir?"

"What?"

"We have a situation outside the compound."

"So? Handle it."

"Control respectfully asks that you pick up on line one."

Preston groaned and snatched up the receiver. "This had better be damned good."

He listened to what Control had to say.

His face grew pale.

Then he nodded his head and said: "You have authorization to use any and all means at your disposal to stop them. *Yes,* including explosives. Keep me advised." He slammed down the phone, turned toward the guards, and said, "Why are you still here?"

"Because I told them not to be in such a hurry," said Annabelle, stepping into the room.

And that's when Preston saw the WorldTech guards relieving his own security of the burden of their weapons. . . .

Down in the lower-level corridor, Psy–4 and Radiant went left while Stonewall, Killaine, and Itazura went right.

Alarms were sounding everywhere.

"I don't know how much longer I can control all this," said Radiant. "Too much is happening at once."

"Do the best you can," shouted Psy–4.

He grabbed her hand and they ran toward the branch in the hallway where Psy–4 had first experienced the feeling of fear and loneliness.

They made a sharp right.

And there was the door.

And there was the wall-mounted hand-scanner.

And there was another door where one hadn't been before, and then suddenly, like a ghost from an old Gothic novel, there was a hunched and twisted figure coming right the hell out of the wall, and Psy–4 lunged for it because it was carrying what looked like a very large gun. . . .

The security towers hit the oncoming robots with everything they had; from heavy strafing with mounted M–60s to hand grenades and rocket launchers.

Nothing stopped them.

Nothing harmed them.

Nothing even seemed to *touch* them.

And just when it seemed there couldn't possibly be any more of the damned things, four more reported sightings came in. . . .

Hidden within the trees and foliage, Singer checked the main HIR unit.

He'd engaged less than half the portable units.

He looked toward the compound, saw the lights in the night, the muzzle-flash of all the firepower, the smoke hanging in the air from the grenades and rockets, and wondered how anyone could manage to see anything through all the fire, smoke, and debris.

Then decided it didn't matter.

And activated the next series of three units.

The magnified images appeared.

If he weren't so worried, this might actually have been fun. . . .

* * *

"Holy shit! Tower Three, this is Tower Five. Are you guys see-ing what I'm seeing?"

"No way, Tower Five, that *I'm* going to be the one to say it."

"Towers Three and Five, this is Control. When you are on this frequency you will observe the rules of—"

"—with all due respect, Control, look out your east window."

"Towers Three and Five, be advised that all personnel assigned to your—oh, *holy shit!*"

"Told you. This is Tower Three—we're getting the hell out of Dodge. Over and out."

All over the compound tower guards were freezing at the sight of dozens of IA–2112 model mining robots running toward the gates.

The IA–2112 models were rumored to be at least twice the size of a normal mining robot.

Those rushing at the gates were easily *eight* times that size; nineteen feet from the bottoms of their feet to the tops of their heads.

That is, while on all fours and running.

Standing straight up, the things had to be at least thirty feet in height.

Most of the tower guards got the same idea at roughly the same moment.

Time to go . . .

Making certain that the guards in the towers nearest him were vacating their posts, Singer readied the first of several mini-ShellBlasters he'd found among the I-Bots' arsenal.

He focused on the closest tower, watching as the guards

threw open the trap door and started running down the stairs.

He waited until they were just past the halfway point, well out of danger, and set the ShellBlaster on his shoulder, took aim, and fired.

The rocket slammed into the top of the tower at the same time the magnified image of the IA–2112 reached the area.

The tower went up in a mushroom of fire, smoke, and metal.

To anyone watching from a distance, it would have appeared that the giant IA–2112 had rammed the tower and blown up.

Singer tossed aside the empty ShellBlaster, checked to make sure the escaping guards were unharmed—they were—then grabbed up an armful of the rocket launchers and ran for the next tower.

The IA–2112 holo ought to be reaching it anytime now. . . .

The phone buzzed again and Preston grabbed the receiver.

"Sir, this is Control again. We have reports of oversized IA–2112 model robots destroying security towers."

"Can you confirm this?"

"Yes, sir. They're big mothers."

Preston rubbed his eyes, glared at Annabelle, then sighed. "All right, then, we don't have much of a choice: Sound the evacuation signal and unlock all underground entrances. I want you to remain at your post, along with any guards whose towers have been reduced to rubble."

He didn't wait for a response.

Annabelle was standing right in front of him.

Preston looked up at her and was amazed by her face.

Usually your One Great Love doesn't look a thing like you remember.

Annabelle looked even more beautiful than he'd recalled.

"Hello, Sam," she whispered.

Even she was unable to hide the pity in her eyes.

"Do I look that bad?" asked Preston.

". . . yes . . ." she said softly, then touched his cheek.

Preston couldn't help it.

He leaned forward, pressing his face into her midsection and wrapping his arms around her.

"I'm so scared, Annabelle."

"Shhh," she said, stroking the back of his head. "It's all right now, I'm here, I'll take care of everything. You don't need to—"

She froze.

Preston could feel her body tense.

"What the *hell* is happening here?" she said.

Preston pulled back and looked at her.

Her face was so cold, her eyes even colder.

She was looking through the glass partition at the computer and the platinum-iridium brain installed in the center of everything.

Preston began to look at it, also, not really thinking about it—he'd seen it enough times—but then he caught a quick glimpse of what had Annabelle so mesmerized; a little thing, really, something Preston had seen every day for five years and so didn't really think about it, didn't actually *see* it, any longer.

A label.

That's all.

Just one of those little stick-on plastic name gizmos that you make with a handheld label-maker.

No big thing, really.

Until now, that is.

His gaze locked on it like that of a condemned man locking on the rifles held by the members of a firing squad.

All over, all gone, bye-bye, he thought, reaching over to touch the label.

The little one that was no Big Thing, really.

The little one he never thought about.

The little one with ROY printed on it. . . .

It wasn't until Psy–4 was about to throw himself headlong into the figure that Radiant caught a surge of familiar energy emanating toward her and called out, "Zac!"

He moved just in time.

Psy–4, trapped by his own momentum and unable to stop his charge, blew past Zac and slammed headfirst into a section of the wall, burying himself up to the shoulders.

Zac fell back against the door and slid to the floor. "*That* had to hurt."

". . . oh, yeah . . ." whispered Psy–4 from somewhere deep in the plaster.

Radiant ran over to Zac, dropped to her knees, and threw her arms around him as best she could, considering the cast. "Oh, Zac, we were all so worried that Preston had . . . had . . ."

"It's okay," he whispered to her. "Now, what say we round up the others and get out of here before—"

"There's something you need to know," said Psy–4, pulling himself from the wall and shaking off the dust, plaster, and chunks of drywall.

Zac grinned a pained grin. "Let me guess—does it have something to do with my birthday present?"

"Yes."

He looked at Radiant, then at Psy–4. "I am all at attention."

Psy–4 cleared his throat and began to explain about Roy.

Of course, Zac would have to settle for the Reader's Digest Condensed version, seeing as how they had less than fifty-eight minutes left. . . .

* * *

The employees of PTSI, having heard the emergency evacuation signal, headed en masse for the underground shelters, only to find, as the huge, electronically controlled iron doors swung open, that there were *things* waiting for them inside.

Each of the twelve underground shelters contained an underground vent for air.

These vents either crisscrossed or passed directly through other, larger vents.

Including a large cement sewer drain.

The robots who'd been hiding under the IPS, Inc., building had wound their subterranean way through the tunnels to emerge, as planned, into the emergency shelters of PTSI.

The evacuating employees, their nerves already frazzled by the explosions and panic outside the walls, screamed at the sight of the robots emerging from the depths, turned tail, and ran blindly through the corridors and offices, smashing windows and overturning furniture, anything at all to either get out of the building or lay hands on something to serve as a weapon. . . .

Itazura, Killaine, and Stonewall smashed through the doors of Preston's office, StunShooters at the ready.

The place was not empty, but it had been seriously trashed.

They saw the scattered papers.

The knocked-over furniture.

The IV stand.

The safe and empty syringes.

And the bloodstains on the sofa and floor.

"He was here," said Killaine. "Zac was in here—recently."

"How can you tell?" asked Itazura.

"Is that or is that not Old Spice I smell?"

"Gotcha."

Then Stonewall spotted the hidden door behind the monitors. "If no one's got any better ideas, I say we try it."

Itazura and Killaine were already heading down the spiral staircase before he'd finished saying "try."

Stonewall was right behind them, pulling the bank of monitors back in place behind him. . . .

Singer just finished blowing up the fifth guard tower—which, to all witnesses, appeared to be the work of an out-of-control, oversized IA–2112—and was just returning to check the HIR unit when he saw a crowd of shadows pass through one of the distant, smoky security lights.

He remained very still, focusing his photoelectric eyes and activating their zoom lenses.

Another rush of shadows.

And this time he saw one of them clearly.

Stompers.

Heavily armed.

He looked down at the HIR unit, activated the remaining images, and was readying to head into the compound when his leg scraped against something. . . .

"So where's the portable chamber?" asked Zac.

Psy–4 looked at Radiant, who shook her head and said, "I was too anxious about Zac and didn't think to—"

"*Dammit!*" hissed Psy–4, smashing his fist into another section of the wall and burying his arm up to the elbow. "Dammit to hell! *How* could I have made such a *stupid* mistake?"

Radiant came over and put her hands on his shoulders. "A lot was happening very quickly and all of us were worried about Zac."

"But—"

"No buts; we didn't know if he was still alive."

Psy–4 yanked his arm from the wall, whirled around, and grabbed Radiant by the shoulders. *"That's no excuse! There is no excuse for a mistake of this magnitude!"*

Radiant placed a hand against Psy–4's chest, punching a hole in his anxiety and calming him slightly. "We've still got a way to buy a little time."

"What?"

She produced a palmtop computer from her supply pouch. "The Catherine Wheel program."

Zac's head snapped up. *"You didn't?"*

"We had to," whispered Psy–4. "We needed to make sure that everything was in complete and total anarchy before we made our move to disconnect Roy from the mainframe."

Zac glared at the two of them "Why didn't you come to me? I would have understood."

"We thought you didn't need anything more to worry about," replied Radiant.

"I'm a big boy, Radiant. From now on, let me be the judge of what I can and cannot deal with, or else—oh, screw it! We'll settle this later." He grabbed the palmtop from Radiant's hands. "I assume, Psy–4, that you preset the initiation time?"

"Yes, but—"

"Shut up," snapped Zac. "I'm also assuming that *this*"—he held up the palmtop—"is programmed with an override sequence in case the need arose to activate the program before its preset time? You'd damn well better say yes."

"Yes."

Zac nodded his head. "Good thinking. Give me everything but the last three numbers."

Psy–4 rattled off the sequence, stopping where Zac had ordered.

Zac entered the sequence, then looked at Radiant. "Can you go back and get the portable chamber?"

"Absolutely."

Zac looked at his watch. "Fifty-two minutes. Which means that the fifteen-minute window of opportunity—"

"—on either side," said Psy–4.

"—on either side is . . . shit—*twenty-two* minutes away, allowing time to set up." Zac looked at Radiant. "You waiting for a good-bye kiss? Go!"

She gave him a quick salute. "Aye-aye, sir!"

And took off at roughly the same time Itazura, Killaine, and Stonewall emerged from the hidden door behind Zac.

Zac whirled around and faced them. "About time."

They were momentarily too stunned to respond.

"Happy to see you, too," said Zac, smiling. "Sorry, but we don't have time for a warm and fuzzy reunion. Killaine, I want you to—first of all, how are you doing?"

"Much better, thank you."

"Good. Radiant's on her way to retrieve the portable chamber. Go after her and run interference in case someone tries to stop her. You up to that?"

Killaine's answer was a quick kiss on Zac's cheek, then she was gone—a blur and a memory.

"Itzy," barked Zac. "Get outside and secure some sort of vehicle for us—I don't give a damn if it's a Jeep, a chopper, or a bunch of Schwinn ten-speeds; get *something*."

"But the vans are parked just outside the compound," Itazura responded.

"Repeat what you just said."

"The vans are parked just outside the—oh."

Zac nodded. "Right. The vans aren't going to do us a whole helluva lot of good *outside* the compound, are they? We have to *get to them* first!"

Itazura shrugged in embarrassment. "Silly me."

Then he became a blur and a memory.

"Stoner," snapped Zac.

"Yessir?"

"Come over here and stand behind me."

Stonewall did as he was instructed. "Now what?"

"Catch me, buddy; I'm getting dizzy."

Zac collapsed into Stonewall's arms, conscious but momentarily disoriented. . . .

"Control, this is Security Kiosk Nine, we need Tower Personnel to confirm a visual."

"Kiosk Nine, why haven't you abandoned your post? The evacuation alarm has been sounding for several minutes."

"Control, are there *any* Tower Personnel still at their post? We *really* need a second visual confirmation on this."

"Control, this is West Tower Six, McPherson speaking, over."

"McPherson, can you confirm whatever in the hell it is that Security Kiosk Nine is seeing?"

"Affirmative, Control, over."

"Well?"

"Security Kiosk Nine appears to be under siege by about a dozen Godzillas, over."

Silence.

"West Tower Six, this is Control. Would you say that again?"

"Yes, Control; Security Kiosk Nine is surrounded by several Godzillas."

"Godzillas?"

"Several of them, Control, yes."

"Godzilla—as in Tokyo, Mothra, Ghidrah, Rodan, and *vs. The Smog Monster?*"

"That would be the one, Control."

"West Tower Six, do me a favor, shoot a rocket at them and see what happens."

"Affirmative." Then, several seconds later: "Went right through them, Control."

"Could you be a little more specific?"

"They appear to be holographic images being broadcast from an unknown source."

"So what you're telling me, McPherson, is that someone has been playing a large-scale practical joke on us?"

"It would seem that way, Control, over."

"Ah, well, *hell . . .*"

Annabelle reached into one of her pockets and removed a fully automatic pistol and pointed it at Preston. "What's going on here?"

Preston held up his hands. "I can explain all of this, Annabelle."

She looked at her guards. "Leave this room and make sure no one else enters until I call you—that goes for you as well, Simmons."

"Madam."

A few moments later, she and Preston were alone in the room.

"Start explaining," she said, her voice cracking.

"I didn't want you to find out, not like this."

"Find out *what?*"

"About Roy."

A single tear slid down her right cheek. "Roy's dead."

Preston stared at the gun in silence, then slowly began to rise from the chair, gesturing toward the computer beyond the glass. "Well, you see, about that . . ."

Beyond the perimeter of the compound, the HIR system ran out of juice.

The robot army disappeared.

As did the oversized IA–2112s.

And the Godzillas that had been giving Security Nine such nervous moments.

For a minute, there was nothing but smoke, sputtering flames, and floating debris.

Then out of the darkness a crowd of shadows came running toward a rocket-blasted section of fence.

Screaming about wreckage . . .

Killaine and Radiant were nearing the section of fence where they'd entered earlier when Singer emerged from the smoke, carrying the portable chamber in his arms as if it were a baby.

Killaine was so proud of him she could have cried.

"Oh, Singer," whispered Radiant, reaching out to take the chamber from his arms. "I don't know how you managed to get through without being shot to pieces, but you'll have to teach me sometime."

Killaine took the chamber from Radiant. "We need your hands free in case there're any security devices still functioning properly—though judging from the mess out here I doubt there are."

The three of them turned and started back toward the main building.

And that's when the world seemed to come to an end. . . .

Itazura was darting around the grounds of the compound, his StunShooter at the ready in case he encountered any security guards.

There were several different vehicles parked all over the grounds.

Of course, most of them were burning right now, having been blasted by panic-fire.

Two guards came out of the smoke and ran toward him.

He got both of them with one blast, knocking them unconscious—as they would remain for the next several hours.

To make sure they'd remain safe, he dragged them into a nearby supply shed.

Then resumed his search.

He saw the truck—unharmed and unguarded—at the same time he caught a quick glance of Radiant, Killaine, and Singer.

Then the whole world blew up. . . .

Annabelle stared at the computer and the mechanical brain, stunned beyond both words and action for the first time in her life.

Roy.

Her son was in there.

Alive.

Alive!

"Annabelle?" said Preston very, very softly.

". . . what . . . ?"

"I did it for us. I wanted us to be a family again."

". . . we were never a family, Sam . . ."

"Then I did it because I wanted us to *finally* be one."

Slowly, Annabelle turned back to look at him.

He seemed so pathetic to her right now, so desperate and helpless and so completely without any grasp of reality.

"I don't love you, Sam. I never did."

"I know, I know, but"—he pointed toward the computer—"don't you think that, maybe, you could *learn* to?"

"You're dying, Sam."

"But we have *Zac* now! Don't you see? If he can design the I-Bots to be so humanlike, then why can't he build bodies for Roy and me, as well? Bodies just like the I-Bots', so human, able to feel, to touch, to give and receive affection."

When Annabelle didn't say anything, Preston came a step closer to her, then slowly began to get on his knees. "I don't want to die, Annabelle, not like this—so weak, so drained, wearing *diapers* under my suit because I never know when—"

"—get up, Sam—"

"—you're the only woman I've ever loved, Annabelle, and I only did what I did with Roy because I saw how much it hurt you, how his death nearly destroyed you—"

"—I'm warning you, Sam, *get up*—"

Preston grabbed Annabelle's other, empty hand and brought it to his lips. "Oh, *please, please* Annabelle, let's do it. Even if you don't . . . don't care for me, at least give me a second chance at life for what I tried to do for Roy—"

It was the "tried" that did it, that tipped off Annabelle.

She looked at the console, then the computer, then Preston. "You bastard," she whispered. "You never . . . you never intended to tell me, did you?"

"I had no choice, Annabelle, things went wrong and he would have been brain damaged and I knew you wouldn't want him, not like that, so—"

"—how fucking *dare* you decide for me that I wouldn't want my son back because he'd be brain damaged! How *dare* you keep this from me all these years! Do you have any idea the . . . the *hurt* I've felt every day and night for the last five years? And all this time you had him here, had him *trapped* in your system like a prisoner and—"

She caught it from the corner of her eye.

A screen-prompt.

<DATA COMPARISON TIME REMAINING: 00:27:42>

"Data comparison?" she said aloud, more to herself than anyone.

It took a moment for the full impact to hit her.

"You *bastard!*" she screamed, slamming the pistol against the side of Preston's skull and knocking him to the floor. "Something went *wrong?* You screwed up, didn't you? You screwed up and didn't want anyone to know about it, so now you're running a Download and Dump. You're . . . you're killing him again."

Preston started to get to his feet.

Annabelle stepped over, slammed a solid Tai kick into the other side of his head, then stood over him, one leg on either side of his chest.

"You're taking him away from me a second time . . . before I ever knew I still had him."

". . . Annabelle, please, there's still time, if we can get Zac—"

She gripped the automatic with both hands and took careful aim.

"Annabelle!" screamed Preston. *"Annabelle, I did it because I love you, PLEASE—"*

There were twelve shots in the clip and one in the chamber.

Annabelle emptied all thirteen of them into Preston's head and chest.

She was still squeezing the trigger over and over when Simmons came into the room and took the pistol from her hands, whispering, "I'm here for you, madam, I'm right here, now, please, we must—"

And that's when part of the wall in the computer room exploded. . . .

The blast that hit the compound yard was like nothing any of the I-Bots had ever experienced before.

As Itazura felt himself lifted from the ground and thrown backward like a rag doll, he thought: *Ain't this a bitch? The Wrath of God and I don't even* believe *in God.*

When the smoke cleared away all Itazura could see were flames and large chunks of twisted metal and other debris raining down.

Killaine, Radiant, and Singer were nowhere to be seen.

Please be all right, he thought.

He pulled himself slowly to his feet, checked to make sure he still had all his body parts, and staggered forward just as he saw the figure walking toward him.

"It's a motherfucker, isn't it?" yelled the figure. "I never thought I'd get to use it."

". . . what was it . . . ?" Itazura managed to get out.

"A Kolikov-Plotnik A–72 military field-issue cannon-launched ShellBlaster," said Gash, unsheathing his sword. "They said it was designed to take out half a city block."

"They were right," replied Itazura, unsheathing his own sword. "Where's the rest of your little Wuss-army?"

"Hanging back, Little Mary Sunshine. I told 'em I wanted first crack at this."

Both of them bowed, then assumed the initial attack position.

"How did you know I was here?" asked Itazura, circling Gash clockwise.

"I didn't," replied Gash, countering the move. "I came here to get Preston, but then I spotted you through the target lens right before I fired. We got business to finish, you and me. My Stompers will follow when I give the signal."

"Right," said Itazura, then jumped to the side and swung his blade up at an arc, connecting solidly with Gash's sword.

Gash countered with a downward-press that brought the tips of both their swords to the ground.

Itazura faked left, went right, and pulled his blade out, snapped it up over his head, and brought it down toward Gash, who scrambled right, twirled his sword in the air, and held it parallel to his chest just as Itazura's blade connected.

The two opponents looked at each other for a moment.

"I'm going to kill you, Mary," said Gash.

"Who's stopping you from trying?" asked Itazura.

And they decided to get serious. . . .

Killaine, Radiant, and Singer had just reached the door when the blast behind them brought down a quarter of PTSI's buildings.

They barely had time to hit the floor before a large, fiery, twisted section of something that might once have been a truck sailed over their heads and slammed into the side of the main building.

Killaine was the first on her feet, checking the portable chamber to make sure it hadn't been damaged, then reaching down and helping Radiant to her feet.

Singer didn't move.

"Singer?" said Killaine. Then: *"Singer!"* She knelt by his

side and started to touch him, but Radiant grabbed her hand and
said, "Don't."

"But he's damaged."

"I know. He—are there any guards around?"

"No," said Killaine. "I mean, there are sections of the tower
and some stray weapons some of them must have dropped when
they were—oh, no."

"He fell on an electron gun and accidentally discharged it,
Killaine. The charge was low, but it . . . it's enough."

"Oh, no, *Singer* . . ."

He turned his head slightly then managed to work one of his
arms behind his back and pull the gun out, tossing it away.

Killaine started to touch him again.

No, he signed. *The charge is still . . . still potent enough to
jump to another host.*

"We can't leave you here, Singer," said Killaine. "I know that
there . . . there has to be something Zac can . . . can do for—"

Singer's hands moved more slowly than before, jerking and
twitching so that some of the words he signed were indecipher-
able: *You don't have have all that much left only twen-twen
moots.*

"Come on, Killaine," snapped Radiant.

She couldn't take her eyes from Singer's face. "You'll
be . . . you'll be all right, you hear me, Singer? *YOU HEAR ME?*"

Go on. I'll . . . I'll wait here if you don't mind.

"*Killaine!*" Radiant shouted. "We've got about fourteen minutes!"

Killaine shook her head and bit her lower lip, turning away so
neither Radiant nor Singer would see the tears forming in her
eyes.

She grabbed the portable chamber and leaped to her feet.

"Come on," she said coldly, the warrior once again. . . .

* * *

"What the hell was *that?*" Zac shouted, hanging on to Stonewall as the violent ripples of the explosion outside traveled along the floor.

"I have no idea," said Psy–4.

"Someone's launched a military field-issue ShellBlaster," said Stonewall. When Zac and Psy–4 looked at him, Stonewall shrugged. "I mean, I've only *read* about them, but that's my best guess."

Zac—far less dizzy now but in serious pain because the anesthetic was rapidly wearing off—checked his watch again and said. "We can't wait any longer."

Psy–4's eyes grew wide. "But they should—"

"I know," snapped Zac. "They'll be here in a minute, but we've lost too much time as it is." He lifted the palmtop and said, "Give me the last three numbers in the sequence."

Psy–4 stared at him.

"Psy–4," said Zac, the warning in his voice clear.

Psy–4 gave him the numbers.

Zac entered them then pressed the INITIATE key.

"All right," he said to Stonewall. "We've hit 'Piss on Subtlety Time.' You got something on you that'll blow away part of this wall?"

Stonewall reached into his pocket and removed a small grenade. "We'll have to take cover at the other end of the hall."

"Fine," said Zac, already on the move. "Just make damn sure it doesn't land *too* close to the wall; we don't want to damage the mainframe."

"Yes, sir."

"Stonewall?"

"Yes, sir?"

"Call me 'sir' one more time and I'm going to get irritable."

The three of them took cover.

Stonewall activated the grenade, then tossed it.

It landed six feet from the wall.

"Perfect," he said.

Then came the explosion. . . .

The Catherine Wheel program was designed with one simple task in mind: To have a computer so intensely focus all its energies on following one directive that anything not directly associated with that directive was basically ignored.

On the night that Zac and the I-Bots had broken into PTSI, the now-late Sam Preston had initiated the Catherine Wheel program to concentrate solely on changing every security code in the compound every ninety seconds.

Everything else, the computer ignored.

The CWP was, in essence, a carefully controlled electronic obsessive-compulsive disorder.

Which is why no one dared run it for more than five minutes; after that, the disorder would be free to spread throughout every mainframe hooked into the system.

Neither Zac nor Preston were ever able to figure out why the CWP could not be controlled for more than fifteen minutes.

Not that it mattered at the moment.

The second Zac Robillard hit the INITIATE key, every computer in PTSI's mainframe focused all its energies on answering the single question that Psy–4 had programmed: *If you were to count every ape, gibbon, gorilla, and similar primate on Earth, then multiply that number by the exact, precise amount of individual hairs on all of these animals, when would the train traveling from Philadelphia at seventy-five miles per hour arrive in Paris after cataloging every drop of water in the ocean?*

Psy–4 had thought it quite clever, actually.

Because even if Preston's system were to realize it was obsessing on a trick question, it would be too late to shut down the CWP.

Sometimes, Psy–4 could be very mischievous.

But he usually kept it to himself. . . .

Both Annabelle and Simmons were startled by the blast. Simmons grabbed Annabelle and threw her to the floor, shielding her body with his own.

When it became apparent that the blast was confined to the computer room, Simmons rose, then helped Annabelle to her feet.

They watched in shaken silence as, behind the glass, Zac Robillard entered the computer room along with two of the I-Bots.

A few moments later, two more I-Bots joined them.

Annabelle broke away from Simmons and looked for a door that would lead into the computer room, but there was none.

Preston had made sure that Roy was totally isolated from any outside interference.

"Simmons," she snapped. "Break the glass!"

He grabbed a heavy piece of equipment from the far wall of the room and heaved it into the window.

Aside from the thunderous noise of the console top striking the unbreakable glass, there was nothing.

Annabelle saw that Robillard and the I-Bots had been startled by the noise and were now looking up at her.

Breathing heavily, Simmons leaned against the remains of the console and said, "It appears to be unbreakable, madam."

Annabelle glared at Zac, scanned the console, saw the button marked INTERCOM, and pressed it as she spoke into one of the microphones. "Zac!"

"Hello again, Annabelle."

"What are you doing?"

"What's it to you?"

She couldn't believe the arrogance in his voice.

"I never doubted you'd solve the equation."

Robillard smiled at her. "I'm assuming that was your idea of a joke?" He signaled the I-Bots to get to work.

One of them set a portable chamber on the floor by the computer.

Another removed a series of electrodes and connector cables from a pouch around their waist.

The other two were busy laying out a row of computer-repair tools.

"Zac," said Annabelle. "Zac, listen, that . . . the brain in the computer—"

"We're taking it, Annabelle. The glass in front of you is shatterproof, and if you want to waste time calling up the blueprints for this building, you'll discover that it would take you at least four minutes to move through the corridors in order to get to us. I've had it with you."

He turned toward the I-Bots; all of them checked the time.

"Zac!" This time Annabelle shouted into the microphone.

He ignored her.

"Zac, listen to me," she said.

Then saw her own guards appear at the blasted-away section of wall, electron guns and automatic weapons at the ready.

"NO!" she shouted.

The guards looked up at her.

"That's right," she said. "I don't want them harmed or detained, understand?"

The guards, looking puzzled, nodded up toward her, then backed off.

Robillard looked genuinely surprised. "What are you trying to pull, Annabelle?"

"Nothing," she said. "Just, please listen to me, all right? The brain inside Preston's computer, it's . . . it's been imprinted with my son's consciousness." She hated the way her voice cracked on the last few words, the way she could feel the tears in her eyes, hated how weak and vulnerable she must look to Robillard right now, but none of it mattered.

Not anymore.

"His name was Roy. Preston and I had a brief affair when the two of you worked for me. Roy was the result of our affair." She leaned forward and clutched the microphone with both hands. "Zac, please . . . please *save* him."

"That's the idea," he said flatly.

"Can you really do it?"

"Yes," he replied.

Annabelle released a long, staggered breath.

Robillard looked at his watch, then at the computer. "In three minutes and fifty seconds, Annabelle, the entire mainframe of PTSI is going to suffer the equivalent of a nervous breakdown. We don't have time to deal with your goons. Call away all your guards and private security soldiers."

"Yes."

"Pass the word along that we are not—repeat *not*—to be fired upon or stopped."

"Yes."

The brain was now being physically detached from the computer and transferred to the portable chamber.

"You can *really* save him, Zac?"

"Yes, Annabelle. And that is precisely what I'm going to do."

She smiled at him. "Thank you."

Robillard nodded, then said: "This isn't over, you know?"

"I know."

"I'll never come back to WorldTech."

"I understand."

"Fine."

"Just as long as you realize, Zac, that I'll never stop hunting you."

"I figured as much."

"I'll catch you eventually."

"Try it."

Annabelle wiped her eyes. "But for now, I'll let you go safely, because you have my son. Take good care of him, Zac."

"I will."

"Because I'll have him back one day . . . and the two of us will enjoy looking at your stuffed fucking head hanging on the wall of our living room."

Robillard laughed.

Annabelle sneered at him.

Then the skylight shattered, glass raining down, a cable dropped into the computer room and a figure came sliding down, spraying automatic gunfire in all directions, taking out the guards in the hall and destroying a section of the computer.

Janus swung around and threw himself from the cable, landed solidly on both feet, pulled a grenade from his pocket, and shoved the business end of the gun against Zac's temple.

"You double-crossed me, Annabelle," he shouted.

"Danny?" said Killaine, staring at him in shock.

"Hello, Janus," said Annabelle.

Janus kicked out with his left leg, hooked his foot into the handle of the portable chamber, and pulled it over. "I've got half a mind to kill your dear old Zachary and blow the rest of this place to hell," he shouted.

None of the I-Bots dared to make a move toward him while he controlled that chamber.

"I warned you, Annabelle—never screw me. I can be one nasty son-of-a-bitch when I choose to."

"So I see."

Annabelle hoped the panic she felt wasn't evident in her voice.

Janus slowly turned to face the I-Bots, using Zac as a shield and moving the portable chamber with his foot.

"Okay, you pieces of mechanical shit," he said. *"Move! Into the hall—NOW!"*

He snapped his head toward Killaine, who felt a pain in her center that defied any she'd ever known before.

"You're . . . you're *Janus?*" she croaked.

"What? You develop an affection for the hump and braces?"

Then he did something that no one else but Killaine saw.

He gave a quick grin and winked at her. . . .

Itazura and Gash moved toward a blasted section of gate, their swords colliding so fast and furiously that the blades could barely be seen.

Finally, Itazura pulled back, bent his legs, and jumped into the air, executing a double somersault over Gash's head and snap-kicking his opponent in the small of the back before landing behind him.

Gash screamed.

He fell one way.

His sword went another.

Itazura stood over Gash, sliding his own sword back into its sheath. "I'm sorry I had to do that," he said. "But I'm kind of pressed for time." He knelt beside Gash. "Don't worry about that numbness you're feeling right now. I haven't crippled you or any-thing like that. Just don't move from this spot, all right? I'll make sure to send an ambulance for you."

". . . no . . ." Gash croaked.

He reached out for his sword.

Itazura laughed. "You're in no condition to continue the fight."

". . . I don't wish to fight with you any longer . . ."

"Then . . . what?"

Gash stared directly into Itazura's eyes. "Can we call this a matter of honor?"

Then Itazura understood.

"I'm sorry, Gash. I can't do that."

". . . yes, you can . . ."

"No, I *really* can't. It's a programming conflict that can't be overridden."

Gash turned pale. ". . . *programming* conflict?"

"Bites, doesn't it?" said Itazura. "You've been playing whup-ass with a robot all along and never knew it."

He rose, then he turned and walked away as Gash screamed: *"A FUCKIN' ROBOT! YOU'RE A FUCKIN' ROBOT? COME BACK HERE! I'LL PULL YOUR HEAD OFF WITH MY HANDS! WRECKAGE! WRECKAGE! I WANT MY WRECK-AAAAAAAAAAAGE!"*

"Too bad," shouted Itazura over his shoulder. "But we all need a nemesis to keep our lives interesting, don't we?"

He looked beyond the gates and saw no sign of the crowding shadows.

Maybe the Stompers couldn't stand to see their leader fall to a Tin Man. . . .

* * *

In the hallway, Janus looked around, made sure all the guards were dead, then pushed Zac away. "All right, there's a chopper by the east gate and a truck just outside what's left of the west end of the compound. You've got a better chance of getting out of here if you split up and take different types of vehicles."

They all stared at him.

Killaine approached him cautiously. "Why are you doing this?"

"She double-crossed me."

Killaine shook her head. "I don't believe you."

"I don't care right now," yelled Janus, then let fly with a burst of gunfire into the ceiling. "That was for the benefit of any approaching guards."

"Come with us," said Killaine.

"Oh, right—like *that's* going to save me now."

Zac was the next to speak. "You don't have to help us, Janus."

"Well, *duh*. Thanks for clearing that up."

Killaine grabbed his arm and turned him to face her. "Why are you doing this?"

"Tell your friends to start getting the hell out of here and I'll tell you—*only you*."

Killaine cast a pleading look at the others. "Please?"

They began to scatter.

Killaine shouted, "Radiant—remember Singer!"

Then faced Janus again. "We're alone and there's not a lot of time. Why did you—?"

"I only lied to you about my name and the scoliosis," said Janus. "Everything else I told you was the truth. I was a carny as a kid, I did time at the Ohio Pen for running a flat store, I love kids and wish to hell I could protect them all from *chronos* . . . and I'm crazy about you." He pulled her close and kissed her on the lips.

Killaine didn't fight it.

She didn't want to.

Janus pulled back and began leading her toward the exit where the others were waiting for her. "Listen to me, Killaine. I never, *ever,* not once in my whole miserable life gave a thought to the state of my soul because I never believed I had one . . . until I met you. I've done things for money that would make you sick—"

"—I don't care, Janus, I don't care, I love you and—"

"—and I love you, too, for what it's worth, but I *refuse* to poison you with what's inside me—don't look at me like that, no one's being noble here, I'm just stating a fact. Violence is not just something I do, it's what I *am.* I could try to rein it in, and who knows, I might be able to for a while. But it always rises to the surface, Killaine. Always. And it's black and it stinks and it infects everyone and everything around me and I won't do that to you! I never understood what genuine decency was before I met you, and I almost wish I *still* didn't understand—but I'll never regret having known you. Never." He pushed her outside.

"Janus," said Killaine. "You can come with us, we can use someone with your—"

"I would grow old, Killaine. I would get sick. And I would die. And somewhere along the line I would start resenting you. I love you more than anything I've ever had or ever will have in my life." He looked behind him. "Guards are coming." He slammed a fresh clip into his weapon and, not looking back at Killaine, said, "I wish we could have gone on the carousel together," then opened fire and ran toward the new wave of guards, hosing the area and tossing the grenade, then somebody screamed and the entire hallway went up in fire, smoke, and debris. . . .

* * *

Zac, Radiant, and Psy–4 took the chopper.

Roy was with them, safely functioning in his new, temporary home.

Killaine, Stonewall, Itazura, and Singer took the truck, a military-style transport with a green canvas tarpaulin tenting its bed.

Stonewall drove, and Itazura rode up front with him.

As they sped through the night, Killaine held Singer's head in her lap, watching as the red glow of his eyes slowly faded.

The equivalent of a human stroke, Zac had said.

Like the robot in the Scrapper Camp, there was nothing anyone could do for Singer.

And so Killaine held him in his last minutes of life and wept for not having known him better, or longer, or, ultimately, at all.

Maybe she wept for herself, as well.

For all the loss and guilt and pain she'd had to absorb over the last few days.

She was pulled out of herself by the touch of Singer's hand against hers.

She wiped her eyes, leaned down, and whispered, "What is it? What do you need?"

Not here, he signed.

"What do you—?"

Not in here. Not in darkness and hiding.

Killaine couldn't find her voice.

Under . . . stars. I want . . . stars . . . under.

She nodded her head, understanding.

"Stop!" she screamed. "Stop the truck!"

Stonewall braked and drove the truck to the side of the road.

Itazura jumped out, ran to the back, and threw aside the tarpaulin. "What is it?"

But Killaine was already climbing out and down, cradling Singer in her arms.

"He doesn't want to die in there. He wants to die under the stars."

Itazura shook his head. "Killaine, look, I know how you must feel, but—"

Her glare silenced him.

Itazura started to say something else, but then Stonewall placed a massive hand on his shoulder.

"Let her go, Itzy. This is something she has to do alone."

Killaine walked across a moonlit field and began heading up a small hill.

She reached the top, and she saw the glory of the night, the acceptance of the stars above, and finally understood what Radiant meant when she spoke of the "silent poetry of the world."

"I wish we'd had more time together," she whispered to Singer.

He managed to squeeze her hand.

Just a little.

"Can you ever forgive me for the way I treated you all this time?"

He tapped her arm.

She looked down at him.

Nothing to forgive, he signed, the light in his eyes dimming more.

Killaine had to fight with everything she had in order not to break down. She didn't want Singer to see her grief, not at the end.

"Is there . . . is there anything I can do for you?" she whispered.

Singer held up two fingers: *Two things.*

"Name them."

He pointed toward the sky, then made a circling gesture with his finger.

Killaine puzzled over the gesture.

Singer made the circling gesture again, only faster.

"Flying?" whispered Killaine.

Singer managed a nod.

"I don't understand what—"

He pointed to the sky again, then managed to sign two words: *Use me.*

And Killaine understood.

Roy. Singer wanted his body to be used for Roy.

"I promise you, my friend. I promise."

Then Singer placed two fingers against the area where his mouth would have been if he'd had one and reached up and placed the same two fingers against Killaine's lips.

She understood his wish at once.

Tell me the rest of the story.

Killaine looked up at the stars. "Well, the girl with no name prepared a magnificent feast for her relatives and . . . and everyone else in the village. The feast lasted for days, and even those who had arrived feeling angry or sad or resentful of a neighbor left with full bellies and bags of extra food and more happiness and hope than they'd known in years. When it was done, when the girl with no name had finished cleaning up and storing the leftovers, one of her aunts took her aside and said, 'Where will you go now?' 'I don't understand,' said the girl. 'Well,' replied her aunt, 'now that you have given everyone enough food to last throughout the winter—and a fine feast it was, my dear—now that you have done so much for us and the village, you need not stay here any longer, not with all the money you've inherited.' Then the girl laughed. 'What is so funny?' asked her aunt. 'May I have a name now?' 'Why not choose it yourself?' 'Because I think I may have done a foolish thing, but I don't care.' 'What foolish thing is that?' 'I have no money left,' replied the girl. 'I spent all I had on the feast.'

"Then the girl began to cry, so embarrassed was she by her foolish behavior, but her aunt took the girl into her arms and whispered, 'You have not done a foolish thing, my dear. You have given of yourself in a way that few of us ever have. And because'"— Killaine's voice broke and the tears began streaming down her face—"'because of what you have done, and for all that you've given us, there is only one name worthy of you. From this day forward, my dear, your name shall be a reflection of your soul. From this day forward, you shall be called Grace.'"

Killaine looked down at Singer as the last of the light faded from his eyes.

She looked up at the stars and the night, wishing that she knew a prayer.

Then she slowly turned and made her way back down to the truck where Stonewall and Itazura waited in respectful silence.

"Is he gone?" asked Stonewall.

"Yes," whispered Killaine, lowering her face and kissing Singer where his lips would have been.

"He was a good friend," said Itazura, his own voice breaking. "I'm sorry he died."

Killaine shook her head, her tears spattering gently on the shiny metal of Singer's stilled face. "He gave up his life," she said. "And he never even knew his real name."

"He was a robot named Singer," whispered Stonewall.

"No. He was a lamb. His name was Grace. Never forget that."

A F T E R   A L L

"I have some rights of memory in this kingdom . . ."
—*Shakespeare,* HAMLET

Time was, he knew happiness, hope, and acceptance.

But now, even though he had all those things and more again, Roy thought he'd settle at the moment for just being able to get his new hands to do what he wanted them to.

"Darnit," he said aloud, still not used to the sound of his new voice or the feel of his recently installed voice box.

"Such language," said Itazura.

"I sorry," replied Roy.

"We gotta work on your sense of humor, kiddo."

Annabelle Donohoe stood at her office window, gently fondling the locket.

She was not even aware that Simmons had entered the room and stood staring at her.

"Madam?"

She blinked, then looked at him. "What is it, Simmons?"

He shrugged. "I was . . . concerned. You've not been out of your office all day."

She smiled, staring out at the night.

Time was, she'd have been consumed by anger and her desire for revenge.

But now . . .

"It's odd, Simmons."

"What's that, madam?"

Now it was Annabelle's turn to shrug. "I should be three times as driven to locate Robillard and the I-Bots as I was before, but, somehow . . ."

"We'll locate them again, madam. We always do."

She shook her head. "I know. But let's not be too intense about it for the time being."

"May I inquire why, madam—if it's not overstepping my bounds?"

"You may, and it isn't." She turned away from the window with a wide, genuine smile on her face and in her heart. "He's alive, Simmons. My son is alive and *out there,* in the world. And even though I can't see him, can't touch him, can't hold him . . . I *feel* him near me. Does that make sense?"

Simmons remained silent.

Annabelle turned back to the window. "I want to wait a while before going after Robillard again. I want my son to have some time to enjoy the new world Zac has given to him."

Her hand came away from the locket.

"But just a *little more* time." She grinned her typical grin. "A mother's patience can only be stretched so far."

Outside their new temporary headquarters in an ugly white house on Oceola Avenue in Nashville, Tennessee, Zac Robillard was making a final check on the contents of the new truck.

"Everybody comfy?" he called into the trailer.

The Scrappers who'd been of such help to them during the siege at PTSI all nodded their agreement.

Stonewall and Radiant brought out the last of the documents that Zac had requested.

"Thought we could use a little road food," said Radiant, loading three bulging picnic baskets into the cab. "I can't believe we're going to Washington."

"Testifying before Congress," said Zac, still having a hard time believing he was going to do it.

One week ago legislation had been introduced to appropriate funds for the creation of "training centers" for all the so-called Scrappers in the country. The idea was that the out-moded, homeless robots would be rounded up and—instead of destroyed and recycled—trained to perform "public work" tasks; public sanitation, security, crossing guards, and other occupations that were becoming increasingly difficult to fill because of the low pay.

Zac had spoken with a congressional representative last week and suggested naming the legislation "Singer's Law."

He was scheduled to testify before Congress in two days, and Washington was abuzz with anticipation of hearing from the "reclusive" grandson of Benjamin Robillard.

Zac figured it wouldn't hurt to be accompanied by Stonewall, Radiant, and the baker's dozen of robots who now waited in the back of truck.

It was the least any of them could do to honor their fallen friend's memory.

"Well," said Zac, rubbing his still-hurting shoulder. "Methinks it's time we hit the road. Everyone say their good-byes?"

"To everyone but Psy–4," said Radiant. "I think he's still hiding from Roy."

Zac grinned. "Yeah, well—he did tell Roy he'd be his new daddy." Then Zac and Radiant laughed at the same memory—of Roy, arms outstretched, stumbling around in his new body after Psy–4 and calling out, "Wait for me, Daddy, wait for me!"

"All set," replied Stonewall.

"I think Singer would be pleased," said Radiant.

Zac nodded. "Well, let's just make damn sure the law gets passed."

A few minutes later, they were on their way.

* * *

Killaine sat alone in the living room, looking at the pillow that Stonewall had made for her. It was covered with happy little puppy dogs.

She liked it very much.

Itazura came into the room and saw her sitting there alone.

He joined her on the sofa, putting his arm around her shoulder. "How're you feeling?"

She shrugged. "Sometimes better, sometimes not."

"Have you, uh . . . have you talked to Roy yet?"

Killaine shook her head. "I . . . I don't know if I can. Even with the new voice circuitry and faceplate, I still look at him and think he's Singer."

"Pardon me for saying so, Killaine, but I don't think Singer would want you to act like this."

"I know." She sighed and looked out the window. "Do you think he made it out alive?"

Itazura blinked. "Okay, you switched gears on me. Who're we talking about?"

"Janus."

"Oh."

Killaine looked at him. "Do you think—"

"It's hard to say," replied Itazura. "He's a damned clever guy. He very well might have gotten away. The news reports have never mentioned anyone matching his description as a casualty of the disaster."

"I hope it doesn't make me sound like a Judas," whispered Killaine, "but I hope he got away."

Itazura leaned over and kissed her cheek. "For your sake, I hope so, too."

"What's this?" asked Killaine, reaching down to take a small paperback book from Itazura's hand.

"Huh? Oh, some damned book Psy–4 gave me: *The Theory of*

Mechanical Race Memory. It has to do with an argument we had a while ago."

"Oh."

"Hello."

They both looked up, startled, to see Roy standing a few feet away, drumming his fingers nervously against the sides of his legs. "I got lonely."

"Can't have that," said Itazura, rising to his feet. "Hello, Roy. I must be going. I've got a pressing appointment with some plumbing pipes in the basement."

"Itzy," said Killaine.

"What? Did you know there's a fungus down there? It's purple. It appears to be breathing. I think it's developing a rudimentary language. I have decided to call it Victoria."

Roy made a metallic laughing noise. "You're funny."

Itazura bowed. "Well, it's good to know that at least one person in this household has some taste when it comes to—" He froze, eyes wide, mouth hanging open.

"Itzy?" said Killaine. "Itzy, what is it?"

He turned toward Killaine and whispered, "You haven't talked to him about—?"

"No."

"Has anyone else told Roy about—"

"Not that I know of. Why?"

"Look."

"What's wrong?" asked Roy.

And as he spoke, his hands signed the same question.

"How did you learn to do that?" asked Killaine, rising slowly to her feet and walking toward him.

"Learn to do what?"

Learn to do what? asked his hands.

"Sign," whispered Killaine.

"I dunno."

I dunno.

"Itzy," said Killaine, not taking her gaze from Roy's face. "What's going on here? Is this your idea of a joke?"

"I swear, Sis, I *swear* I had nothing to do with this."

"Roy," said Killaine. "Can you . . . can you say something to me without speaking?"

"Huh?"

Huh?

"Talk to me with your hands. Don't say anything out loud, okay?"

Okay.

Killaine and Itazura looked at each other in astonishment.

"Roy," said Killaine, slowly, very calmly, "Is there anything you want to know about, well . . . about anything?"

Yeah.

"And what might that be?"

Who is Singer?

Again, Killaine and Itazura exchanged astonished looks.

"So we have no race memory, huh, Itzy?" asked Killaine.

Itazura was speechless.

Roy tapped Killaine's arm. *Do you know Singer?*

"Yes, Roy, I . . . I knew him. He was my friend."

Could you tell me about him?

Killaine nodded her head, holding back any further tears as she at last touched the newest member of the family, putting her arm around his shoulder and leading him toward the kitchen where she intended to share some milk and cookies with him.

Was he nice? signed Roy.

"He was wonderful," whispered Killaine.

Tell me 'bout him, please?

"Okay, shhh, listen: Time was, robots like Singer were a wonder to humankind, the culmination of its dreams of merging the mechanical with the humanistic in order to form the basis for a more enlightened and advanced society."

Huh?

Killaine smiled at him. "They were way cool."

And soon, she was able to look at him as Roy.

Only Roy.

Her absent friend would have wanted it that way.

Later that night, in what many would call the "wee hours," a moth fluttered near the bright front porch light of the I-Bots' current home.

It neared the hot bulb, circled, hovered dangerously close.

Then it sensed something about the house, maybe emanating from somewhere inside.

It moved closer to the bulb and the fruition of its life.

Then—and no one was there to guess why—at the moment when it should have slammed its body against the light and screamed its insect scream as wings burst into flame, it veered to the side, circled the light one last time, and flew off into the darkness.

Choosing to live a little while longer.

Choosing life, if only for one more day.

And knowing that, after all, there was another day to choose.